PS-BZZ-062

High praise for the ... **wing**

"A tour de ...

"Compulsive and un-put-downable ... A nail-biting read, glittering with ideas which just might be real."
—*Eastern Daily Press*

"Dazzling ... brilliant ... There are clearly many more marvelous adventures to be had in Ryhope Wood ... and I confess that I eagerly anticipate another visit."
—Gahan Wilson, *Realms of Fantasy*

"An enthralling, absorbing tale. Holdstock's brilliantly evoked, mysterious forest ranks alongside Gormenghast and Middle Earth as one of modern fantasy literature's most outstanding creations."
—*South Wales Evening Post*

"All roads lead to Ryhope—Mythago Wood—and out from it through many strange dimensions.... Such depth of wonder, grief, and mystery Holdstock manages to evoke in *The Hollowing*!"
—*Locus*

"Extraordinary adventure by a fine writer [with an] astonishing power of invention."
—*Australian SF News*

"Brilliant ... In the end we come to understand exactly how much resonance of the mythic past continues to influence the present."
—*Fantasy & Science Fiction*

"Absorbing, frightening, and completely original."
—*Western Morning News*

"Powerful storytelling and strong characters ... Reveals a world where dreams and legends become real."
—*Library Journal*

The
HOLLOWING

Robert Holdstock

A ROC BOOK

ROC
Published by the Penguin Group
Penguin Books USA Inc., 375 Hudson Street,
New York, New York 10014, U.S.A.
Penguin Books Ltd, 27 Wrights Lane, London W8 5TZ, England
Penguin Books Australia Ltd, Ringwood, Victoria, Australia
Penguin Books Canada Ltd, 10 Alcorn Avenue,
Toronto, Ontario, Canada M4V 3B2
Penguin Books (N.Z.) Ltd, 182–190 Wairau Road, Auckland 10, New Zealand

Penguin Books Ltd, Registered Offices:
Harmondsworth, Middlesex, England

Published by Roc, an imprint of Dutton Signet, a division of Penguin Books USA
Inc. First published in Great Britain by HarperCollins Publishers. Previously
published in the United States in a Roc hardcover edition.

First Mass Market Printing, July, 1995
10 9 8 7 6 5 4 3 2 1

For Wendy, Brian, Alan, Marja and Robert,
  fellow travelers in the realm . . .
and for Hilary Rubinstein, with much appreciation.

Acknowledgments

My thanks, for a variety of reasons, to Chris Evans, Jane Johnson, Sarah Biggs, Malcolm Edwards, Andrew Stephenson (chats scientific), Dave Arthur (chats mythic) and Garry and Annette Kilworth. And of course, to the unknown author of *Sir Gawain and the Green Knight,* and the long-forgotten dreamer who inspired the tale.

Contents

PART ONE: FROM THE UNKNOWN REGION

The Green Chapel: 1   *3*
Out of the Dark   *9*
Moondreaming   *17*

PART TWO: IN THE WILDWOOD

The Green Chapel: 2   *35*
Out of the Pit   *40*
Oak Lodge   *53*
The Wildwood   *60*
Ghosts   *71*
The Green Chapel: 3   *77*
Old Stone Hollow   *82*
Lytton   *96*
Echoes   *106*
Genesis   *112*
The Green Chapel: 4   *122*
Jack   *126*
Inside the Skin   *136*
The Hunted   *149*

x   *Contents*

White Castle   *167*
The Green Chapel: 5   *176*

PART THREE: *LONG GONE, LONG TO COME*

Spirit Rock   *179*
Old Man, Old Lake   *193*
To the Forgotten Shore   *203*
Bosky   *243*
Skin of Stone   *252*
Glamor   *263*
The Triumph of Time   *283*
The Green Knight   *296*

Appendix   *315*

"Now certainly the place is deserted," said Gawain.
"It is a hideous oratory, all overgrown,
And well graced for the gallant garbed in green
To deal out his devotions in the Devil's fashion.
Now I feel in my five wits, it is the Fiend himself
That has tricked me into this tryst, to destroy me here."

From *Sir Gawain and the Green Knight*

One of the deep silences fell on them, that seemed so much more natural than speech, a timeless silence in which there were at first many minds in the overhang; and then perhaps no mind at all.

William Golding: *The Inheritors*

PART ONE

From the Unknown Region

The Green Chapel: 1

Each dawn, since the hollyjack had come to the cathedral bringing her strange dreams, the boy had started to think of waking as the opening of petals, or a form of budding. At this time the light was not green, it became green later, but he could never wait to wake, and in the same way that flowers opened to the sun, and leaves turned and unfurled, so he unfurled, so he opened. At first curled up on the inscribed marble floor, arms and legs gathered in for warmth during the night, now he began to straighten, then stretch, face to the open sky where the roof had been, mouth agape and damp with dew.

His eyes remained closed but he knew the cathedral was not yet green, it was still in *stark* light, and the world was not yet *quick*. And like the pores of the leaves, still closed, the water stayed inside him. He liked the feeling of the water. It pressed painfully against his belly, but he kept the water with him, waiting for green light. He rolled on the hard, cold marble, touching the grooves in the slab, the hidden names of the dead carved in the floor that guarded their bones. He listened to the cathedral stir, to the forest beyond begin to wake, to the hollyjack as she woke and moved restlessly, like a bird, in her nest of vegetation at the end of the aisle, against the great outer doors of the church.

The hollyjack had been here for days, now, weeks perhaps. She had changed his dreams. He could dream more widely, and feel his way over great distances of the forest,

peering up from the roots, or glimpsing the ground as he
flowed through the branches. She still frightened him, but
until she had come he had been unable to see anything at all.
With her arrival he had seen how like a leaf he was, unfurling with the new day. But last night, the dream last night
had been startling. He didn't want to let it go.

The sun moved over the line of the trees. The ragged
edges of the cathedral's fallen roof caught its warmth, its
light. On the cold marble the brilliant edge of the green light
spread, moving like a growing thing, an unfurling plant, toward the unfurled boy.

He felt it touch his legs. He woke fully and cried out as
the light spread across him and birds fled from the nest
where the hollyjack chattered. The bones of the dead below
him shifted as roots prowled among them. The cathedral
shuddered into life, from nave to chancel. The rotting wood
of the pews began to steam, and he could smell this; and the
carved dancing men drew deeper into the knots and rings of
the old trees, their night of freedom and exuberance finished
for a while.

He let the water go, now, adding his own moisture to the
heavy dawn as his belly deflated. The water stank of nettles
as it passed, and this mingled with wood sorrel and anemone
in the rising steam of the chapel. He was relieved, out of
pain, and felt at last that it was time to open fully. To open
his eyes. To let green light shape him for the day.

The hollyjack had left her nest. He saw her moving up the
ivy-covered wall toward the high arch of a window, where
tree branches reached into the ruins of the cathedral and
stone faces grinned down at him. She hesitated for a moment, glancing back at her nest, and at the boy, then had
gone, outside into the forest.

He wanted to call to her, to tell her about his dream, but
it was too late. He stood and stared through the leaning
trunks of oaks at the rows of rotting wooden pews, some of
them crushed, others raised above the floor as the forest
grew from below them. The altar space was a distant grove
among white-flowered thorns, the gold cross sparkling
through the leaves. Saplings were sprouting everywhere,
coming up from the crypt below. Only the marble slabs, with

the names and dates of the dead, defied the forest as it struggled to emerge into the cathedral, keeping a clear channel to the high altar. Since the hollyjack had come to him, he had begun to imagine how the roots and branches in the crypt, and the bones themselves, were all entangled, all pushing at the floor, a great pressure ready to erupt upward.

It had been *such* a dream. It had been his first *real* dream since he had come to the forest. He said the words aloud into the decaying church. *Real dream.* For so long his dreams had been of endless snow, and endless forest, and endless running, and endless water, an endless flight across unchanging lands. All that had *broken* with the first dream of the unfurling leaf. And now this one. He had begun to remember so much again.

"They danced!" he shouted, staring into the brightening sky, through the crossing branches of the trees, through the green light. As if to answer his cry, one of the carved wooden faces on a pew moved slightly, then stretched forward from the end of the stall, poking out into the aisle. It turned and peered at the shouting boy, who watched back through the sunlit mist that hung heavily in the great space. It looked like the hollyjack, branches extending from its mouth, leaves around its face. As quickly as it had stretched to look at him, it withdrew and was silent again. The boy blinked, then laughed. He was still dreaming. Last night that same figure and twenty others had come all the way out of the wooden benches, small, gnarled shapes with willow-thin arms and legs. They had led a wild dance up the stone walls and into the branches, among the stone faces in the high eaves, which had laughed and twisted too, stretching out from the pillars and cornices of the cathedral, peering at the wild activity below them and around their vaulted positions.

In the stillness of the new day, the boy went to the hollyjack's nest and peered through the small hole into the stinking mass of rotten wood and foliage, grass, bracken and dead birds that the creature had compacted against the tall cathedral doors. Above those doors, half of a stained glass window began to glow purple and red as it was struck by first light. He liked the shape of the knight with his lance and silver armor, but now—another question! He was so full of questions these days—now he wondered what the knight was fighting—he could just see the creature's legs—what was missing from the shattered area of the window.

Away from the nest, he went into the gloom of the sacristy and looked at his disjointed reflection in the cracked mirror. His hair was long and filthy now, falling in a lank, black mass around his pale, smooth face. A new thought occurred to him (he smiled at the pleasure of it) that he looked like the picture of an Apache Indian boy he had seen in a book at school. The boy in the picture had worn animal skins. The boy in the mirror was naked. The picture of the Apache now blurred and shifted in his mind, then faded. The chapel boy's teeth were still white when he grinned, shifting his head across a distorting fracture in the glass.

The deep scratches on his chest and right arm were healed, now no more than bright red lines. They no longer hurt. The skin around them was still yellowed with bruising. He could hardly remember the attack, now, it had been so fast, and at dusk. He hadn't even seen the creature, just heard its awful laugh. He thought of it as the giggler.

He was grimy with dirt and remembered that he should wash, so he thought of the well, but the well was at the edge of the clearing outside, and the wood was dangerous there. When the giggler had snatched at him and ripped him, it had hurt him badly, and when the hollyjack had tried to help him it had torn her leaves before retreating into the deep bosk of the wood. She mightn't help him again.

The moment of apprehension faded as fast as the memory of the Indian boy from the book. He was suddenly on the ivy "ladder," hauling himself up the stonework to the open roof, over an empty gallery, then across a broad sill that was carved with intricate rose and leaf patterns. He held the long neck of an ugly stone animal, and peered back down into the body of the church, swinging gently in the vast space and watching the wooden seats below, but they were quite life-less now. Then he had clambered over the gargoyle and out onto a branch, crawling into the daylight and slipping down the twisted beech tree and onto the slate roof of the porch. The clearing stretched around him, ending at the wood. A few granite headstones poked from mounds in the tall grass and nettles. The stone well was half in shadow. The crowding wood was dark, crushing, and he felt a tingle of apprehension again. The giggler came and went, usually at dusk, but he couldn't be sure it wasn't there now, watching him from the shadows. He needed to drink, though.

Without really thinking, he reached the well and drew up the bucket, splashing water into his mouth and over his body, liking the cold touch on his bruises. Some impulse, faintly remembered, made him rub water between his toes.

Something moved suddenly in the dark wood, startling him, and he scampered back to the open door of the porch, yelping at the stings he received from the dense nettlebed. It was only the hollyjack, in fact. She hovered in the gloom, then stepped quickly past the well, crouching against a headstone. He knew that her eyes would tell him of fear, but her eyes said nothing. They gleamed from deep in the holly leaves that wreathed her face. The thin twigs that stretched from each side of her round mouth were wet. She had been feeding, then. She was fat, these days, and her body often moved as if she was being kicked from inside.

In her hands she held a selection of colorful fungi. She offered these, and he came forward and picked carefully, knowing that some would make him dizzy and sick. The rest he ate gratefully as the hollyjack quickly examined those he had rejected. She was trying to learn.

The hollyjack was disturbed. Her mouth flexed and she made bird noises. Her long fingers stroked her body leaves restlessly, almost nervously. He wanted to go back into the chapel, to safety and security, away from the strange men and creatures who so often prowled among the trees. But he sensed that the hollyjack needed him, so he stayed in the shadow, listening to furtive movement in the woodland and the fluttering of wings in his friend's body.

He realized quite suddenly that she was inviting him to dream again, and his heart surged.

He had had a dream last night, in the cathedral . . . as he ate the last of the mushrooms he struggled to recall the details. There had been wild dancing. The green men in the church stalls had slipped out of the wood and run amok. He was like a leaf, unfurling at dawn. The giggler had stepped from the wood and walked into his dreams, hiding there . . .

But as he tried to remember these things, so they faded, leaving him blank again, empty and restless, lonely and isolated. The details had gone.

A bigger dream was on offer, now. The way the hollyjack crouched and trembled, watching him and chitter-chattering in her funny way, all of this told him that she had heard something. Big Dream, he wondered as he chewed, or Little Dream?

When he was full he left the porch and went over to the hollyjack, curling up in her twiggy arms. The prick of holly leaves made him shudder, but after a while the mixing of blood and sap soothed him, and although the inside of her body shifted and fluttered restlessly, he felt himself slip out into the wood, flowing softly, spreading widely, connected to the forest around him through her roots, now embedded in the earth of the graveyard, and touching the tendrils of wilder trees.

She was sending him on the Little Dream, and he heard his father's voice again, for only the second time since the hollyjack had come. His father was in the wood. His father was coming closer. He was looking desperately for his son. There was someone with him, a man like a bear, dark-featured and fierce. There was excitement, running, they were afraid. The wood shifted around them, tripped them, snagged them, sucked them deeper. The giggler was watching them, but they weren't aware of it.

Then he touched his father's dreams again, his memories, and he shouted with pain at the anguish he felt, the sadness. The hollyjack wrapped her arms more tightly around him, soothed him, rustled and twittered at him with her voice. Blood and sap mingled more deeply. He lay back in the hollybush and started to cry. But he dreamed his father's dream for a while, feeding on it, bringing himself close again to a man he remembered only as a picture. He moved out of the cathedral and into the wood, a wraith, anxious to touch the man who was searching for him.

Out of the Dark

It was to be an evening of rain and strange encounters. There would be a return from the dead, and the beginning of the ending of a life.

Richard Bradley hastened along the road to his house, at the edge of Shadoxhurst, hatless and drenched by the torrential and freezing late September downpour. The whole town had become dark. The few shops had their lights on, and at four in the afternoon this made a depressingly wintry scene. Richard was wearing only his suit, the collar of his jacket drawn tightly around his neck in a vain attempt to stop the rain coursing down his back. Bedraggled and fed up, he broke into a run as he neared his cottage, then slowed abruptly as he saw the woman dart away from the back gate toward the fields.

She was wearing strange clothes. She too was saturated, he could see, her dark hair plastered to her scalp. He didn't see her face, only the army trousers, tucked into muddy, black boots, and a full and heavy-looking green anorak drawn tightly around her neck. She had something slung across her shoulder, and although it was hard to be sure, Richard thought it was a short bow and full quiver.

He quickened his step, puzzled by the fact that she had been at his back door, but by the time he reached the gate she was a bulky and distant shape, running through the downpour toward the stream that led to Ryhope Wood, on the estate. The rain made the wood seem grim, as always.

He opened the back door and peered inside the house, noticing the wet footprints that led across the kitchen and into the small parlor. The footprints were small. He assumed at once that they were those of the woman, but what on earth was she doing here? Nothing looked disturbed. The cash box, clearly labeled as such (it contained only coppers), was still on its shelf.

Richard followed the footprints. They ascended the stairs and showed clearly, though slightly faded, how the intruder had looked into each room. The carpet had dried the wetness from her boots by mid-landing of the return, but downstairs, on the bureau, he found a note, which he read with astonishment.

Why aren't you here? Everything's OK with Old Stone Hollow. I really hoped you'd be here. I miss you. It's been too long.
IMPORTANT: Lytton reckons he knows how to locate the boy's protogenomorph, but we need YOU there. Come to the Station. I'm going back into the wood by the old brook, taking path through Huxley's Lodge. Follow me the moment you get back. This may be our only chance to find the true Cathedral! Just do it! I miss you.

The note was unsigned. The paper was wet where she had held it, the pen, a cheap biro, flung on the table. She had rested a hand on the polished wood and he placed his own hand upon the vague outline, noting its smallness, the details of her fingerprints, three of which were crossed with scars.

A thought had occurred to him, that he should fetch the police, but he stood there unwilling to do so. He just looked at the handprint, and the note, savoring its strangeness and its incomprehensibility. And remembering the image of the woman, wet, dark-haired, bulky with clothes, but fast, running along the bridleway toward the wood that had so fascinated Alexander's young friend Tallis Keeton, before she and her father had so tragically and mysteriously disappeared, over a year ago, now.

Alex came bounding up to the front door and rang the bell. Richard folded the note and tucked it into his trousers pocket, then opened the door to the wet, excitable thirteen-year-old. The boy ran straight to the kitchen and poured himself a glass of orange juice, then crashed upstairs to get ready for the school play.

On impulse, Richard followed his son to the "treasure house," as he and Alice called Alexander's room.

"Do you want tea?" he asked from the door, watching the boy poring over some typewritten sheets.

"No thanks. Had crisps and two Lion bars."

"Well, that sounds healthy enough." Alex didn't respond. "We'll be leaving at six, if they want you there at six-thirty, so don't lounge around reading for long."

"I'm not reading—I'm memorizing. Mr. Evans and me wrote a new scene today."

"Mr. Evans and *I* . . ."

Alex groaned tiredly.

Richard looked around the room, reaching out to flick one of the many model planes that were suspended from the ceiling. Alexander's costume—he was to play the red-bearded Lord Bertolac in the third year's production of *Sir Gawain and the Green Knight*—was draped around a tailor's dummy. The red beard and hair had been fashioned from two very old wigs and looked hilarious upon the boy. Another pupil would be playing the Green Knight himself (who was, in fact, Lord Bertolac in otherworldly form) as the change of costuming was too difficult.

There was something about Alex's den that both embraced and unnerved Richard. It was a difficult feeling— there was so much obsession here, so much passion, from the paintings of knights, with odd insignia and helmet crests, to the drawings of dinosaurs and the carefully ordered trays of fossils and crystals, gathered from all over Britain, all labeled and all imbued with mystery. Chunks of iron marcasite from chalk pits were questioningly labeled "Spacecraft remains?" The intricate patterns of fossils were related to Star Creatures, lost in the chalk seas in primordial times. Models, in plastic and wood, were everywhere, and the boy could tell a story about each one.

It was an imagination inherited from his grandfather (along with a love of toy soldiers), but a trait completely missing from Richard himself, although he tried hard to re-member what had been his own childhood dream: he had walked, lazed in the sun and swum in the freezing seas off the Welsh coast. He had very little to show for growing up.

He realized that Alex was watching him anxiously. He asked, "What is it?"

Alex said simply, "You can come in, if you want. You can test me."

Feeling awkward, for no reason he could identify, Richard turned to go downstairs. "I'll test you in the car, shall I? I'd better get some tea going."

Leaving Alexander to memorize the final few lines of his part in the heavily adapted play, he went down to the kitchen, taking out the note and re-reading it. It had an odd, foreign quality to the language—*Lytton reckons he knows how to locate the boy's protogenomorph.* It had an American twang to it. And what on earth was a *protogenomorph*?

The rain drummed monotonously. He heard the sound of the family car, an old Rover that roared and spluttered as the engine was turned off. Alice struggled out onto the curb and cursed the rain.

He had hidden the note before she entered the house to begin her relentless domestic routine and preparing for the evening out. She had little time for idle chat. Richard pre-pared tea and wrote two letters, but he was distracted and disturbed—indeed, he was enjoying a welcome if vicarious experience.

The note had surely been intended for someone else, not for Richard Bradley. But he couldn't get over the odd and thrilling sensation that nine words in the woman's hand gave him.

I really hoped you'd be here. I miss you.

Alice was half asleep in the passenger seat, her head rocking as the car bumped slowly over the uneven road, leading back to Shadoxhurst. The headlights cut a bright path through the rain. Houses appeared gray, windows reflecting dully; trees were dark, looming shapes that appeared and disappeared from vision in seconds. The road curved across the country;

two foxes scampered across the path of the car, casting gleam-eyed glances, hesitating as the vehicle approached.

Behind Richard, Alexander stared at the night land, awake, alert, excited. He was still dressed in his Lord Bertolac costume, all but the bushy beard. His performance had been warmly applauded.

In fact, it had been a spectacular performance all round, from the mad chase around the stage for the Green Knight's severed head, which took on an unintentional role of its own, to the sub-Gilbert and Sullivan words of the songs, all written by the children.

Even now, Richard found himself singing the "Wild Man's" Song:

> *"I am a Mountain Wodwo,"*
> *"I live on leaves and fish roe . . ."*

There had been no subtleties, of course, simply an adventure, with monsters and supernatural entities. The Green Knight's beheading, his magical return to life and subsequent challenge to Gawain, to meet a year later at the Green Chapel (an ancient burial mound) for a return stroke, were powerfully played; the three attempts at seducing Sir Gawain by the enchantress Morgan le Fay, disguised as Lady Bertolac, were excruciating, as the boy playing Morgan couldn't keep the pitch of his voice constantly high. Alex's innovation to the story had been to make the pagan Green Knight the guardian of a fabulous talisman. At the end, Gawain, disguised as a hunting falcon, tricked the monstrous knight out of his chapel, entered the mound to the fairy Otherworld and stole the treasure.

Alexander had been singled out for special applause. Richard and Alice had felt very proud of the lad and joined heartily in the encore, a refrain from the final song ("One bloody nick at the side of my neck—All for the sake of My Lady's Green Girdle").

Headlights cut through the dark, swinging across trees, hedges, walls, briefly illuminating a land that was silent, saturated and sleeping.

The man who suddenly staggered in front of the car was

wearing only a dressing gown. He waved both hands helplessly as Richard swerved to avoid him. He was holding what looked like a round, white mask.

For a second, in the headlamps, the man had been startled like a wild animal, frozen in the road. Then he flung himself aside to escape hurt. Richard saw only his white body, naked beneath the gaping gown. He had been thinly bearded, and everything about him had glistened like oil, the effect of light on rain-drenched skin.

The car stopped heavily and Alice woke up abruptly.

"What the hell is it?"

"A man just ran into the road. I nearly knocked him down."

"You should drive more slowly," Alice said predictably.

Richard was already outside the car, peering into the darkness behind. He listened through the rain but could hear nothing.

Alice said, "I'll drive, shall I? That way we might get home safely."

"I didn't *hit* him, Alice. And he *did* run into the road . . ." But Richard was disturbed by the man's appearance. "I just thought for a minute . . ."

He got back into the car and sat quietly. As Alice woke more fully from her drowsy state so her shock and her irritation passed away. "Let's go home."

"I thought I recognized him. I only glimpsed him . . ."

"Probably a farmer's lad, drunk. As you said, you didn't hit him, so let it alone. I'm cold."

"He was wearing a dressing gown. Gaping open. Did you see him, Alex?"

Behind him the boy nodded palely. His eyes were wide and he looked upset.

"Alex?"

"It was Mr. Keeton," the boy said quietly. He was shaking. Richard went cold as the man's face became clearer to him. "It was Tallis's father," Alex repeated. "It was Mr. Keeton."

"Nonsense," Alice said, but she frowned when she saw the look on her husband's face. "Jim Keeton and Tallis disappeared over a year ago. You know that, Alex. He hasn't come back, now. If it was Jim, then it's his ghost."

Richard was trying to remember something from those distressing days, when the countryside had been searched and no sign of the two Keetons found. "When Jim vanished ... wasn't it in the morning? He'd run out of the house in his dressing gown. Don't you remember what Margaret told the inquest?"

Alice shrugged. "I remember. But they've been gone for over a year. You're not telling me that a year later he's still wearing his dressing gown ..."

Richard looked round in the darkness. On the small back seat of the car his Red Knight son was hunched, knees drawn up, eyes wide as he stared at his father. He was crying silently.

Five hours later, James Keeton came to their cottage. The rain had eased, but he made a miserable and bedraggled figure, standing at the bottom of the garden, staring at the dark window where Alexander watched, the mask held against his chest. He opened the gate and ran quickly to the back door, tapping on the glass. Alex struggled to see the man from his bedroom, but Keeton had moved through the rain to stand outside the dining room. Like a bird, tapping with its beak, Keeton kept tapping with his fingers, pressing his face against the glass, hand raised, tap-tap-tapping as he peered into the darkness of the cottage.

Alex stood on the landing, shivering. His pajama trousers came undone and he struggled to tie them more securely. He listened to the noise of the beak on the glass downstairs, and remembered his friend Tallis's tales of birds, and bird creatures, and nights filled with wings. He slowly descended the stairs, and in the dining room approached the half-moon face of the man outside, coming closer until he could see the beard and the curve of pale flesh above, stepping right up to the window where the half-naked man tap-tap-tapped in slow desperation. Alex gently tap-tap-tapped back. Keeton's nose was squashed against the glass. A trickle of rain ran down between eyes and windowpane. He held the odd piece of rotting wood in one hand, and Alex saw the crude face, the moon-like curves, the cuts for eyes. He recognized it as one of Tallis's masks. It was Moondream. He pressed his hand against the glass where the mask watched, remembering his lost friend.

The water on the pane, outside, mingled with the tears that Mr. Keeton shed.

"Don't run away," Alex called, and the man closed his eyes. He seemed to slump against the glass and continued to tap with the mask, as if he were a weary Punch and Judy man, using the cold-eyed wood to entice the children's fancy. Moondream tapped the window and Keeton sank down into a huddle; mask-face and man-face disappeared from view.

Alex went outside with the Persian rug from the hallway and wrapped the heavy fabric around the freezing man. Mr. Keeton was silent, now, hugging the mask and watching the dark, damp night through eyes that were unpleasantly blank and watery. Alex tried to help him stand, but he wouldn't move.

"Don't run away again. Promise? Stay here."

The man made a strange sound, then curled more tightly into his saturated dressing gown and the thick, dry rug, pulling the knotted ends around his neck.

Alex went upstairs and woke his father.

"Mr. Keeton's come home. But he's very sad. I think Tallis must be dead."

Moondreaming

There was something very curious about James Keeton's condition. When he had been bathed, shaved and his hair brushed, only a desperate, haunted look in his eyes suggested any difference to the robust and over-nourished man who had disappeared, presumably to live rough and wild, one year and fifteen days ago. His wife, Margaret, was very distressed, hardly touching her husband, but staring at him as he was examined by a local doctor, and talked to and tested, but without responding in any way.

Keeton's skin was scratched in places, and his two big toes very bruised. The growth of beard, now removed, had been that of four or five days. His dressing gown, though the pockets were torn, once dry was as good as new—not the raggy robe that might have been expected from a year in the wild.

Oddest of all, the elastoplast on his index finger covered an almost healed cut. The day before he had disappeared, Keeton had cut himself carving a shoulder of lamb for the family lunch.

Had he been looked after somewhere during his absence, only to be returned to his original appearance (minus pajamas!) a few days before, to run blindly along the country lanes around Shadoxhurst? Only James Keeton could answer that question, and Keeton was saying nothing. He rocked slightly in the armchair, and seemed, at times, to be looking into the far distance. He cried silently, and his lips moved, but no sound emerged.

The doctor made a tentative diagnosis of shock, inducing a temporary catatonic state. He might emerge from it at any moment, or he might become dangerous, to himself if not to others. He should be taken to hospital for further and more expert examination, he advised.

Throughout all of this, from two in the morning to the new day, Keeton held firmly onto the crude mask, his grip tightening like a child's when Richard tentatively tried to take it.

"Tallis was always making those things," Margaret murmured from across the room. She was pale, exhausted with confusion. "Which one is it?"

Alexander said, "It's Moondream. She told me more about it, but I've forgotten."

At the sound of the boy's voice, or perhaps at the mention of the mask's name, Keeton's unfocused gaze hardened and he sat up straighter, his lips smacking together for a moment. When Alex put his arm around the man's shoulder, Keeton curled into the embrace; apparently relaxed.

At his own request, Alex drove with the Keetons to the infirmary, fifteen miles away, near a secluded village on the county border. Richard and others from Shadoxhurst spent the next three days searching the countryside for any sign of Tallis, but for a second time they found nothing. The owners of the Ryhope Estate scoured the edges of Ryhope Wood and the area adjacent to the mill-pond, but reported that they, too, had found no traces. Twice, Richard went across the fields to the wired-off road, and stood where the old road entered the gloom, to the ruins of Oak Lodge where his son, and other children, had once played. High, barbed-wire fencing and notices of the prosecution of trespassers, were unfriendly reminders of the detached and hostile attitude to the local community that now resided in the Manor House: the two children (now in their thirties) had inherited the property after the death of their father.

Alex was a regular visitor to James Keeton over the next four weeks, and Richard and Alice both became concerned at what appeared to be the boy's insatiable curiosity about the silent man. Keeton sat immobile and silent, staring into space, the Moondream mask either clutched to his chest or propped up on the mantelpiece of his small, private room, overlooking the woods. But although Richard talked to his son, tried to discourage him from the obsessive visiting, Alex would not be persuaded. He could cycle the fifteen miles to the hospital in just over two hours. His homework suffered. He was always glad if Richard drove him to the secluded place, and seemed unbothered by his father being in the room.

What Alex did was to whisper stories to the frozen man. As he spoke, he stroked Keeton's hands. Sometimes he held the mask up for him, and invariably Keeton leaned forward to peer through its eyes. It was the only voluntary movement he made. Everything that Alex did sounded reassuring. He told jokes, wild adventures, he talked of Tallis.

"Come back, Mr. Keeton. Come back home," Richard heard him saying once. "I know you're still wandering. You can come back now. Everything is safe."

In the car, driving back to Shadoxhurst, Richard asked his son what he had meant by those words.

"It's just a feeling," the boy said. "His body's here, but I think his spirit is still wandering, still searching for Tallis."

"This sounds like a fairy story."

Alex shrugged. "Sometimes he whispers things that make me think he can see other lands."

"Like the land of the Green Knight, eh?" Richard said, and then the implication of what Alex had said struck him. "He *whispers* things? He talks to you?"

"Not to me," the boy said, shifting in the car seat and staring out at the darkening landscape. "But he talks ... Not very much, and always in whispers. It doesn't make much sense, but I think he's wandering somewhere, searching hard."

A month to the day after his committal to the infirmary, Keeton recovered consciousness dramatically. By the time Richard and Alex arrived at the hospital he was in a state of high excitement. He didn't appear to recognize Richard, but began to talk almost incoherently to the boy, even as he peered through the face of the mask on the mantel-ledge.

"I can see her, Alex. I've caught up at last! She's on the other side of the mask. I'm not sure if she knows it's me, and she can't hear me, but she's there, among big trees, with several riders. She seems well. But she's so grown up."

Richard watched and listened as the older man poured out his vision to the thirteen-year-old.

"Her face is scarred. She's become so tall. I think she must be a hunter of some sort. They're in a deep wood, near a river, among stone ruins. An old man is with her, and he keeps crying. There's something very strange in the trees—like a creature ..."

"May I look?" Alex asked.

Keeton passed the boy the mask and Alex held it to his face, peering *in* through the eyes, turning slightly as if adjusting his view. From his expression it was clear that he had seen nothing but the room. Keeton took the mask back and placed it on the mantelpiece, touching the smeared moon-shapes, the crudely gouged eyes. His white shirt was saturated with sweat, his gray flannels creased and drooping. His hair had turned completely white in the last month, a startling change that occurred overnight, as if a ghost had touched him and he had been unable to respond.

He sat down now and sighed deeply. "Alex?"

"Yes?"

"It was her. It was my little girl all grown up. Wasn't it?"

"Yes," Alex whispered.

"Oh dear," the man said, then slumped a little. "Oh dear ..."

And then he was silent. Within moments he had slipped away again.

He came back two weeks later, raving and angry, screaming as he stared inward through the eyes of the mask. He had to be sedated. Thereafter, every three or four days he would emerge from his catatonic state and address an aspect of the reality he could experience through his daughter's childish creation.

As often as possible, Richard took Alex to see him, aware that the two of them shared a rapport that was quite exclusive. Keeton described wild visions, of journeys across marshlands, of great snows, of thudding and frightening skirmishes, fought out in bloodstained mud, of fires on hills and mad dancing at fire-lit dusk. And as he described these visions he seemed at peace, as if he knew that his daughter would return to him.

The periods of lucidity were short-lived, however, the longest being only five hours. And the longer the lucid phase, the longer the time in silence, empty of dreams, empty of life. Quite often, at weekends, Alex would beg to visit the hospital, only to be frustrated and saddened by a day of sitting with a dead man. Not even the touching of the precious mask could draw a flicker of response from James Keeton.

Alex must have heard the rows between his parents, but said nothing, just became more withdrawn himself. Alice had become increasingly angry and concerned at the time Alex was spending at the hospital. She wanted to end the relationship. Richard argued that there was a special trust between the two, and that Alex might be the channel through which the man would return to full sanity.

"What the hell is the attraction? They hardly know each other—"

"I know. I don't know what the attraction is. Perhaps it's Tallis, a link with her. All I know is, Alex seems to comfort the man, and he's happiest when they're talking, sharing visions."

"Visions!" Alice's frustration made her face contort, anguish and anger aging her. "We've got to put a stop to it, Richard. He's not himself anymore. I don't recognize him."

"Give him time, Alice. If he *can* help Jim . . ."

Alice, exasperated, closed her mind to the argument. "You're a fool."

Alex, certainly, heard it all, and sometimes he would try to reassure both parents, but only by touch, never with words.

One night, in the early spring, he crawled on all fours into his parents' bedroom, reached up and tugged his father awake. Richard peered over the side of the bed and groaned.

Alex silenced him with a finger to lips and beckoned him to come downstairs. Blearily, Richard followed, as Alice slept restlessly and full of her own unexpressed—perhaps inexpressible—pain.

At the back door Alex pointed into the March night. "There's a fire by the wood, people dancing. They've got drums. It's very weird."

Now that he looked carefully, Richard could see the faint, flickering glow of light from near Hunter's Brook, at the edge of Ryhope Wood. When he investigated his tall son with his fingers he could tell that Alex was wet with rain, and cold with night air. He was also dressed in jeans and windcheater.

"Have you been *out*?"

"Come and see! Bring a stick. They're all dancing with sticks around the fire."

"Have you been *out*?" he whispered again. "At three in the morning?"

From the far distance the sound of drums swelled on the night breeze. It was an odd rhythm, faintly audible, a fluctuating murmur in the cold night.

"Come and dance! *Please,* Daddy. Get a stick. Do it for Tallis."

Richard stared at the pale features of his son. "For Tallis? What do you mean by that?"

"I was dreaming of her. And the fire. Then I woke up. It might help Mr. Keeton to find her again."

Confused, very cold, aware that he was operating in a game that he didn't understand, Richard nodded. "What sort of stick?"

"Anything. Anything wooden. Tallis's call was always wood."

Richard went upstairs and dressed quietly, then explored the playroom, searching behind cartons, trunks and camping equipment until he found his old school cricket bat. "Willow," he said as he closed the door, walking down the path with Alex. "Will that do? It's signed by Fred Trueman."

Alex had no idea what his father was talking about. Impatiently he said, "Let's go!"

Six months before, Richard had watched a rain-saturated

woman in army fatigues run along this bridleway. Now he used a heavy torch to illuminate the way to the small fire that burned by Hunter's Brook.

The air pulsed dramatically with the fierce drum sound. As he drew closer he could see dark shapes twisting wildly in front of the flames. He was reminded of Indian dancing from Western films, but there was no chanting or singing, just the rapid, turning dance of eight or nine cloaked human figures, whose death-white faces caught the firelight as they spun.

The land dropped slightly to a muddy brook, then rose again. Alex scrambled up the slope in the darkness, an eager shape picked out in the beam from Richard's torch. As Richard struggled through the freezing brook, gasping as cold water soaked his feet, he became aware of the sudden ceasing of the drum beat. At the top of the rise he stared at the fire close by, but the figures had gone now, and the March night was still and silent, save for the murmur of wind.

Alex ran to the fire, crying out and running around the flames waving his stick. As Richard flashed the torch around, he picked out the tall, feathered pole that had been pushed into the ground. An odd twig-doll dangled from the top, clattering against the wood as the wind whipped up. A light but steady rain began to fall, driving in gusts at Richard as he stood and watched the fire. The glowing embers sizzled as they were quenched.

"They've gone!" Alex cried again, staring toward the woods.

"Let's go home," Richard said.

Alex turned back to him. "We should dance. Dance round the fire."

Richard raised his cricket bat and looked, by flamelight, at the faded scrawl that was the signature of his cricketing hero. The face of the bat was dented and discolored from years of use at school. Where the handle joined the willow blade there was a deep split, making use of the bat dangerous.

"Alex—"

"Daddy! Dance with me! It'll bring them back . . ."

"I'm afraid I'd feel rather foolish."

"That's what you always say! That's why you never do anything!"

Alex ran to the feathered pole and knocked the twig-doll down, turning it in his hands, examining it minutely. He was shuddering, and Richard realized the boy was crying.

The rain suddenly started to fall more heavily, and the fire hissed and spluttered, burning more brightly before dimming. Disappointed and distressed, but unwilling to take his father's hand, Alex followed back through the pitch-dark of the night, back along the mudtrack, to the dark house where Alice slept.

Richard crawled gratefully back to bed, but slept badly, his dreams centering around dancing and fire. He was not a man given to intuition or premonition, but he felt nevertheless an eerie sense that something was about to happen.

The phone woke him at six in the morning. He stumbled out onto the landing and snatched the receiver from its cradle, groggily acknowledging the caller. It was Margaret Keeton. Her husband was awake and raving. He kept asking for Alex. The specialist in charge of his case felt that this might be a last moment of lucidity before a total collapse; so could the family and friends come at once?

James Keeton was standing at the mantelpiece. He was fully dressed and stooping slightly to peer in through the moondream eyes of the ragged mask. He was calling softly for his daughter. He was hardly raving, but Alice took one look at him and turned, walking stiffly away down the corridor. "I'll go and keep Margaret company at reception. She's had a night of this. She must be exhausted."

Alex went up to the man and touched his arm. Keeton looked round, glanced over at Richard and smiled.

"Where's Margaret?"

"Downstairs. Shall I get her?"

Keeton shook his head. "Poor Margaret. She's aged . . . This must have been a hard few days." He stroked the mask gently, then seemed to change his mood, a glow entering his eyes. "I think she's coming home," he said to Richard, then repeated the words to Alex and squeezed the boy's shoulders.

"Tallis?"

"Yes. Tallis. Coming home—but I'm afraid—I'm afraid she's coming the hardest way of all." A moment's shadow, then a vigorous voice again. "There has been such a battle, Richard. Crows on the field, feeding on the dead, and ragged folk dismembering and carrying off the corpses. Through these eyes I can see her, but she's so old now. Such a full life led. I wish I could have been with her. I don't know if she even hears me."

He turned to the mask and called again. "Tallis?" And after a moment, the name again, and again, before a sad yet smiling resolution. "She can't hear me."

Aware of Alex, Keeton rested a hand on the boy's shoulder, then took down the mask and placed it against Alex's eyes. "What do you see? Do you see anything? Perhaps she'll speak to you."

"I can't see anything," Alex confessed.

Again, Keeton placed the mask on the mantelpiece, then went to the armchair and sat down heavily, letting his breath out slowly, his eyes half-closed as if with effort.

He watched Richard for a moment, then asked, "How long was I away?"

"Away?"

"Before I was brought to this place."

"A year, Jim. We thought you were dead. We thought—suicide."

Keeton laughed dully, shaking his head. "Why not? There's no life left, now. I've lost her, Richard, just as I lost my son before her. There's nothing, now. I didn't believe her when she told me stories of the wood, what a strange place it is—but she's gone there, and she's gone for good. Four days ago she went away. She won't come back. And I'm a dead man, as good as. I've seen what's happened to her—"

"She's been gone for a year and a half, Jim. She was gone a year when you turned up again." Richard felt awkward. "You were gone for a year yourself . . ."

"Four days," James Keeton repeated. "And a lifetime." But now he frowned, watching Richard curiously. "A year?"

"A year. Not that you'd have known it from looking at you. You've been in hospital for six months."

"A year," Keeton said, savoring the words, his eyes

closed. "Dear God, it was a strange place. The stream into the wood. Ryhope Wood. I saw her riding. There were four men with her. I tried to follow, but they were too fast, and I was so cold—and then the strange place, and the gentle ghosts, and they took me by boat across the sea to a lovely island, but I was so unhappy and they brought me back. A moon-faced girl showed me the way from the wood. And when she left me, a demon started to laugh and tear at me, and then the rain ..."

"What strange place? Can you tell me, Jim? Can you remember?"

Keeton's eyes opened, looking wild for an instant, then with a long sigh he said, "It comes over me and traps me. It's as if everything is sucked from me, all energy, all thought, all hope, all intensity. I become empty, clinging by a thread. I am aware of you, but can't respond. I don't even have the energy to scream inside."

Richard realized that the subject had changed. Keeton was talking about his existence *now,* how it felt to be home.

"Time means nothing," he went on. "Alex's voice is soothing, but even that is just like water, lapping over me. There is no pain, Richard, no anguish. And then suddenly there is a flow of energy and Tallis is back. She's on the other side of the mask, do you know that? The mask is her, and the eyes can see her. When she's close I can hear her, see her, almost touch her. I've watched her in glimpses, growing old, fighting, loving. She bore three children. Three. But they all died. She's nearly gone now. When she goes, I go too. I have nothing left."

"You've got us," Alex said. "Especially me."

Keeton laughed and hugged the boy.

"We don't want you to go, Jim," Richard said. "We want you to come home. Come with us. Keep yourself well."

"If I could I would," Keeton said. "But I have no control over the ebb and flow of my life. Margaret means nothing to me anymore, and she knows it, and I feel it is the same with her. When Tallis went away, part of me went with her. First Harry, now her ... Whatever is beyond that mask controls me."

Nonsense, Richard thought, looking at the scrap of wood.

But he couldn't bring himself to articulate the dismissive word aloud.

A male nurse came into the room and spoke briefly with Keeton, then Richard, and left. Richard, weary of the other man's sentimental ramblings, aware that he was really addressing everything to Alex, excused himself for a while and went down to sit with Alice and Margaret. But he had been downstairs for only a few minutes when he began to feel uncomfortable, even alarmed. The two women talked quietly together.

"I'm going back up," Richard said, and hastened away from reception, taking the stairs three steps at a time, breaking into a run along the stark, gray-carpeted corridor.

Breathless, he arrived at Keeton's room, and saw the man again standing at the mask, stooping to peer through the eyes. Behind him, Alex was a hunched, crying shape. Tearful eyes turned on Richard, and the boy shook his head, mouth quivering.

What was happening?

Richard stepped into the room.

Keeton said, "Tallis?"

Then more loudly, "Tallis!"

A look of relief touched his face. "We were worried about you," he said through the eyes of the mask. "We thought we'd lost you."

And a moment later, smiling, Keeton added, to no one in particular, "Well, thank God for that."

He turned from the mask and went to the window, looking out across the grounds of the hospital. Then, with a small laugh and a sigh, he came to his chair, sat down, closed his eyes . . .

Richard went over to him . . . "Jim?"

"He's dead," Alex said.

Richard felt quickly for Keeton's pulse. "He can't be."

"She came home," the boy said, trembling as he spoke, looking very frightened. "That's the end of it. Mr. Keeton found what he wanted. Tallis came home."

Alex had crossed the room and was peering through the eyes of the mask. Richard felt for the pulse in Keeton's warm wrist, found none. He listened at the man's mouth, stretched open an eyelid, then dragged the body down onto the floor, stretching it out.

"Get a nurse!" he said, but Alex kept staring through the mask. "Alex! Go and fetch help. I don't know how to do this. Alex!"

Thump.

A fist to the dead man's chest, then a more controlled, careful placing of one hand over the sternum, and a thump with the other. Dear God, how should it be done? Press, then hit. Press, that was right . . .

"Alex!"

He pushed down on Keeton's chest, four times hard, then opened the man's jaws and pressed his own mouth against the cooling lips. He inflated Keeton's lungs, then watched the air drain away.

"I don't know what to do. I never trained . . . Alex, for Christ's sake get some help!"

As he shouted his son's name, as he turned in desperation, aware that footsteps were pounding along the corridor outside and that a cacophony of screaming and shouting had erupted from the other rooms, as he looked desperately to Alex for help, so the boy screamed "Mr. Keeton!" A second later he was *blown* across the room. The air stank suddenly of wet earth and wood and for a moment the space between mask and boy writhed and rippled, like the distorted reflection in disturbed water. There was a distant sound, like harsh laughter, then all air was drawn from the room and the windows rattled, the door slammed back on its hinges.

Frozen with shock, Richard watched Alex hit the wall and slump. In the instant before he collapsed his eyes were wide, his face a mask of terror. Then he fell forward, folding into himself, curling up like a leaf, and Richard was on him in moments, unrolling him, cradling him.

Laughter—echoing, then dying—mocking laughter . . .

"Alex! Alex!"

The boy was still conscious, but his whole body was shuddering uncontrollably. Wet, empty eyes stared up at his father. His mouth worked, his tongue licked his lips.

"Alex . . . what happened? What happened?"

Alex stared at his father blankly, his gaze unfocused.

Then, like a small child, he reached up and put his arms round Richard's neck, drawing himself closer, curling into the heavy frame of the man, nestling there.

A male nurse was at work on James Keeton.

"What happened? What's that smell? Oh Christ! Adrenalin! I need Adrenalin—"

"He suddenly collapsed," Richard said, as he crouched, cradling Alex in his arms.

"He's gone," the man said anxiously, shaking his head. "He was so fit. This isn't right. I'll keep trying. *Where the hell's the Adrenalin?*"

Two female nurses ran into the room, one to look after Alex. Richard stood up and bit back his own tears, watching the black eyes of the boy, the wet lips moving silently. The nurse whispered to the lad, then looked up.

"You'd better go to your wife. She and Mrs. Keeton are walking out in the grounds."

Richard nodded dumbly. But instead of going downstairs, he felt impelled to go over to the mask, to pick it up—

("He's dead. I can't get him back. Damn! Get Doctor Warren up here.")

It was an odd and eerie sensation, but where before when he had handled the mask it had tickled his senses, making the hair on his neck prickle, now he saw just a childishly-daubed piece of bark. It was quite lifeless, rotting; dead-eyed and meaningless.

Later, when he went over the events of that morning in his mind, Richard could no longer be sure that Alex had been *blown* across the room. He had run back and struck the wall in his excitement or panic; he had stunned himself. Everything had been happening so fast, with such urgency, that the boy's movements had taken on a surreal quality.

Nevertheless, something had shocked him, something so startling that it had caused him almost to fly backward with surprise.

Alex slept, then woke and was silent for the next few hours, not responding to his parents' attentions. Then he slept again, deeply, restlessly.

By the end of the second day Richard's apprehension had

begun to develop into terror. Alice, grim-faced and cold, talked and talked to the boy, but Alex just responded with incoherent murmurs. His eyes were wide, almost depthless. He stared at things without thought, without real sight. He seemed immune to suggestion. He was in his own world, a new world. The only words he used, at this time, were "chapel" and "giggler." When he murmured "chapel" he seemed agitated, perhaps puzzled. But "giggler" was a sound he used in his nightmares, waking screaming this word, or name, shrieked from lips that were flecked, wet, the expression of a boy terrified by his vision.

He no longer read books. He no longer took interest in the radio, or music, or the events in Shadoxhurst. His models meant nothing. He sat in his room, surrounded by the treasures of his imagination, and stared at the insubstantial air in front of him. The Bradleys kept him away from school, and when the school's inspector came to interview them it took no more than five minutes to convince him that Alex was seriously ill.

Perhaps it was this humiliating and embarrassing visit that broke the wall of resistance in both Richard and Alice. A day after the inspector's visit they arranged for Alex to be taken to the same hospital where James Keeton had spent his last days.

The boy came home every weekend. The three of them walked, and tried to talk, and Alex was calm, pleasant, responsive to the simplest of things, but without any engagement of intellect or imagination. He might have been two years old again. He showed no wonder, no surprise, no interest. Only at night did he scream. When they walked in the woods, when the light was gentle, Alex would sound wistful and point into the distance.

"Chapel . . ."

Perhaps he was remembering the school play, Gawain, the Green Knight, the woodland chapel below the fairy hill. Richard could never find out, because Alex had no words for him, and quite soon Richard gave up trying.

Late that summer, Alex disappeared. The windows of his room were locked, but his door had been left open— there had seemed no reason not to leave it so—and he had probably walked out of the hospital at some time during the night. His day clothes were missing. There was no note, of course. One of the nurses told Richard that for two or three days before, Alex had been more vocal than usual. He had seemed frightened, jumping at shadows or unexpected movements around him. Twice he had locked himself in the small toilet at the end of the corridor, only emerging when his favorite nurse encouraged him out. It was to her that he had spoken his last word, before disappearing from the hospital, a wistfully breathed "chapel." He had been looking into the distance, from his window, over the trees toward Shadoxhurst. Perhaps he had been thinking of home.

His badly decomposed body was found a year later, half-buried in the leaf litter and wild growth of a boggy elm wood at the edge of a local farm. Rooted up by an animal, probably a fox, the traces had been sniffed out by the farmer's dog. The skull had been so badly crushed, by two or three blows, that precise dental association was impossible, but from the size of the bones, the male features of the pelvis, scraps of clothing in the same grave, and the fact that it was found so close to Shadoxhurst, the conclusion at the inquest was that the remains were those of Alex Bradley, unlawfully done to death by person or persons unknown. The police investigation lasted two months, and the file was kept open when local activity ceased.

Alex was buried in Shadoxhurst church in May 1961. His parents' wreath was shaped like Alex's favorite model plane.

Tallis Keeton's moondream mask was buried with the bones.

PART TWO

In the Wildwood

The Green Chapel: 2

It had been raining for hours and he sheltered high on the east wall, curled up below the wide stone arch of an empty window. From here he could see down into the cathedral, where the hollyjack moved restlessly among the saturated trees.

She was upset again. He could tell this easily from the chattering sounds she made, and the way she passed from nest to altar, kicking at the wet benches, gabbling at the wooden faces and watching the boy from behind rain-glistening leaves. The wood in the cathedral rustled continually, occasionally juddered violently as new growth stretched the trunks, the marble floor buckling suddenly as each tree, its roots in the crypt among the bones, thrust a boy's length upward, feeding on the rain and the new life that flowed through the earth.

In the big wood, the giggler came and went, its face thrusting from the edge for an instant only, time enough for the boy in the high window to see a gleaming eye in the black face, a second gouged socket, a grinning mouth, white tusks thin and deadly.

Other creatures hovered at the edgewood too. During this long time of rain he had seen wolves on their hind legs, men with the heads of snarling dogs, a pig of vast size, and bird-men of all descriptions. Most disturbing was a woman in torn green robes. Her hair was a rich and full tumble of red around a noseless face that was as white and dead as a fish, the eyes cold and unblinking, her mouth open and wet. She had watched him for an hour, unmoving, then had stepped carefully back into cover. A minute later the giggler had taken her, noisily and terribly, and fed for a long time while the crows had circled in the rain above the trees, disturbed by the stink of flesh.

Other humans came, peering at the high stone wall of the cathedral. Some had weapons, others were mere shades, cloaked and hooded. One was half-armored, his face covered with metal, the features of a fox, his heavy cloak red around the green bronze. He watched the boy for a long time, then waved and withdrew. The giggler tried for him, but failed to secure the life and retired howling for a while, before it recovered, parted the undergrowth and leered at the watching boy.

Why was the hollyjack so disturbed? She had embraced him and let him travel on the Little Dream, and when he had cried she had soothed him with bird song and thorny caresses. Although she often accidentally poisoned him with her forest offerings, she was always careful with her touch, and never drew blood except when dreaming with him. When the sadness at dreams of his father had passed, she had taken him into her nest, and they had slept for a day or more. When the sky darkened and the rain began to fall, they had both moved back into the sanctuary wood, and while she had explored the area near the altar, he had ascended to the window on the east wall.

She called for him now. She was a bristling, beckoning bush in a thicket of red-berried thorn by the Lady Chapel, gleaming as the rain ran from her leaves. But she was calling for him and he swung carefully down the ivy, touching dog-stone face as he passed it, to pacify it, and entered her embrace again, letting her thorns prick his skin, flowing through her roots into the crypt below the marble, out through the rootweb, past the giggler and the other creatures at the edge.

Where are we going?

Big Dream!

Deeper and deeper through the earth, through glades and hollows, by river cuts and high banks, through beech and elm and lime, willows by lakes, and aspen on chalk downs, flowing through the wildwood like blood through water, spreading, thinning, yet always touching the stone-place and the holly bush.

He came up in a misty place, near a river among silent trees; and the greenjacks were here, the *daurog* as he heard them named. He was in a place older than stone, at a time before words and language, but he felt the presence in the wood of men, though men with eyes and ears only, no mouths or tongues that could articulate, no way of calling save like the birds or wild creatures of the forest they hunted. He peered out into this ancient grove from the face carved in a tree.

The greenjacks were waking from their winter forms, the new growth on their bodies vibrant and sensitive. They moved through the wells of light, scratching at bark, scooping fingers into the earth, or brushing water from the stream along the curving branches that erupted from their mouths. He could see the different forms of the creatures, the oakjack, large and densely leaved, the birch female, quivering and restless, a thin silver shape by the water. Willow and a smaller oak were still rooted, although their heads turned to the light, willow's fringed arms rising as if he was stretching on waking from a deep sleep—and of course, in one way, that was precisely what this family was doing, although it was only the conscious parts of their sylvan minds that had slumbered within the stalking bodies of their winter forms.

There was a hollyjack among them. This evergreen had emerged from hiding, now that the new growth was on her family, and she ran among them, tending to them. She was aware of being watched by one of her own kind, and the hollyjack that cradled the boy quivered uncontrollably as she observed the much younger form.

The greenjacks were moving toward the cathedral. They were advancing steadily through the seasons and the wildwood, closing on the stone-place, but as yet the hollyjack was puzzled by the reason. All the boy could understand from the faint flow of thought, whilst sharing the rootweb, was that the *daurog* were coming for him— and there was great danger if they came in winter.

But the boy was in a waking dream, still, his mind half on his father, half on the terrible creatures who waited for him beyond the sanctuary. Each day he felt a little more alive, although he thought of it as "seeing further." Memories shaped, like images in rippling water that was suddenly still. He felt frightened of the greenjacks, but took comfort in the pricking arms of his nesting friend. He was aware of her own fear, the great fear of the still and silent time of winter, the black time for trees among the heavy white of snow on the earth. A terrible death stalked the wildwood at that time.

Later in the day the skeletal form of the shaman approached the face in the tree, emerging from the darkness of the denser wood. Ghost-of-the-Tree, as the shaman was called, was badly broken. Fragments of bark hung from him like stiffened flaps of brown flesh. One side of his face was ragged, the branch tusks shattered (they would grow back with his own first bud). When he lifted his forelimbs to the watching boy, the fingers were bent, some missing, the nails cracked. He was caked around the mouth and chest with a rust-like paint, the last vestiges of blood from his winter hunting.

But before he fed now, on the reviving nutrients and water of the natural forest, he came to the tree, watching the carved face through those sinister eyes, the glitter of steel encased in wrinkled oak.

After a while, bolder, he approached and scraped the bark face with a nail. The thornwood entered the hard skin of the tree, creating a new cut among the old scars.

There are not sufficient seasons to prevent us from finding you. We'll find you soon—

The thought flowed through the rootweb, frightening and threatening at first, yet perhaps it was more of an exhortation, a fervent wish. The greenjacks were gentle. They were lost on this journey and exuding desperation. Whatever they wanted from the boy in the cathedral, they could not communicate it clearly. They were just coming to find him. The seasons would not stop them.

Boy and hollyjack flowed away from the face in the tree. The rain fell steadily, pouring from ledges and stone faces, pelting the trees inside the cathedral where bush and boy curled together.

Don't let me go. Hold me. Don't let me go—I want to see him again.

The hollyjack closed over him; rain filtered through the leaves of her crown and dripped onto the boy's closed eyes. He flowed with the Little Dream again, drawn by the feelings of confusion and anguish from his father.

The man was alone and frightened. He was hiding in a clearing, striking at shadows; the bear-man was gone, and his father was lost. The power of his fear and his loneliness writhed like a twisted vine through the rootweb, and the boy followed this scent and surfaced at the edge of the glade, his head full, now, of the lost man's inner voice, memories that were fresh in the man's mind, recent events that had much to do with his son . . .

Out of the Pit

The drive from his London flat had been long and tedious. Beyond Oxford the traffic had been slow and Richard had been unable to pick up the Home Service on his new car radio. He had been forced, instead, to fill the car with the sounds of rock and roll coming from either the Light Program or Radio Luxembourg. He had enjoyed Procol Harum (though the lyrics to "A Whiter Shade of Pale" left him bemused), Pink Floyd and the jaunty sounds of The Kinks with "Waterloo Sunset," but he couldn't get away, it seemed, from a syncopated piece of trivia called "Puppet on a String" and an appalling piece of crass commercialism called "I'm a Believer," and their performance, as he drove the last few minutes to Shadoxhurst, had been punctuated with his cries of Dear God, oh dear God, this can't be called Music!

You old man, he lectured himself as he finally stepped out into the cool country air and stared over the thorn hedge at the small spire of Shadoxhurst church. He ached from the drive. He was thirsty, hungry and haunted.

He was home for a short break from work, back to the house, back to bad dreams. But for Richard this trip was an annual pilgrimage—his fifth—that he felt he had to make.

The footpath to Shadoxhurst was overgrown with early nettle. He kicked through the weeds, crossed an open field, and clambered over the locked gate of the small churchyard. It had rained earlier in the day and everything was fresh and moist. His desert boots soon became saturated as he approached his son's grave and knelt down, his heart torn between grief and peace.

Someone had put fresh flowers in the small porcelain pot on the green gravel. Bird droppings were smeared across the name on the granite headstone and Richard spent a minute or so cleaning off the lime. His fingers, touching the sharply inscribed letters of the name, felt only stone.

He's not down there, not all of him, only part of him. What happened? What in God's name happened?

The loss was too much, and the return to the village too strong an event to resist: emotion surged; and for a while he sat, letting the sodden turf saturate his skin through his jeans, and cried, and missed Alex, and thought of Alice, long gone Alice.

He was startled by the sounding of the church bell. It was three-fifteen. The bell rang a second time, then was silent. A moment later the side door of the church opened, closed, and was noisily locked.

Richard returned to his car and drove to his house, parking on the street and spending a few minutes greeting neighbors. It was clear that his absence from the village, and from the house, was a source of criticism. But he had found it impossible to stay here after Alex's body had been found, and had moved to London, where he now worked in a bank.

Entering the house through the back door he was at first overwhelmed by the smell of damp. During the winter there had been a leak in the bathroom ceiling, and the carpets were encrusted with fungus. Giant spiders scuttled across the enamel of the bath itself. He trod the floor warily, but the soaking wood was firm. Below, the ceiling of the utility room sagged badly, and he sighed as he thought of a peaceful holiday now inclining toward repair work.

Everything otherwise was as he had left it. He had fresh bedding and a bottle of wine. The bookshelves were full of old favorites. There was no television. He would not miss it.

Inside the front door was a scatter of letters. He picked them up and leafed through them, the accumulation of nine months' absence. Among them were two scrawled notes on paper that had been folded and not enclosed in an envelope, and as he opened the sheets he was disturbed by the hand-writing on one of them. It seemed familiar.

The first note, written in a robust, upright style, read: *"Mr. Bradley—I have some information for you of urgent interest. No one in the town knows your forwarding address, but I'm told you return here regularly. I've left an instruction with the manager of the Red Lion. I'll drop by just before Christmas and hope to catch you then."*

It was signed *Alexander Lytton.*

The second note, in a slanting but precise hand, read simply, *"You're a hard man to pin down. But we'll keep trying. Believe me, Mr. B, you'll want to talk to us. I don't want to be more specific right now. We need to talk. If you come back to the house in the next few months, can you go out to the brook, where the bridlepath crosses it, and tie a green ribbon to the signpost there? And check to make sure it stays? One of us will notice it and stop by. We move in and out all the time. Sorry to be so mysterious."*

It was signed *Helen Silverlock.*

When the Red Lion opened, at six-thirty, Richard went into the lounge bar and ordered a pint. He was served by some-one he didn't know, but Ben Morris came down later and greeted him.

"Showing your face again, eh?"

"Time to come home, Ben. Time for a holiday."

"There were some folk looking for you, a few months back."

"Yes, I know. They spoke to you. Left a message or something . . . ?"

"Last summer. Strange pair of tourists, strange dress. The bloke was small, sturdy, a Scot, very irritable. The woman was very pretty, like, long black hair. A right head-turner. She was American, no doubt about it. Not a hippy, though. Not a student. But both of them queer, like. Odd clothes. They were looking for you but wouldn't say why."

"What did they ask you to tell me?"

Ben nodded and frowned. "If you came home, you were to tie a ribbon out by the old track, by the brook. Nobody knew where you were, Richard. You didn't leave an address . . ."

"I know. I wanted to be away. Did they say anything else? Did you get an idea where they worked?"

Ben shook his head. "He was some sort of scientist, working out on the Manor grounds, there. I heard them talking about 'The Station'. That's all. As I said, queer, like."

It was a fine May evening, very tranquil, very warm, the light almost lucid. Richard walked along the bridleway to the brook, found the signpost, and tied a strip of green rag, torn from an old shirt, around the top. Two riders galloped over the hill, from Ryhope Manor, he imagined. Ryhope Wood, on the Manor estates, was shimmering, a solid wall of green and orange, just across the fields, beyond the rights of way. Alex had been fascinated by Ryhope, as had his friend Tallis, but probably only because it was reputed to be haunted.

Having left his marker, he returned to his house and began the process of unwinding, with fish and chips, red wine and *Cold Comfort Farm*, a school favorite of his.

Two days later, she was waiting for him when he returned from a shopping trip to Gloucester. She had found the green ribbon and arrived in Shadoxhurst as fast as she'd been able. Finding the house open she had entered and called for Richard, but then gone outside and sat down against the base of the elm at the bottom of the garden.

As he stepped through the gate she rose from the ground, startling him. She was dressed in a dull brown anorak and baggy trousers, tied tightly around hard working-boots the color of mud. Her long hair was jet black, save for a silver streak at each temple. Her skin was tanned and her eyes an intense green. For a second she had seemed a part of the tree and its root system, but now she stood, breathing hard and extending a friendly hand.

"I'm Helen Silverlock." She tugged the streak of white and grinned. "My grandfather named me 'Frightened of Foxes' but I buried that one years ago. I left you the note. I *guess* you're Richard Bradley?"

"Yes, I am." As he stepped closer to shake hands he became aware of her smell, stale breath and the damp, rather rank scent of wet undergrowth. Her gaze was startling, flickering over Richard's face in a penetrating and inquisitive way that unnerved him slightly. As his grip curled around her fingers, he felt the scaly, bark-hard skin on the back of her hand, and was so taken aback that he broke the greeting prematurely and obviously.

She smiled at him, rubbing the skin—which was almost black. Had she been burned?—and said, "It's OK. It doesn't cause me pain."

"Looks nasty."

"Necessary," she said cryptically, and then, as if slightly embarrassed, put her hands into the deep pockets of her strange anorak. She was not tall, and her American accent gave him no hint as to where she was from in the States. As they walked to the house he asked the question.

"Nebraska. A small town called Watanka Lake. I'm Lakota Sioux. Not pure blood, but not far off. I've lived in Brazil for four years, and here in the U.K. for over a year now, so home seems a long time ago . . ."

"Well, you're more than welcome in my own damp and humble home," Richard said as he let her into the house.

She confessed that she'd already entered once. "I forgot where I was. Back home it would have seemed normal . . ."

Richard was easy about the intrusion, but then he began to remember the running woman of eight years ago, the intruder who had scrawled a note to him, an incomprehensible message. And connections, nagging connections, began to be made.

Helen sat at the kitchen table, biting her lip and clearly not totally at ease. Richard offered tea, coffee or red wine.

"Not wine," she said. "Coffee, if it's made from beans."

"I'm afraid I only have Camp Coffee. It's a liquid. Quite thick. Quite strong."

She grimaced, showing her teeth and just a hint of tongue, but smiling too. "Tea would be just fine," she said.

"I agree."

As he poured water into the kettle she asked, "Do you have a TV? A paper?"

"No TV, I'm afraid. And I've chucked my paper away. Why?"

She shrugged, loosened the zip of her overcoat. "This is going to sound odd," she said. "But what's today's date?"

He had to think for a moment. "It's . . . I think it's the eleventh. Yes, the eleventh of May. Does that help at all?"

With a laugh, walking over to the window and peering out at the evening, she said, "Just helps me orient."

Richard leaned against the sink, watching his odd guest. He noticed a film of moisture on her forehead and, unsure as to whether she was hot or just nervous—she was behaving nervously—he suggested she shed her coat. Without response she unzipped the anorak and tossed it on the floor by the back door, returning to her chair at the table. The heavily lined, baggy trousers were tied about her waist with a belt of gadgets. Her undershirt was a startling affair of green webbing, a body stocking that hugged her slim frame like a skin. Watching the man watching her, looking at her body, she smiled sympathetically. "It keeps me warm, it keeps me cool. It's based on what the astronauts wear on Apollo."

"I was staring," he said, reddening. "I apologize."

"I don't mind if you stare. It's OK."

With a laugh he said, "You look and sound as if you've just beamed down from the Starship Enterprise."

"Isn't that a neat show? I miss it. I miss a lot of TV. Did you ever see *The Twilight Zone*?"

"My son did. I watched it with him sometimes. The program I always liked was *Quatermass*. Did you see that in America? *Quatermass and the Pit*?"

She shook her head. "I certainly heard about it. Some of the British guys at the Station grew up on it. Ancient Martians, right?"

"Ancient Martians," Richard agreed. "The Station?"

"That's where I'm based. Old Stone Hollow Station, Hollowstone for short."

The kettle boiled and Richard made the tea. His heart had started to race. Helen watched him, more relaxed now. The evening sun, through the window, made her hair shine. The musty, dank smell of her clothes was heavy in the air, but the scent of the tea became stronger for a moment. He was too aware of the gnarled skin on her right hand. He thought of the hand as ruined, but she flexed it easily, the black scales stretching like a lizard's. He was more aware of her eyes. She seemed so familiar with him. Indeed, she seemed familiar *to* him. He thought of her note. He thought of the running woman. The thought nagged its way to expression.

"How long did you say you'd been in England?"

"About a year. In *England*."

"You wouldn't have been in Shadoxhurst in 1959, then?"

She seemed startled, frowning, then quickly said, "Damn it. No. No I wouldn't. Why? I was still at college. Why?"

Disturbed that he had alarmed her he turned and stared, then brought the teapot to the table. His head was in a spin—he consciously thought this as he tried to clear his thoughts—and he tried to visualize the writing on the note that the running woman had left all those years ago. Although he had long since lost the scrap of paper, he was sure that the writing was similar to Helen's. And the running woman had been small, short-haired and bulkily dressed.

What had that note said? He struggled to remember. Some of it came back. "Do you have any idea about . . . premorphs?"

"Pre-morphs?" She looked puzzled.

It wasn't the right word. "Proto-gamma-morphs?" he suggested hesitantly.

"Proto *gamma* morphs? You *have* been watching too much *Star Trek*. No. It means nothing . . ."

But for a second her face clouded, a moment's concerned thought before she again shook her head and confirmed, "No. Nothing at all. Why?"

"I feel I've known you before," Richard said bluntly, and Helen laughed.

"Great line. I've only heard it a hundred times."

"I feel I've known you before," he insisted solemnly, watching her face carefully. She was upset.

She stared at the table, good hand covering the black scales of the other. "Please don't," she said quietly.

"Please don't what? I'm not making a pass. I feel I've known you before. You're very familiar."

"Don't," she insisted. "Just pour the tea. Don't talk about it. Not yet. I didn't come here for this. I'm not ready—"

"But I'm sure it was you—"

She erupted with anger. "Stop it, Mr. Bradley! Stop it now! You don't know what you're doing. Shut up about it!"

Her fury was heavy in the room. Her eyes had widened and her whole facial demeanor had knocked the breath from Richard's body. She had not just been angry: she had been terrified, and had covered the fear with a look of such draining aggression that he was incapable of speech for a moment.

It was she who spoke finally and her words were an apology. Then: "I came to tell you something."

"Tell me then," he said stiffly. "You've obviously been after me for some time. Tell me what you have to say."

"Don't be angry with me. Please! I didn't mean to upset you, Mr. Bradley. I can't explain yet, but you were touching difficult ground for me."

Her candor softened him and he regretted the bitter tone that had touched his words. "Please feel free to call me Richard."

"Richard," she echoed, "I bring you tidings of great joy, yet great difficulty. Greater than I'd realized, since you're obviously in deeper than you know. And I've been in the deep end for a year, now ..."

"You're not making any sense, Helen. What tidings of great joy?"

"We've found your son," she said in an urgent whisper, leaning toward him, trying to instill confidence.

Richard's heart stopped. He banged the cup into its saucer, his face reddening, her words touching anger in him again. "Alex? Alex died a long time ago. What is this? What are you doing?"

"Please!" she said urgently. "Just listen to me. Alex *isn't* dead. We've located him. He's not dead. He's alive. We've made contact with him. He's been communicating with us since late last summer. He's still alive, Richard."

Confused, wanting to feel anger yet aware that the certainty of the woman's words, her assurance, were pointing up his own uncertainties about the fragile, sad remains that

had once been discovered in the woods, he drew breath and
closed his eyes.

Dear God, he thought, I'm beginning to have hope again.

Then he grew black. Alex was dead. Whatever this
woman was talking about, whoever they had found, it was
not his son.

"Who's we? 'We've' found him?"

"We're explorers. I'll come to that later."

"What does he look like? Alex? How does he look?"

Helen looked confused, now, shaking her head, angry at
herself. "I'm not making a very good job of this. Lytton
should have been the one to talk to you. Richard, it's not as
easy as perhaps I'm making it sound. I'm sorry. It's hard to
know how to approach it—"

"Approach what?"

"We've made *contact* with your son. But we haven't exactly *found* him. Not yet, at least."

"He's telephoned you?"

"No. Nothing like that. We *have* found him. We're going
to need your help to bring him home ..."

Tears stung Richard Bradley's eyes and he stood, facing
the garden through the misting window, hands in pockets.

Six years since Alex's body had been found. Six long
years, six empty ones. He could still remember the stink of
the wood as he'd trudged with the police through the saturated bracken. The skies had been overcast, a dull, depressing rain falling. Beneath the trees it was stiflingly humid.
Their footsteps, crushing through the undergrowth, had been
the only sound in the world. A solemn group of men had
stood around the cordoned area where the litter had been
swept away and the distorted torso exposed, its empty skull
upward, the face no more recognizable than a crushed pile of
autumn leaves.

"I'd given up hope," he said from the window. "I can't
believe you. My son went away. He's never coming back.
It's too painful to give me this hope again. You shouldn't
have come."

There was no sound from the woman save for the gentle
clink of her cup returned to her saucer.

He went on, "The bones were very corrupted. Very rotten.

They were an inch or two too short. Or were they? Who could tell what changes had occurred with a skeleton so decayed? The forensic tests were done hastily. They all knew it was Alex. It was easy to bury him and give up anguish. If I've had doubts about his being dead, they've ceased to gnaw at me. So I suppose I've accepted it."

"You've accepted that he's not coming back, not that he's dead. I spoke to the barman at the Red Lion. I know about your doubts. Forgive me, that's why I was so blunt. I thought you'd be glad of the news."

"What news? You've brought me no news. You can't give me evidence of Alex. You confuse me."

He had turned from the window, angrily watching the calm woman at the table. She leaned forward.

"You said the bones were rotten—what exactly was said about them at the inquest?"

"They were woody."

"They weren't bones," Helen said dogmatically, her eyes alive with certainty. "It wasn't Alex. We have a word for what it was. A *mythago*. A false thing. And the boy we've located *is* Alex. Believe me." Her face darkened. "The only problem is ... we don't know where he is *exactly*."

Suddenly suspicious, Richard came back to the table and leaned down on it. "The *boy*? How old is the boy who's been speaking to you?"

"About thirteen," Helen said.

Richard laughed sourly, walking away from her. "What is this? What sort of sick game is this?" But he couldn't look at her as he chided. "If Alex is alive he's nineteen, twenty years old, now. He's a man."

Why was he crying? With disappointment? Anger? He didn't want to be angry with Helen Silverlock. He didn't want her to go. Perhaps hope had surfaced for a moment, but her words had dashed those hopes again.

She said, "He's still a boy, Richard."

Perhaps he was retarded ... perhaps he sounded like the boy he'd been, even though he would be bearded, deep voiced ... NO!

Helen went on, "We've learned a lot from him, including where he lived, this house, and we feel him strongly. He's a boy, and he's not complete. His mind is not complete. But he has strength, and he is drawing his world back to himself. It may take a long time, and it's dangerous. He's in great danger. Dr. Lytton doesn't know if we *will* be able to help him, but we can't do anything until we get our hands on him. That's why we need you. We want to help you, and Alex too. But you have to be involved, which means one weird trip."

After a moment Richard sat down, tried to pick up his cup but the china rattled so badly in the saucer that he abandoned the simple act. "You've hit me where it hurts," he said with a thin smile. "And I think you have something else to tell me. I can sense it. There's something very wrong. Where is it you *think* Alex is?"

"He's built himself a defended site in a ruined cathedral. The cathedral is in the heart of Ryhope Wood—"

"Ryhope? I doubt that. It's on the Estate. An unpleasant and dangerous stretch of wood. But it's far too small to have had a cathedral built within it."

Helen Silverlock laughed delightedly, shaking her head as she watched the man. "You'll be surprised by what can be found there. But I'm not the person to show you. There's more than a ruined church, Richard. And Alex is there too. We can get him back, with your help. But he's a long way in. Maybe three months ..." she said awkwardly, watching him.

"Three months?"

"Maybe three months to get to him. It's hard to tell. There *may* be a shortcut."

"Three months? In Ryhope?" Richard was laughing at the absurdity of what he was hearing.

Helen ignored him, finishing, "And we don't know what's between the edge and the guarded zone he's constructed. There's an anomaly, an abnormality, something we can pass through, but can't *access*."

"Lost," Richard said kindly. "Totally lost."

"Who?"

"Me."

Helen stood and fetched her coat from by the back door, shrugging it on and zipping it halfway up. "It's late. I have to get back, and you need rest." She seemed undecided and disappointed.

Richard toyed with the cup, half-watching the woman, very much wanting her to stay, despite the pain he was feeling.

She couldn't be right. He shook his head. Alex would be twenty! They had the wrong boy. She couldn't be right.

"I've got to go," she said. "If you change your mind, leave another marker. And have good walking boots, weatherproofing, a good book, any medication you need, some food, a good brandy, two changes of clothing, and a rucksack, a good-sized one. Have them ready."

"I have a job in London. I have to be back in two weeks."

"You won't need that much time."

"You said three months. Three months to find him. I don't understand."

"I know. I know you don't. I'm sorry, but it's as hard for me at the moment. Will you come to the Station? It's not far. Six or seven hours' walk. Come tomorrow?"

He shook his head. "I don't know. You have a boy at the end of some sort of communication network and the boy is thirteen. And my boy is twenty. And unless his voice has failed to break, they can't be one and the same. Is it possible he's older than you realize?"

"Maybe," she said with a shrug. "I doubt it. We think he's in a timeslow."

"Something else I don't understand."

"Sorry."

She turned to go, opening the door to the gathering dusk. "Helen?"

Glancing back, she hesitated and smiled. Richard stood and went over to her. "Thank you," he said. "I'm sure your intentions are quite genuine."

"I'll come back," she said defiantly, smiling. "Don't you worry about that!"

As she walked down the path he called out, "Next time he calls you, ask him what stick I danced with round the fire. It was our secret."

"That's a good idea," she said dully, mocking him.

He called again, "I'm being honest with you. I'm not sure

I believe you've found what you tell me you've found. But I'll know him when I hear his voice. I'll know him. If you can arrange it."

Helen had zipped up her coat and was running along the bridleway, toward Hunter's Brook. Richard recognized the gait, and his confusion was compounded.

Helen Silverlock *had* been here before, despite what she'd said.

Oak Lodge

At dawn, a grim gray mist hung over the land, a subdued and flowing sea in which the dark features were the taller trees of the fields and woods.

Richard stood in his bedroom, fully-dressed, hands in his pockets, and stared at the wreathed land, thinking moodily of the woman, her message, her enthusiasm, her strangeness. Crows circled close to the house, flapping and vanishing through the wraithed branches. One detached itself and swooped toward the garden, gliding low over the gate and rising toward the bedroom window with the merest flap of its wings. Richard could hear the scrabbling of nestlings in the disused chimney and waited for the great bird to continue its curve, up to the roof, but the creature came straight on and smashed startlingly against the window. The whole pane shook. The crack of beak on glass seemed deafening. When Richard opened the window and stared down, he could see no sign of the bird, but its dreamlike and dramatic action had disturbed him and he went downstairs.

At nine o'clock he rang Alice in London. She had just arrived at work and was tetchy and tired. She became almost hysterical when he told her, as simply as he could, what Helen Silverlock had implied to him, but when she heard that the boy was thirteen years old she laughed scornfully, then began to get angry. She wanted to know why he had *really* called her.

"For just that reason," he said. "I thought I should keep you informed."

"You have something on your mind. What is it, Richard? Why don't you be honest about it?"

"I rang to tell you what I've told you," he said wearily. "Goodbye, Alice."

He put the phone down, wondered if she would call back and when the phone stayed silent went back upstairs and sorted out his weatherproof clothing.

By midday the gray gloom had been replaced by a bright and overcast sky, a fresh wind bringing the land alive. Richard trudged in heavy boots along the bridleway toward Hunter's Brook. He had not brought a rucksack. He intended only to look a little more closely at the wood where Helen had said she and her team were stationed.

The stream was in wild flood, and along its edge he could see the spoor of deer, probably from the Manor park. A high wall bounded the Estate on most sides, but a right of way passed over several fields, and here the boundary was marked by fences and a stile. Ryhope Wood was a dense and solid wall of trees to his right as he crossed the field toward the old road. He followed this to the wood itself, and was mildly surprised to find that it ended abruptly, overgrown by dense bushes and scrub elder. A "Keep Out" notice had been recently fixed on barbed wire.

He walked on round the wood, conscious that he was now on private grounds. The Manor House was hidden by trees, half a mile away; the only sign of life was a gallop, five riders exercising the horses from the Manor's stables. They crossed open land, then turned and came back, thudding past Richard without taking any notice and passing away toward the ridge where an earthworks had been built, long in the past.

Was this where Alex had come to play with his friends, Tallis and the rest? Tallis had always been so quiet, a mysterious girl existing in a rich fantasy world of story and invention. Alex had always wanted to play rougher games, when outside, exploring woodland being one of them. But he had never talked in detail about Ryhope, only referred to it darkly as a place where "Tallis talks to statues."

What had he meant?

Years after the boy's death, Richard began to miss him again, and to miss the lost opportunity of knowing his son, of sharing his mind games. Alex had always liked comics, and they had read together in peace, or watched TV, but had so rarely spoken or explored ideas. Alice had always been too busy doing things, arranging for trips, for picnics, for journeys to London, for schoolbooks and clothes. She had known Alex's strengths and weaknesses and had been nurturing him toward areas of intellect and interest where he might do well at school, such as playwriting and biology. Even so, she could not have known the inner boy, the adventurer.

He felt sorry for himself, sat for a while head bowed and thought back over the years. He allowed himself tears, and the wind, freshening and gusting, made the enclosed scene all the more mournful.

Alex had been in his grave too long. The pain had passed away too many years ago. The tears, the melancholy, were short-lived, and Helen Silverlock was standing before him again, mysterious and inviting.

An intense curiosity now began to push away the sorrow. The edge of the wood was thorny and grassy, too solid, too dark. It was as if it had never been broken by the passage of people or animals. Sunlight caught the sign across the road, and Richard's interest was piqued.

He eased himself through the barbed wire and entered the gloom of the undergrowth, brushing at branches and ivy as he felt his way carefully along the hard surface underfoot that told of the crumbling road. When the wall of a house suddenly loomed before him he was startled. He touched the brick and pushed through the stifling tangle of creeper and briar, following the wall until he reached the back of the house. Sunlight dappled above him now, and by its flickering light he could see the blackened, rotting shape of a tall wooden idol. It was leaning heavily against the house. If there had ever been carved features they were long since obliterated by rain and time, but he thought he could faintly discern a gaping mouth and the outline of a wide, blind eye.

Crouching, he crawled below the statue, still feeling along

the brick wall, and after a moment stepped into a cleared space, now grassy and filled with flowers and nettles, extending from what had once been French windows. He saw, too, that people had been here recently.

He stepped into the house. The vegetation in the room had been scythed down and the smell of fresh sap was still strong. Through the covering of nettles and ivy he could see the fragmentary remains of furniture. A tree, a substantial oak, grew in the middle of the room, and Richard was puzzled: this was old; had the owners built their house *around* the oak?

He was startled as birds moved noisily above him, where the ceiling had collapsed and branches entwined, and stepped outside again. A small beaten path led from this glade to what had once been a backyard, and here a wider space had been cleared, bounded by thick saplings, but quite light. A ramshackle shed still stood here, and he could see the remains of a fence and gate forty yards away, where the trees grew thick and dark again. The garden area spread away from the creeper-covered hole of the back door, through which he now passed.

Inside he found the kitchen, a heavy marble work-surface, and the remains of fires and food on the floor. He saw, too, the gleam of light on a tracery of wires, and investigated more closely.

There were five wires in all, each the thickness of fuse wire. They had been run to and from various points, out around the perimeter of the garden clearing. There was no electric charge in them. They were just higher than Richard's head and did not seem designed to trap anything. Where they joined the house they were attached to tiny terminals, and around each terminal a gold spiral had been impressed upon the brick.

A sudden wind gusted and the wood swayed restlessly, then was still again. In the sudden silence Richard heard the sound of electricity deeper in the house, and he followed the murmur to its source. In a box in the middle of what might have been a parlor—he could still see the wallpaper and a sodden, fungus-covered armchair below the ivy—he found a small machine, like a miniature radio. It had two needle dials, one of which was flickering. Gold and copper wires led from four sockets into the ground around it, and from a fifth vertically to the exposed laths of the ceiling where the plaster had fallen. The machine emitted the faintest smell of ozone.

As he stepped away from it, the needle on the active dial registered something strongly, then faded. As he approached again the needle quivered but remained essentially inert, only to react suddenly with great swings to the extreme, even though Richard had neither moved nor breathed. It was not responding to him, then.

At this same moment the birds outside fled through the foliage and something crashed away from the house, making a sound that might have been a cry, or perhaps laughter.

Unnerved, suddenly claustrophobic, Richard kicked his way through the tangled undergrowth and out of the overwhelming gloom of Ryhope Wood, back to the field. His head ached and his vision was askew. He rubbed his eyes but they kept watering, the edges of his vision blurred. He was getting a migraine, he imagined, something from which he suffered when he was very stressed.

Oddly, he felt quite relaxed at the moment, merely a little spooked.

He lay back on the damp ground and watched the swirl of grim, gray clouds above. Slowly his vision returned to normal. The breeze made the moisture in his eyes sting with cold.

The gallop was returning. He could hear the drum of hooves, the shouts of delight and encouragement as the five riders stretched their charges to the limit, galloping up the slope, a hundred yards or so from where he lay.

As they passed, Richard still stared up into the sky, but he was aware that one horse had reined-in and was now trotting toward him. He sat up and stared at the young, gray-faced man who rode around him, watching him with the pallor and arrogance of the Manor's new owners. This was the eldest son, a man of thirty or so. In his green parka and flat cap he might have ridden straight from Windsor.

"These are private estates. What the hell do you think you're doing here?"

"I'm walking," Richard said. "Or rather was. At the moment I'm resting. Good morning."

He had meant it to sound dismissive, but the rider kicked his horse forward and came threateningly close. The horse watched Richard through big, tired eyes. Steam was coming off its coat. It was a magnificent animal, seventeen hands at least, gleaming black, its mane tight and trimmed. It watched the man on the ground as if sorry for him.

"The right-of-way is half a mile to your left. Return to it at once."

"The road into the wood . . . that was once a right-of-way too, I imagine. Where did it go exactly? There's a ruined house in the wood . . ."

The horseman came closer and leaned down, waving his crop menacingly in Richard's face. As Richard started to stand up in alarm, the young man thrust the short whip toward the bridleway. "Over there! The right-of-way is over there! If I catch you trespassing again I shall have you arrested."

And he turned and galloped toward the Manor.

Exasperated and angry, Richard walked slowly back to his house, kicked the kitchen table and poured himself a large glass of red wine.

It was an hour later that he finally noticed the message pinned to his kitchen noticeboard:

A cricket bat? You danced around the fire with a cricket bat?

That evening he wrote a brief letter to his parents, and an almost identical note to his place of work.

If you don't hear from me for a while, please don't be anxious. I'm teaming up with some people for an expedition into what I'm told is a pretty remote place, and it's hard to know if I'll get back in time for autumn. I can't talk about the trip in detail, except to say that I've just realized it's something I need to do: full story when I get back. Just one thing: if anybody from a place called Old Stone

Hollow should call you, take what they say very seriously,
even if you think it sounds a bit bizarre.

He took the letters to the Red Lion to be posted, had a
glass of light ale, then returned home and slept well for a
few hours, the result of the nocturnal distraction and alertness that had kept him awake the previous night. Nevertheless, he was up at three in the morning. He dressed quickly,
then packed his rucksack with brandy, apples, sandwiches, a
compass, an adventure novel and changes of clothing; an
hour later he was walking through the same heavy mist that
had encompassed the land the morning before. Now, though,
he walked with purpose and at first light, when he arrived at
Hunter's Brook and found the signpost, he spread a tarpaulin
on the ground, sat down, then curled up to keep himself
warm.

He felt strangely relaxed. The chill on his cheeks reminded him of his school days, and camping on the moors,
or along the Wye Valley.

He knew without knowing that someone would come for
him.

The Wildwood

He was being shaken gently. He opened damp eyes, glimpsed the huge, dark shape above him, and for a second thought that he was being attacked by a wild animal. He yelled with fright and twisted away, looking for a rock or piece of wood with which to defend himself. When no pursuit immediately occurred, he turned back to observe the new arrival.

The man was wearing a heavy bearskin robe, dark brown and black fur splattered with mud. His hair was long and jet black, as was his beard. A red and green feather hung, tied with twine, from a single ringlet on his right temple. Intense brown eyes sparkled with humor from below heavy brows. His boots were dun leather and filthy, their tops fringed with circlets of yellowed animal teeth, which rattled as he moved, crouched on his haunches. From his mouth came a powerful odor of cheese and wild onion.

He was watching Richard, grinning.

"You sent for me, sir?" this behemoth roared with a throaty chuckle, like a smoker's laugh, Richard thought as he wiped dew from his face. The man's accent was French. He extended his hand, quite slim-fingered and cool, not the brawny paw that might have been expected, and Richard shook it. "You *are* Richard Bradley?"

"What's left of him. You've just scared the living daylights out of me."

"I'm Arnauld Lacan, and I'm quite harmless. Good morning! I'm watching the edgewoods for a while and I noticed your summons on the way-marker. Good man! Helen will be glad you've come."

Glancing at his watch, Richard realized that he had fallen asleep for three hours. It was seven in the morning.

"Where is Helen?"

"Beyond Hergest Ridge, looking for a *trickster.* It's a long way from the Station. She went off yesterday, so she might be away for some time. But we think everything should be all right."

Richard reached for his pack, conscious both of the powerful smell of animal sweat coming from the friendly man before him, and of his words. "Why shouldn't everything be all right?"

"It's too deep to be sure," Lacan said with a concerned frown. "It always makes us nervous to go there. But she's been beyond Hergest Ridge before and come back OK. She knows what to watch for. Are you stiff?"

Richard reached out a hand and the other man hauled him upright. As he stood he realized how tall the Frenchman was, probably six feet four. Without being asked, Lacan twisted Richard round and ferociously massaged his shoulders, powerful fingers stretching and bending the joints of his shoulders and back. "Better?"

"Ça va mieux," Richard muttered as the pressure-shock faded.

Lacan laughed loudly. "A man who speaks my language!" he said. "I think I'm going to like you!"

He probed around in his own pack, a bulky affair of stitched hides, and finally proffered a long, dark piece of bone and meat, which reminded Richard of a charred turkey drumstick. "How about some breakfast before we journey?"

"What is it?" Richard asked queasily.

"Bear. Very rich, quite dry, very good."

Richard stared at the tatters of flesh and sinew being waved below his nose. "May I ask from what part of the bear?"

With a grunt, Lacan sniffed the offered gift. "That's a good question. Hard to tell, after all this time. Does it matter?"

"I think I'll stick to apples and cheese," Richard said quickly.

Lacan shrugged. His smile was ambiguous. He returned the dry joint of bear to his pack, then indicated Richard's own rucksack. "Customs inspection. Do you mind? It's what you English would call 'a formality.'"

Hesitating for only a moment, Richard passed the pack across to Lacan, who undid the buckles and reached inside. "Aha!" he said, withdrawing the brandy bottle. But his smile vanished as he stared in disbelief at the label. Without looking at Richard he muttered, "And this, I suppose, is what you English would call 'medicinal.'"

"Best I could find. Sorry."

Lacan sighed sadly. "So am I."

The bottle was replaced, the pack returned. Then more seriously, "Come on. We have to get you into the wood. It's a slow process, learning to go deep. Lytton is very keen to talk to you as soon as you are acclimatized. That will take a few days, perhaps, and you must be ready. First, I have to check some instruments at the old Lodge. But I'll have you comfortable by nightfall. Don't worry."

"I'm not worried—just intrigued. Who found out about the cricket bat?"

"The *cricket bat*? Is that some sort of ridiculous English animal? Sounds preposterous."

"Helen thinks my son—Alex—is still alive."

"We all think Alex is alive. One of us has talked to him. But not me. Come on, now. Save your questions."

Richard hefted his rucksack onto his back and followed the enormous man along the bridleway. Lacan walked fast, hair and pack bouncing with each stride. He constantly paused to smell the air, and used his hands like an insect's antennae, waving his slender fingers as if sensing for a change in the breeze.

They crossed into the private estates of Ryhope Manor and left the path, ascending the fallow field to Ryhope Wood. As Richard had begun to suspect, Lacan led the way through the tangle of wire to the ruins of the house in the wood, following a narrow path that Richard had previously missed and which led directly to the small garden. In the parlor, Lacan broke open the back of the small radio-like machine, pulling out a roll of white paper covered with ink marks. The Frenchman unfurled a few feet to scan the recording.

"Looks like one of those hospital traces," Richard said. "An EKG?"

"Very like," said Lacan distractedly. He seemed puzzled. "Something has been generated. Someone has been here. There has been activity."

After a moment Richard said, "I was here yesterday morning. I came exploring. I noticed the needle on one of the dials started to dance around. It didn't seem to be in response to my own movements . . ."

Lacan scratched curiously at his long beard, staring at Richard and thinking hard, then shook his head and furled up the roll of white paper. "You came here? Then maybe it *was* you. You've had an effect already. Quite remarkable!"

"What *is* this place?"

Tucking the record into his pocket, Lacan looked around at the ruined room. "This place? It's where it began. Where it began in *this* century, at least. A man called Huxley lived here, with his family, a wife and two boys. They didn't own the house, they rented it. Huxley's father had been a good friend of the then Lord Ryhope. But something which had been quiet for four hundred years woke up again when George Huxley began to study here, not in this room, but in another part of the building. We're trying to find what that thing was. The house is called Oak Lodge. The wood around us is very old, very old indeed. This crude piece of equipment," as he spoke he loaded a second roll into the back of the machine, "this little item is my own adaptation of Huxley's 'flux drain.' It's a monitor. Very simple, really. It monitors life, new life, spontaneous life, the life of heroes, ghostly heroes which we call *mythagos.*"

The odd word was vaguely familiar to Richard. Of course: Helen had used it, just a day or so before. He repeated the word aloud, questioning it.

"There are some things you should know," Lacan said, leading the way outside again. "You have to start understanding soon, if you are to help get Alex out of the wood, and it will take some time. Sit down. Perhaps a little of that brandy would help . . ."

George Huxley and his family had occupied Oak Lodge for twenty-five years, until his death in 1946. He had died leaving two sons, Steven and Christian, but they had both disappeared from the area in 1948, and had not been heard of since. Huxley's wife, Jennifer, had died tragically some years before.

Huxley's training had been as a scientist, initially in the field of psychology (he had studied with Carl Jung for some years) but later broadened his horizons to include research into the dating of archaeological remains and the variability of time. He was a man fascinated, even obsessed by myth, and by the spiritual presences in the wood. He had been a jack-of-all-trades. For many years his collaborator and colleague had been another academic, Edward Wynne-Jones. The two men, during the thirties in particular, had explored the odd nature of the forest and its startling occupants. They had documented its inner realm to the extent that was possible in their day, leaving a crude map, a fragmentary journal and many unanswered questions.

From one small, semi-cryptic passage in Huxley's research journal, which was now in the possession of Old Stone Hollow, it was clear that he had kept a second record, a private journal in which he had recorded aspects of his research, observations and discoveries that he had not wished, or had been too ashamed, to share with the world.

No trace of that second diary had yet been found.

Ryhope Wood was primary woodland. It had been untouched, essentially unmanaged, for eight thousand or so years, a tiny stand of primordial wildwood that Huxley believed had survived by *defending* itself against the destructive behavior—slashing and burning in Neolithic times—of the human population that was settling around it. Over the millennia, the concentration of time and spirit in the wood had made it into something more than just trees and bracken, dog-fern and bramble. It had become an entity, not conscious, not watching, but somehow sentient and to an astonishing degree timeless. It communicated not through the normal channels of plant and animal life—the transpiration, the pheromones, the ecological balance of its predators, prey species and decomposers—but through the eyes and ears and mouths of *mythagos,* and it was these spirit forms, solid and substantial, though destined for short lives, that gave time, perspective and fascination to the wildwood.

The word "mythago"—Lacan pronounced it with the stress on the "a"—was Huxley's coinage, and derived from "myth imago" or image of a myth. From the moment of first human consciousness, Huxley had believed, the need for heroes, heroic acts and a belief in the mythological attributes of nature had been the empowering force behind human psychological development. Archetypes common to all human life across the globe had arisen spontaneously in the collective unconscious and each culture had fleshed them out with human or animal attributes appropriate to their own environment and social situations. These characters, often based on historical figures, more often on imaginary but *needed* figures, had become an integral part of the human mind, existing just across the mysterious boundary between full awareness and that state of acknowledgement of an underconscious process at work—dreams, rituals, visions— that might be called intuition and insight.

Listening to Lacan talk, Richard experienced no real difficulty in accepting either the existence of ancient wildwood, or the persistence of archaic memory. But he balked for a while at Lacan's further explanation, that the combination of the two primitive states, powered by the dual tensions between the right and left hemispheres of the human brain, and the aura that existed within unspoiled organic structures, as represented by Ryhope Wood, could produce the solid *forms* of those mythagos. They condensed out of nowhere, to become real, to become aware, to carry language and purpose, to live a brief life in unnatural conditions before dying and soaking back into the vortices of the forest.

All mythagos were shaped by the moods and needs of the creator. A gentle Hercules would die quickly. A compulsively brutal version would forget the code of honor of the Mycenaean Greeks and become a killing machine. It was a complex creative process that begged caution, but told much about the existence of a realm of "sylvan" time, as well as being able to answer many questions about the nature of the human mind in the past.

At the edge of his vision, the woodland seemed restless. Richard became aware of occasional movement and it broke his silent contemplation. Lacan had gone back into the house. Richard found him in the room behind the old French windows, checking the tracery of fine wires, polishing the unobtrusive lenses of the cameras positioned around the walls.

"This was Huxley's study," Lacan said. He slapped the dark tree that grew from the floor, then reached through the ground ivy to take up a decayed book, its spine too faded to read the title. Tossing it aside, Lacan went on, "It's a room that is visited often, but by a ghost we can never photograph. As you can imagine, this house is a powerful focus for activity. The echoes of the family that lived here are still in the wood, and they come back to touch the place before dying. We can glimpse them occasionally." Lacan's eyes shone as he looked around, balanced precariously on a sagging floor beam. "Such an amazing amount of magic starts with this room, Richard. It has been Lytton's obsession for many years, now. For myself . . ." He caught his words and glanced at Richard defensively. "Well, never mind for myself. We all have our dreams."

He escorted Richard outside again. "We've excavated the place. You see? We've opened it up like an archaeological site."

Now that it was explained to him, Richard could see how the cleared spaces around the house formed a pattern. Lacan and his team had cleared "trenches" through the woods. The Frenchman pointed down one narrow pathway. "Through there is a stream. Huxley refers to it in his journal. It was his own route into Ryhope. In his own time the stream was at the woodland's edge, with a field between here and the house. From his study, he could watch the big trees at that edge, and he saw many creatures and other mythic entities. Then, at some time in the last twenty years the whole wood *grew out*. At an astonishing rate! It consumed everything in its immediate vicinity, including the Lodge. It is as if it needed to take Huxley into its heart, to *eat* him."

"Didn't the owners of the Manor think that strange?"

Lacan grunted as he swung his leather pack onto his shoulders. "Now there's a question. And a good one. The Ryhopes know more than they pretend, but they say nothing, give nothing away. It's very peculiar."

He walked down the wide path away from the Lodge, and then entered the wood itself. Richard followed at a distance. As Lacan was consumed by shadows he called, "Come on. Let's get to my camp. It isn't far, by an old stone shrine. You need to rest, to acclimatize."

"I'm fine," Richard said. "I'm not tired at all."

"You need to rest. You'll need to adjust. Your eyes especially . . ."

"My eyes?" Richard queried. He strode quickly and nervously after the other man, into the gloom. "Adjust to what?"

There was silence for a moment and Richard stopped, staring into a well of light that marked a clearing in the trees. Lacan was a tall silhouette in the clearing, watching him. He stepped back to Richard, brushing aside the foliage. Green eyes gleamed intensely as he breathed softly and smiled. "To sights they have never seen before. To a light that illuminates from within."

And adding only, "Be patient. Write things down. It's cathartic!" he set off across the glade again.

Lacan's camp was a tiny clearing in a stand of beech, from the center of which grew a gray monolith, deeply carved with the crude shape of a horse. Tatters of leather still draped over the stone, tied in places around the yellowed, weathered fragments of bones. This, then, was the horse-shrine.

The light was quite intensely green. Lacan's shelter was an A-frame, made of poles stacked against the low bough of a large tree, a perfect roof-beam. The poles were tied with creeper, filled in with turves and covered finally by strips of black tarpaulin. Inside this cramped hut were two sleeping bags, skins, bones, brittle wooden weapons, tins of food, empty wine bottles, a clutter of machine bits and a small camping gaz.

"Not much, eh? But very comfortable when all there is to do is sleep. And this is your sleeping place, my friend. I will be leaving you for a while. But don't worry. We know you're here, now. We'll keep an eye on you."

Lacan vanished for a while, returning with a plump, quiescent wood pigeon. He seemed triumphant. "There are traps all around," he said. "Before I leave I'll show you. This beauty was almost waiting for me. What do you say, Richard?" He held the bird by its breast, allowing the flapping of wings. "Shall we honor that beauty and let her go? Or shall we eat her?" He looked anxiously at Richard. "You must choose. You are the guest in my house, such as it is."

Richard stared at the bird, so calm in the big man's hands. "Let her go. I have plenty of dried food. I can last without a killing."

The Frenchman shook his head, sighed with mock displeasure, then laughed and turned away. "You are the sort of house guest I usually cannot stand—the one that gives the wrong answer!" His right hand twisted suddenly. "But on this occasion I forgive you."

Grinning broadly, he tossed the bloody head into the undergrowth and began to pluck the pigeon. "Now you must make a fire. Wood smoke is better for flavor than butane. You *do* know how to make a fire, do you my friend? You just put two sticks together and rub—"

"I know how to make a fire," Richard agreed, not knowing whether to smile or frown at the man's performance.

After they had eaten, Lacan took Richard through the tight woodland, showing where he had set his traps, three in all, designed to snare rabbits and small birds. "We all become a little prehistoric in Ryhope Wood," he said.

"Surely not . . ."

"But fresh meat is so much better than our supplies. If you see equipment, you mustn't touch. It's very delicate."

"I shan't."

"You will need two days here, two full days. To acclimatize. So I shall leave at dawn and be back for you at dusk, day after tomorrow."

Back at the clearing, Lacan used Richard's tarpaulin to make a second crude shelter, long enough to cover his tall body, all but the booted feet. Richard was to have the comfort of the A-frame. He huddled below the turves, feeling the moisture rise through the earth, feeling chilled, feeling as if he was alone and exposed at night. The fire burned vigorously, and Lacan idly kicked wood from a small pile with his left foot as he relaxed himself below the weatherproofing.

"You may have disturbing dreams. It's how it begins."

"Thanks."

He stayed awake for an hour, then began to doze, still crouching. Movements in the woods alarmed him at some time after that, and he eased out of the shelter and stood, by the glowing embers, watching the pitch darkness around, and the glimmer of stars visible through foliage and cloud above. Whatever was in the woods was moving very deliberately. He hissed Lacan's name and the Frenchman stirred, muttered irritably in his own language. "Go to sleep."

"There's something in the trees."

"Of course there is. Go to sleep."

"We've got company."

"Then get down or it might shoot an arrow at you."

Richard dropped to a crouch, alarmed by the words and startled by the sudden swift movement of a figure around the edge of the clearing. His eyes, adjusting slightly to the darkness, were able to discern the full form of the watcher. A moment's gleam of eyes, the quiet withdrawal into cover, the surreptitious movement away from the glade. Richard reached for more wood and piled it on the dying fire. Crackling, smoking, the flames took again and Lacan groaned, kicking feebly as if to smother the noise and light with earth that his boot could not find.

"Go to *sleep*."

In the event, Richard didn't dream at all. He woke at dawn to find Lacan brewing coffee and cutting thick slices from a hard loaf. "But don't worry," Lacan said, half apologetically. "I have something very special to go with it ..."

This turned out to be an over-ripe brie. "Some home comforts are always necessary. But my supplies are low. Thankfully, English cheeses can sometimes be quite good."

So they breakfasted, and Lacan produced water for washing and paper for comfort. Again he said, almost wistfully, "I've been too long here. I'm going *bosky*. I shall have to get out for a while, go and experience some of your exciting English night-life."

"Not in Shadoxhurst you won't."

Again, the instruction to remain within the glade. "It will be very boring. Think of it as a test of character."

"I brought a book. Helen suggested I did."

"Good. I repeat, if you wander away from the glade you are in trouble. You'll get lost."

"In Ryhope Wood? Hardly ..."

"In Ryhope Wood! Definitely! Do this our way, Richard, or I'll take you back home now. This is no joke."

"I don't intend to joke. And I'll stay here. And see you—tomorrow evening?"

"I'll bring some wine," Lacan said with a friendly pat on Richard's shoulder. "I'd brought some before you came, to greet you in case you made the right decision, but someone must have drunk it while I was sleeping."

And with that he shrugged on his pack, picked up his staff, and walked deeper into Ryhope Wood, his last words a grunted "goodbye," the sound of his movement through the forest loud for a few minutes, then suddenly gone.

Ghosts

Alone in the horse-shrine, sitting in a light-well close to the huge, carved monolith with its equine image, Richard began to realize how *wrong* it felt to be here. He could hear nothing but the breeze and the birds. Surrounding him was a claustrophobic darkness, through which the thin shafts of sunlight illuminated only color and shape, without perspective, without definition. He felt trapped. By late afternoon he was panicking, stumbling his way back along the path which he felt sure was the track he and Lacan had followed the day before.

He walked for over an hour. This was not possible! The trees crowded in on him, the atmosphere heavy and resinous. He veered off the path and tangled with sharp thorns. He felt stifled and sick, increasingly enclosed, increasingly afraid. He called out, then screamed out, and the woodland shook to the startled flight of birds, then was abruptly silent.

Again he shouted for Lacan, then ran on, ducking and weaving, trying to keep as straight as he could, desperate to find the ruins of Oak Lodge and the way out of this forest prison.

He came back to the horse-shrine, emerging at a run into the clearing, thinking it to be the garden of the Lodge, then stopped in shock as he saw the carved monolith, the A-frame and the drifting ash from the dead fire.

From the corner of his eye he saw someone, or something, move fleetly through the undergrowth. Startled and frightened, he swung round, but the wood was still. He could hear nothing. It happened again, then: a ripple of activity to his right, vanishing as soon as he glanced that way.

"Who's there?" he called nervously. There was nothing but silence and dappled light.

This was the beginning of his waking dreams.

He built the fire again and made himself a pan of stew from Lacan's supplies. He regretted for the first time that Lacan had guzzled the entire stock of wine. He made himself tea instead. He started to feel feverish, his vision blurring, his head beginning to buzz. When he closed his eyes he felt better, but whenever he stared into space the swirl of activity and colorful movement dominated his peripheral vision. It was not nightmarish, nor frightening, but alarming in the extreme. Although he had never taken LSD, he knew of the effect of hallucinogens, and imagined that this was how it must be experienced. Had he unwittingly eaten magic mushrooms? The thought of last night's meal of wood pigeon came to mind. Had Lacan, in his culinarily unpredictable French way, stuffed the bird with the fungal contents of its own crop? Feeling sick at the thought, Richard reminded himself that hallucinogenic drugs took effect quickly, not twenty-four hours later.

He could not resolve the images. It was as if he saw the activity of people and creatures in a thin strip of highly distorting glass at the corner of his eye. The more he concentrated the more he realized that these were indeed human figures, shifting and blurring as if in a heat haze. Sometimes they came close and seemed to be peering through the glass at him. Sometimes they moved too fast. Faces passed his awareness in an instant: here a bearded man leading two enormous horses, there a youth in long, blue breeches, singing in a wild way; then a cloaked woman, her briefly-sensed glance, as she hesitated before hurrying on, one of sensuousness and curiosity.

There was a new vibrancy in the glade, now, a tension in every leaf, a murmur in every branch. He knew he was being watched, and he sensed the hair on his neck prickling as his adrenaline surged. He was anxious, reacting instinctively to an unseen threat. He crept into the A-frame and curled up, staring out into the clearing, mouth dry in anticipation. When he closed his eyes there was peace of vision, the clutter of figures and the sensation of movement fading. But birdsong became intrusive, and as he listened so he realized that the cries and calls from the canopy were wrong, that they mocked him, or taunted him. Sudden crashings and cries from the deep of the wood were startling and frightening. Toward dusk he removed one of the strong poles that formed the side of his shelter and used a knife to sharpen the point. He stoked up the fire. Glowing embers streamed skyward, seeming to illuminate elemental creatures that hovered, staring down at him, just out of true sight.

He began to hear incomprehensible sounds, recognizing them as voices, the murmuring of languages, the laughter and shouting of strangers, but the words were incoherent, a blur of sound, surging and ebbing, like the babble of noise on a foreign beach.

What was happening? Lacan had talked of furthering his sight. What exactly had he said? To learn to see the light . . .

What *were* these living dreams, these edge visions? What had Lacan fed him, or set him up for?

At dusk a wolf glowered at him from the far side of the glade. Richard watched it silently, despite the panic he felt. He held the sharpened stake forward and prayed that the fire would keep the beast at bay. After twenty minutes of silent contemplation, the wolf rose onto its hindlegs, a massive, gray shape. It used its forelegs to break off a small branch and examined the implement carefully, hefting it and testing the broken edge. To Richard's astonishment it then stalked around the edge of the glade, upright and slightly hunched, murmuring and growling before abruptly disappearing from sight. It had seemed to be saying his name.

Richard had no difficulty staying awake and alert for the rest of the night, although in the morning he was frozen, his shoulders aching. He realized he was drifting in and out of a restless half-sleep in which an odd, disturbing dream of Alex running along a woodland path pursued by a hollybush haunted him. The boy, in his dream, had hovered at the edge of the clearing, watching him excitedly, before the hollybush had absorbed him and dragged him into the undergrowth.

He had wept whilst in this semi-conscious state and the moisture was now cold on his cheeks. With first light he felt more depressed and despairing than he had for years. An incapacitating loneliness smothered him. He thought of Alice, of their first years together, and succumbed to bitter regret that he had let their relationship drift into such remoteness. He thought of his small flat in North London, and the piles of newspapers and magazines that were never tidied, the TV that was always on, the phone that rarely rang. He became conscious, again, of the silence of the place, two large rooms which were never used to entertain his acquaintances. What had happened to him? He had slipped away, he realized, not for the first time. He had become isolated in his life. He had ceased to have direction, to make initiatives. Like a bear in the longest of winters, he had hibernated for the last six years, living off the decreasing supplies of mind-fat, of old memory.

With a sudden, angry shout he snapped himself out of the mood of incriminatory self-pity, crawled from the shelter and beat the fire with a length of wood, making gray ash swirl up in the new light.

A sudden movement in his peripheral vision startled him. He swung round, but of course there was nothing. And yet, there had been something eerily familiar about the human shape that had suddenly walked toward him then darted away. Something in the way it moved . . . He couldn't summon the image back, and the distortion had been too great to resolve the features clearly, and yet, again he felt that Alex had been watching him.

"I've had enough of this," he muttered.

The wood was restless, Richard was unnerved. Determinedly he began to retrace his steps to the edge, pack slung over one shoulder, crude spear held tightly in his hand. There would be no turning back this time, no disorientation. He'd had enough. If Lacan, if Helen, had anything more to say to him they would have to come to Shadoxhurst.

"Enough is enough!" he declared, ducking below low branches, keeping his attention firmly on the narrow but beaten track.

Oak Lodge was just ahead. He could see the clearing in front of it, a place where the light was intense.

He stepped into the horse-shrine, faced the gray stone and screamed his frustration. "How? Why? Where did I turn?"

A figure darted in panic from the A-frame, the sudden movement shocking Richard. It was a young man, his skin stippled and whorled with blue tattoos, his face quite black to the mouth line and lined with red below. His clothing consisted of a short, hide kilt, leather shoes and crossed bands of green fabric over his patterned chest. A long braid of black hair, gleaming with bits of bronze, hung from his right temple. He grabbed at a pack and a long knife before whirling round twice, shouting loudly, defiantly at Richard, then streaking away into the undergrowth.

Someone blew in Richard's ear. He turned in panic, bringing up the sharpened spear.

Lacan stood there grinning, a brace of red-furred hares slung over one shoulder, a tied bunch of wild garlic on the other.

"Been for a little walk?"

"Take me home," Richard said, shaking.

Lacan ignored him and held up the hares. "Look at these. Aren't they magnificent? Look at the nervous elegance of their sweet faces, the perfect and refined shape of the fore-paws, the exquisite color of the fur. Mountain hares, my friend, of the *finest* breeding. Which makes them French, of course. I shall make a meal fit for Vercingetorix himself!"

"Lacan, get me out of here! For God's sake take me home."

"Why? Because a tattooed Prince from your Wessex of five thousand years ago has called you by the ghost name *pukk katha 'nja*—" he laughed. "Condemning you, incidentally, to spew up demons in the shape of rocks every time you wish to speak! Great for hangovers! Shout back at him, my friend. Don't be afraid. It's good for the soul."

"I don't know what you're talking about. I just know I'm scared. I'm claustrophobic. Lacan—I want to get out of this place! I'm hallucinating. I can't sleep. I need a drink."

"A drink! *Now* he talks some sense. I need a drink too. Don't worry, I know where we can find one."

Furious, Richard hauled the Frenchman back. "Lacan. Take me home! I don't know what's happening to me!"

Frowning, but reassuring, the big man placed a hand on Richard's shoulder. "It has happened to you fast. Faster than usual. Perhaps it is because Alex is in the wood. Lytton said you should stay here for two days, to acclimatize, but I think I must take you deeper right now. If we walk fast, if we encounter nothing more sinister than that wild, ghost-singing youth, we can be at Old Stone Hollow in four or five hours."

"I want to go home," Richard said, hardly finding the breath to speak, feeling his despair rise as tears.

Lacan shook him gently, then squeezed the lobe of his left ear. "I know you do, my friend. But by this evening, fed, well-wined and surrounded by good company, you will feel very differently. If you don't, then I will take you home personally. That is a promise. But trust me for the moment, Richard. There is nothing to be afraid of. Truly. You'll soon get used to what is happening. Will you trust me?"

Helpless, Richard nodded. "I'll trust you," he said dully.

Lacan laughed in his falsely enlarged fashion and walked to the A-frame, Richard following. "What a foolish man you are, then! But I *still* can't help liking you. I must be going bosky. Come on, we must hurry, or those other drunkards will consume all the Burgundy."

The hollyjack was fat with birds, crows by the sound they made as they shifted inside her. She had extended her nest until now it was a massive structure of dead wood, yellow grasses and thick briar, covering the whole of the double doors below the broken window where the knight challenged the half-glimpsed monster. She shrieked now, rather than chattered. Her activities were directed solely to expanding the fat sphere of the nest. Alex watched her curiously, usually from the high window where a rain gutter, stretching out over the graveyard, gave him a position to swing from. Whenever she looked up at him and bristled her smile, he called down his name.

"Alex! It's come home to me. Alex! My name. It's come home. I'm *Alex!*"

Chatter-shriek-chirrup. (That's a good name. Has it brought good dreams with it?)

"Yes. I dreamed I was playing in fields. I ran through long grass, full of thistles. I flew *kites*. I caught fish in the pond near the fallen stones. I lived in a small house, which was very dark, but it had a big fire. My mother was always writing letters. My father walked up and down a lot, and watched cricket. He seemed very sad. I made things with wood. I'm *Alex*. I'm going home."

Flutter-shriek-chatterchatter-rustle. (Your father is looking for you. He's in danger. The daurog are calm now, but the seasons are changing quickly again. Call to him to be careful.)

"He can't hear me. I'm going home, though. He's coming to me. My name is Alex. Alex has come home. The giggler won't get me now."

He swung down the ivy ladder and ran past the fat hollyjack, tugging at her leaves mischievously, to stand and stare at the figure in the window.

A name was close here, too, a certain recognition. He was waking from a long sleep. He felt his eyes open and his head expand. At first it was strange, but soon he began to grasp that a form of memory was returning. His name had come home, a bright bird that had flown through the wildwood and entered him, like an old friend. And now he knew the knight in the window, and the creature that he was killing, but the name still eluded him, even now he had become conscious of searching for it. And the faces at the edgewood were familiar too, all save the giggler, which changed so much that he could never be sure if the creature was there or not.

But the other inhabitants tickled his imagination now, suggested stories to him. They brought thoughts of sea voyages and great monsters, sword-fights and silver armor, wild rides in the night, with baying hounds, and great castles encased in rose briar and blackthorn.

He began to name things, feeling the words and the identity flow into him from the air as if they were a fine rain, drizzling through his hair and eyes and ears, into his mind. He screeched with pleasure as each name returned, "Gargoyle! Crucifix! Gravestone!" And as he remembered the faces at the edgewood, "Robin Hood ... Lancelot ... Jason ..."

Some of these names frightened him because when they had appeared to him they had horrified him—they had been death's heads, or wolf's heads, on the bodies of men, and although the names should have been comforting, the men were not.

Nevertheless, as dawn crept through his head he alarmed the hollyjack as he scampered past her through the sanctuary trees, sending one of the uplifted pews crashing to the ground from the thin branches that supported it, shattering the small face at its end.

The dancer.

The whole bench was rotten. Alex picked up the pieces of the face. They were soft, like fungus, crumbling at his touch. He joined them together and placed them safely at the side of the wooded nave. He thought of taking the shattered dancer down to the bones and stone vaults below the floor, but he had heard something moving about down there, occasionally thumping at the marble slabs as if trying to get through to him, like the trees, and he kept the heavy door closed and barred with a branch.

The hollyjack shrieked suddenly. He turned quickly, staring at her from the altar, close to the golden cross that gleamed from its protective thicket of thorn. She seemed rooted. Her arms were over her leafy body and her branch tusks clattered. She was watching him in earnest, but a moment later she turned away and scurried awkwardly to her nest from which, for a long time, came the sound of her chattering, a sound of pain.

Helpless, Alex left her in the nest, leaving her sanctuary through the window, by the stone falcon, and dropping to the wet grass of the graveyard. Everything was still. He went to the well and drew water, drinking and staring at the wood a few feet away. Someone was standing in the cover, hardly breathing. He could feel the gaze on him, detect the shallow intake of breath, the betraying thump of the heart. When he moved slightly, as he lapped water from his cupped hands, he glimpsed dull gray fabric, a shawl and long dress, and red hair in a wild tumble. The glitter of watching eyes eventually resolved from the sparkling points of light that were wet leaves. These eyes were fierce, yet the hesitancy suggested fear. And a name came to him, drawn from the figure, finding a roost in his head.

Guinevere . . .

At once, as if the name on leaving her had released her from a spell, she screamed and ran. And at once the wood a few paces away erupted into a second flurry of movement. Alex backed toward the cathedral as the giggler broke through the tangled wood, a giant, stooping form whose stench emanated suddenly from the undergrowth, and whose voice rose from a growl to the braying laugh that haunted Alex's waking dreams. The woman stepped out into the open for a second and Alex grimaced at the face below the flowing hair, the twisted features, the vile mouth. This was not the beauty of his story-dreams. Her clothes were the rags of shrouds. She seemed to stare at him with pity, or perhaps uncertainty, but a moment later she had vanished into the wood and for a long time the sounds of the hunt told of her speed, and the giggler's determination.

Alex withdrew to the porch roof, below the ascent to his sanctuary. Rain came and went, and there was further furtive movement: a boy, then a figure in red uniform, then a hooded man. All of them glanced out from the wood, then retired: but not before he had named each of them, a whisper of recognition, a second's delight.

Suddenly the giggler grinned at him, fresh blood on its white face and teeth, the briefest of apparitions in the undergrowth, so quick that Alex could hardly grasp it. It chuckled as it withdrew, moving heavily away to the right.

A touch on his hair made Alex jump with fright. The hollyjack had eased herself down the ivy rope so carefully, because of her size, that he had not heard her approach. She crouched on the porch now, shaking like an aspen in the wind. There was something very final about her. In as much as Alex could tell her expression from the oddly shaped eyes, deep in the twisted wood of her skull, he perceived anxiety. She wanted to show him something.

She led the way to the ground and reached around in the grass until she found a place in the earth where she could root. Alex curled into her, and flowed with her on the Big Dream ...

It was the height and the depth of summer and the daurog moved through the stifling wood like shadows in the green. It was thick with heat. Where the forest thinned they passed through the deep wells of light, raising faces to the sky so that the sun shone on their polished tusks, emerging now from full, thick leaf on their fat bodies. Oak and Ash led the slow journey to the cathedral. Hazel and Holly kept to the fringes of any clearing. Beech, Birch and Willow walked slowly, using tall staffs to keep touch with the ground. Behind them, moving carefully, always watching, always listening, always feeling for the eyes and ears that came to him through the rootweb, the shaman was a sinister presence, never quite visible, taking deep root quite often so that he trailed behind the family, catching up with them by moonlight, as the others of the group formed into a spinney to rest.

The shaman had carved a face on his thick staff. Sometimes when he pushed the gnarly wood into the earth, Alex was drawn up to the face, and the shaman watched him, silently and closely, scratching the face with thorny nails, then clattering his tusks before walking on.

They were in summer, then, and safe. They were closer than before, and searching for the stone place, for Alex. But there was something wrong with them, an emptiness that could not be conveyed, only touched. They sought something more than Alex, and they were in great pain.

Now he reached again, journeying on the Little Dream, feeling for his father, and touching the man, expecting to find sadness but finding a new joy. He was close and he was with a woman, not his mother. They were dancing by a fire. There was contentment and excitement in the air. The boy edged closer, came closer, and slipped back into the earth, draining toward the dancing man, expanding through the giant roots, curling around the deep stones, the hollow tombs, the bones of the dying-down and the being-born that littered the vast wood. When he could hear the sound of song and pipes, feel the drum of the dancers in the earth, he rose from the rootweb, and called for the man he loved . . .

Old Stone Hollow

(i) The Bone Yard

Five hours later, Lacan led the way out of the tangle of dark wildwood into clearer, lighter forest. Tall columns of stone rose among the trees, ivy-covered, weathered, some carved with the shapes of armored men, others inscribed with glyphs and symbols reminiscent of those to be found in the Minoan remains of the Aegean. Further on, they passed below four corroding bronze pillars, each decorated with the faces of lions, one fallen at an angle and resting against an oak.

Lacan led the way carefully, taking a winding path through these majestic ruins. A huge wooden building, steeply thatched, had slipped to one side, folding into itself. Elm saplings had begun to penetrate the roof. Fallen idols, crudely hacked from stumps and sarsens, littered the ground before it, and Lacan ducked below the cracked, oakwood lintel to snatch a photograph of the interior.

The place was known as the Sanctuary. It was a collection of shrines and temples, and according to Lacan was dangerous.

"At least two *hollowings* lead away from here. We're not sure where exactly. We know a safe path and we keep to it. But this is where Dan Jacobi went missing, over a year ago. There's his marker ..." Richard saw the gray and rotting doll, hanging loosely in an ivy trail from a tall column. "I think he must be dead by now," Lacan went on. "I have a feeling for such things. But it's still all we can do to stop his wife going after him. She won't believe he's dead. Good for her! All love is blind to reason, and maybe that's why some people are so strong."

"A *hollowing*?" Richard asked. "What *is* that, exactly?"

Lacan was impatient to continue. He brushed aside foliage, and walked in the lee of an immense, marble wall, from which spectacularly grotesque faces peered out through the forest.

"A hollowing is a way *deeper*," he said unhelpfully. "We are going further into the wood, but there is a way under us. Not in physical space, you understand. Just *under*, going to other planes, other lands, other *otherworlds*. It's dangerous to enter a hollowing. The wood is criss-crossed with them, woven with them. Another system of space and time. The only ones that we know are safe are close to the Station. We know where they come out. But there are many others. Helen will show you, later."

His voice had faded as he strode ahead, out of sight, striking at branches with his staff. Richard struggled to keep up, noticing the furious activity in his peripheral vision, alarmed by this and distracted by the sense of being watched from within.

Suddenly Lacan was in front of him, a huge, broad back, blocking out the light. The Frenchman urged silence. Ahead, Richard could hear the sound of rapids. This was beechwood, the land sloping gently down, the light intense in places, shifting. Two figures moved slowly through that light, approaching the river. When Richard came closer he saw that they were children, crudely cloaked, flaxen-haired, each carrying a painted staff. Their movements were so deliberate that it took a moment for him to realize that it was sluggishness, not caution, that governed their actions.

"It is not pretty, up ahead," Lacan whispered. "Not pleasant at all. Harden your heart against these two. And just remember—they exist in other places. They are alive, they are not alive. These are dying—"

"Dying? Why?"

"Because this is a dying place," Lacan said coldly. "We

made it so when we built the Station. We made it so when we set up the protective field to keep ourselves apart from the wood. These mythagos, these helpless creatures, are drawn here, drawn to us, and the closer they come the more their lives are drained. You must remember something: they are just dreams. Like dreams, they seem so real for a while, and then they disperse and are soon forgotten. Harden your feelings until you can understand better."

He walked on, skirting the frail, shuddering figures. As Richard passed them, forty yards distant, one turned slowly. A sweet face, full of pain and puzzlement, watched him. The boy's head shook slowly, then his eyes closed and he subsided slowly, kneeling, then hunching, to remain quite still.

His companion was standing in a thin stream of brilliant light, looking up at the sky. Gradually her arms dropped and she remained immobile, stiff, not breathing.

"Who are they?" Richard asked.

Lacan shrugged irritably.

"Who knows? If you're that interested we can set up a study program. That's what we're good at here. Hold your breath. We're coming to the bone yard."

They were in sight of the river. The sound of it, fresh, powerful, clean, was a welcome sensation as Richard looked around him. To right and left, the wood was filled with the rotting figures of what Lacan had called "mythagos." He stared in numbed horror at the wooden bones. He was reminded of sculpture. Faces, skulls, shapes, their limbs were cracked, their postures awkward, as if they had died crawling, reaching for the river, heads thrown back with the effort of gasping for air. It was as if a graveyard had been unearthed and scattered. Leaves sprouted on drooping jaws. What appeared to be piles of firewood were hunched, agonized figures, their ribs returning to the earth. Colored rags of clothing, and the dull reflection of metal ornaments, suggested the rotting vestments of these sad dead.

They were all facing toward Old Stone Hollow, Richard noticed.

"They are drawn to us," Lacan murmured again. "It is a function of these creatures. They are compelled to find and touch their maker, their creator, whichever one of us it might be. We have had to defend ourselves powerfully. But each time one of these things dies, someone in the Station dies a little too. There is a connection which we don't yet understand."

Behind them, the cloaked girl began to sing to the sunlight, her voice faint, very weak, very final. Lacan watched her for a moment, then turned away quickly, looking very grim. "Come on. There's nothing we can do for her. And besides, I'm hungry."

(ii) Sciamachy

"There is something wrong," Lacan murmured as they came in sight of the rough palisade that marked Old Stone Hollow. "It doesn't feel right."

"In what way?"

"It's too quiet. There should be someone to hail us."

They were on the slope of wooded land that led down to the turbulent stream. A flimsy-looking rope bridge spanned the river. The gate through the palisade was open, revealing a wide compound, several tents, and the end of a turf-roofed longhouse, from which smoke rose. But for the moment, Richard's attention was taken by the two odd figures that stood outside the wall, one on each side of the gate: they were made from poles, simple structures that suggested crucified men, leaning forward. The heads were grotesque bulges on the skeletal frames, draped with skins, rags and the black, rotting carcasses of carrion birds. Unquestionably, Richard realized, these hideous scarecrows were designed to discourage entry. Indeed, as he looked from his vantage-point at the trees around the compound, he could see masks, shields and weapons slung in the branches, and the shapes of totems rising behind the tents. The door of the longhouse was framed by the extended, elongated and lurid blue effigy of a tusked boar.

The defenses of Old Stone Hollow were not, then, restricted to the thin barrier of electronics and infrared that could be glimpsed as gleaming traceries extending between trees and bushes.

At the far side of the cluttered compound was dense

scrubwood, white with elderflower, and otherwise colored by pennants tied to branches. This wood separated the clearing from the awesome rise of a rock face, a cave-riddled cliff that towered against the bright skyline and cast deep shadow over the Station below, making Old Stone Hollow seem uninvitingly gloomy.

There was a slow, cautious approach behind them, as they watched, and something—someone—stumbled and was still, although a piece of rock rolled for a while down the slope.

"Lytton?" Lacan called, and his face registered his concern. "McCarthy?"

There was no response. When the breeze shifted, though, the scent of beef stew came on the air. Someone, somewhere, was cooking.

They crossed the bridge, Lacan warning Richard of the dangerous nature of the river, which was often a "throughway" for "Wild Riders," and entered the compound. "Wait here. Watch the bridge approach," he said before moving swiftly to the canteen tent, a small, green marquee from which the smell of the stew was emanating. He emerged a moment later, chewing, shook his head, then checked the other tents and the longhouse. "Deserted!"

Finally he hacked his way through the tanglewood below the looming wall of rock and called into the deep overhang, his voice echoing clearly.

While Lacan was otherwise occupied, Richard strolled warily around the Station. By the back wall of the rough longhouse were piled weapons, armor, helmets, bits of wagon, the broken hull of a narrow boat. It was a junkyard of the past, fascinating and repelling at the same time. An Etruscan helmet still contained the mummified skull of its owner; the patterning on a browning long bone proved, on closer examination, to be an intricate series of pictures of canoes on a river, each action dominated by beasts, animals, or unidentifiable half-human shapes.

The longhouse itself had a fire in its center. Richard stooped and entered the smoky interior. Light flooded the room from gaps in the turf roof, and from the slatted windows that had been shaped in the wattle and daub of the walls. There were tables here, and charts on crude frames.

Chairs were scattered about, and there was a sectioned-off dark-room and a clutter of photographic equipment. This, then, was the research center.

Richard was hailed and he stepped out of the lodge. Lacan appeared again from the undergrowth, tugging at his beard and shaking his head. He looked worried.

"McCarthy is here. I'm sure of it. I can see signs of him. I think he must be slipping away. He'll need help."

"Slipping away?" Richard asked, then realized he meant "going bosky."

A thought occurred to Lacan. "The lake. Of course! He'll be there. It's the natural place to be."

Richard dropped his pack and followed along the bank of the river, which eventually narrowed and deepened, flowing between sheer, mossy rocks and stunted trees. Holding on to each other, and grabbing at roots and rocky prominences, they waded into the freezing water and edged through the ravine.

The confinement suddenly ended and the river opened out into a wide, ice-blue lake. It was cool here, and across the shimmering water the woodland was in the bite of winter. Richard could see snow on the dark trees, a stone tower rising above the branches and the wrecks of ships piled in disorder against the length of the rocky shore. The middle of the lake was hazy, the forest beyond visible as if through frosted glass. Richard didn't know it then but Helen told him later that this was "Wide-water Hollowing", and was believed to connect ancient seas, meres, streams and lakes, from Tuonela to the Aegean of Odysseus, from the magic waters of Manannan and the lake of Excalibur to the river gorges of the Lorelei. None of the teams at the Station, however, had yet risked a journey to the watery worlds of legend beyond, and most of their understanding was guesswork, based on the mythagos that had come through to their own world of Old Stone Hollow.

Just off the shore, where Richard and Lacan crouched, a small boat bobbed as the breeze sent waves against it. Two fishing lines stretched out from the lakeside, one of them flexing under tension, suggesting that its bait had been taken. Lacan strode to the fiberglass rod and reeled in the catch, holding it up on the hook. He looked at the five inches of thrashing juvenile perch with silent disappointment before returning it to the water.

"I have no time for *morsels!*"

A few minutes later they found McCarthy. He was hunched up in the rocks, totally naked, his hair draped with green vegetation, his body streaked with blue and black dyes, which at first glance looked like bruises. He was staring blankly out across the water. He appeared to be shivering.

"Is that what you mean by 'bosky'?" Richard whispered.

"First signs," Lacan confirmed quietly as they watched, adding in a whisper, as he fiddled with the bear-tooth necklace around his broad chest, "It's very sad, Richard. Very disturbing. He will become more and more primitive, wearing animal furs, and charms, becoming very *strong* in smell, very wild in his look. It is a most unpleasant change. We must resist it at all costs."

Richard glanced at the big man, almost unable to believe what he was hearing, thinking Lacan must be making a joke. But the Frenchman was impassive, impossible to read. He said, "You see? He's sitting there dreaming, listening to the wood. There's nothing to hear. Not in *here,* at least," he tapped his right ear. "But there is so much to hear more deeply. McCarthy is a talented *sciamach*. They often go first."

"Sciamach?"

"Shadow dreamer. They use the wood, they probe the wood, it's a sort of journey ..."

Stepping into the open, Lacan shrugged off one of his heavy furs and flung it at the dreaming man.

"Get dressed."

His words, abrupt and angry, seemed to shake McCarthy from his daze. He looked up through watery blue eyes and smiled.

"Arnauld! What's happening?"

"Put the fur on. Quickly. You'll die of cold."

McCarthy stood awkwardly. Richard noticed the huge scar across the left side of his torso—he had been gored by a boar, Lacan whispered—and he looked like a wasted man, all ribs, pelvis and prominent knees. When he tugged the dark fur round his shoulders he looked pathetic. He was still trembling. He reached a hand through the cloak to shake Richard's. His face was deeply etched, very drawn, and in the way of dying men his teeth seemed too large for his mouth, his eyes loose in their sockets. But he seemed at ease, was content to be led and followed Lacan obediently back to the Station, not complaining as he waded through the cold river.

McCarthy's speciality was dreams, although from the brief summary of his area of study Richard gathered that he was no psychologist. As he drank tea, and almost literally came back to earth, he talked of "lucid dreaming," "dream travel" and "dream correspondence."

"Ghosts," he said, as his enthusiasm returned, "dreams and creation—Ryhope Wood resonates with all of these things, and condenses them. If I can find the key to mythago-genesis, I can unlock the Big Dream, the First Dream."

"I wish you luck," Richard said encouragingly, again not understanding a word.

Lacan laughed. "I can't understand him either," he said loudly, bringing the hint of a smile to McCarthy's morose features. "He speaks in tongues. But I like him! He may not be able to unlock the Big Dream, but he unlocks a very good *cassoulet!*"

When the Station at Old Stone Hollow had been established, three years ago by the time-standard of the world outside of Ryhope Wood, there had been twenty assorted scientists and anthropologists, all gathered in by Alexander Lytton, all with a specialist field, all made privy to the secrets and oddities of the realm of the wildwood. They had been divided into ten teams of two, but only five of these duets remained extant. Three had disappeared more than two years ago and were presumed dead. Helen had lost her husband, Dan, although under circumstances that were unclear. McCarthy had been unable to save his partner from a lance wound, inflicted when they had been exploring one of the medieval castles that could be found in the deeper wood. Alexander

Lytton and Arnauld Lacan had proved to be so temperamentally unsuited to each other that they had willingly and gladly separated and were the only two members of the research establishment who went on solo missions.

Helen was currently beyond a zone named Hergest Ridge, but was with Elizabeth Haylock, a specialist in first millennium Europe, and Alan Wakeman, a palaeolinguist and expert in "glyphs." Two Finlanders were due back within a matter of days.

Helen's team were several hours overdue at the Hollow, but McCarthy, before his temporary lapse into the *bosk* (it was his first, it would not be his last) had sensed the three of them returning, quite close, quite safe. They were vibrant shadows in the wood, and McCarthy could communicate with those shadows, although in a way which was unclear to Richard at the moment.

Exhausted by walking, made tired by wine and McCarthy's gamey and substantial stew, Richard slept in the mid-afternoon. He awoke to the sound of voices, hailing the camp from a distance, and went out into the Station in time to see Helen carefully crossing the rope bridge. Haylock and Wakeman were already entering the compound.

Helen looked wretched, her clothes matted with mud, her face a tracery of thorn scratches, nothing serious enough to worry about. She greeted Richard very wearily, but managed the echo of an amused smile as she said, "How's the man who dances with cricket bats?"

He noticed that moss was growing on the blackened bark of her right hand. Aware of his helpless glance, she covered the blemish, rubbing at it self-consciously.

"I really have to wash and rest," she murmured. "I've been two weeks in the wild—"

Richard was astonished. *Two weeks?* He'd only seen her the day before yesterday!

"—I'll talk to you later. I'm really glad you've decided to come."

"I'm glad to see you too," Richard said. "I've got a lot to learn. A lot to talk about."

"And a lot to see," she added as she walked tiredly to one of the sleeping tents. "And a lot of traveling."

Wakeman and Haylock had unpacked onto a trestle table, displaying their finds, some of them quite gruesome. Stripped of their over-clothing, stretching their limbs after shedding the weight of their equipment, they made a strange pair, naked but for the tight, green body-webs both were wearing. Elizabeth Haylock was a tall, robustly-built woman with an angular face and restless eyes. Her hair was in a long, black pigtail which draped over her right shoulder as she talked to Lacan. She seemed shy of Richard, or perhaps uncomfortable with simple social graces. When he was introduced, and asked about her speciality, she was sharp; when he admitted his lack of understanding she seemed impatient. Perhaps she was just tired. He understood that she was also an expert on the Late Pleistocene, a part of the Upper Palaeolithic characterized by wide-scale treks of the hunter-gatherer clans, and the laying down of two separate streams of mythology, of which later echoes could be seen in the richly painted Magdalenian caves of the Pyrenees.

Her rambling words, her apparent hostility, blunted Richard's relationship both with the woman and with her conversation. She walked off after a while, and emerged from one of the tents wearing a towel and carrying soap and a scrubbing brush. She joined Helen in the river, which earlier Lacan had called dangerous, and floated lazily in the turbulent flow, seemingly quite unbothered by the prospect of Wild Riders passing.

Wakeman too was distracted and exhausted. He was in his fifties, tanned, wore his gray hair in a ponytail, and was intricately tattooed with Celtic symbols on each of his muscular arms. A powerfully-built man, he reminded Richard of the sort of wrestler who appeared on television on Saturday afternoons. Wakeman was triumphant over a find relating to his own speciality: the Urnfield and Wessex cultures of the Bronze Age (a term he hated). The bronze mask was very tarnished, and quite battered, but the face it depicted was imbued with a terrible evil, and was unquestionably, he thought, related to a particular magician of the third millennium B.C., a terrifying specter who used the riverways of Europe to trade in the then current form of spells. His name, Wakeman believed, had been *Mabathagus*.

Possession of this mask then, was dangerous, and Lacan was not happy that it had been brought into the Station. He pumped up the generator power and made a circuit of Old Stone Hollow, checking the wires, ribbons and talismans of the defenses.

(iii) Spirit Ghyll

An hour later, Lacan led Richard between the highly-colored warning poles at the back of the Station. The path wound tightly through a scrub of knotty hazel and elder in full, white flower, into the deep shadow cast by the high, over-hanging rock wall. It felt suddenly cold below this great cliff, and the smells of earth, damp and vegetation were concentrated powerfully. Richard could hear the distant sound of rushing water, but the scrub was heavily silent, eerily deserted. Their movements became loud.

Lacan indicated markings on the rock and as Richard's eyes became accustomed to the shade, so he saw the painted patterns for the first time. The activity of his edge-vision intensified, a swirl of color, the sensation of two figures running toward him, a ghostly movement that set his hair prickling and caused him to glance round.

Lacan watched him curiously. "Have you seen such designs before?"

Lines painted in parallel, complex spirals, rows of brilliant blue circles, cross-figures and stylized human forms and faces. The underhang was a tapestry of primal patterns and surrealism. Everything seemed to flow toward the earth, gathering toward the place, behind dense bushes, where the sound of water was a constant, distant murmur.

"Some of them are like rock carvings," Richard said. "Those old tombs, the megalithic ones . . ."

Lacan nodded, satisfied. "Some of them are very like that indeed. Where I come from, in Brittany, the tradition is even older than in this country. But there are patterns here that are like those of the Bushmen. In the Kalahari there are caves and rock faces with the same sort of configurations. It's like two cultures fused together. Have you ever been to the Kalahari?"

Richard hadn't, although he was familiar with the rock paintings from school studies. Lacan beckoned him on, pushing through the brush until the low cave itself opened before them. "This is only the beginning," he said. "There's much more inside. Be careful."

The open cave lowered and narrowed as they edged through. It became a cramped passage, curving and dropping in alarming fashion into the earth. They crouched, then crawled below the oppressive weight of rock. Richard could hear the sound of rushing water, far away, deep down. The damp, depressing smell of wet stone and stale air, familiar to him from potholing days in the Yorkshire Dales, was at once comforting and threatening.

"This leads the way to a most dangerous hollowing," Lacan said. "We've lost three good people through it, right at the beginning of the expedition. And more mythagos emerge from it to our world than from anywhere else. Look there . . ."

Lacan had suddenly pointed the torch at three hollow-sticks wedged into a crevice in the rock. The passage had widened slightly, and two narrow tunnels led away into the darkness, one above the other. One of the wooden figures was clearly female: the carver had shaped crude breasts on the thick twig that formed the body. All three had winding-sheets of green cloth tied around their middles, pouches to contain the relic that gave power to these spirit guides.

"We're coming to the main chamber. It's very slippery."

A moment later the crushing rock lifted and Richard was able to straighten into the echoing, cathedral space of Old Stone Hollow. Lacan switched on the lamp that was placed here, and a pale yellow light set sudden illumination and deep shadow to the cascade of shape on the rock walls and the formations of thin stalactites on the ceiling. Water gushed from a narrow crevice to the right, tumbling through a fine mist of spray into a wide ghyll. The floor was strewn with fallen chunks of the roof. The mouths of smaller tunnels opened everywhere.

All of this, impressive though it was, Richard took in at

a glance. Because above him and around him was a swathe of movement and color that was breathtaking in its expression and overwhelming in its power.

He had seen the prehistoric cave paintings in Les Eyies and Niaux, and of course knew of the paintings at Lascaux and the Spanish Altamira, but these startling images of animals, elongated, deformed, yet brilliantly executed and astonishingly colored, were like nothing from those ancient shrines. As he stared at them, so they seemed to move, to shift and extend further, their bodies draining down toward the deepest part of the cave, as if, again, being sucked by the mouth of the earth itself—or perhaps running toward it. Odd, disturbing patterns, dizzying to focus upon, seemed to interweave with the spirit creatures. They appeared to dart between the pounding legs, to pass straight through the ethereal and stretched bodies of bison, stag, horse and wolf. And other forms between these stampeding creatures reminded Richard of men, hunters dressed in strange garb, not at all the sticklike figures of the Bushmen caves with their stylized weapons, but rather shapes that drew as much from the world of trees as from the world of human beings. And yet it was clear that they too, as they hunted, as they ran, were moving into the shrine, apparently racing inward toward the swirling "pot" at the cavern's deepest point.

Richard slipped and slid across the wet floor, bracing himself on fallen boulders, and cautiously peered into the deep well. Someone had fixed a rope to the rock, the cable dropping into the darkness. It was then that he noticed the vague shapes of humans in the rock itself. He used his torch to pick out the details more clearly and realized they were hollowsticks, but petrified now, hardened by the calcium-rich water that had been dripping steadily upon them.

"Who were they?"

"From another age," Lacan said. His own torch ranged restlessly about the well, picking out other stone dolls, perhaps as many as twenty. "They're very old, more than a hundred years from the amount of petrification. It's where we learned about the spirit guides. People went down this swirl-hole, reaching for unknown lands, knowing that they needed to mark the place of their departure to ensure their safe return." He reached out and ran fingers down the smooth stone that now covered the dark figure below. "These have obviously failed. Their makers are trapped somewhere."

A thought occurred to Richard, something puzzling about several of the figures. They were *inside* the well, and they seemed to be facing into the claustrophobic darkness. Could they have been the guides of people *emerging*? he suggested. Maybe coming *from* the hollowing to Lacan's own world, and marking the way back?

"It's true," Lacan agreed, turning his dark gaze upon Richard approvingly. "That's what Lytton believes, when he isn't attributing everything to George Huxley. Our own world is the spirit world as far as some mythagos are concerned. They emerge to touch their maker, the mind from which they were drawn."

It was bitterly cold in the cavern, and even Lacan was shivering through his bearskins. He led the way back through the crawl space to the welcome airiness of the overhanging cliff, below the confusion of painted symbols. "As you have seen, Richard, this is a dangerous place. Avoid it, and avoid following anyone or anything *into* it. But whatever you witness here must be reported at once. We are three good travelers short."

Lytton

A beautiful twilight spread across the Station at Old Stone Hollow, the sky on fire, the canopy bright with dusk color. The painted symbols and shapes on the wall of the overhang, where Richard walked with Helen, deepened in tone as the light caught them, so that the ochres began to round out, to burn redly on the bodies of the animals, those that caught this last of the light.

They returned to the compound and sat at a trestle table, quiet and relaxed, save for the conspicuous shift of movement at Richard's edge-vision, the glimpses of a world forming from his mind in the vampire wood around him.

A few minutes later an odd breeze started to blow through the camp, a pulsing wind tingled with ice and movement. Birds flew in panic, and the screen of trees rippled with movement. The hanging masks and artifacts clacked and knocked against the poles.

From somewhere in the camp, one of the team called, "Elementals . . ."

At once Helen rose to her feet. "It's Lytton," she said. "He attracts elementals like some people attract flies. We'll have to be on our guard."

Lacan was already scanning the twilight skies, turning in a slow circle, one of his hand-sized machines held against his chest.

"He's coming from the north," he called suddenly, and there was a general movement toward the trees at the edge of the great overhang. The breeze grew in strength, and from the branches, eyes watched the camp, tantalizing faces that flickered in and out of vision.

Lytton, Richard discovered, was returning through a hollowing which opened between the fallen boulder and the curved trunk of a lightning-struck elm. It was a narrow gap, leading to a bright glade, now tinged with evening's orange. It was easy enough to see how the wind, and an oddly formless flow of shape, was coming from that area.

Something pinched his cheek and Richard slapped at it, turning quickly and in time to see a pointed face and quizzical eyes. Then his hair was tugged and blown as if by a sudden breath. He tried to follow the shape, but it had vanished.

He saw Helen struggle irritably with thin air, then look to the river where the waters became turbulent for a few seconds, a fish thrashing, perhaps, or something invisible exalting in the cool flow.

"Here he comes ..." Haylock said, her voice calm.

Lacan called out, "There's something behind him. It's coming up fast!"

The generator whined and Richard got the sense that extra power had again been pumped into the circular network of wires, beams and cables around Old Stone Hollow.

Between boulder and elm, the air pulsed, the view shrank, then expanded, whitening, as if looking into snow, then becoming intensely red. A man's shape was silhouetted there, frozen, one arm reaching out from its body, but as if hurrying. It hovered in the frame, a shadow against the red glow, immobile. Behind it a fainter shadow began to grow, looming up into the trees, then bending toward the frozen image. of the running man.

A second later the tableau broke, and a tall, thin figure stumbled into the Station, yelling violently, the space around him contracting dizzyingly, almost swallowed, colorless, before becoming once again the twilit glade, the stone, the dark tree.

The ground trembled. Lytton turned and stared anxiously back to the hollowing, then grinned and shouted, "Close, but not close enough, damn your eye!" After a moment he relaxed, ran a hand through his gray-streaked hair and tossed his slim backpack to the ground. His shirt was made of skins held together by bronze pins down the front. He was wearing the army-issue trousers and boots that Helen sported. As he walked into Old Stone Hollow he waved a hand at the air behind him, then slapped at his cheek. Richard sensed laughter and curiosity from the bushes near to him, and subtle, flowing movement, not unlike the movement of the cave paintings, half there, half not there.

Lacan, staring at his machine, pronounced, "It's gone." Then with a slap on the new arrival's shoulder, he asked, "What have you been dragging up this time, eh, Alexander?"

"God only knows," said Lytton with a grim smile. His way of speaking was very deliberate, and his accent distinctly Scottish. "One of Huxley's nightmares, I imagine. But I've some good photographs." He passed a small camera to Lacan, who took it and peered at it as if he had never seen such an object before. "I need to change," he went on, pulling the restraining pins from the ragged skin shirt as he walked over to Richard. "Mr. Bradley, I presume. Of course." He shook hands.

His eyes were like ice, a pale gray. Richard couldn't engage with them. He sank through them. Lytton looked old, his lean features heavily lined. His teeth behind the engaging smile were yellow and bad. But those eyes, the depthless feel to them, that gaze was disorientating. He was shorter than Richard and smelled rank. His ribbed torso was heavily scratched, but very tanned. He exuded strength and certainty. He was very curious about the other man, and slightly apprehensive. "I shan't be long," he continued. "I lost my shirt and had to rifle a corpse for this uncomfortable piece of rabbit skin. No sense of style, the Jutes. Not in 800 A.D., at any rate. I'll just freshen up. Then there's something I'd like to show you. You're not in any sort of hurry, are you, Mr. Bradley?"

"Not at all."

"Of course you're not!"

He smiled again, slapping Richard's arm in a curiously stiff show of welcome, then stripped off the shirt and his heavy army gear before walking naked (and unconcerned) to the river, there to stretch out in the cold flow, his voice a murmur of pleasure, punctuated only by his irritated shouts as one of the elementals prodded or probed too close to him.

"As I'm sure you've been told," Lytton said later, his words slow, the tone dropping as if always making statements, never questions, "I'm plagued by Huxley's damned elementals. They must like my blood!"

He was leading the way through the undergrowth along the side of the cliff. The path began to rise steeply, away from the deep cut of the cave, and they dragged themselves up through wiry trees, stumbling on the mossy boulders that stuck from the ground like broken teeth. The sounds of the camp dropped away, behind and below. The wood was restless, bird life—or perhaps Lytton's attachments—frantic about them. The twilight played tricks with perception. The sun was brilliant as it sank low, although there was something almost diffuse about the orb, about the clouds reflecting the intense orange light. Stretching away, to the side of him, as Richard climbed, the canopy was a misty sea of shape and silence, a few tall trees probing the heavens, bony, storm-racked limbs spread out above their smaller charges.

Dressed in faded Levi's and a rugby shirt, Lytton grunted with effort as he picked his way up the steep and tangled incline. When he stopped for breath, he smiled and patted at the large, leatherbound book below his arm. The covers were new, the pages inside were old and crisped with time. "Have you read much of George Huxley's journal? Did Lacan instruct you?"

"A little."

"You have a treat in store, Richard. Truly, Huxley was a man of genius—" He broke off sharply, pointing through the trees. "Look! Look there!"

A sudden flight had signaled the dusk departure of an immense heron from its nest in an elm standard high above the wood. Its throat feathers were blood-red, its back striped with black and gray. It sailed out over Old Stone Hollow and disappeared into the glow of the sun.

"Mag*ni*ficent!" Lytton said with admiration. "Do you know what nature of bird you've just witnessed, Richard?"

"A heron. A bloody big one."

"A bloody extinct one! It was hunted out of existence by tribes living in what is now the Atlantic basin, west of France and Spain. But that was in the last interglacial, fifteen thousand years ago. Can you *imagine,* Richard? Fifteen *thousand* years. And now someone, some *thing* in this place, has brought the bird with it. A lost legend, a forgotten hero, a creature associated with that hero, and there it is, exquisite in its flight, beautiful, timeless, a brief glimpse of something our world has lost."

His voice was still breathless, but his pleasure at this giant heron radiated through the wide smile on his face as he watched its last shadow in the distance.

Richard said, "Lacan would smack his lips and wonder how it tasted."

Lytton laughed and turned away, climbing again. "You're not wrong there. The man's a true barbarian." Then he slapped at the air in front of him. Richard smelled something rotten and felt a brush of icy breeze. "*Damned* elementals!" the Scot shouted furiously, reaching for a sapling as he hauled onward. "Do you understand the notion of them, Richard? Do you know what we *mean* by an elemental?"

"Something fairy-like?" Richard suggested. His legs were getting tired, but he could see the leading edge of the overhang through the foliage. The climb was almost at an end. Lytton brushed irritably at his left shoulder where, if the light was a certain way, Richard could just discern the small, hunched shape of an elfin-faced creature, lank hair waving. It was riding backward, staring at him and grinning.

Lytton had been highly amused by that answer. "Fairy-like! Indeed! But what exactly *is* a fairy? Have you ever cast your mind around that question, Richard? Something with wings out of a Victorian fancy, perhaps? Not in the least! Then maybe a wee, green guardian of pots of gold? That's the Irish for you, boundlessly optimistic! But a leprechaun's no fairy. A fairy is something corrupt, Richard. Something shriveled and shrunken. Something so old that the flesh of myth has withered from its bones, and the bones of its story dissolved to a thin marrow." He spoke slowly, his voice almost a growl. "Like the terrible creature which rules them, elementals come from the first of times, the worst of times, the time of the first forests, the first fires, the first *language* that consisted of more than simple signals. Do you get my drift? The time of first insight, first irrational fear. First nightmares, if you will. Lacan calls them 'shape- memories,' from the earliest time of human consciousness. They are all we have left of the savannah, of the great lake cultures around Olduvai, of the long walks out of Africa. But because they *are* so old, they are *tenacious,* by God. They have lingered in our minds, as unshakable as our shadows on a bright day. And in this place, this wildwood, they condense and exist as easily as an English rain."

Lytton led the way from the tree-line onto a grassy slope leading to the cliff edge. Dusk was deepening and they would be staring into its reddening mask on the horizon. Both men were exhausted with the walking and talking, but Lytton drew a deep breath, his eyes closed, smiling face to the heavens. Richard had been about to respond to the mini-lecture on "elementals" with a question concerning the role of toadstools, but thought better of it.

"Come on," Lytton said suddenly, taking the book into his hands. He brushed irritably at his left shoulder. "Is there something there?"

"There is."

"Damn! Anyway, let's sit, talk, and look at the world George Huxley has made."

And as he strode to the edge, he lit a cigarette, choking as he drew the first smoke.

"Are you beginning to understand us, Richard?" Lytton asked in his slow, Scots drawl. "Has Lacan been a good instructor to you?"

Sitting close to the edge of the overhang, Richard felt overwhelmed again by the spread of forest before him. As he stared into the great distance, regular shapes began to expose themselves among the billowing waves of the trees. He could see the crenellations of a medieval castle, the broken point of a spire, the solid columns of totem trunks, nearly as tall as the great elm standards. In the farthest distance, the wood seemed to burn, and beyond that flickering illusion of fire, the suggestion of mountains.

In answer to Lytton's question he could only say, "I understand his words, but not how they add up. I just can't grasp the whole of *this*—all in one tiny patch of woodland . . ."

Richard had accepted the vastness of Ryhope Wood as if in a dream, but every hour or so the incomprehensibility of it struck him with surging, stifling power. It was a dizzying feeling, sickening. He was a *real* presence in an unreal world, listening to talk of spirit-guides and space-time warps, of elementals and a dead boy, now alive, and who had not aged at all over seven years. He lived a lucid dream, a dream of need, because that boy was his son, and he missed him and longed for him, but he was caught in this dream, fully aware, between sleeping and waking.

He realized suddenly that Lytton was watching him with a curious intensity. The Scot raised his eyebrows, asking, "A dark twilight of the soul, is it Richard? What are you thinking? Tell me about it."

"*Is* my son alive? Is Alex alive? Is it possible? I saw his dead body."

Lytton nodded and ground his cigarette into the sparse turf, then stared out across the wilderness. "Alex is most certainly alive, and if I could show you where he's hiding, I'd do so, and gladly. I can show you a *bit* of him, that castle, the fortress. We're pretty sure it's from Alex's mind, and not Huxley's. Did he have an interest in knights and jousting?"

Richard thought of the models, the castles built of tiny bricks, the stacks of books on Arthur, and the paintings of Green Knights and Red Knights, even a knight dressed in gold, and one called the Ghost Knight that Alex had made into a Christmas presentation when he was eight, a silly little play, but wonderful fun for proud parents to watch. "Yes," Richard said with a smile.

"I'm not surprised. The castle is like the White Castle on the Welsh Marches, near Ludlow. Do you know it? The site of a fortress for thousands of years, mentioned in the

Mabinogion, the old Welsh tales of Celtic adventure. In the manner of Hamlet's father's ghost, Alex haunts that castle. McCarthy has glimpsed him in the passages. Lacan too, I think. It's a place from which he watches us at times, and it was there that we first contacted him, first heard him talk, so to speak."

"Sciamachy . . ."

"Indeed. The contact of shadows. It's a two-week walk to the castle, although it doesn't look it, and you'll go there with Helen. But as to where he *is* . . . all I can tell you, Richard, is that he is out *there* somewhere, hiding from us and defending against us, and against the creatures that would gladly render him to corrupted flesh and bone. He is in great danger. But you already know that, because Helen would not have kept it from you."

"No. No, she didn't . . ."

"You can't see him, but we have an idea how to approach him. What you saw, all those years ago, the remains of the boy, they were probably, yes, probably a *form* of Alex. But they weren't Alex. He's here, around us, and he's destroying what Huxley has created."

The words took Richard by surprise. Lytton indicated the wilderness. "Do you not *get* it yet? Everything you *see* is Huxley. The wood was here from the first seed after the ice, yes, of course. And people came and went and seeded the wood with the products of their myths. Yes. *Yes.* But not until Huxley was it *shaped.* Whatever the man did, he touched its very heart. Huxley is dead, but lives on around us. We are living *in* the man, in the mind of Huxley himself. And somewhere out there, somewhere at the heart, is the key and the clue to what he did, thirty years ago. But Alex . . .

"When Alex came he began to disrupt everything. He is like a tumor at the heart of the world, eroding, destroying the subtlety and the beauty of Huxley's creation. His mind, roaming free, is like a fire, burning and charring. It's an evil thing. That's why I want him *out* of here, Richard. And *bloody fast*! That's why we need you. He'll come to you . . . I'm sure of it. And when he does . . ."

Lytton was suddenly angry; his words had taken on a tone of menace and Richard was disturbed. Very pointedly he said, "And when he does . . . *what*? What will you do? What are you implying?"

For a second the fire continued to burn in Lytton's narrowed eyes. Then he frowned and shrugged. "I apologize. Huxley's hurting and it grieves me. You may grieve too." He glanced up, spoke softly. "You see, there's something I have to tell you, something else about Alex. It may be bad news for you . . ."

"Go on."

"There is something wrong with the boy. His mind . . ." Lytton tapped his temple, squinting at the other man as he growled the words. "Something lacking, or something . . . twisted. We can't be sure, Richard. What the boy is creating, what is generating in the wood around the cathedral, is warped. It's not right. He has defended himself against these creatures, but it can only be a matter of time before those defenses fail. This is a dangerous enough place as it is, without seeding it with the twisted and cruel products of a child's grimmest imagination."

Imagination. The key word. Richard thought about his son, that sad, blank face that had stared at Alice and him during the long, final year of the boy's life. He relived the pain, the attempts to draw something, some imaginative response from a child who seemed to have shed all emotion, all feeling, all fun, as a snake sheds its skin.

Lytton reached out and gripped Richard's arm, a reassuring squeeze. "I'm sorry if that hurts. It's best you know."

"I knew," Richard said. "Something happened to Alex, a year or so before he died . . . vanished. He was staring through a mask, trying to see into Ryhope Wood. I thought it was a game. A madman's game. But he was struck by something. I only caught a glimpse of it . . ."

Lytton was excited, his eyes intense again as he listened. "I need to know everything," he said. "Every detail. A mask, you say? I need to know about it. Everything, Richard. The more we understand about the boy, the quicker we can winkle him out of hiding and send him home. Come on. Come on."

He was standing, brushing at his jeans, impatient to be on the trail again.

Richard stared at the castle walls, now just shadows among shadows. He thought of Alex coming home. He tried to feel what it would be like to have him home again, as if he had never been away, the same age, the same bright-smiled child, the same enthusiast, the same little boy, longing for someone to help him with his models.

It was too much for him, too powerful, and Lytton came back and crouched down, staring impatiently out across the forest, but waiting until the sadness had passed.

Echoes

In the warm longhouse, Richard relaxed with the smell of fresh turf and the sweet woodsmoke that came from the central fire. Lytton unfurled a map of Ryhope.

"This is the perimeter, the easy part of Ryhope Wood to draw, though you still won't find it marked on any Ordnance Survey map."

Ryhope was more-or-less circular, though a deep path cut into it from the southeast, leading to a millpond. Two streams flowed into the wood, only one flowed out. Inside the perimeter were bands and enclosures, with names like Oak-Ash Zone, Elm Track, Primary Genesis Zone, Quick-Season Gorge and Wolf Caves.

Lytton tapped the map. "There are four ways into Ryhope that we know. One is across the pond, a difficult entrance through a thick stand of oak. It's the place where Huxley's boys saw various apparitions back in the thirties. Huxley's own entranceway was here." He tapped a stream marked "sticklebrook." "He found he could penetrate quite deeply by following the stream for a while. Ultimately, of course, the wood turned him around, disorientated him, but he managed to map the zones near Oak Lodge, and found the Horse Shrine, which is a very powerful site. The other two entrances into Ryhope are 'hollowings,' which run into different planes and different times, if we're not careful. One here is where we think the girl got lost, your son's friend, Tallis. From what you tell me, she probably went in through Hunter's Brook. The fourth way in is through an abandoned Roman tin mine, just here." He indicated the solid edge of the wood, on the side facing the village of Grimley. "The workings were abandoned in about 200 A.D., probably because of what was happening to the miners ... The shafts are deep, but were sealed in antiquity."

Now Lytton unrolled a second chart, smiling as he saw the expression of complete bemusement on Richard's face.

"The underlayers," he said. "Otherworlds we think are accessed through hollowings."

The map showed five Ryhope "perimeters," one above the other in a staggered display, connected by thin tubes that curved down between them, some connecting adjacent planes, others running deeper and usually ending in a question mark. Old Stone Hollow Station was clearly marked on the top plane and, like some ancient and mystical site radiating ley-lines, seemed to be the source of several hollowings.

"We're in the top plane—topwood. It's the Ryhope that Huxley knew. Here we are, at the cave. Two hollowings leading from here are short, and have been successfully explored. One drops to a dark lake-filled land, in three-wood, probably from Slavonian legend. And this one ... where does this one go?" He twisted the map slightly. "Oh yes. To a valley filled with stone tombs in two-wood, late Neolithic Europe. But the hollowing that leads from the cave must go very deep indeed, the same with Wide Water Hollowing. So far we've detected five levels of underworlds. There's more than a lifetime's exploration here, Richard, and all we can hope to do is establish safe routes down and back, so that later explorers can at least have more than a hollowstick to guide them."

Richard stared at the confusion of tracks, tunnels and shafts for a while, then gently rolled the chart up again to expose the simple plane of Ryhope Wood. He had seen, previously, the small spire marked in the outline, and pointed to it. "You think Alex is in topwood?"

Lytton cocked his head and raised his eyebrows. "That's not easy to say. He *seems* to be. But the cathedral itself might exist in more than one level. The question is: in which wood is Alex hiding? If he's deep, then we'll need to find a

hollowing. If he's in topwood, then we should be able to get
to him directly. The problem is, we can't. There's something
blocking us, Richard, a barrier, about five days in from the
Station. If it *is* Alex putting that barrier up, then perhaps—
just perhaps—he will let you through. Are you willing to
try?"

Richard was surprised at the question. "Of course. I'll try
anything, now that I'm here. Never mind that I hardly understand a word, that my vision is full of dancing, my dreams
are like some prehistoric commedia dell'arte, chaotic, colorful, confusing—frightening. If Alex is alive, then I want him
back. Just tell me what to do."

"You'll get used to the dreams," Lytton said kindly. "And
the chaos at the edge of vision fades in time as well. That's
just part of the process of *generation*." He smiled broadly.
"Mr. Bradley, you're creating life, although you don't know
it. Out there, the wood is listening to you, feeding off you,
enriching both itself and its underworlds from you. It's
drawing out your dreams, your memories, your fears." He
slapped the back of his hand against Richard's chest. "It's
giving them *flesh,* but ennobled and empowered by the form
of the Hero!" He laughed quickly. "I like your metaphor of
the *commedia.* It's more apt than you might think. Wait until
you are an audience at your own show! It can be quite enthralling!"

As night closed over the Station, and a second generator
powered-up to bring light to the compound, an odd and mu-
sical wind began to blow from the cave, carrying with it the
distant sound of voices. At once, Lacan started recording.
Helen went through the scrub to the overhang, to observe
and to listen. Richard, finished for the moment with Alexander Lytton, sat with Elizabeth Haylock, the sketchy map of
the wood spread out between them on a trestle table, and
shivered as the voices rose and fell in eerie pitch.

"They sound in pain," he said.

"It could be no more than distortion . . ."

"Can you recognize them?"

She shook her head. One voice, deeper, began to chatter.
The words ebbed and flowed, but were meaningless. Then

there was an anguished cry, high-pitched, falling away in volume, lowering in tone.

Soon the wailing from the cave passed away, and Helen returned. She came to the table where Richard sat and glanced grimly at Haylock.

"One of them sounded like Ben Darby."

"Oh God."

"You said you always wanted to know ... I might have been wrong."

"I *do* want to know. Thanks."

"Need to talk?"

"Not necessary. Thanks anyway."

Helen went into the longhouse. Elizabeth Haylock stared at the overhang for a while, then rose and walked stiffly to the river. She lay facedown on the bank, trailing a hand in the cold water. After a few minutes she stood again, walked along the river bank, searching for something, in fact a long stick, and crossed the bridge with this simple weapon, striking angrily at the vegetation as she was consumed by darkness and the forest.

Richard followed Helen to the lodge. She was eating a sandwich and writing notes in a thick pad. A mug of tea was cooling beside her. "Elizabeth's just crossed the bridge. She seems very upset."

Glancing up, Helen nodded, swallowed her food and motioned Richard to sit. "She'll be OK. Ben was her lover. He's long dead and she knows it. We found his body a year ago. But his ghost pursues her in more ways than one. He and his partner must have passed through a timeslow, so he's still alive in the wood, just for a while. Sometimes the echoes come through."

"Did the same thing happen to Dan?"

Helen watched Richard, her eyes narrowing slightly. "Lacan told you about Dan, did he?"

Richard nodded.

She took a huge bite from the sandwich, staring into the middle distance, then scrawled a few more words on the pad. "He knew the risks," she muttered eventually. "We take risks just by living here. But Dan'll be alive, still. I'll get him back. Lacan is wrong. McCarthy is wrong. They say there's no shadow of him in the forest, but I don't think that can be right. Dan knew the risks— he'll have been on his guard. Don't talk about him anymore. Please?"

"I'm sorry. I didn't mean to distress you."

Helen laughed. "How English. There's no need to be sorry. I'll tell you about Dan later. I just don't want to think about him now, OK?"

"OK."

"Now. Have you made your hollowsticks? You'll need to make four or five. You'll find wood behind the longhouse. You need hair, blood and . . ." she smiled awkwardly, "semen? If you've got any to spare. It's a good spirit link."

"Witchcraft," Richard murmured and she raised her eyebrows, nodding enthusiastically.

"It also works!"

Richard hesitated to point out that three hollowsticks by the cave entrance did not seem to have been effective, indeed, that Dan's token up in the Sanctuary ruins was growing fungal with age, but Helen saw his reservation and intuited his doubts. "They work more than they don't. And sometimes it takes time to call the traveler back. We use the hollowsticks to mark our passage through the hollowings, to know who has gone. In this world, Richard, time is strange, so patience takes on a new meaning."

Richard fetched twigs and twine from the small pile behind the research lodge and shaped five little effigies, ready for the incorporation of his "body relics" later.

"Do you need any help?" she asked, mischievously.

"I can manage, thanks."

"I'm sure you can."

When Helen had finished her notes she cracked a beer— Richard took a second—and relaxed more, recounting her trip out to Hergest Ridge. She soon grew tired and went to the river's edge, splashing her face with water and singing softly to the night-dark across the flow. Richard was entranced with her voice and went over to crouch behind her. The song had an eerie tune, and the words were in the language of the Lakota. When she had finished singing she told Richard to look away and quickly used the river.

As they walked back to the tents, Richard said, "Was that a folksong?"

"A charm," she said, and smiled. "A trick. It's the only way to catch a trickster. And catch him I will! Mark my words."

And with that she ducked into the tent where she kept her pack, to sleep.

Genesis

The hares had hung for two nights and a day. At *reveille* Lacan, dressed only in torn-down denim shorts and his magic tooth-necklace, began to prepare the feast for the evening, skinning the creatures, talking to them, loudly celebrating their elegance, and issuing instructions to everyone, as they woke and emerged from the tents to wash, as to what they should each do for him.

"This meal is *Lièvre à la Royale* and only a Frenchman with an intense Celtic ancestry can do it justice. Ah, Helen—good morning—when you've finished your womanly ablutions, your job is to make a rich sauce of the congealed blood—brandy will thin it out—"

"I'll make a rich sauce of *your* blood if you give me *that* job . . ."

Irritably, Lacan hacked the head off one of the hares. "Then sacrifice some carrots and cloves of garlic, finely, very very finely."

"Much better."

"I wish them to be *practically molecular!*"

"No problem."

Richard was told to build a fire in the pit where meat was barbecued. McCarthy accepted the task of thinning the jugged blood. Lytton and Haylock gathered wild herbs and edible mushrooms before settling to a study of artifacts and a further hour's conversation with Richard about his son's last years in Shadoxhurst. Lacan fussed and sang, bellowed and criticized, but the morning passed and the "first operation" was declared a success: the hares were slowly braising.

Richard made only one mistake. Watching Lacan from outside the blue ribbon cordoning off the cooker area from the "uncivilized" part of the Station (Lacan's little joke) he said, "Of course, the *true* Celts would never have eaten hare. It would have been sacrilege. Did you know that?"

Lacan looked up sharply, his eyes wide with surprise, then scowling. He leapt the "cordon bleu" and grabbed Richard by his shirt lapels, glowering down at him.

"Which *madman* told you that?"

"It's a known fact," Richard said evenly, trying not to smile. "The hare was a sacred animal . . . to the *true* Celts. They worshiped it."

Lacan breathed slowly, gaze meeting gaze, then he released Richard and smoothed his shirt. "Well, of *course!*" he said loudly. "Of course we worshiped it. We worshiped it alive. We worshiped it dead. Best of all, we worshiped it when *cooked!*" He shook his head despairingly as he returned to the cooking area, muttering, "Foolish man . . . he knows *nothing* about worship . . . he must be going bosky . . . it happens . . . perhaps I'll ignore him . . . maybe he'll go away . . ."

Richard had slept late, his dreams disturbed by thoughts of Alex. After talking to Lytton again, he looked for Helen, and found her at the lake, swimming. "It's freezing!" she called. "But wonderful. Come on in."

He stripped naked and shuddered and shivered into the cold water, finally diving headfirst to get the shock over and done with. The lake was crystal clear. Helen trod water, her limbs an unnatural pale hue, but slender and shapely as she slowly cycled. When he surfaced in front of her she was smiling. "You need to lose some weight."

"In water this cold I'm glad of the blubber."

"Swim with me . . ."

She somersaulted in the lake, legs kicking as she dived deep, then surfaced, yards away, striking powerfully toward Wide Water Hollowing and its warning markers. Richard's best stroke was the crawl and he followed in her wake, soon warm enough to enjoy the cold. When they stopped, bobbing vertically in the deep water, Helen peered downward. "There's a castle below us. Can you see?"

Richard dived, descending as far as he could before the pressure-pain in his ears was intolerable. He saw the walls and weed-covered structure of a stone building a long way down. A mass of sinuous movement in one place resolved itself as eels. Two vaguely human figures seemed to be crouching by one of the ramparts. He was astonished at the clarity of the ruins, at how much light reached them. But they were too far down to explore without proper equipment.

Breathless, he surfaced again, to see Helen on her back, stroking lazily to the shore.

When they were dry they sat by the water and pitched stones across the shimmering surface at the haze that marked the hollowing. Richard asked, "What's come through in your time?"

Helen shrugged. "Boats, mostly. A selkie, a serpent, but mostly boats. They usually end up on the far shore—I guess they don't like the look of this one. The most dramatic was a Viking longship, wonderful sail, bizarre creature carved on its prow. It had only two men crewing it, one dressed in white skins and helmeted in gold, the other holding the ends of the sail in his hands, guiding the vessel. We didn't recognize the legend, and the mythagos vanished into the deepwood as soon as they'd beached." She pointed further round the lake shore. "The vessel is over there, somewhere. Lytton uses it when he sails round the lake calling for Huxley, which is something he does frequently." She glanced at Richard, jade-green eyes curious. "What do you make of Lytton?"

"Scots—obsessive—bad breath—romantic—probably brilliant . . ." He thought of the uneasiness in the conversation above Old Stone Hollow, the evening before. "He's angry with Alex. He seems to think the boy is a *malignancy,* destroying some unseen and subtle structure in the wood. I'm sure he doesn't mean it."

Helen's laugh was sour. She took her jacket from around her shoulders and shrugged into it, looking hard at Richard. "He *does* mean it. He's frightened of what Alex is doing. He *does* mean it, and you should never let that thought leave you. Don't trust him. Listen to him, yes. He understands Ryhope Wood better than any of us. He's the one who called us together in the first place. He knows Huxley, and mythagos, inside out. Yes. But Richard—be careful of him. Watch him."

"He wants to get Alex out of the wood. He wants to help him."

"He wants Alex out of *Huxley*—he'll do anything to achieve that."

Richard stared across the blue water. Everything was so quiet, so peaceful, so remote. He had just thought this when, distantly, Arnauld Lacan's voice roared faintly, another demand, another irritation during the preparing of his brace of hares.

Helen frowned as she listened. "Something about 'the first removal of the fat being completed'?" She shared Richard's grimace. "Thank God all I had to do was cut vegetables."

"He's a good man, is Lacan."

"Yes he is. And a good friend." She was suddenly wistful. "He'll never find what he's looking for. There are times when I feel very sad for him."

"What *is* he looking for?"

Helen looked down, shook her head. "If he didn't tell you, I shouldn't talk about it. Sorry. It's a sort of rule, here. A part of the ritual."

"That's OK. How about you? What are you seeking?"

"Me? Trickster. As I told you last night. That Ol' Trickster Coyote. Old Man Fox himself! The haunter of conscience. The first deceiver. The laughing friend, the gloating foe. Trickster. He's here, I'll find him. And when I do, I'll . . ."

She smiled, breaking off her flow and tugging at the silver lock of hair that grew from her temple. "I'll find him," she repeated. "He and I have something to say to each other."

"Everybody's looking. Everybody's seeking. Everybody's dreaming."

"That's why we're here. You too. Except that, unlike us, your goal is not a mythago."

"Yes, I know. I was astonished when you found out about the cricket bat so fast—"

Again, Helen laughed. "It took a wéek! McCarthy encountered the shadow of Alex on one of the castles."

Richard remembered Lytton talking about this and said, "Sciamachy?"

"Something like that. Alex is in difficulties, but he *can* move through the rootweb. He's got help. Someone's helping him. When he appears, it's literally as a shadow, but someone like McCarthy—and sometimes me—can communicate with him. We ask a question, we get a dreamlike reply. Like talking to someone who's in a lucid dream? When McCarthy asked the shadow about the fire-dance, it unleashed a storm of emotion. A lot of memories, almost overload. That night was important to your son. More important than perhaps you realize."

Richard whispered, "I let him down. I wouldn't dance. I was embarrassed. And he was so desperate for me to dance."

"You wouldn't dance? Why you old *square*." She smiled. "It was more than that. It was the moment when he linked with the heartwood. We all do it, we all get trapped. If there's a significance in that evening, it's to do with the dancing figures, the fire, not your cricket bat! We'll find out eventually. For the moment, only one thing is important."

He glanced at Helen, then looked more deeply, drawn to her looks, her eyes, and the warmth and strength she offered him. Beads of lake water had formed on the braided locks of dark and silver hair. She breathed softly, watching him, then said, "Do you believe Alex is here? In your heart? Do you believe us? We won't find him unless you do."

"I so much want to. The cricket bat—how else could you have known? Unless you can read my mind."

"We can't read minds. Talk to ghosts, yes, but not read minds."

"I do so much want to believe he's alive. I gave him up so easily after the accident. I gave so *much* up so easily . . . But I saw him dead and I buried him. Something came for him, struck him through a mask, took him away from us. When he finally died—oh God, I'll say it. I'll say it. When he died I was *glad*. It was such a relief. Like a depression lifting. I felt free again. I felt there was something to live for again. But that didn't happen."

"Alice drifted away . . ."

"And I drifted on. I stopped living. I just started to get old." Helen's hand was a gentle touch on his shoulder, then she shuffled closer and put her arm around him, surprising him. "Is this OK? Does it bother you?"

"No. Not at all."

She squeezed him harder, grinning at his discomfiture, his reserve, looking hard at his profile, teasing. "Then why are you so stiff?"

"You can tell *that*? Without looking? Amazing."

"Why are you so *tense*?" she corrected with a laugh. "Don't you do this in England? Get close to a friend when you know they're sad?"

"Maybe I've been thinking of more than friendship—" His face burned as he said the words, wondering where in the name of heaven he'd found the nerve to blurt out such an obvious truth.

Helen hesitated, then glanced away, thoughtful for a moment, but her arm held him tightly. "That's OK," she said suddenly. "Why not? I'm attracted to you too. I was attracted to you the first moment we met, all those weeks ago."

"Three days ago, if you don't mind."

"Three days, five weeks—I've been in *deep*. I've had longer to think about you than you have about me. You're a hard man to shake off, Richard Bradley. You feature in my dreams. I like that. And I think Dan will like you too. And it's OK, before you start getting edgy. He's not the macho, possessive type."

"Not a Jack Daniel's and Marlboro man, then?"

She laughed. "No way. The occasional Southern Comfort and lemonade, maybe. Marijuana, of course, but then who doesn't? But how about you? I know Alice left you. You still on your own?"

"A regular bachelor boy. Cliff sang about me and no *body* but me."

"Cliff Richard? He's too pretty. Mick Jagger, now . . ."

"The Stones? With you all the way. The only music I'll dance to, these days. But I still have a fondness for The Shadows . . ."

Helen laughed loudly. "Then, Mr. Bradley, have *you* come to the right place!"

A horn blast brought everyone running to the river's edge, through the gates of the compound, and a great cheer went up as two bulky figures appeared among the trees at the top of the slope. They came down through the bone yard, and again the man raised the bone horn to his lips and emitted the deep, sonorous call, laughing as Lacan shouted to him to be silent.

They came over the bridge and flung their packs to other members of the team, then stripped down to sweat-stained skin suits. They were Finnish mythologists and had been coming home for some weeks, vaguely tracked by McCarthy. Their arrival was sudden and unexpected and a special delight for Lacan, whose *Lièvre à la Royale* was sumptuously ready to eat. The woman of the new team, Pirkko Sinisalo, had an arrow nick in her right wrist and Elizabeth Haylock led her to the medical tent.

A few minutes later they came over to meet Richard, Pirkko reeking of antiseptic, her partner, Ilmari Heikonen, holding a half-finished bottle of *snapsi,* ice-cold and fragrant, which Richard happily tasted. They had been searching for Tuonela and the hero Vainamoinen, but had ended up on the tundra of an early Siberian myth-cycle, fighting for their lives against mammoth hunters.

As dusk drew close, music started up on an old gramophone, a loud country song, up-tempo and jaunty, made unusual with the voices of Lacan and Helen adding their own accompaniment.

The hare was served, so tender that it melted from the bones, so tasty that everyone forgave Lacan for his temper and his tantrums, and the jobs he had given them.

After the hare, and the compliments, and Lacan's voluminous and voluble acceptance of his culinary genius, there was dancing to Breton jigs and waltzes, supplied by Lacan on a set of ancient bone bagpipes, which he played with immense vigor and much foot-stomping, and Ilmari on a violin. Richard was quietly pleased that Helen danced with him early on, taking him through the steps of the country dances that, familiar in tune, he had only ever seen, never tried. The coals from the fire, plus dry wood, had been used to create a bonfire in the middle of the clearing, and the occupants of Old Stone Hollow wheeled and skipped around the flames, voices adding hysterically to the singing and guitars from the scratchy records.

"What, no cricket bat?" Helen called, as she waltzed with Lytton, who kept roaring out words of song in such a broad Scots accent that it sounded like a battle cry. Haylock's black hair flowed around her like a veil as she and Wakeman pirouetted, the man holding himself rigidly upright, like a robot, his movements sudden and jerky. Richard and Pirkko, dressed only in the body webs against the heat of the fire, performed a sort of sedate Regency to the slower Breton rhythms. Pirkko sweated, kept saying things to Richard which he couldn't hear, pressed close to him and laughed familiarly. He concentrated on Lacan and McCarthy, tussling with each other as they danced awkwardly, the small Irishman trying to control the monstrous Frenchman as they twirled together, at arm's length, scowling and insulting, stumbling and laughing.

The dancing stopped abruptly, almost shockingly. Ilmari Heikonen was screaming at them to be quiet. He was by the gates through the palisade, pale and frightened, illuminated by the fire.

"Turn the music off!" he shouted, and the strains of the Celtic dance ended suddenly, leaving an eerie silence broken only by the crackle of burning wood and Heikonen's words. "There's something coming toward us. Out by the Sanctuary. It's coming fast, through the roots . . ."

Richard had never seen such activity. Within moments everyone was jacketed up, swinging cameras and monitors onto their backs and running to the river. Helen flung Richard's heavy jacket to him, and he struggled into it, following, confused, behind the others, over the bridge and up the dark incline toward the Sanctuary, stumbling as he went, aware of the torchlight ahead.

Suddenly the wood was very silent. Lights flashed in the dark, spread in a wide arc. Helen was breathing hard, leaning against a tree. Suddenly she shouted, "He's here!"

At once two figures slammed themselves against trees, hands outstretched, scraping against the bark. Richard noticed Helen rubbing the blackened, coarse skin on the back of her own hand. He smelled blood.

"It's rising. Concentrating," came McCarthy's voice.

Then Helen's, "It's the boy. He's hesitating. He knows we're here ..."

"It's your son," she whispered a moment later. "He's aware of you. He's probing for you. Quickly ... we might get a chance to see him." She dragged Richard forward.

Lacan bellowed: "He's shifted through the web ... to the right, forty degrees ... He's in the Sanctuary!"

Helen changed direction, running between gray stones and carved columns, following the flash and flicker of torches ahead. Bulky shapes crossed in the light, or loomed up and scrambled away, each trying to find a position, to feel the flow of whatever energy Alex was projecting. Their voices merged and mingled.

"Here!"

And then a flight of birds and a wild crashing through crisp undergrowth.

"He's rising again!"

"But where? Where?"

"He's close! Who's got his shadow? McCarthy?"

"I'm with him. He's stretched thin—he's searching very hard. I can see his trail—he's frightened."

All around him Richard could hear movement among the trees and the ruins, but suddenly he felt cold, isolated, standing with his back to an oak, facing the somber shadows of a wood whose outline was broken, high above, by a fragmentary moonlight.

And then someone called him "daddy."

The voice had seemed to come from the edge of the world, but had shocked him. It was a boy's voice, a whisper only, not recognizable, yet powerful. A single word, a dream word, and he felt weak and leaned heavily back, staring at darkness.

It started to rain, warm and sticky. The tree against which he was leaning began to ooze and he pulled away, shocked by the unpleasant sensation. The whole glade rustled and trembled as the sap squeezed from the leaves. The atmosphere became heady, heavy, quite stifling, and the air pressure built until his eardrums began to hurt.

From the corner of his eye he saw a camera flashbulb triggered, a brief glare. The air was sucked slowly from his lungs so that he gasped.

An immense and ghostly face rose suddenly from the dark ground, a gray luminosity in the night, a half-glimpsed image of eyes and nose, a flop of hair, a mouth that worked silently, the gigantic visage of a boy thrusting up into the glade. As it rose, so it dispersed, fragmenting at the edge, but re-forming and leaning toward Richard, who backed again into the weeping tree. The specter's eyes were wide, and in the glowing gray shape he could see what looked like tears. The face rose further and shoulders and arms appeared. A hand swept through him, tenuous fingers seeking to touch him. The figure began to enlarge then, spreading thinly through the trees, expanding unnaturally, then silently bursting, like a flock of white birds scattering in sudden alarm.

The pressure in the glade changed and the sap-scented air freshened. Helen came up to Richard and took his arm. "What did you see?"

"I saw Alex. His ghost. His face."

"Are you *sure* it was Alex?"

"He called to me," Richard said. "I think he recognized me. And he *did* sound frightened."

Before he could say more, before he could allow the sudden sadness to arise and express itself, Lytton called out in a low voice, "Let's get out of here. He'll have seeded the glade, and this is a primary genesis zone. Did anyone see where he came through?"

Lacan said, "The arch. It must be a hollowing."

"Good! Then we've got him!"

Helen tugged at Richard, an urgent gesture. "Don't wait around."

"A seed?" he asked as he followed.

"Genesis," she murmured stiffly. "Alex has come to have a look at you, but he's generating mythagos and we don't like what he generates. It's how we'll follow him, though ... McCarthy will have seen shadows of the land between us and the Cathedral. We should be able to follow Alex home ..."

The team moved back through the darkness. Richard listened to the glade behind them, but heard nothing.

In the night, though, the silence was broken by an almost human cry of pain and frustration, coming from a distance, lasting moments only.

The Green Chapel: 4

The hollyjack was in pain. She was certainly close to death
She had returned to her nest and lay there, emitting sounds
that made Alex sad. He kept whispering, "Don't die. No
yet. Don't die . . ."

It was dark, the sky laden with storm clouds, a cold wind
blowing through the roofless sanctuary, this huge cathedral.
Alex moved restlessly below the trees, waiting for the rain. He
watched the dark maw of the nest, calling to his friend, but she
was beyond his help now. He didn't fully understand.

She had told him that what was happening to her was
merely part of her life and death, even though she had escaped from her own troop, and had not been with a male for
several seasons. He knew only that there would soon be carrion birds. They would not harm him, they would simply fly
to occupy the high nests of the wildwood. But the hollyjack
was so weak she feared for her sapwood. She was already
dry to the point of cracking.

Alex was so confused. He had left the Little Dream
abruptly, dramatically affected by the sight of his father, who
had looked so old, so different to the man of his recent
dreams. He had surfaced in a place where there were
traps—he had felt a pulse of hostility, like a raw wound, a
savage threat to him from among the men around him. The
anger had not come from his father. From his father there
had just been desperation and longing, and the man had
called to him, and Alex had answered, calling that he wanted

to go home, that he longed to go back to the house with its shadows and its warm smells of food and the pictures and models on the walls and shelves.

He could see the house as if at the edge of his vision, not quite clearly yet, but it was welcoming, an old friend struggling to be remembered. He belonged there. Something terrible had happened to him, though. His father had seen it, and on one of his journeys to the Little Dream, Alex had glimpsed the terror through his father's eyes, a boy blown across a room, a dead boy, a vacant boy, a boy buried in the rain. Something bad had happened, and that something was out in the wood, waiting for him. The giggler had struck once and it could strike again, if it could just break through the defenses of the sanctuary.

The giggler had followed him through the wood just now. It had flowed behind him as he'd surfaced to see his father, and had run amok, dispersing the men and women who had set the traps. It had laughed and screamed, then skulked back through the rootweb to the cathedral again, to hover in the leaf shadow, waiting its chance. Or perhaps just waiting . . .

The hollyjack was silent. Alex walked up to the nest, conscious of the powerful smell of rot and decomposition that flowed from the round entrance. The hollyjack stirred in the darkness. Alex could hear the distant sound of cawing crows, muffled, painful. The hollyjack gasped, and her tusks clattered. Above the nest, stray light from the storm sky struck the shattered knight . . .

"Gawain . . ."

The name came to him just as thunder rolled and a sudden, freezing wind gusted through the cathedral. The light shifted on the colored glass. The green legs of the monster shone briefly. Behind the headless figures, the green chapel beckoned, its dark doorway in the fresh green mound like a gate to peace. Alex smiled. "Green Knight," he said. "I remember . . ."

The glass shook as a second peal of thunder rolled across the sky, followed by a strike of lightning and a further crash of sound.

The hollyjack screeched. Birds erupted from the nest, a

hundred of them, flowing like a black cloud from the bower. White-billed and black-winged, they struggled to the entrance and filled the air, brushing Alex back as they streamed into the thunder, swirling, crying, circling above him as they found birth and freedom.

When the nest was silent, Alex crawled into the soft interior, reaching to feel for his friend. She was still alive. Thorn-tipped fingers brushed his skin and she rustled. Alex wanted to fetch her something, anything that would help her recover. "Water? Shall I get water?"

She emitted a feeble chatter, and he left the sanctuary, racing through the storm to the well. Lightning broke the dark cover and he watched the wood anxiously as he raised the bucket, then carried a scoop of cold liquid in a leaf pouch back to the nest. When he got there, the hollyjack had crawled out onto the marble floor, and was partially entwined with an oak root. She looked like a small bush, but raised her head and opened her arms to embrace the boy, who curled into her empty belly-space, aware of the gnarled backbone and the black feathers that were scattered between her browning leaves.

She sipped the water messily. She was very weak. When he dreamed the Big Dream with her, it was faint, a hazy view of the greenjacks as they made their way through the wide woodland, and the shifting seasons.

The shaman led them, his summer growth now browning with an encroaching winter, the flowers and grasses that decorated his body withering and losing color. He stood in a rain-swept dell, watching the watcher, while around him Oak and Ash, Hazel and Willow, moved through the thickets, making slow progress toward the cathedral. They were agitated. Soon they would start to shed their leaves, grow monstrous and transform. Winter Wolves.

How far from the cathedral were they? Alex had no way of telling. But he felt his soul touched as the shaman scratched the face on his staff, and sensed a new direction, a new path through the forest.

What do they want with me?

To touch you. To enter the sanctuary. To pass through the chapel.

Why?

They are incomplete. They are searching for full creation. They are drawn to the source of creation. This place is at its heart.

Her chattering, whistling words were so soft in his mind that Alex could hardly experience them. He knew, though, that his friend needed to rest, and to grow in strength. She was an evergreen, and he was aware that she did not go through the shedding and renewal of strength of others of her species. But there was no nourishment in the marble slabs above the crypt. Alex rose and helped the daurog into his arms, but she was too leafy, and the leaves pricked and drew blood whichever way he tried to carry her. So he used ivy to make a sling, and hauled her to the window, lowering her to the porch, and then the ground. She found a soft-earth place, behind a slanting stone, and put down deep roots, folding into herself, quivering violently for a while, before becoming still.

Alex watched the thundery skies and felt the cold wind, but he sat beside her, watching the wood, protecting her as she struggled for life.

At some time during the night her arm reached out, and fingers touched him gently, and he heard his father's voice, and the sound of running and horses.

"We'll soon be safe," he said. "My father is close, and coming closer. We'll soon be safe . . ."

Jack

Very early the following morning, Richard was woken by Lacan shaking him roughly. It was dark, damp and cold in the tent and Richard's sparse beard was wet with dew.

"I've come to say *au revoir*," the Frenchman said. "I'm getting an early start."

Surprised, Richard could only repeat, *"Au revoir?"*

The big man was a heavy, featureless shape crouched over him. "You'll go inward in an hour or so, with Helen and Lytton, maybe McCarthy. For myself, I like to take the Otherworld by surprise."

Dazed with tiredness, distressed by what Lacan had just said, Richard propped himself up on the bunk. "I don't understand. I thought you were coming with *us* . . ."

"Alas, no. There is something else that calls me."

Richard shook his head firmly. "I'm sorry, but that's just not possible. Quite out of the question! Consider yourself under tent arrest, Lacan."

"Alas . . ."

"You're upset because I didn't eat bear for breakfast . . ."

"You want some bear? I have plenty . . ."

As Richard's eyes adjusted to waking, he saw that Lacan was suited-up, his backpack in place, lucky charms dangling from neck and jacket flaps below his heavy bearskin cloak. He had tied his hair into a ponytail and his high forehead was streaked with green and brown camouflage. "You're still tired, eh?" Lacan said. "Still the visions?" He indicated the side of his eye.

"I feel exhausted. I wake wearier than going to bed."

"Bad dreams?"

"Indescribable." He swung his legs from the crude frame, rubbed his eyes vigorously, then stared at the big man. "Where are you heading? I'm sorry to see you go—"

"A big journey," Lacan whispered. "I've been planning it for some time. I'll be gone maybe six months, maybe less. I'm going in through the cave. I'll be OK. I have a nose for returning to where there's good, French wine!"

Perhaps Lacan saw the sudden concern that shocked Richard as he realized that his friend was about to enter the most dangerous of Ryhope Wood's hollowings. Lacan's hand was a firm and friendly grip upon the tired man's shoulder.

"It will be a great adventure! There are so many underworlds where Old Stone Hollow can emerge. I feel very *lucky*. Please *don't* worry about me. This sort of exploration, my friend, is what life in Ryhope is all about."

He hugged Richard, kissed his cheeks three times, grinning all the while. "The dreams *will* get easier. Write about it. It's good catharsis! And when you find your son, everything will be easier still. For all of us! Trust Helen. She's a fine heartwooder. She has an eye for you, too. Trust me! And McCarthy has seen much of the trail that Alex left when he came last night to visit—"

He stood and turned to go, but Richard reached out and grabbed his sleeve. "Arnauld?"

As if sensing what was coming, the Frenchman stood quite still, quite silent, staring out into the new day.

"What is it?" he asked eventually.

Richard's voice was a mere whisper. "What are you looking for? Can you tell me?"

Lacan glanced back, his features dark behind bushy hair, flowing beard and heavy fur hood. His eyes sparkled, though, and not with excitement. His breathing was slow as he said, quite simply, very softly, "The moment of my death."

Embarrassed, uncomfortable with himself both for this potentially offensive show of curiosity and for the curious-ness of the answer it had elicited, Richard said, "I don't understand—but I hope you find it . . ."

"Thank you. Me too. It would be good to live again."

He paced out of the tent into the pale dawn. A moment later Richard called after him, "If you ever need help, just whistle! Do you hear me? You *do* know how to whistle, don't you, Lacan?"

The Frenchman's raucous laugh sent birds panicking through the trees.

They left within the hour, Lytton leading Helen and Richard the way over the bridge and up the wooded slope to the Sanctuary. McCarthy paced along behind, dreamy and distracted.

Once at the Sanctuary they quickly assessed the damage that Alex's "seeded" mythago had caused: four deep slashes in the trunk of an ash, oak branches broken savagely, one showing the unmistakable pattern of a bite, long, pointed teeth, wide-jawed.

"We are beginning to reconstruct your son's childhood pleasures," Lytton said with a smile. "His imagination is loose. It affects everything he creates. This was a reptile of some sort." He cast a thoughtful look at Richard. "Did Alex, maybe, have a passion for dinosaurs?"

"Show me the child that doesn't."

"Indeed," Lytton agreed with a vigorous nod. "This one was small, though. It has left traces of itself. Can you see?"

Richard looked to the upper branches of the battered oak and saw strands of greenish hair. There was a torn fragment of clothing, thick linen, also green. "Two creatures?"

"I think not. Alex is creating oddities, combinations of passion and myth. What did you say was his favorite Arthur story?"

"Arthur? You mean King Arthur? All of them. He went through a phase of wanting to be Sir Lancelot. There was a series on the TV. That and Robin Hood were great inspirations."

"But those serials were very shallow. He must have read more in the genre."

"As I've told you, *Gawain and the Green Knight* always

intrigued him. He performed one of the parts the same evening we found Jim Keeton running along the road."

He looked up at the trailing green hair in the tree. Suddenly the idea of the monstrous form that had ravished this
glade changed into something almost comical. And yet, its
power was manifest. "Half-reptile, half green-bearded giant?"

"Why not?" Lytton said pointedly. "There are odder
things in Ryhope Wood than that."

A few minutes later, and with an awkward formality, Richard placed the first of his hollowsticks at the base of the
Greek arch where the hollowing opened, adding his own
crude figure to the three others. Lytton said, "Don't hang
about, now. We've got a long trek ahead of us. Come
on . . ." and stepped between the stone pillars, somehow
melding with the background, then fading.

The moment he had begun to blur, McCarthy followed
through, then Helen. Richard hesitated, watching as space
seemed to swallow her bulky shape. For a few seconds, his
heart racing, he stood nervously in a fragment of Ancient
Mycenae, below dancing figures in marble and lush creeper,
and then he, too, summoned his courage and took a few
steps forward—

The light changed. It was still deep forest, but this was
high summer, and the light was brilliant, blinding, the heat
suffocating. A high earth bank rose to the left, and somewhere ahead a river broke over rocks. There was no sign of
the others and Richard called for them, suddenly concerned.
A moment after his second cry, Helen stepped naked into the
light, from the direction of the flooding water. She was
gleaming wet, her hair saturated, her face a solemn signal of
her irritation. Silently she reached for her shirt, which was
piled with her other clothes against the roots of an oak.

"I'm glad you finally decided to come!" she said angrily,
wringing out her long hair as she watched the man across
this dazzling glade.

Astonished, Richard could only protest: "But I only
waited a few seconds."

"Don't!" she said sharply, tugging on her trousers.

"Didn't you hear what Lytton said? Don't ever do that again! Do you understand? I've been waiting a day and a half for you. The others have gone on ahead. McCarthy saw three colossi which might mark the edge of Alex's defense zone. Lytton thinks they can get that far without your help."

"A day and a half . . ." Richard repeated.

Helen sighed, running fingers through her drying hair. "I didn't know it would happen. Some hollowings are more time-friendly than others. Richard, don't make assumptions about this place. Please? I want to get on. I want to get moving. We had no idea whether you'd chickened out or were just getting up courage. Do you see?"

Richard did see, and apologized. But he added, "If you were getting worried, why didn't you just step back?"

She looked grim as she hefted on her backpack. "I tried."

"And failed?"

"And failed. This is a way in only. And that's bad news."

"But Lacan—"

Richard was confused. Lacan had told him that hollowings were two-way gates. Why should the rules have changed?

As Helen led the way to the river, all she would say was, "This is a fragile, tentative land. It's in a state of flux. It's changing all the time with the minds around it. The rules are flexible and that's that. I don't know what the *hell* happened here. But this hollowing is different and there's no way back through the Sanctuary. And that's bad news. And I'm worried! And so is Lytton. Apart from that, and your abysmal time-keeping . . ." She glanced over her shoulder and smiled. "Everything so far is going well."

Richard had lost her again, and floundered in the cold and the darkness, uncomfortable with the constant sheen of wet on his beard, his legs aching with the effort enforced upon muscles from constantly keeping balance on the rough and slippery terrain of a wildwood. He was sitting on the moss-slick and softening trunk of a dead and fallen tree, enjoying dappled sunlight in an otherwise stifling gloom, when Helen's distant cry eased faintly through the heavy silence—

"Where are you? Richard! Come over here! Come this way!"

He found her crouching below a gray, overhanging rock. Whorled patterns were faintly visible through the lichen, which grew in rosettes across the towering face of the monolith. The remains of a tall man were crushed below the stone. Helen was turning the shriveled head in her hands, peering at it matter-of-factly.

"It's a Hood," she said, then added, "Robin of the Greenwood? We call them Hoods. This one has very obvious attributions, almost certainly a child's. Probably Alex's. Interesting bow, though." She nudged the longbow with her toe. Richard noted only the dark stained shaft, the red fabric tied around its ends, the small white feathers that radiated from its center. "Did Alex know a lot about archery?" Helen asked.

"No. Not that I remember."

The dead man had been more than six feet tall and of substantial build. What remained of his clothing consisted of brown leather and dyed cotton, the predominant color red. Around his neck he wore a thin chain of crude silver on which was threaded an amber stag's head, penny-sized and exquisite. The cause of death was all too clear—he had been disembowelled. His corpse was already corrupting, the limbs breaking away (as had the head), fungal growth intruding through the shriveled flesh, ground ivy struggling to drag the remains down again into the soft ground.

"Murdered?" Richard asked.

Helen shrugged, then stooped to part the clothing and examine the open wound. "A tusker, I think."

Richard was astonished. "An elephant?"

"A boar!" she said with a laugh, but sobered quickly. "Which might still be around. Not a good idea to argue with the big pigs. When they condense—become real," she added with a glance at Richard, "they tend to have one particular mythical attribute: they're bloody gigantic!"

She tossed the skull to Richard and shrugged on her pack again. The head was light, like balsa wood. But the shock of touching it made him drop it, and the shriveled bone cracked as it struck his foot, spilling gray, dusty remnants of a mythago brain.

"It isn't very interesting," Helen said again. "A very obvious phenomenon in Ryhope. There are hundreds of them in the wood, the stereotyped Robin Hood. It's a combination of race memory and enriched imagination. Everyone has a similar idea about Hood. Errol Flynn has a lot to answer for! I'm still intrigued by the bow, though. Everything else suggests a child's mind has generated the figure. Children have great power in this place. But that bow . . . It's not right . . ."

An hour later the wood changed character. It became very noisy with the chattering and shrieking of birds high in the brooding trees. The temperature of the dank and misty underwood dropped, becoming icy. Helen was agitated. She circuited the light wells, keeping to the gloom, persistently glancing up at the heaving foliage, then holding her hand out to Richard in a gesture that clearly said *stay still*.

"What is it?" Richard asked. His frozen breath spread before him into a half-lit grove of hornbeam and juniper. An animal track led away from the moody place, toward more open wood, and Helen beckoned Richard to follow her into the misty brightness.

But as Richard began to follow he heard movements in the grove, and a fleeting sound, high-pitched and human, the sound of pain. He dropped his pack, watched where Helen was going so as not to lose her again, then stepped between two trees into the flower and grass of this dell. The bird cries increased in agitation, the sound of their wings became louder as they took to flight.

A hump at the side of the dell resolved into the figure of a man, back arched up from the enclosing earth, arms spread to his sides. He was dead, Richard thought, and as he drew closer, peering down, he could see how the earth itself was open around his torso, and strands and tendrils of vine and sucker were swathed around him, dragging the corpse back into the body of the wood. His face was scarred with flat fungal growth, his hair, which was fair and long, seemed to be rooting into the bracken. There was a dull gleam of metal around the body's neck and checkered red and yellow showed through the weeds on the torso, the remains of its shirt. The man's mouth was open and Richard glimpsed furtive movements in the hole. The eyes were closed, tightly, an expression of great pain. He could see no wound.

There was a sudden step behind him and he started with fright. Helen grabbed him by the shoulder. "Get the hell out of here. *Fast.*"

"He's dead. Another Hood, I think."

"Another Hood nothing. Quickly, Richard. Get away from here."

Behind him the dead man, perhaps still dying, uttered a high, slow moan and shifted slightly in the sucking earth.

Helen was back on the track. "Did he see you?"

"No. His eyes are closed. He's dying."

"He's being born! Come on, let's put distance between us. If he sees you he'll fix on you. It's a Jack, and I don't like his colors. He's bad news."

Being born?

Richard stumbled away from the dell, recasting the image of the corpse in his mind. Not being sucked into the earth then, but pushed out of it, the gray and green fungal growth being absorbed into the skin, not absorbing the decaying flesh.

"A Jack? As in Beanstalk?"

"As in Giant Killer," Helen called back stiffly. "Didn't Lytton show you Huxley's diaries?"

But before Richard could recapture a sudden memory of the dead man's writings, a more concerning thought struck him: *his pack!*

He turned back and ran to where he had dropped the bulky backpack. Snatching it up he turned to follow Helen again, into the thinner forest, away from this icy womb. He caught a glimpse as he rose of a shape, mansized and stooped, standing deeply in the shadows of the grove watching him. It leaned an arm against a tree-bole, breathing hard. Light caught its eyes, which were narrowed, sinister, and staring.

Richard was in no doubt that it had seen him.

Huxley had written:

13th May '28. A Jack has come to the edgewood and watched the house. The boys are at school, and Jennifer in town. It seemed unsure at first, then, like all mythagos, it came toward me as far as the gate. I might have hoped to see a goose below its arm, the glint of a golden egg, but this particular echo of folk myth was hungry, bloody and heavily armed with whatever it had been able to find in the wood: this meant crude spears, a heavy club, two knives in its belt. Its clothing was reminiscent of Northern British Roman, the leather kirtle and short trousers especially, although it was warmed by a heavy sheep skin round its shoulders. There was something of Hercules about the Jack in this form. Its long hair and wild eyes made it seem less intelligent than the tricky customer I have come to expect.

And later, in summer 1930:

Jack be nimble, Jack be quick . . . Jack change shape! In the Oak Ash zone I encountered a Celtic bard, a gentle creature who carried a complex set of bone pipes, elbow pipes of a very early design, and indeed his own story was linked with their first invention and use in magic. He told me four tales:

And one of them:

Finally, a Jack tale—I have called it "Jack His Father"— close to the "core legend", I think. Jack is a shapechanger. His name in the story is Cungetorix, son of the clan chief Mananborus, who was an historical figure. This early legend contains only an ingredient or two of the later folk-tale about the Beanstalk that it will become in the telling.

All of this Helen whispered to Richard as they rested in good, thick cover, catching their breath after an hour of running and weaving through the forest, away from the source of the Jack.

She went on, "Jack His Father is one of the very few tales that George Huxley was able to interpret from his encounters in Ryhope. Mostly he saw mythagos as glimpses, or brief and incomprehensible meetings. But Jack His Father is a tale of the British trickster, so it interests me—and it means our pursuer is not to be messed with . . ."

"Can you summarize the tale? I suppose it would be useful to know what we're up against."

Helen took a long drink from her water bottle, listened to the wood for a moment, then leaned forward, arms around her knees.

"Very briefly: it's a tale of mutual trickery and Jack's revenge. While Jack is out in the fields, sowing wheat, a raiding party attacks and slaughters his father and three brothers, taking their heads. Jack doesn't know this, but when the raiders come for him, he knows he's in trouble. He bargains for his life with three seeds which he claims are magic: one will grow into a house in which there will always be a feast cooking; the second will grow into a boat fit to sail over any magic lake. The third is the seed of a tree which will grow so high that from its top a brave man can see the fabled Isle of Women. The warlord believes Jack and offers in exchange the prize of all the pigs captured in his raid; the best singing voice that Jack could wish to hear; and offers also to make Jack a better man than his father. Jack accepts; the seeds are revealed as wheat, to the warlord's fury; but then Jack is given his father's head: his father was the best pig captured in the raid; his voice sang sweetly as he begged for life; and since his father is dead, Jack is now the better man.

"But Jack invokes the Crow Goddess to exact revenge and she shapechanges him into his father's gory head. Strong-winged geese carry the head to the warlord's camp, where it first shapechanges into the feasting house, then the valiant ship, and finally grows into the giant tree. The warlord, being greedy for the Isle of Women, climbs to the top, but the Jack-in-the-tree keeps growing, snaps off at its base, and the warlord falls to his death on the rocks of the very isle he has coveted."

Richard digested the tale. "So we're on our guard against—what? A house, a ship and a huge tree?"

"Against a shapechanger," Helen said. "It's how Ben Darby probably died. From now on, Richard, assume that nothing, however simple, is as it seems."

Inside the Skin

Unnerved by the incident in the juniper grove, Helen ran
through the beech forest like a deer, apparently unconcerned
at the noise she made as she crashed through the choking underwood. She was an occasional figure in the distance, half-
lit, tenuous, no more substantial than the flicker of a shadow
but it was enough for Richard to follow.

After an hour they stopped to rest by a fall of water in the
cool protection of rocks, huddling into the moist shade. The
sound of the fall made it difficult to hear whether or no
the Jack was following and Richard went up onto the overhang, where the air was warmer. The wood was quite still
and he listened hard, but the only movement was a furtive
rustling close by that resolved into the figure of a tiny man
who watched, hesitated, then fled, uttering a bird-like cry.

When he reported this to Helen she dismissed the small
man, but was concerned at the silence behind them. "Is i
possible? He can't have . . ."

"Can't have what?"

"Overtaken us. Not already . . ."

"The Jack?"

She tugged apprehensively at her long hair as she stood
above the waterfall and stared into the distance.

"He's fast. I should have remembered that about him
He's nimble Jack. He'll wait for us, somewhere ahead, so be
vigilant."

They camped that night in a crumbling wooden building

that had once been used as a shrine. It was in a clearing in the wood, and had begun to dissolve into itself, the dark thatch rotting. Carved beams supported a thin, stone lintel on which the traces of painted runes could still be discerned. Inside, there were stone heads and limbs, and the shattered remains of patterned urns. It was an easy enough place to barricade against roaming wildlife, and a low door in the back made a convenient escape route, should anyone try and enter. It had seemed unwise to sleep in so open and obvious a location, but Helen shrugged off Richard's concern as soon as she was satisfied that this structure was not a manifestation of the Jack.

"It's going to rain."

And rain it did, for most of the night, and although the air became damp, the thatch was intact enough to keep them dry.

Richard woke early, startled by the dead, gray face, blank-eyed and gaping of mouth, that was staring at him. He shouted out in alarm and crawled across the floor as he emerged into full consciousness.

Helen, in her body web, was sifting through the pottery urns. She grinned as Richard finally calmed down and stared at her. She had placed the votive offering by him out of a sense of mischief, she confessed.

"You nearly gave me a heart attack!" he complained.

"Revenge, that's all. That's a powerful snore you have there, Mr. Bradley."

"I was snoring? That's not like me."

"More impressive than a tusker. Boar, not elephant, that is." She cast an amused glance at him. "These are Urnfield. Lovely designs, excellent craftwork. The urns are full of stones painted as eyes"—she held out a handful of the oddities—"and shards of reflecting crystal, including some lovely amethyst and opal. I think this must be the shrine that the Hunter-Child Vishenengra sought, to win back sight for his family, blinded in a Kurgan raid. It's a sort of *argonaut* adventure from all over Europe and West Asia, but going back five thousand years."

Her certainty, her knowledge, was quite startling. How

could she tell this from such a corrupted and shattered place? Helen reminded Richard that all things in Ryhope Wood were connected with legend, not just the heroes, be they Palaeolithic hunters or chivalrous knights, but also the structures and landscapes associated with the lost tales. At some time in the past, this crude shrine had been not *real* but mythic, a place of aspiration in the dreams of people, a place unreachable, unattainable except in story.

She had recognized the eyestones from a legend mentioned briefly in Huxley, circa 1940.

"This is a magic place, but I don't remember how. The Guardian hides from visitors, watching through the eyes of the Dead . . ."

They looked as one at the stone heads, and Richard felt a sudden shiver of apprehension. Helen's earlier tease suddenly seemed far less amusing.

"I suggest we get out of here," Richard said, and she agreed.

They scrambled for their packs and Richard ducked out through the sloping doorway, stepping into the damp but bright glade and almost screaming with shock as a huge horse snorted in his face, then shook its head with a rattling of chains. It towered above him, black as coal, decorated with crescents of bronze, polished bone and colored ribbons, stamping restlessly on the ground as its rider held it back. The tip of the man's lance was a broad and saw-toothed stone, tied firmly to the heavy haft with cord and now pressed painfully against Richard's throat. Against the restless light through the canopy Richard could see that the warrior was partly armored. His hair was cut short, spiked with chalk along the right side and worn in three long, feathered braids from the left.

Further movement at the edge of the glade announced the cautious arrival in the clearing of two more tall horsemen, leading their mounts from the scrub. The lance tip was prodded at Richard again, indicating that he should move to the side, and he complied quickly. Helen was silent, still in the shrine, but Richard was helpless against this huge man. He hoped she was ready for the attack, or already making good her escape through the small door at the rear of the structure.

The horse-lord's two companions dropped to crouching positions, lances across their knees. They were both bare-armed, bodies protected with dull-colored leather corselets. They wore heavy trousers and boots. Feathers and grasses, tied in bundles, decked them from braids to belts.

The horse-lord slipped down from his saddle blanket—there was no saddle as such, and no stirrups on the trappings—and stooped to enter the shrine. Suddenly afraid, Richard stepped forward, intending to call out, to draw the man's attention away from Helen. A spear sliced the air across his eyes, and struck the door beam with tremendous force, quivering there. Both the other men were standing, and a second spear was drawn back and ready for flight. The two horses grazed the long, wet grass unconcerned.

Richard put up his hands in a gesture (he hoped) of supplication, but called anxiously, "Helen?"

From the shrine came the murmur of the man's voice. Richard heard him say one word several times: *Kyrdu.* He talked on. The eyestones were shifted, sifted, the pottery shards of the broken urns clattered about. *Where was Helen?*

Richard looked around, scanning the edge of the wood for movement that might indicate her lurking, hiding presence, but there was nothing, just these wild men, now relaxed again, crouching down and staring across the clearing as their horses fed.

The horse-lord suddenly appeared from the shrine, bent low, then straightening and examining a handful of the stones and crystals. He was looking for treasures, no doubt. Under his arm he carried the stone head. Behind him, stepping out into the glade, came Helen. She glanced at Richard and motioned him to be quiet.

The warrior placed the eyestones in a pouch which he tied at his belt. He tossed the head across the clearing to one of his men, who reacted with total surprise, the momentum of the catch sending him sprawling backward, to his friend's great amusement. The head was then wrapped in cloth and slung over the grazing horse, which reared up and whinnied at the sudden weight.

"Are we in trouble?" Richard asked Helen.

As if reacting to his voice, the tall man suddenly came over to him, glowering at him, pushing him back. But then he worked the spear from the door-post, checking the stone point with his fingers, and appearing satisfied. His breath was fruity, although his body exuded a stale, sweaty smell.

Helen said, "No. We're not in trouble. But they are. Our friend here has just taken the head of the god Mabathagus. Remember the mask Wakeman brought back? Same necromancer. I should have recognized it last night. These three will pay dearly for what they're doing. But with luck, not before they've helped us to the ravine and the colossi."

They were three of the Sons of Kyrdu, part of a cycle of adventure that had been widely told across the forests and tundras of northern Europe, as far as the Altai Mountains in the east and the rocky coasts of Ireland in the west. These men were *Kurgans,* not the earliest form of the legend they embodied, but the first that had begun to draw influences from other cultures. The Kurgan people had been farmers and raiders, and like the Norsemen who were a much later reflection of their ethic, they were an odd mixture of rustic, warrior, land-grabber and superstitious monster.

An early form of their story had entered North America, probably with the Clovis Point hunters, and was best preserved in Iroquoian mythology, although it had been rapidly subsumed into a simple tale of a raiding party on another clan's totem land, elements of which Longfellow had recorded in his account of Hiawatha.

It was a rich cycle, with elements of quest, of revenge and of hubris. The five sons—these three were all that remained at this fairly late stage of the story, the raid on the shrine— were determinedly seeking the way into the Underworld, to plunder the treasures they believed to be hidden there. On the way they accumulated talismans of various forms, but the stealing of Mabathagus and the Skinning of the Drum, whatever that would turn out to be, was one of the actions that would contribute to their terrible fate. The head was reputed to carry far sight and silent thought, an aspect of the "long gone long to come," and Kyrdu's sons wanted that facility for the moment when they would cross Black Pike Lake.

Mabathagus, rising from the earth, would have something to say about the act of vandalism.

That fate remained in the future. From the brief, cautious exchange in the shrine itself, Helen had determined that these raiders were aware of the ravine, and the wooden colossi that probably marked the entrance to the zone where Alex had erected his best defenses. The Kurgan would accompany her there, and Helen had agreed to trade for the privilege: their presence would be protection against the Jack, which she was convinced was now dogging Richard's trail.

For the moment however, they stayed in this silent, wet clearing. The Sons of Kyrdu had spread blankets and were seated now, busy with industry, one working an awl through a long strip of leather, the other re-securing the stone head of the spear he had launched in front of Richard by way of discouragement. These were Herkos and Kyrki. The horse-lord himself, Etherion, picked through the contents of Helen's pack, but dismissed everything as useless. Richard heard her say "damn," and she glanced his way, looking apprehensive. "Can he have a look at what you're carrying? I don't want him getting ideas about *me* . . ."

"Of course. He can have what he likes."

But as he saw Richard preparing to offer his own back-pack for consideration, the man shook his head. He drew a slim, stone knife and cut one of the long, silver locks from Helen's hair, braiding it with facility in his big hands, and using a thin twine to tie it to his own front lock. It dangled there, silver at the end of black, and he smiled broadly and nodded at the woman.

"It's a little bit of my spirit to protect him against the 'shadow that comes from shadow.' He's just paid me an enormous compliment. And do you know what, Richard? I actually feel complimented."

"Good. Now let's get on."

"Unfortunately . . ."

Their time at the shrine was not finished. There was a sense of expectation in the air. The birds around the glade began to fall silent. The awling stopped, the spear was laid aside. The three dark men watched the light through the canopy, ears pricked and expectant. Helen sat quietly, just inside the temple itself, waiting out the hours, waiting for the murder.

The drum started. It was distant at first, but came closer. It was high in frequency, like the Irish bohdrain, a single skin round a wooden frame, beaten with a bone. The drumming circled the clearing. The horses twisted against their tethers, and Kyrki stroked their muzzles, calming them as he watched the woods, alert for movement. The other two stood and drew their short, bronze stabbing swords.

The man who ran suddenly into the clearing was wizened, bent double, clothed in swathes of brown rags, with a fur hood drawn tightly around his weatherbeaten face. He beat the wide drum frantically and screamed at the three men, twisting where he stood, using the drum as a weapon, thrusting it at each of them in turn, as if its sound would stop them in their tracks.

The Sons of Kyrdu circled the wild man, wary, unsmiling. They seemed genuinely afraid of him, but purposeful in their movements.

"Time to go," Helen said, and left the shrine.

Richard stepped out after her and edged away from the confrontation. She stood at the edge of the clearing, watching the dance. "I don't want to be a part of this." Her face was full of pain. "It won't be pleasant . . ."

Richard looked back at the warriors. Kyrki had snatched the drum from its owner and sliced it into tatters, stripping the leather away from the frame. The other two were unfurling the old man, as if in some bizarre party game. He twisted and screamed as the rags came away, until his gray, scrawny body was exposed, naked and richly tattooed with distorted figures and strange faces. Suddenly he stood still, his hands resting against his skeletal thighs, his head drooping over a hollow chest. Kyrki stepped toward him, bronze skinning knife drawn.

Richard followed Helen into the dense undergrowth, into the welcome darkness. The old man's shrieks followed them for a while, and then there was a sudden silence. Helen turned and without a word put her arms around Richard, holding him very tightly. She was shaking. Richard felt sick, and as the old man's ululating death tones seemed to echo everywhere, he asked, "Will they kill us too?"

"No. Of course not. Be quiet, Richard. Just hold me."

Richard realized she was crying. She felt very small against him. In silence they stood against a leaning oak, the breeze shifting, the smells of the wood fragrant, calming. It was very still, very peaceful. Slowly Helen's anguish dissipated.

"It's one of the things I find hard, very hard," she said softly, still with her face against Richard's chest. "The violence. So much of myth, so much of legend, so much of it is turned around deeds of heroism, and bravery, and revenge, and war ... and it all comes down to one thing: death. Violent death. The duels between heroes. The burning of saints. The skinning of old men. Dan hated it too. Even a good and chivalrous knight can become a killer in this place. We don't get innocent Jack, the Beanstalk boy with his pleasant trickery ... we get Jack who kills, Jack who tricks, Jack who murders for gain." She trembled suddenly and Richard put a hand against her neck, welcoming the closeness and the sudden deeper contact she initiated. "God I miss him," she whispered. "So much. So much. I miss him so much ..."

If Richard had thought she was talking about "Jack," he soon grasped her meaning.

"He'll come back," he said, pointlessly. "As Lacan told me, time plays silly tricks. He's probably on his way home even now."

But she shook her head. "I've been deluding myself. He's dead. Trickster's got him. It's happened again and I've been a fool to insist otherwise. There are some things that you know in your heart, Richard. And in my heart I've always known that Dan's dead."

She drew away and sat down against the swollen root of the oak, folding down into herself, head below her arms, the sounds coming from her faintly and sadly. Distantly a drum was being beaten and deep voice shouted words which suddenly resolved into Helen's name.

The Sons of Kyrdu were calling her back.

Kyrki welcomed Richard into the glade by beating gently with the handle of his skinning knife on the new drum, the thin, stretched skin colorful and patterned with symbols of the moon, reindeer and swans. The sound it made was faint, as if the skin was tired, or distant, singing out its pain from another realm. The others had stretched sections of tattooed skin across their round shields. A red carcass lay sprawled in the door of Mabathagus's shrine. The horses, distressed by the strong stench of raw meat, were almost out of control, twisting, rearing and whinnying as Herkos held their tethers.

"Come on! Time to go!" Etherion shouted, smiling. Not in those words, of course, but his gestures and intentions were clear enough.

Helen stepped into the open, silently gathered up her pack, and grimly followed the riders into the woodland opposite.

Richard was glad to leave the place. He was gladder still of Helen. Her calm behavior in the presence of these Bronze Age Kurgan mercenaries was very reassuring to a man who would have preferred to be running in the opposite direction.

And when it came to running, these men were more demanding than Helen herself, moving as they did at a fast jog through tracks that hardly existed, their horses snorting and trotting behind at the end of a short tether. There was no open country. All packs were slung over the animals, which made running easier, but too often the Kurgans ran so far ahead that Helen and Richard lost sight and sound of them. Etherion, perhaps honoring his promise to help the woman, was impatient with the two outsiders, but always waited for them to catch up. Richard noticed how he feasted his eyes upon Helen, but he seemed afraid of her, sharing smiles and looks, but not touching. What Helen thought of him wasn't clear. Richard assumed she was keeping him happy. He knew—it was not hard to realize—that Dan's was the only face she saw with love.

Etherion used sling-shot to bring down a plump pair of red squirrels, which he spit-cooked in the evening, when a very welcome rest from the relentless wildwood run was called. The fur was stretched over improvised drying frames, the entrails cleaned and twisted into a thong, also to dry, the flesh warmed over the wood fire. Kyrki produced dried plums from his pack and some thin cakes of mashed grain, perhaps emmer wheat, unleavened, in any case, and very dry, very bitter.

The squirrel was strong in flavor, and demandingly tough. The raw skulls were carefully detached from the carcasses and put in a pouch with some earth. Richard assumed the idea was to make a necklace, but Helen said they would more likely be bartered in communities where animal totems were held in reverence.

Etherion wanted to reach a place, which he called the Silent Marshes, before evening of the next day, and so they left the small encampment literally at first light, and ran on. The Sons of Kyrdu smelled the air, and listened to the woodland breezes, watched the flights of birds and discussed shadows in clearings, using their daggers to make points to each other. They had sought long and hard for the shrine of Mabathagus, and having found it they now seemed to be well aware of where they were going. Some guiding voice, some insight, some reading of the forest entrails had told them their location in the legend-heavy wood. The band moved cautiously toward the ravine, but Etherion was alert to the changing conditions, the land around him, the elements of myth that were in constant flux and shaping his quest, and that of his brutal brothers.

They reached the ravine in mid-afternoon, after stopping to rest in a grove in the middle of some young hazels. It was a welcome break as far as Richard was concerned, but Kyrki had scouted on ahead and his voice suddenly hailed the band from a distance. At once the other Kurgans packed the horses and led them away from the hazel grove at a fast trot. Helen and Richard followed, increasingly excited as the wood opened out ahead of them.

Kyrki was standing on a prominent spur of rock, a tall, dark shape, peering down the steep, forested slope to the gleaming thread of a river below. The far side of the ravine was close, a vertical wood of oak, elm and hazel standards.

His voice echoed in the narrow space as he called to his brothers.

For the next few hours the horsemen picked their way carefully along the lip of this gorge, Etherion looking for the way back into the forest, Helen scouring the descent for a suitable passage to the river below, and the colossal wooden statues that McCarthy had clearly seen in his dream.

"There!" Helen said at last, pointing ahead and down into the forested gloom.

Against the contrasting light and gloom, for a moment it was hard to make out the shapes. But slowly the three figures below resolved into more than shadows, although only the tops of their heads could be seen at this distance. They were braced across the river, and for the moment seemed small.

When the horsemen were almost above the statues, the Sons of Kyrdu abruptly turned away from the edge and with no smiles, but loud exhortations which Richard took to be expressions of good luck, led their steaming horses back into the deep wood, seeking the open land that led to the Silent Marshes. Kyrki rattled his horse chains, Herkos howled and Etherion grinned at Helen, who raised a hand in a gesture of parting. Richard, however, just felt relief. He was not at all sorry to see them go.

They descended the steep side of the ravine, dropping from tree to tree, clinging on to each other, passing their packs between them, often slipping and coming perilously close to a head-first tumble to the river. As they descended, so the size of these wooden constructs became clear. Colossal was right. When Richard came level with their blind heads it was an eerie experience, particularly since the third figure was turned slightly, and seemed to be listening for him. The wood of their bodies was dark, cracked and was already beginning to sprout seedlings. The figures were naked, that at the front stooping forward slightly, as if peering up the ravine. The middle figure watched the sky through hollow eyes, its mouth a leering gash. They might have been three naked giants walking in single file up the river, legs braced across the water. When Richard reached the bank, he could see how the feet of the monsters seemed to grow from the land, joining at the belly. They were trees, then, that had been trimmed and carved to create these gargantuan shapes. They stood a hundred feet high, and looking up at them, against the skyline, they seemed to move and creak, as if straining to draw their legs from the deep rocks. Almost immediately Richard felt a familiarity with them, something about them that suggested a painting he had seen, perhaps, but the thought refused to resolve.

Behind the figures the gorge narrowed suddenly to form a roofless cavern, dark and deep, the source of the icy water that flowed below their towering forms.

This, then, was the way into Alex's domain. Not a hollowing, but the gateway to a place that seethed with the boy's lost passion, and which was convoluted and impassable, a block to the normal passage of human travelers.

And at once, as Richard thought of this, it occurred to him why the colossi were so familiar! "They're his soldiers!"

"His soldiers?" Helen followed his gaze upward.

"His model soldiers. Of course! I bought him a set of Second World War 'Desert Rats' to play with. He had an obsession with them. My father gave him cannons and tanks. They fired matchsticks. He was obsessed with soldiers for a couple of years, encouraged by his grandparents! And being Alex, he used heat to soften the plastic of the models. They were only three or four inches tall, of course, but he twisted them into all sorts of attitudes . . . marching, searching, dying, hiding. He made a real army, set it up in a model wood, around a brick castle. I recognize these figures, the attitudes . . . they're his *men*. No guns, no clothes, but the postures are right. Why *are* they naked? That seems odd . . ."

"Not odd at all," Helen said. "When Alex created these monstrosities, he drew on several parts of his unconscious: personal imagination was just the model; forgotten folk-lore was the shape. These giants are part of an older myth."

"Which one?"

"I wish I knew," she said with a quick glance at him. "But one thing I do know. I hope they stay rooted!"

Above and behind them there was a furtive movement in the trees. Rocks slipped and tumbled down toward the river. Richard watched as the boulders came to rest, leaving a sudden silence. A hundred yards away, a flight of birds took noisily to the air. A tree bent out into the ravine under the weight of something leaning on it, then was still, as if the creature was aware that it had been seen.

"It's the Jack," Helen said, ending their moment of rest. She clutched her pack and stepped into the water, wading awkwardly toward the wooden giant, to the gap below its oaken legs. Richard followed apprehensively, stumbling through the cold stream, aware that the earth was shaking slightly and alarmed at the lumps of moss and rotten wood that fell from the cracks and crevices of the huge figures above him. He was glad to enter the narrow gully, with its wet ferns and slippery floor, and ducked with relief into the tunnel through the rock, scrambling toward the bright, yellow light at the far end where Helen was already emerging into the new land.

The Hunted

Lacan was right. There is a catharsis in writing about the events that have not just surrounded me but overwhelmed me.

I tried to keep a record in Old Stone Hollow, but was too fascinated and confused by the supernatural (no other word fits) that my record at that time consists only of fractured thoughts and fragmentary descriptions. When I followed Helen through the gully, away from the Colossi, I found even less opportunity for reflection, since we spent long hours running the forest tracks as we strove to catch up with Lytton, and the castle where Alex's ghost had once been seen. But I am aware now, as I was then, that a new vigor had crept into my soul.

From the moment I emerged from the narrow gully and the cold river, I knew that Alex was close. I could almost touch him—and yet there was nothing to touch. I could speak to him, but there was no child to speak to. I could embrace him—he seemed to be embracing me—but there was only the land, and the strange figures that littered that land, and the shadow of my lost son, reaching for me.

Helen was sitting on the bank, among the drooping and scintillantly yellow branches of a willow which formed a sort of bower in which she rested, half-naked, squeezing water from her clothing. Striking though this vision was,

*it was impossible to ignore the two huge effigies that rose
on each side of the river, facing the gully, as if guarding
this entrance to Alex's world.*

*The figures were made of straw, each the height of a
tree, but both beginning to rot with the weather, to fragment with the rain. One of them was the martyred Christ,
the once-extended arms now lost, so that just the stumps
remained. Crows had nested in the socket of the left arm,
below the drooping, ruined head. Across the stream was
the figure of a second martyr, arms behind its back, body
flexed. Black rods of thorn, emerging from the straw, suggested spears or arrows. The head was gone, but the identity was clear, for here was St. Sebastian, shot to death by
arrows.*

*As soon as we could we left these effigies of agony be-
hind and followed the river into the deeper wood. The land
was rising toward hills which we had glimpsed distantly
and Helen had pointed out the fires that burned on the skyline. We found few traces of Lytton, the vaguest of tracks,
until we came upon a fire, set back from the river, below
a rock overhang, where traces of a bark and branch shelter
could be seen. The fire had been constructed between
stones, on one of which was a small pile of half-burned tobacco, the leavings of Lytton's pipe.*

*There had been a skirmish. Helen traced the slash-
marks in the trunk of one of the trees, and pointed out the
furrows in the damp earth near the river, where someone
had slipped or been dragged. And when we searched the
area around the rock, I found a shallow grave, its head
marked with a crude cross.*

*Without a word, Helen scooped the dry earth away, and
exposed the contorted face of a man, his skin greening
fast, his teeth now brown and fragile. He had been pistol-
shot through the left brow. By uncovering part of his
torso, a rustling metal breastplate was revealed, and a
colored linen shirt. The creature looked just like one of
Cromwell's Ironsides, a trooper from the Civil War in England.*

*I covered the corpse, remembering the boxed set of
model Royalists and Roundheads that I'd bought for Alex*

one Christmas, forty soldiers on either side. We had re-enacted the battle of Edgehill on the dining table. Somehow, as is the way with such things, a small patrol of plastic American GIs entered on the side of the Parliamentarians, and Alex had won the skirmish.

Many legends, many heroes, came out of those bitter years of Civil War in the sixteen hundreds. There were as many heroes from Cromwell's army as there were from the more romantic Royalists, but Alex had always been fascinated by the rigor of the commoners' army, and less romanced by the swashbuckling reputation of the King's Own Men.

Whatever this unfortunate soldier had done, Lytton had dispatched him dispassionately.

Alex was everywhere, in the high hills, with its earthworks, over which we toiled during that first day's journey, in the crumbling fortresses that peered grayly through the matted greenwood, in the falls of water with their huge stone guardians, in the rattling chariots and steaming horses, colorful riders full-cloaked and armed, that broke noisily across our path, clattering or galloping along their own roads, too busy in the pursuit of adventure to stop and hail travelers from another time. In all of these things I recognized a reflection of the land around Shadoxhurst, of Alex's dream-castles, created from fairy tale and our family explorations, on holiday, of the wonderful Norman fortresses along the border between Wales and England. Alex had always seen faces in rocks, or bodies in the hills—it was a game he had played, fitting features to the vision, a sleeping giant here, a witch petrified in limestone there.

The land beyond the gully pulsed with that life. Each hill hid a giant, whose movement was reflected in cloud shadow. Each woodland stirred as creatures rode through the hollow trunks, inhabiting a world out of sight behind the bark. All rocks watched us with eyes behind the cracks and holes formed from frost and rain and water. For Helen, the experience was frightening. She was continually apprehensive, edgy, sometimes deeply fearful. For me, there was a strange comfort. At least, there was little fear from the land itself—it was Alex.

It's so hard to describe, but I felt, for a while at least, that Alex was guiding me. He filled my dreams, but I would have expected that. He was a strong presence in my life again, perhaps I could say in my heart. I seemed to smell him*—socks and stale sports gear, the odor that had pervaded his room— and to hear him too, a clatter of activity, running through empty rooms with new model planes, or plastic knights, singing at the top of his voice. All this in a claustrophobic wood, where the only real sound of any permanence was water, the languages of birds, and the murmuring, barking, chittering signals of deer, fox and weasel.*

For the few days in Old Stone Hollow, Alex had been a sadly remembered loss, talked about by madmen in a mad world into which I had gone willingly, and which I kept at bay, as one always strives to keep the incomprehensible at bay. Not even the encounter near the Sanctuary had fully impinged upon me, although the feeling of Alex calling to me had been a terrible and saddening moment in the dream. At that time I was fascinated by Helen, and I will write here that I miss her, now, more than I can express. Like Alex, she continues to haunt my dreams, but I suppose it's too late. In Old Stone Hollow something happened to me, something fast, something of which I had had no previous experience. I can't use a word like love. I came to love Alice, after we had married because we had feared breaking the relationship that had existed for so long. I came to not love her. I probably never felt more than affection for her. I simply don't know. But when Helen came to me, that night in Shadoxhurst, and when she emerged again from the wildwood, wild and naked, wild and swimming, my God, I had such feelings for her, sexual, yes, but more than that: I felt strong in her presence, I felt vibrant with her.

And she, too, was not backward in coming forward about her attraction to me. Dear God, I must have seemed so fumblingly shy. After Alice walked out on me I had only two, tentative, terrible relationships with women. I must have been such a bitter man, such a detached man, not a lover to linger with. Those years in London are like a bad dream. A form of limbo. Suddenly there was Helen, an American Indian (not pure blood, I think she said) who reminded me of Cher from the pop duo Sonny and Cher, who was attractive to look at, whose presence excited me—such a good feeling!—who at first seemed abrasive toward me, but who was fond of me and let me feel that fondness. I thought Alex dead. I didn't believe in life after death. Helen was a stronger need than Alex, even in this unnatural realm where I should have known that the impossible might be happening, that the lad might truly be alive.

And then we passed beyond the gully, and it was like living inside Alex's skin. Like being in my private room, aware that my son was behind me, watching my every move, hearing my every sigh, my every word, and gripping my shoulder, urging me forward. The presence of Alex was so powerful that he came back to me. I began to flounder, to cry, to need the boy so much. And Helen, in those first hours of our journey, comforted me greatly. She seemed to understand what was happening. "My God, we're going to find him," she said, and for the first time I was not chasing a dream, for the first time it was not a photograph of Alex that was being talked about, but the real boy, the living boy. He was here. He was alive. And he was close.

Helen said that previous explorations of this part of young Alex Bradley's mental landscape had led to confusion, to circularity, to unwitting, unwilling return to base. But now Helen and I, following Lytton and McCarthy, entered more deeply than anyone before, save the sciamach, McCarthy, whose shadow had flowed with the clouds and wild beasts, to reach as far as the castle, although not to the cathedral itself, where Alex was hiding.

I began to have such hope . . . and yet though I felt comfortable in this place of family memory, the darker products of Alex's imagination also populated the confused and entwining landscape, and on the second night of

*our journey we encountered two of the more threatening
of the boy's mythagos.*

Lytton and McCarthy had marked their route well, and with
more than tobacco ash; they left chalk arrows, and on this
occasion a short note, which Richard discovered, rolled inside a tube of bark and marked, where it was hidden, by a
cross. It was hard to read, because it had been written in
such haste, but Helen managed to decipher it by firelight.

> *"You are entering a part of Alex that has been influenced
> by Conan Doyle. This is the Lost World, even though it is
> not located at the top of a plateau. Last night our camp
> here was attacked by a small, ferocious reptile, the size of
> a child, with murderously sharp teeth, a* velociraptor, *we
> believe they're called, like a small version of a tyranno-
> saur. There were four of them and they reacted satisfy-
> ingly to fire. Since memory of such creatures cannot exist
> within the human unconscious, these are creations from
> his own learning.*
>
> *"An* ursine *of immense proportion, a form of cave bear,
> has its den close by. It will attack if provoked. Don't un-
> derestimate its speed. McCarthy did, and only just es-
> caped. It runs faster than a hound, but fortunately is
> reluctant to climb trees. I am fascinated by this mythago-
> genesis. It defies Huxley's understanding and account of
> the process, which is that a mythago is a remembered
> hero, a hope figure, or a place of aspiration, such as a
> castle, or a cathedral . . . unless, of course, such beasts
> are part of Alex's private hope, but I cannot work out the
> mechanism. Be on guard, and hasten to find us. Alex's
> castle is close. Once there I can give you two days to
> catch up with us before the final strike for the cathedral.
> There is something moving between our parties, however:
> a shapechanger. McCarthy senses it through the shad-
> ows. We are being hunted. Take special care."*

"Hunted? Could he mean the Jack?" Richard asked as
Helen finished the note.

"Of course he means the Jack," she said, scanning the scrawled words again. "It's got ahead of us. Damn!"

She was agitated and irritable and Richard kept both his curiosity and apprehension concerning the giant ursine to himself. They were in a place of massive trees, with wide spaces below the heavy canopy, a hard encampment to defend. Lytton had made a windbreak of dead wood in the overhang formed by a low bough. The river flowed on the other side of a raised bank.

During the early evening, the creature moved cumbersomely from its den, among the rocks on the high ground behind the encampment, and padded down to the river. Breathless, Richard watched it from cover, hoping that Helen, who was at the water's edge, washing, would hear it coming. The beast was familiar, its body bearlike if huge, its long muzzle thrown up into fleshy ridges. Overlapping canines pressed outside its mouth. Its shoulders were covered with a thick shawl of spiked, black hair, on a body that was otherwise gray and brown.

Close to where Richard crouched in total silence, waiting his moment to warn Helen, it rose onto its hindlegs and browsed at the foliage twenty feet above the ground, its stomach rumbling loudly, its breath a series of muffled snorts. When it dropped to all fours again, it hesitated halfway down, front paws with spreading claws held expectantly, the whole beast hunched as if listening.

When it moved on to the river, Richard followed it, spear held firmly. He wished sincerely, at that moment, for Lytton's pistol. There was no sign of Helen by the flowing water. The cave bear approached the tree-fringed river and drank.

There was a furtive movement opposite and it reared up to its full height, arms extended. The wood was suddenly full of chattering and three sleek lizard shapes dropped from the overhanging branches onto the huge beast. The bear screamed in an oddly human way and turned, slashing at the reptiles. One of the wide-eyed lizards had its teeth in the bear's neck. One hung onto the black shawl with tiny hands, slashing with a blade-like hind claw at the ursine's eye. The third was kicking at its bulging and exposed paunch, trying to rip through the hide with its glinting knife. The whole attack held a fascination for Richard, probably because of the thought that these were *living dinosaurs,* engaged in the hunt: he eased down the bank, crouching in cover to watch. the kill. Absorbed by the bloody mayhem by the river, he failed to notice the narrow, grinning face that was staring at him, until the reptile chattered suddenly and dropped toward him, killing jaws open.

He cried out as the sleek body swung down, ducking away from the claws that flashed before his eyes, narrowly missing him; the creature's whip-like tail struck him across the face. A second later, a bloody iron point erupted from the wide jaws of the creature and the dinosaur wriggled, gurgled and finally went limp. Behind it stood Helen, lowering her spear before working the point out of the skull.

"You should pay more attention!" she said angrily to Richard. "This vicious little bastard had been watching you for over a minute."

Richard watched as the hind claws flexed in the death throes, six inches of razor-sharp curved horn. "Thanks. That's one down; only three to go—"

By the river, the ursine had broken the back of one of the rapacious reptiles. It used the limp body to thrash at the others.

Then, unexpectedly, a fifth reptile appeared, running like a sleek bird along the river bank, nervous, jerky, its long tail horizontal until it stopped, at which point the tail undulated stiffly. It glanced at the humans and uttered a croaking taunt, then ran to join its kin. Oddly, the two dinosaurs had detached themselves from the bloody fur of the giant mammal, leaving it to lumber away, still roaring with pain. They were spitting and tail-flexing at the newcomer. Richard sensed their panic, as they circled on the spot, watching an animal that was identical to them, but which they clearly did not recognize. The bear appeared suddenly close to Richard, but it ran heavily through the trees toward its den, shaking its massive head to alleviate pain, spraying blood to right and left.

By the river, the fifth reptile rapidly grew and changed its shape, and as the two killers turned to flee it hunted them down, so fast that its actions were a blur. It bit through each neck, severing the head, then stood on its hindlegs, the corpses in its hands as it tore and nibbled at the muscle and tissue of the bloody necks.

It was ten feet tall. There was a human quality to its face and limbs, though the tail, held almost vertically, quivered and flexed at the tip. It was a lurid red on its belly, bright yellow and green on face and back, the colors of the Jack that had been born in the hornbeam glade.

As it ate, it croaked a challenge to the woods, certainly intended for the human observers.

Richard withdrew discreetly, following Helen who had fled the location long seconds before. A last glance at the river afforded him the glimpse of a man, shaggy-haired and clothed in colored rags, standing by the water watching the wood, the dead dinosaurs held easily in his hands.

"Why didn't he take us? The Jack—why is he taunting us?"

Helen had rolled up her sleeping things and filled her pack, then squatted down behind it, an arrow nocked to her bow, her iron-bladed spear to hand. "I don't know. Part of its nature would be my uneducated guess. We can't move until dawn, in the meantime let's defend ourselves as best we can."

In the event, the night passed swiftly, with only the grumbling roar of the wounded bear, high in the rocks, disturbing the snatched sleep of whichever one of them was not on watch. With first light they followed Lytton, cautious and apprehensive, but nothing was waiting for them, although Richard could not shake off the feeling of their tracks being dogged quietly. It was an understandable anxiety, he imagined.

Helen's apprehension did not lighten. On the third evening they heard the sound of fife and drum coming from a clearing in the wood, and she skirted widely, anticipating danger. Richard crept close to the small fire and saw the three tunicked soldiers, seated in the fire's glow, one of them practicing the thin flute, a second drumming happily on his side drum, the third smoking a long, clay pipe. They were British soldiers of the eighteenth century, redcoats, and in Alex's mind would probably have been associated, from the Grimm brothers' tales, with giant dogs whose eyes were as wide as saucers. Indeed, the baying of a hound sounded later, but by that time they were ensconced inside the walls of an old tavern, huddled in the canvas tent as the night's dew formed. Empty oak barrels, stacked against one wall, were a tease to Richard's appetite for a pint or two of strong beer.

For warmth they slept in the same roll of blanket. They had come to this arrangement without really addressing it. Although intimate, in its way, it was also too practical for either embarrassment or exploitation. In the morning, Helen's arms were round Richard, her breath soft in his ear, the flop of silver hair tickling his nose. When he stirred, stiff and damp with dew, she murmured softly and tugged him back. "This is too comfortable," she said. "Let's have a few more minutes."

This welcome lie-in was rudely interrupted moments later when the bushes outside the ruined tavern were crushed violently and a tall shape peered over the wall, startling them. Against the brightening sky it was hard to see detail save that the figure was a man, a tall, lean man of huge height, carrying two staffs. He peered at the tent quizzically for a few seconds, then spoke in a deep voice, guttural words whose intonation suggested a question. He repeated the query, frowning at Richard's silence. Again he spoke, a single word, "Helpen!"

Richard called up to this fairytale figure, "We don't need help. Thank you for offering."

He laughed huskily, then reached over the wall and with a hand the size of an armchair picked up one of the tuns, shaking it then discarding it with a sigh. A moment later he withdrew.

From the doorway Richard watched his unsteady passage through the trees, his short cloak ragged, his breeches tied with leather in the Saxon way, his face gray with a bristling beard.

"What the hell is *he*?" Helen whispered.

"A Long Man," Richard said, and there was little else to

add. That the visitor was a Long Man was obvious: he was the living reflection of the chalk figures that could be found on the English downlands, and whose origins and identities and functions remained a mystery.

Just before he was out of sight, the Long Man turned and called again, pushing aside the foliage with one of the staffs, bending the high branch easily. When Richard shook his head he shrugged, then turned and reached out his arms, a tall pole in each hand, an absolute image now of the Long Man of Wilmington, in Sussex. He stepped forward and faded, both poles following him into obscurity.

Behind Richard, Helen gasped and laughed at the same time. "He carries his own hollowing!" she said. "We should have made friends with him . . . he could have saved us hours!"

A distant rumble, a freshening breeze, told of the storm approaching. They had set off from the ruins, anxious to make the rendezvous with Lytton, but had gone no more than half a mile when the thunder came closer, and the sky darkened to such an extent that they lost the track below the canopy in the gloom and the constant, wind-whipped motion of the undergrowth. When the first rain began to trickle through the foliage, Helen led the way swiftly back to the tavern. They re-erected the tent and crouched in misery as the heavens opened and the downpour began.

For a while there was nothing but the drum of the rain, but the hound that had bayed in the distance grew closer, its cry a mournful sound at first, then more of an angry challenge to some hunted beast. Helen had folded into a tight ball, her arms around her head, as if blocking the sound, but after a while she looked up, drawn and misty eyed, a grim set to her features. Richard grew concerned and asked her why she was frightened, and she replied quite simply, "Trickster."

She wouldn't talk further, not for the moment. Richard established only that, although she was hunting Trickster, she could not be sure whether or not he had risen from the earth in the wood at her own instigation. The Jack that dogged their steps, the shapechanging relic of pre-Celtic myth that shadowed them like a lie, was probably Alex's creation, imbued with the darker side of the frightened boy, who was protecting himself so intensely against the products of his own imagination.

She could not be sure. She had expected to encounter Trickster in its AmerIndian form, yet this Jack was quintessentially European. This, however, might be the trick that Trickster was playing on her, hiding himself from her in confusing guise while he waited for the moment to destroy her, as he had destroyed . . .

At this point she slumped again, then looked up sharply at Richard, reaching for her bow and quiver. She said, "It's an odd story, and I can only explain it in the simplest of terms."

"Good. Then I'll understand it."

"Five hundred years ago, Trickster destroyed my family; it didn't end at that time. The destruction has continued down the family line to the present day. And I'm going to stop it. Or die trying. And that's my story."

She brushed aside Richard's question, his concern, his offer to come with her. Heavily dressed in weatherproof jacket and leggings, her head protected beneath a hood, she tested the bow, selected six arrows, and went out into the rain, walking fast toward the awful baying of the giant dog.

If it *was* Coyote, she would have a fight on her hands.

When two hours had passed, and the sound of the dog had been swallowed either by distance or death, Richard followed Helen through the wood, calling for her. Emerging onto open land, where tall, wild grass was being crushed by the heavy rain, he saw her distantly, coming back toward the stone shelter. Stray light, penetrating the thunderclouds, caught on her rain-drenched waterproof. Her head was down, she was walking normally. As she came close Richard could see that she was unwounded.

Back in the shelter she ate food and tried to dry her saturated hair.

"Coyote?" Richard asked.

She shook her head. "I let it go. It was what Lytton calls a wild-hound, an early form of dog. You see them regularly. They're solitary animals, more inclined to help than hinder.

All for food, of course." She smiled distractedly. "The story of the dogs' downfall."

After a while she relaxed. In her absence Richard had built a ditch around the squalid shelter, the floor was dry, and it felt warm with the small fire that smoldered at its center. Richard asked her what had happened five hundred years ago, and why she felt she could end the curse today, in 1967.

"Because I carry the curse in my head," she said. "As do all my family. Trickster is in here." She tapped her skull. "And he shares his spirit between all the minds of my family. There's only one of him, and if I can just entice him out ... if I can just make him come out of the shadows ..."

She was in a dreamy state, her eyes closed, her body swaying. For a moment she sang, but so softly that Richard strained to hear the words, then realized they were in an older tongue than his. When the song had finished she began to speak, eyes open but watching the long-gone, her voice rhythmical. The story was entrancing, *chanted* by the speaker as the rain lashed down.

Richard established afterward that it was more than a family story, passed down from generation to generation: it was literally a family *dream,* and the dream of a family that had been regularly attacked, abused and destroyed by Coyote. When he came to record the story he could not recapture the sense of time and land that she had elicited in his mind, the rhythm of a lost land, reflected in the rhythm of her words.

The first dream is still with me, though I haven't dreamt it for years, now.

When we are children, the past is closer. It passes through the lands in our heads more easily.

Young Grandfather, who was named Three Crows Flying, was a fine hunter, and later a flier with eagles, which we would call *shaman.* He was born in the time before horses, when the great plains were covered with grass, and the best hunters were the fastest runners, or the most skilled at setting hidden nets and blind-alleys of wood for a single buffalo.

At the best time of summer, the grasses were very high. When the buffalo came down to the tribal lands, they entered the grass like a man entering water, slowing down wading carefully. At this time the herds would spread thinly. The calf and the cow would follow the bull, but the families would move widely, leaving great passages in the grass, the trails which the hunters followed.

No hunter would follow any trail that led to the setting sun, or the rising sun. Those buffalo had a special spirit.

The hunters would dance in the great flat place, where the herd had gathered and the grass was trampled, and by song, by dance and sometimes by courting coup, they would select the high-grass trail to follow. They would run through the tunnel toward their prey on all fours, never allowed to stand high, because this would bring them above the grass, and make them vulnerable to the dark spirit that watched the herds from the distant rocks.

Young Grandfather became a fine hunter. If a buffalo turned back along its track, it was considered right for the hunter to lie down and let the beast walk over him. It was a painful and humiliating thing. But when this happened to Young Grandfather, to his surprise Coyote appeared at the edge of the grass track, disguised as a musk rat. "Next-Buffalo-Meal is walking away from you again. You can hunt him, now. He will not trample you. I have done this, and this is my gift. But don't forget you owe me a name."

"What name?" cried Young Grandfather.

Coyote revealed himself for what he was. "The name that was stolen from me at your birth. If you don't yet know this, you soon will."

Sometimes the hunters would take up their coup sticks and arrows, their feathered lances and stone skull-crackers, and run across the hills to dance war. On one occasion Young Grandfather had stumbled in a snake-hole, and his enemy was screaming above him and about to crack skull. Coyote bit the enemy and the black stone club whistled like sling-shot, a skin's thickness from Young Grandfather's eyes. Young Grandfather used his granite club to break the enemy's knees, then his jaw, then open his head to the crows. Coyote ran with him afterward, disguised as a gray dog.

"I have saved your skull, and this is my gift for you. But don't forget my name. You must remember that you owe me a name."

The day came when Young Grandfather was growing old. Not so old that he couldn't disturb his wives in their sleeping skins, but old enough that the paint ran in many furrows on his face. He wished to fly with eagles, so he went out to Coyote Rock, to remember his birth.

When he had been born, White Eagle, his father, had stepped from the lodge and stared around the wide land. Three crows had been flying toward a high rock and woods where the carcass of a coyote lay, gored by a buffalo. He took the child up to the rock. But the coyote was not quite dead yet, and it watched the man and the child as the crows settled and began to feast.

Coyote said, "I'm glad you've come with the new child, to give him my name, the name of the first thing you saw when your child was born."

"I saw three crows, flying to eat," White Eagle said. "The boy will be named after them."

Coyote was furious and the picking crows flew up to escape the slashing claws. "He must take my name or my spirit cannot rest. I saw you come from the lodge. I saw you look up at me. You watched me haul myself to this place to die. The crows were still in the north wind. You saw me first. He must take my name."

"Never!" said White Eagle, and Young Grandfather was then named for the crows.

The coyote died, his spirit entering the woods as his bones bleached. And from here, over the years when the people passed this way on the hunt, he crept out to watch over the child, and then the man, who had not been named for him by words, but who was tied to Coyote by first sight.

Now, years later, the spirit of Coyote came out to sit with Young Grandfather, in his new paint on the old face, at his new age, searching for eagles. Coyote said, "I ran with you through the tall grass when you were a child who wished to be a man."

"I remember you. You saved me from a trampling."

"I remember you when you first went below the skin of your first wife. You were very clumsy."

"I don't remember you. And I had no complaints."

"From the look of you, the grass-hunting time is finished, and the inside-the-skin time; and the skull-cracking time is finished too."

Young Grandfather shook his head as he thought of his wives. "Not the inside-the-skin time, but the others, yes. All finished. I wish to fly with eagles, and with crows, to see the tribe and their hunt-trails through other eyes. I wish to see the long-to-come through the eyes of other dreaming things. But something stops me."

Coyote chuckled. "You have the name of crows, and not coyote. You have the wrong name. Your father was at fault and I killed him."

"My father ran up onto high rocks and fell."

"I pushed him. He gave you the wrong name. It's not too late. Here I am."

Young Grandfather had been expecting this. He knew from his father, from his grandfather too, that to take Coyote's name would be to be in Coyote's grasp, and Coyote was tricky. Sometimes his visions would be real. Sometimes they would be lies. It was the same with young women and old men. It was a dangerous thing to take Coyote's name, and no matter how sincere Coyote sounded, sitting there on the spirit rock, with the sun setting and the feathers in his gray hair waving in the wind, Coyote could not be trusted.

Young Grandfather scratched in the earth on the rock and found the skull of the dead coyote. "You must come back into the eyes and the ears and the jaws of these bones," he said to the spirit, "so that I can honor you, and take your name."

Coyote hesitated. Was he being tricked? No, the old man was too eager to fly with eagles. On the grass below, the lodges were spread widely, and smoke rose from every teepee. Children were making games, their laughter thin on the late evening air. Coyote sighed and went into the skull, and Young Grandfather carried the bones reverently to the village. There were many drums in the night, and a great fire, and a tall ash-pole with the spirits carved upon it and the dead coyote was placed on the ground. When the drums stopped, Young Grandfather drove a buffalo horn through the skull, then buried the bones in the earth where a stream split and made an island.

"May your ghost stay there forever," Young Grandfather taunted. "I will never take your name. Now at last I can fly with eagles."

Coyote was furious. The buffalo bone, stuck through his skull, had made him insane. He danced on the island and screamed, but he was trapped.

But a time came when Young Grandfather's youngest daughter came to the island at night to give birth. She had lost her way in the darkness, and Coyote had sung sweetly, and rustled the leaves on the trees to make it sound like a good shelter for her labor, so she had crossed the water. As she crouched and felt the weight of the child, Coyote whispered that she should tug the buffalo horn from the ground and lean on it. She did so, and Coyote was freed from his buffalo coffin. Coyote helped with the birth, still singing softly, but as the child put its head into the world Coyote pinched its cheeks to open its eyes. He jumped into the open eyes and entered through the bone. When the child slipped out onto the soft skins of its cradle, it grinned. "Now I have my name," it whispered.

The mother was terrified to hear the newborn speak, but after a while she thought it must have been the pain in her loins and the cool of the wind making her dream, because soon after this the child began to cry, like any child.

But Coyote was now in the blood of the family, and already planning his revenge for Young Grandfather's trickery.

The rain had stopped and they shook out the tent, preparing to move on. As they worked, Helen said, "We became the most wretched of families. We were known as the Mad Dog People, because nothing ever went right for us, and sometimes we killed each other in a fury of desperation.

"Coyote took the best of our hunters and made them crazy with potato whisky. He danced round the best of our warriors during battle and made them kill each other. Our children were sometimes born with the heads of dogs; the most beautiful of our women would mutilate themselves, or start to bay like hounds as soon as they were married. Coyote caused starvation, even when there was plentiful game and fish, interfering with nets, cutting lines, warning animals. He distracted fathers and warrior sons during war-party raids on other tribes, and left them with their skulls bashed open and the crows on their eyes. He brought disease and cancer. He struck children dumb, and our mothers blind. He dried up their milk. He caused fire in teepees, even in the rain. He appeared as a disembodied dog-skull, the jaws grinding, and when we saw that we knew that Coyote had come to claim another prize. For generations my family has been terrified of the dreamworld, where this malevolent shadow stalks us. We never know *when* he will strike."

No one had known what to do. The old rituals were long-since forgotten, and the precise nature of the magic that Young Grandfather had used to torment Coyote in that time-before-horses had died with him.

Then Alexander Lytton had visited the university where Helen and Dan were teaching, and she learned of his obsession with a strange wood in England. He had been looking for an expert on Palaeolithic hunter-gatherer societies. He found a woman and her husband who were specialists in that subject and who were living a nightmare. He had welcomed them to the team.

"So that's all there is to it," Helen murmured as she led Richard into open land, where a white-walled castle gleamed distantly. "If I can get Trickster to come out into the wood, to be made solid, then I can kill him. Dan tried. I think he's failed. I'll grieve for him in good time. I can't think of anything, yet, except destroying the shadow."

White Castle

From images of the ancient plains of North America, Richard suddenly stepped into the early Middle Ages, approaching the castle through patchy woodland, impressed by the height of the walls, suddenly aware that the purity of color was not due to paint but to the white berries of a spreading thorn, grown so completely across the stone that it had covered the castle entirely.

The drawbridge had long since rotted. Across the scum-covered moat, a stagnant pool filled with decaying wood, a felled tree had been placed to make an awkward bridge. Inside, sheltering in the watchgate, Lytton and McCarthy huddled round a fire, McCarthy fussing with food on wooden skewers, Lytton smoking his black pipe and scrawling in his notebook. He glanced up as they arrived, grinning broadly. His rich Scots tones rang out to greet them. "Glad to see you! Did y'have a good journey?"

"Wet!" said Helen irritably.

"Indeed! We saw the storm from a distance. Have you any food, Helen? As you can see, we're down to our last two dormice—tasty enough, but I'd kill for rare roast beef with all the trimmings."

"Can't help you with beef, but I'm happy to go hunting."

"God bless you," Lytton said with a second yellow-toothed smile. "I'd sing a song of luck for you, but I'm so damned hungry I haven't the energy. I saw wild pigs in the woods, across the way, there."

As Helen prepared her bow, and spoke softly with McCarthy, Lytton glanced at Richard. "You look as disheveled outside as I feel inside. I wish I could say that your son was here, but he isn't. This place is deserted. He's discarded it. And nature, as you see from the walls, is regaining it, stone by stone, passage by passage, chamber by chamber. Explore it by all means, but this is a ghost place. First, sit down and tell me how close you *feel* to Alex. We *must* be close. McCarthy here feels his shadow, but the boy is damned good at keeping hidden."

Richard told Lytton of his experiences with the "presence" of Alex, and the Scot mused and pondered, and smoked his vile pipe. "There's something not right," he said. "Something I'm missing. I thought I had your son clearly in my sights, but something must have happened. If you can bear to indulge me, tell me again about his death, about the man Keeton. You saw him suddenly on a road, near his home, a year after he had vanished . . . and he was only days older . . . Tell me again . . ."

Richard recapped the events of that long-gone autumn night in as much detail as he could remember, from the songs in his son's adaptation of *Gawain,* to the state of James Keeton as he had stumbled from the Otherworld, half-naked and very frightened.

Keeton had gone somewhere "out of time," Lytton mused. It had probably not been a form of fairyland—if that had been the case, his return still young would have meant time catching up with him. He would have aged a year suddenly. Keeton had been *suspended* from time, exactly like Alex, or at least, the Alex that could be sensed by McCarthy, probing the sylvan shadows, and Richard himself through his dreams.

"But damn!" Lytton said, leaning back against the wall of the watchgate. "I'm missing *something.*"

"Time might *well* be playing tricks," Richard offered, and for the first time told him of the Helen look-alike who had been at his house on the afternoon of Keeton's return, leaving a message that had been incomprehensible. Under Lytton's questioning he accepted that he could have been mistaken. "But when I mentioned it to Helen, when she came to visit me the other day, the thought seemed to disturb her."

"Did it?"

"I'm not sure it was her. I don't suppose I ever have been. But if it was Helen, then she visited me seven years before she'd even come to England . . ."

"Yes," Lytton said. "And she appeared on the night when Keeton came back from the Otherworld. Like Hallowe'en, maybe a night when the gates went down for an hour or so . . ." He scribbled in his pad. "Time *always* goes forward in Ryhope Wood. Not necessarily at the same rate in different places, but always forward. Nevertheless, there's an odd coincidence here."

McCarthy watched the inner walls of the castle dreamily, singing softly to himself. Richard realized Lytton was talking to him. The man repeated, "The ur-Helen . . . what did she write in the note?"

Richard confessed that memory had failed him. "Something that you had found. Something that needed my attention. Odd words. When I lost the note, I lost the sense of its contents completely. I'm sorry."

Lytton wanted to think. McCarthy, shrinking in his clothes, pale and wan, yet always ready with a smile, nibbled at the thin flesh of their last catch and stared out through the watchgate at the wetland and far forest, where Helen could be seen, prowling the thickets at the edgewood, listening for game.

Richard stalked the decaying corridors of the castle, feeling the cold silence, the dank stone, the sense of being in an abandoned place among dull shadows. He could not even imagine the sound of voices, of laughter, of the growling of the great hounds that must once have lazed in front of the huge wood fires, until required to bound through the forests in search of game. There was nothing here for him, and he started to return to the watchgate.

A moment later a shadow passed swiftly through the chamber, an odd touch of warmth, like a breath on his neck. He realized suddenly that he had lost his way. He passed from chamber to cold stone passage, down worn steps and into a sequence of wide rooms, where traces of the wooden partitions could still be seen. He called out for Lytton, but his voice was deadened by the stone walls. He was suddenly back in the main hall, a vast space, echoing to his quickening pace. It smelled of woodsmoke, and he saw the smoldering logs in the wrought-iron gate. On the wall above them he recognized the stone carving of a knight and a giant, clashing swords above the leering, foliate face of a Green Man, replete with branches for its mouth, and fruits and berries in a fringe around the face.

The atmosphere in the Great Hall suddenly became stifling. Richard reacted to sudden movement in the air, half-aware of hounds, of swirling cloaks and skirts, and the steamy aroma of food in clay pots. He saw nothing of this activity but the smoke in the fire and the cracked, gray carving above.

And then, whispering startlingly from the shadows, a child's voice urged at him, "Go back!"

"Alex? *Alex?*"

Somewhere a drummer struck the taut skins in a staccato, military beat. The stone carving shifted, rustled, and as Richard called his son for the third time, the foliate face stretched forward, peered down at him. "Go back!" it hissed, and Richard stumbled toward the doorway. The face twisted on its long stone neck, eyes gleaming in the gray rock, stone leaves falling noisily as the giant head trembled.

"Go back where?" Richard shouted. "Alex? Are you here? Go back where?"

The face withdrew and a sudden cold descended. The side-drum had faded, the fireplace was empty. Only Richard's skin was hot, burning with the shock of the encounter. He ran quickly through the passageways and abruptly found himself stumbling into the light, where the skies still drizzled rain.

Lytton was just outside the castle gate, staring toward the distant wood. "Richard!" he called without turning. "Quickly! Something's up."

"Alex *was* here!" Richard called, as he scampered over the muddy courtyard and into the sheltering gate.

He stopped and drew breath as he saw Helen running toward the castle, shouting, pointing to her right. As she came close, stepping awkwardly across the narrow bridge, she looked at Richard, breathless and excited: "The cathedral—Alex's cathedral! It's over there ... I've seen it!"

"That close?" Lytton gasped. "So soon?"

McCarthy struggled to his feet, running out into the light rain and staring into the distance, his eyes half closed. He walked quickly to the thorn that draped the high walls, and crouched down, his hands running down the broad, ridged wood of the lower branches. He was tracing shadows, hunched and cold, feeling his way through the earth toward the defended site.

"I can't touch the shadow!" he called. "He must have put up another barrier."

"It's there!" Helen cried. "I saw it when I climbed a tree to get woodcock eggs. It's *there*!"

"Then let's fetch him out," Lytton said. "And let's do it *quickly*. Are you ready, Richard? Are you ready to face your lost past?"

He grinned coldly as he slung his small pack across his shoulder and followed Helen to the open land. Richard said nothing, but caught McCarthy's quick glance, a look of uncertainty, of apprehension. There was something of a warning in the frail Irishman's expression. Richard whispered, "Is Lytton still armed?"

McCarthy held up a hand with four fingers raised, indicating the number of rounds. "It's only a pistol. But he's a bloody fine shot."

"Go back!" the green face had said, and it occurred to Richard that he had been urged to leave the castle because Helen had now seen the way to the cathedral, and the castle itself was becoming dangerous as shadows crept back into the lifeless shell.

Lytton had not heard the drumming. It had been sound for Richard's ears only, a memory of the legends of ghostly drummer boys, and as such, a certain signal from Alex that he was close to his father again. But "Go back!" ...

The whispered words unnerved Richard as he entered the woodland, following Helen as she pushed through the lush summer growth toward the light again. It was too still in the wood, too quiet. Was this simply anticipation affecting him, making him dread the moment of contact again with a boy from his past? His stomach churned violently, his legs shook, and he stopped for a moment, listening to the others ahead of him. He felt tears in his eyes and the pulse of blood in his temples and a moment later was sick. He wiped his mouth with wet leaves, then jumped as a gentle hand touched his shoulder.

"What is it?" Helen asked. She recoiled slightly from his breath, but touched a finger to his cheeks, her eyes watching his. "I guess that's an idiotic question. I can imagine how hard it's going to be to see him again. If you don't think you can face it just yet ... if you need some more time ... to watch from a distance for a while?"

"I don't know," Richard confessed awkwardly, still shaking. "He whispered to me. In the castle ... he whispered 'go back'. I wonder if he meant go back from here? I remember in his school play, the words were used as a warning."

"Against what?"

"The Green Knight, I think. Someone was trying to stop Gawain entering the Green Chapel and finding its secrets."

"But Alex *wants* you to find him. You've felt this strongly. He wants you to help him out ..."

Distantly, Lytton called loudly, summoning Richard. Helen kissed Richard quickly on the cheek, whispered, "Courage!" and led him to the edge of the wood.

The cathedral rose high and ruined, gray through the heavy mist that drowned the steaming land. Richard crouched beside Lytton and followed his pointing finger to one of the arched windows, below the craggy line of the wall where the roof had been torn away. A boy's face watched them over the stone sill. A second later the head vanished, but reappeared lower down in a circular portal where once there had been stained glass.

"I can't get a touch," McCarthy was saying. "He's not allowing contact."

"Call to him," Lytton said, pushing Richard forward.

Richard called out his son's name twice, and a moment later came an answering cry, not a word, more of a sob, a high-pitched sound that was filled with longing, and relief, and fear.

"My God ... he's in danger!" Richard gasped, and ran

from the cover of the undergrowth, through the grass, to the gaping doorway of the side porch.

Lytton came after him, crouched low. The saturating mist swirled about them as they entered the bleak and deserted interior of the ruin, Lytton running to the center of the space, Richard touching one of the broken columns that marked the side aisle. Helen came through the door, looking quickly round, then up to where the boy had just been glimpsed.

"This isn't right," she said.

Outside, McCarthy yelled, "Get out of there!"

"Daddy! Go back!"

The sound of his son's voice startled Richard. For a moment he couldn't locate the source of the words, and then the small figure stepped forward, a gray statue, up on the altar space. It had seemed to detach from the stone, to come away from the hard surface, and now raised its arms sideways. The boy's eyes sparkled, his mouth stretched wide, though not in a grin, nor a grimace—something oddly expressionless. But it was Alex, long-haired, naked, undeniably Alex, a small boy, frail in build, watching his father with an expression that suddenly shifted into anguish.

"Alex! Come on, lad. Get out of here!"

The cathedral shuddered, the walls bending inward, the floor dropping so that the rising columns seemed to buckle. Helen yelled and grabbed at Richard. The boy on the altar started to scream, and Richard pulled away from Helen, only to feel her foot kick his legs from under him so that he sprawled headlong.

Lytton was running toward the altar. Alex screamed again and crouched defensively as the man raced toward him.

"Don't touch my son!" Richard bellowed, and struggled to rise.

Lytton's first shot stunned him. The second made him cry his pain. The bullets penetrated Alex's head, blowing muddy tissue across the altar. The boy kept standing. The cathedral seemed to be falling down around them, and Helen was tugging at Richard, her words meaningless, even though he knew she was shouting at him to *get out, get out!*

Lytton emptied the final two shots into the brain-dead boy on the altar, then swung his staff so that it crushed the skull, then knocked the small figure sideways. The walls around him flowed down and bulged, gray stone melting into an organic flow that began to swell and surround the screaming man, tendrils of liquid rock reaching out and wrapping around him. The shape of the boy was absorbed into the floor. A new human figure erupted like new growth to tower over the struggling form of Alexander Lytton.

Dark, piercing eyes stared across the shrinking cathedral from below a shock of green hair, above a body that was clad in colored rags.

"The Jack . . ." Richard hissed.

Stone tendrils probed for him and he used his staff to strike them away. The whole building was drawing into the Jack, a giant trap, shrinking, now with its human prey.

The door through the porch was closing down, but Richard felt a final tug on his shoulder and this time turned and followed Helen through into the rain, where McCarthy stood in shock at the woodland edge. He shouted, "Alex is close. He's shouting for you! That's not Alex in there!"

A moment later the earth itself rose up around him. McCarthy screamed once, struggled, shouted "Christ!" and was gone, sucked down below the yellow grass.

Richard ran for his life. He glanced back once to see that the cathedral now had the shape of a grinning stone head, watching him below flowing hair. From the huge open mouth two snaking branches erupted and raced toward him, sprouting side shoots as they came, full-leafed trees that formed a consuming tunnel as the tendrils bore down upon him. Somehow, somewhere above the roar of the earth and the rustling of this hunting growth, he could hear Lytton's death agony, shrill and desperate.

Where was Helen?

He saw her in the distance, leaping the moving earth like a cat, outrunning the snares the Jack was sending at her. There was a moment when she hesitated, caught sight of Richard in the distance and waved at him furiously: Get the hell away from here!

And a moment later she was gone.

A towering man-shape loomed in the mist, stepping forward, arms outstretched and holding two tall poles. Richard sobbed with exhaustion and fear as the Long Man barred his way. But then the figure beckoned, shouted words that could have been "Come on!" The Long Man turned his back and braced his legs apart, the poles held to each side.

Aware that everything behind him had suddenly stopped, that all was silent, that the Jack-chapel head had disappeared beneath a tangle of hawthorn and oak from which the hedges grew, he ran at the Long Man's back, and grabbed for the figure's shoulders. Long Man and frightened man stepped forward together, and the world closed around them.

A moment later they were stumbling against a red-brick wall, startling pigeons in the trees and a wild cat, that hissed, spat, then bolted into the dense undergrowth. The Long Man brushed himself down, peering up and around at the glade. But Richard recognized instantly where they were.

"Oak Lodge," he breathed. "You've brought me back to the starting place."

The Long Man rubbed his eyes as he looked nervously at the ruined house and the rotting wooden statue that leaned against the wall. Perhaps he could feel Lacan's defenses. In any event, he didn't like this place. His expression showed it. He picked up his staffs and stepped away from the wall of the lodge.

"Thank you," Richard called. "Thanks for bringing me home . . ."

Alex. Oh God, Alex. Was it you! Or the Jack? What happened? Helen. I've lost you. Helen! What happened? This can't have happened!

The Long Man shook his head sadly, long hair waving. By word and gesture he invited Richard to follow him back, but Richard shook his head, too disturbed by what had happened to contemplate returning to the nightmare.

The Long Man grinned, touched a finger to his right eye, then turned and stepped between his poles. The air popped, sending a gust of wind around the small clearing that had once been a garden, and the giant had gone.

Crying softly, suddenly very weary, Richard left the wood and stumbled along the bridleway to Shadoxhurst, to his house, to the silence of the grave.

He's gone!" Alex screamed, and erupted from the sharp embrace of the hollyjack. He climbed the creepers to the high window and stared out across the wood.

"Don't go!" he cried. "Daddy! Don't go!"

There was no movement. Everything was still. His father had been close—Alex had shouted his warning about the giggler, setting his trap, and his father had escaped the snare.

But he had *gone*—just *vanished* from the Little Dream. He had been running. There was the tall traveler. And his father's shadow had disappeared from the wood, just yards from where Alex was sheltering behind his defensive wall.

He had been so close ...

The hollyjack whistled from below. Alex went back to her and cried in her arms. She was very weak. She clattered and chirruped.

Winter is coming. There will be danger. We must draw deeper, to protect ourselves.

Alex closed his eyes. The wood in the chapel shivered, then seemed to freeze. Light caught the broken colored glass above the doors, a last glimpse of the knight and the monster, before the shadows closed in on him. The window had grown—the glass had filled out, the colors deepened. He could see so much more of the scene of battle.

Something was not right. The knight—Gawain—not right.

The hollyjack trembled.

They slept for a long while.

PART THREE

*Long Gone,
Long to Come*

Spirit Rock

(Two months later ...)

There's a fire up by Hunter's Brook—they're dancing by the fire—"Daddy—wake up—there's a fire—"

"They're dancing—"

"Daddy!"

Richard woke with shock, yelling out into the pale dawn light. The room was cold and damp, dew-encrusted. The window was wide open and he could see rolling clouds, threatening rain. It was four in the morning. The crows were flapping and cawing in their roosts and Richard's head was pounding as the image of Alex, reaching out to shake him awake, began to fade.

He was fully clothed, having slept sprawled on two blankets on the floor. The bedroom was a mess. Downstairs, from sitting room to kitchen, the chaos was far worse. In the month since he had resigned from his job in London and returned permanently to Shadoxhurst he had become a slob through distraction. He walked the perimeter of Ryhope Wood every day, and filled his evenings in the local pub, writing an account of his experience at Old Stone Hollow and points beyond, and getting very drunk.

The more he wrote, and the longer he stayed out of the wood, the more dreamlike the events became. It began to seem as if he had been the audience at a film. The characters were vivid, but they were all actors. Arnauld Lacan,

McCarthy, Alexander Lytton—a fine cast, certainly, but they were now playing other roles in other films. Ryhope Wood was a small, dangerous, marshy woodland, far bigger than it seemed, but surely just a wood, tricky, deceptive, but as tame, in its way, as everything in England. His son was not hiding there. His son was dead. His bones were in the earth. Even Helen had become an artificial memory of beginning love. She filled his waking dreams and occupied his thoughts obsessively: they had grown so close, in those few days in the wood, but now she too was dissembling into image, voice, laughter, becoming detached from him.

But the dream—it had been so real—it had been his first real dream since coming back here.

Standing stiffly, rubbing the small of his back where it ached from the hard floor, he staggered to the window and greeted the misty dawn. He saw, at once, the column of smoke that rose steeply from Hunter's Brook before being whipped by the cross-winds. Was that a figure standing on the gray skyline? He squinted, trying to make out the detail, and a moment later the shape had vanished.

"Christ! Oh Christ—Helen!"

He tugged on his shoes and windcheater, walked groggily down the stairs and splashed cold water over his face. He was unkempt and unshaven, but gave no more thought to this than to the ants that crawled over the sink where his dirty crockery was heaped, ready for cleaning. Outside, he relieved himself against the elm at the bottom of the garden, then walked briskly along the bridleway. Soon he saw the orange lick of flame below the shifting smoke, and as he came over the low rise toward the brook and the trees, he saw the crouched, black-caped and hooded figures, one in front of the small fire, two below the trees, mostly in shadow. The mustached face of the nearest man was very bronzed. Slightly oriental eyes watched Richard from below the hood. Somewhere in the trees there was movement in the mist and Richard was distracted. When he looked back at the crackling fire, the hooded man was standing and holding out a wooden object. Richard approached cautiously.

It was a cricket bat, six inches long. Richard was astonished. He accepted the gift, and was at once aware that the other man was pleased. His companions stood and drew back among the alders at the edge of the stream, pulling their capes about their slender frames. The hooded man beckoned to Richard, who followed him to the brook and along its dry bank.

A human shape, covered in leaves, lay on its side on a crude litter of poles and cross-woven twine. The body didn't move. One of the caped figures brushed leaves from the face to expose graying-black hair over deathly white skin. A further brushing aside of leaves revealed an arm in splints and the curve of hips, unmistakably female.

When Richard looked more closely he could make out the dead body of Elizabeth Haylock.

Across the brook two further dark figures appeared among the trees, then ran quickly toward Ryhope Wood. The mustached man clapped his hands and said sharp words. Both language and gesture were clearly designed to communicate "She's all yours now."

Then he followed his friends, away from the stream and onto the grassy rise, where more hooded shapes rose from cover and joined the easy trot back to the wood. There were nine in all. Before he vanished from sight the leader turned, a silhouette against the brightening day. He raised both hands vertically, watching Richard and uttering a shrill, broken cry.

What had happened?

Richard pocketed the tiny cricket bat and leaned down over the woman's corpse, nervous about touching it. The leaves on the litter by her face shifted, as if blown. A moment later she groaned and her eyes opened slightly, focusing painfully on the brook. Richard cleared the hair from her face and she turned to look at him. When she saw him she allowed herself a thin and pallid smile.

"Richard—am I out?" she whispered.

"Of the wood? Yes."

"Thank God. Oh thank God . . ." She grimaced with pain. "I'm in a bad way. What happened to the Pathanan?"

Richard glanced at Ryhope wood, thinking of the small figures. "Gone. Can you walk if I helped you?"

"Sorry—sprains in both ankles. *Christ,* I'm cold. Please get me warm. Please . . ."

She drifted into unconsciousness again, and mercifully remained so as Richard dragged the litter along the bridleway—he hadn't wanted to leave her alone while he went for help—taking nearly an hour before he was able to unroll the damaged woman onto a blanket and haul her into the relative comfort of his sitting room. He called the doctor and made tea. Elizabeth revived again and allowed herself to be stripped and examined. Her ankles were bandaged and her arm placed in a better splint. She would go to the hospital for a proper cast the next day. Given painkillers, antibiotics and strong tea, she began to feel human again.

The doctor, although curious about her clothing and general condition, did not question Richard too closely. And as soon as he had gone, Elizabeth appeared to relax. Richard helped her to the bath, where she soaked for an hour, unbothered by his presence as he sat on the toilet seat, helped wash her back, and waited for her to talk.

She was very thin—Richard remembered her as being quite robust—and her face was lined, her breasts badly bruised. She had shallow but extensive cuts on her legs, and Richard replaced the iodine that had now washed off. To compound her physical deterioration, she seemed mentally exhausted, distant and depressed, speaking in a slow, quite breathless whisper.

"What happened to you?" Richard asked after a while.

"The wrong sort of hero," was all she would say. "It doesn't matter. Don't push me on it. The Pathanan found me and helped me, thank the Lord. I was just trying to get out— just trying to get away. I've had enough." She lay back in the water, one hand gently touching the deepest bruising on her chest, her eyes closed.

"They were camped in Oak Lodge, coming right to the edge." Hesitantly, she added, "I think they were looking for you. They were carrying a little cricket bat. It was a gift, either came from Helen or Alex—"

"They gave me the bat. Nothing else. Just the bat— and you. No message, no hint of anything else."

Elizabeth sighed again. "Someone wants you back in the wood. But there's nothing there now, nothing to go back to."

Again Richard asked what had happened, and wearily the woman said, "It all went wrong. We lost too many, too much. Maybe if you'd come when we asked it wouldn't have risen again. It overwhelmed us." She opened her eyes slightly, frowning. "That wasn't meant to sound like an accusation. Sorry. I *can* understand why you didn't want to go back. The way I feel now—" She rubbed her face with her hands. "If this is how you felt, then it's not surprising you hid from us."

Confused, Richard leaned forward, his gaze on Elizabeth's face as she breathed softly and soaked her aches away. Her words were coming out in a jumble—he didn't understand "risen again," or being "asked again." Was she delirious?

"When was I asked back? I left the wood two months ago. I went back to London, couldn't face the job I was in and came back to live here. I've not heard from any of you, from the Station, for two months."

Elizabeth Haylock frowned from behind half-closed eyes. "Didn't you get Helen's note?"

"Helen's note? No."

"Damn. She said she left the note for you here. You were out."

Even as she spoke, a memory of 1959 screamed at him, memory of a previous encounter with Helen on a rainy day, the woman running from the house, leaving behind a scrawled note, now lost.

"When *was* this?" Richard asked.

"About a year ago. Station time, that is. This will probably come as a shock, but you've been gone from Old Stone Hollow for nearly three years . . ."

He felt more alarmed than shocked. Three years to his two months—so much had happened, then, while he had been suffocating in isolation.

The note—could it have been the same one? He asked if Elizabeth knew what message Helen had brought him, and his mind raced as she said, "It was something Lytton had worked out—how to find the protogenomorph. Alex's, of course. It's most likely to react to you, so it would have been good to have you in the wood. Also— forgive me for gossiping—but Helen was missing you. You made quite a hit." She became aware that Richard was very pale, very shocked, and sat up in the bath, using her good arm to draw a towel around her shoulders and over her breasts, perhaps self-conscious for the first time.

"Are you OK?" she asked.

"Yes. *No!* I don't know what to say. Is Lytton alive? I saw him killed by a Jack."

"I heard about that. It spat him out. He did some good work. Helen came to tell you about it . . ."

Confused, almost dizzy, Richard held his head in his hands and said, "I think I *did* get the note. It sounds like the same one. Only I got it eight years ago! *My* time. 1959, to be precise. Helen had short hair, right?"

"In 1959? No idea."

"I meant when she brought the note, a year ago . . ."

"That's right. She'd cropped it back after getting a tick infestation."

Too much, too fast . . .

Lytton alive! An odd fury crept into Richard's heart. He had spent weeks trying to forget the moment, the wonderful moment when he had seen what he believed to be his son. And the same painful memory was linked to the sight of Lytton's murderous rage—the man had started to kill Alex *before* he'd realized the trick. He had wanted Alex out of the wood with such a passion that it had never been his intention to rescue the boy.

But when he said this to Elizabeth she simply shrugged. "Helen told it differently. He was killing the Jack, not Alex."

Helen had made her own slow way back to the Station, and McCarthy and Lytton had turned up later. Although they had been tricked by the Jack, they *had* been close to where Alex was hiding, and it was when McCarthy had been submerged in the shadow world of the wood, unconscious and half-eaten by the wood, drifting in the flow of stored memory, quite bosky, that he had seen the inner shadow of Alex, the primal shadow that Lytton called the "protogenomorph"—"The first form of the dreaming mind of the boy, or something. A reference to first consciousness. McCarthy saw it playing near a Mask Tree, which Lytton thinks is a focus for it. He thinks it leaves Alex to explore, and returns to him. It's quite literally the boy's "free spirit," so if you can find it, and follow it, you'll find Alex.

"Help me up, please."

Richard lent an arm and Elizabeth eased herself out of the bath. As he wrapped his towelling robe around her battered body, she said, "Eight years! Christ! She *said* she felt something was wrong. She must have gone through one hell of a hollowing—but then how the hell ... how did she transit back? It doesn't make sense."

"Everything about that evening was strange, that much I remember. Strange all round. An odd note from a cropped-haired woman. An odd play at school. And it was the night James Keeton came back from the dead."

"I've had enough," Elizabeth Haylock said, her voice almost forlorn. "I need to sleep. I need to repair. Then I need to go. There's nothing left in the wood for me, now. Everything I once loved I saw killed ..." She glanced at Richard. "It's not the same for you, though. Maybe you should go back."

"I've made up a bed for you."

Richard supported her as she walked painfully to the sitting room and sat heavily on the couch. He was burning with curiosity. "Where's Helen now? What happened at the Station?"

"I don't know where Helen is. She vanished. Wakeman's dead, McCarthy too. Lytton was taken, probably dead. Nobody has seen Lacan since he left through the cave, the time you were with us. Heikonen drowned, we think, trying to retrieve a Finnish talisman from the lake, and Sinisalo went crazy and went deep. It all fell apart. Something came through out of Old Stone Hollow. It affected everyone, and it all just fell apart. I think I'm the only one who got out."

She slept. Richard sat in an armchair and listened to her breathing, the words she murmured in her sleep, and her cries of pain, coming not from her broken body but from her broken memories.

At midnight he abandoned the vigil and went to bed. He lay awake for ages, staring at the moon, thinking of Helen and his son and the broad, good-humored Frenchman.

Three years!

Lacan had expected to be gone on his own journey for six months, so he was far too long overdue. The thought of his loss brought tears to Richard's eyes. Should he have stayed with them? Should he have waited for Alex to come back? If he had stayed, would Alex have returned? Perhaps he should have *believed* in his son more. And yet, in a way he *had*. How could he have known about the trickster figure of the Jack, drawing his own needs from his mind, making them real . . . ? He should have *believed* in his son. The voice had been there, warning him. Not everything had been deception.

He drifted into sleep. His last thought was that he would invite Elizabeth Haylock to stay for a few days, after taking her to the hospital. He would piece things together with her.

He woke, in the dark, to the sound of horses and murmuring voices. Light flickered in the garden and he went to the window, looking down at the torch, held by a cloaked rider on a gray mount. The man saw him and called out a warning. There was a sudden flurry of movement in the house below and Richard ran downstairs to where Elizabeth Haylock had been sleeping. The couch was empty. At the back door he watched helplessly as the band of riders cantered back toward Hunter's Brook, the flame from the torch streaming behind the leader, Elizabeth held in the arms of one of the riders, slumped or curled against him, asleep perhaps, or unconscious— perhaps content?—he would never know.

She had been removed from him, and from her own world, and this time she would not return.

He ran frantically along the bridleway, shouting at the raiders, not thinking of the possible consequences of his action, but by the time he reached the edge of the wood the torch had long since vanished into darkness. He eavesdropped the silence. He brushed through the undergrowth, a night shadow between two worlds, listening for horses, or voices, hearing only the breeze.

At first light he went back to his house and cried, partly for the woman, whose terrible journey to freedom had so suddenly been frustrated, partly for himself, for the loss of a contact with both Alex and Helen that he realized, now, he had needed desperately.

From Richard's notebook:

—many signs of activity in the ruins of Oak Lodge. A large pit, filled with charred wood and bones—axe and knife marks on trees, dried excrement (both human and animal) and discarded raggy clothing, all suggest that the place has been in regular use recently.
No sign of Lacan's machinery, although there are traces of the wires he used to create the boundaries. Usual feeling of being watched, but feels like a girl . . . No sign of her.

—round and round in circles again, but suddenly came to the Horse Shrine. The monolithic stone was overgrown with ground ivy, which I cleared to expose the carved image of the horse. Found a feathered arrow, point missing, and two rusting cans, the remains of Lacan's encampment. From here I can at least begin to follow the right path to Old Stone Hollow.

—back to the shrine again, but this time climbed a tree and saw a high cliff in the distance, and am hopeful that this is the Station. Have made a friend of a Roman legionary carrying a treasure and shared his food. He's a splendidly tanned man, black hair cut short, face weathered and full of good humor. His helmet is lost, but he carries a bronze-bladed spear carved with running animals, and a well-used and battered short sword, plus an equipment pack complete with tin and copper kitchen gear. His "treasure" is the Eagle standard of the Twentieth Legion. He himself is Catalonian, of a local royal birth, banished by his father. He joined the Legion in a town called Burdigala, which I think is Bordeaux, and was separated from his troop after a terrible skirmish. He carries the standard as a rallying point for the scattered men of his army.

—he shared crusty bread, made very palatable by dripping olive oil onto it, strips of very tasty dried meat and spiced sausage, and used leaves from his pack and water from the brook to make a sharp drink that tasted remarkably like spiced wine. All the time we ate he talked and *gestured, made maps in the air, quizzed me and laughed. I learned this little about him, but not his name. His name he will not reveal.*

—*the Roman accompanied me along the river and probably just as well. Bone-armored man, heavily painted, wild grasses attached to arms, shoulders and legs like bunches of quills, dropped on us from the heavy bough of an old willow. Murder clearly in mind, and the Catalonian dispatched him with great ferocity and determination, a massive strike from his spear, and then a series of punitive stabs, demolishing the stone axe of the opponent and splitting his bone corselet as easily as a butcher cuts through the breast cartilage of a chicken. One grass-bedecked head left hanging from the branch, turning in the wind. The Catalonian made a charm of one of the bits of our assailant's protective bone, I thought for himself, but he presented it to me, an animal's tarsal, now scratched with the sign of Mars.*

—*the cliff again, seen from a high bank through tall beeches, closer now. To my surprise, the Catalonian knows the place and is frightened of it. He calls it Spirit Rock, or Ghost Rock, and describes it as the scene of a terrible massacre, perhaps referring to the remains of mythagos at its perimeter. When I tried to question him more closely he became agitated, quite irritable, then whispered (using small signs too) that he believed in the Gods, but had never thought of magicians as anything but market-place charlatans. But many magicians had lived below the rock, and had been destroyed by their own evil charms. The ghosts of that magic remained, like a honey trap for a bear. He advised me against going there, but smiled and seemed philosophical when I shook my head. "You are part magician yourself," he said, and prodded me in the chest. "Make a charm for me!"*

—*the Catalonian pointed me along a trail to Spirit Rock and I have finally broken the circular defenses of this watching, thinking wood. I wrote my telephone number on a page from this notebook, folded it and inserted the paper roll into a section of rush. The legionary seemed pleased. It will be as useful to him as will his image of Mars be to me.*

—going deeper. Claustrophobia is my constant companion, and faces in the undergrowth, so many of which seem familiar. I call for Alex and Helen, and am answered by shrieks, the beating of wings, or silence. Mosquitos and other insects are a permanent and excruciating nuisance. The Roman was good company. I wish he hadn't gone. Where is Lacan? I hope he's not too deep. Where the bugs have bitten me, the skin is raw. I try all leaves, and mosses, to soothe.

—three years and I have dreamed for days only ...
Where is Helen? I feel confused. The buzzing and the biting in this moist heat is infuriating. I am watched from inside my dreams.
Hungry—I have been six days. Very tired and faces everywhere. Someone is calling me from inside my eyes. My arms and hands are weak.

—to write down. The cold.
Lacan has the hare, skin round his ears, and fire, and elegant forepaws. Fire is dancing. The bats. Is elemental of course, and quite corrupt, like bone marrow, and Alexander as the knight.
Cold is coming. Slopes up and down. Is this it? The dying place, the dust, the cold, and the lake and down, swimming. To the castle where the pike rules the lake.

A fire was burning, up at Hunter's Brook. They were dancing round the flames ...

With a cry, his body twisting to relieve the cramp in his thigh, Richard woke from a fever dream, drenched with sweat and frozen. He was in a crude shelter, naked from the waist down.

He knew at once that he had been here for three days, increasingly delirious. The notebook was open and damp, and he read his last ramblings with painful embarrassment. He had a clear memory of writing, and of feeling such *sense* in the entries. The fever, perhaps from the insect bites with which he was covered, had turned him quite crazy, however.

He was starving, and desperate for water.

Through the trees he could see tall stones and recognized them at once, as perhaps he had recognized them days ago, but through the obfuscating barrier of delirium. He was in the Sanctuary. Ahead, the river flowed; and on the far bank of that river, Old Stone Hollow waited for him.

He collected his equipment together and stood, still shaking from the days of fever, still weak. His mouth tasted foul, his face itched with stubble. He walked cautiously into the Sanctuary, looking for hollowsticks but finding none, concentrating on remembering where the dangerous areas had been, the one-way hollowing.

The graveyard was a soft, mossy swathe of woodland corruption, all features gone save for the occasional jaw, or socketed face, that might easily have been the decaying bark of a fallen tree. To walk across the dead was no different to walking in the deep, soft mast of a beech forest.

He slipped down the incline to the river and tears surfaced. He waded through the deep water, hauling himself up to the broken palisade, desperate to hear the sound of voices. And with a sense not so much of foreboding, but of deep loss, he walked into what was left of Old Stone Hollow, moving first to the crumbled ruins of the longhouse, then to the shreds of the canteen tent, where glass shards among the claw-torn canvas told of the last of Lacan's wine. Eventually, he sat down in the mouth of the painted cave itself, below the streaming, running shapes of animals, and gave vent to his grief and frustration, letting all the tears flow, all the anguish frighten the birds with his shouts and sobs of fury.

Later that day, more composed, he wrote in his notebook:

Damage Report: the outer wooden palisade has been smashed down, the poles left scattered and re-erectable. The wooden guardians have been burned. Traces of wires, and infra-red and laser generating equipment remain. The

*generator looks serviceable, but I have no idea how to
service it, or the amplifiers that control the defenses themselves. Plenty of oil.*

*The longhouse has been demolished from the inside with
apparent ferocity and very little subtlety. The roof torn
down and scattered, the walls pushed through in places
with a large battering ram, perhaps a log. Fragments of
maps, chairs and tables litter the place. This house is
renovatable, at least in part. I can make a new roof from
the old turves. The canvas tents have been shredded all
save that over the generator, which can be patched up and
made good. There are several tins of food, stacks of firewood and a good amount of kerosene; also, metal objects
such as a shield, rusting swords and decorations. The
compound is high with grass and thistle, which I shall
leave, making a crazy path through it for extra defense. I
shall search it for other items left after the attack and perhaps also will find a clue as to what happened here. The
good news is that the kitchen garden has flourished, with
tomato and marrow plants, apple trees and scattered
bushes of raspberries and black currants. There is a small
olive tree, a rosemary bush, wild garlic and onions and
potatoes everywhere.*

*The lake: I can see the hollowing. Lytton's Viking boat
hull is out in the water, close to the danger area, apparently untethered but motionless. The sail is furled, but appears to be intact.*

<u>*Proposal:*</u>

1. *I shall use pieces of the palisade to make a defensive wall along the river gully through the
   rocks that leads to the lake, and across the path
   that winds up to the top of the overhang.*
2. *Rebuild one end of the longhouse. Fetch boat to
   safety.*
3. *Learn about generators by trial and error.*
4. *Collect and reconstruct all that remains of the
   electronic defenses around the hollow.*
5. *Build a new Guardian by the river, as grotesque
   if not more so than the previous incumbents.*

6. *Make hollowsticks in case of the need to travel.*
7. *Construct fishing equipment and hope for a good catch.*
8. *Wait for something to happen, someone to contact me, and try to contact Alex or Helen by power of dreams, belief and shouting loudly!*

Salvage: *Heinz Baked Beans x 2*
              Marinated Herring x 2 glass bottles
              Old Oak Ham x 3 (one with spear-point damage)
              Gentleman's relish x 1
              Meacham's Potted Beef x 1 (looks disgusting)
              Cans without labels x 7
              Cote de Roussillon Rouge, 1962, x 2 (cheers, Arnauld!)
              Olive oil 2 pt x 2
              Colgate toothpaste x 2
              Plastic hairbrush x 1
              Silver cigarette lighter (working) x 1 (Lytton's?)
              Leather shoe, left foot, size 7 plus bones x 1
              Mirror glass fragment 6" x 5"
              Effigy in willow of dancing man x 1

When he had finished this "log" he walked again to the lakeside and spent a long while letting his thoughts drift across the bright blue water. Herons stalked the reed banks nearby and he watched them until suddenly they spread wide, black-fringed wings and ascended with much noise, out across the lake and back to their high nests.

At dusk he entered the overhang of the hollow itself and touched the cold stone walls, the fading colors of the running creatures. And it was then that he found the hollowstick. It had been placed at the deeper entrance to the cave, to mark its creator's passage inward. Its legs had been snapped, its body slightly chewed, perhaps by a fox or wild cat, but the black and silver lock of hair was still tied to the roughly painted face at the tip of the curve of willow that formed the body.

Old Man, Old Lake

He had almost finished rebuilding the last part of the long house roof when the central pole buckled and snapped and the whole wood slat and turf structure collapsed below his weight. With a cry more of frustration than pain, Richard tumbled into the grassy, earthy chaos, spat out dirt, sat up and bellowed for the boy.

"Taaj!"

Above him, the sky was graying into winter. His ankle throbbed and he scrabbled for his stick, using it to haul himself up before hobbling out into the clearing. The sprain was almost healed, but each time he jarred the foot he spent a day suffering. It seemed to Richard that in the six months he had been back at the Hollow, not a day had passed without *something* biting him, fighting him or tripping him.

Where *was* that boy? Hadn't he heard the cry?

He rang the bells ferociously. The empty tin cans clattered together dully, and the stones inside them rattled. A system of rope pulleys connected with one set of cans at the cliff top, another at the lakeside. He tugged on the lake-bell several times, hoping that Taaj would hear, but he heard no answering shout.

It had been such a long morning. He had prepared the turfs with pegs for the holes he had so painstakingly gouged in the willow slats. He braced the walls and checked the attitude of each of the supporting poles. The roof should have gone on, over what had once been the Station's community room at one end of the longhouse, as easily as the piece of a known jigsaw. But the central pole had been weak—he could see the black stain of the fungal growth—and several hundredweight of turf and Richard himself had proved too much.

Again he rang the clattering bell and bellowed the boy's name. Then he remembered that Taaj had gone out on the lake, fishing. The boy had seen the movement of large fish during the morning and had returned to the Station excited and hungry. Something had been driving them into the lake—perhaps through the hollowing?— and they had thrashed on the surface, white bellies plump, fins flashing in the gray light. Their backs had been dark purple, like sloe berries. There had been blood-red streaks along the gills. The fish were half the length of an adult man, and one catch would last a fortnight, when smoked or salted.

"Catch the biggest," he said as the boy ran to him, shouting excitedly. "In the meantime . . ."

"You must help me, Rishar! Come and help me."

Taaj was jumping up and down, his brown eyes glowing with pleasure. He was holding the crude ladder on which Richard was precariously balanced, and his leaping action made the whole structure wobble alarmingly.

Richard looked down. "Easy. Easy! Why do you need *me* to come fishing?"

"I can catch the biggest, Rishar—but I don't want to catch the spirit that drives them! Can't you come onto the lake with me?"

"What spirit are you talking about?" Richard asked, and Taaj calmed down, looking apprehensively at the gully to the lake.

"Hold the ladder as I come down," Richard said.

He sparred with the boy for a moment, touching the long hair, making flicking movements at Taaj's feather earrings. The boy ducked and weaved, laughing, then followed his friend into the longhouse. They kept the rods and hooks here, and Richard picked out the best. "There. You'll catch a whale with this lot."

He noticed the second look of apprehension on Taaj's face as the boy whispered, "I don't want to be eaten by the spirit.

I'm afraid, Rishar. I think I have less than the day's fight in me."

"Nonsense," Richard said, again tousling the lad's hair. "What spirit can get the better of *you*?"

All he could think of was the longhouse. He needed the roof. In the six months he had been here he had made Old Stone Hollow into a magic place again, with a protective wooden wall, reconstructed from the old palisade, totems, talismans, a working generator, a latrine, a fire-pit and a longhouse to be proud of. He had rebuilt this lodge in stages, and today he would complete the turfing of the last room, a place for the hanging of furs, fish and game. He had no time to go fishing. Besides, the boy had been on the lake a hundred times before: he was a superb fisherman.

"Listen. *You* catch the fish—*I'll* gut the catch. I know how much you hate doing that job."

Taaj went outside, slightly forlorn, Richard thought. He walked over to the river and undressed, and Richard followed, watching as the boy knelt down in the water.

He went back to the roof, for a while, but an hour later sought his mythago friend at the river, by the new gates.

Taaj was kneeling in the water, a girdle of flowers floating round his waist, a small piece of dark wood held in each hand, turned by his fingers as he sang a quiet, repetitive song. Richard crouched on his stick by the stream and watched the hunting ritual. It was so hard to date the lad to an historical time, but Richard believed he must have been from a mesolithic society, lake-dwelling hunter gatherers.

He was brooding on this point when Taaj "drowned" the flowers, then strained to relieve himself in the water. He came ashore and dressed quietly, fixing his lines, hooks and baits. He smiled at Richard, then ran silently through the gully to the lake.

That had been this time yesterday!

It almost took Richard's breath away as he realized how long Taaj had been gone. All of yesterday afternoon, while Richard had prepared the turfs, then drunk potato mash to go with his dried meats, aware that the boy was away, but not concerned, because Taaj was always vanishing for a day or two at a time. Drunk, and full, and weary with work, he had slept a long night, and in the damp morning had set to the task of putting on the final roof. Only when he had suffered the mishap had he started to *need* Taaj. Only now did he become conscious that Taaj's words had seemed strange, that the boy had been in a strange mood, that for the first time in their short relationship the boy had *asked* for something and Richard had refused him.

With a terrible feeling of foreboding he hobbled to the river, shouting for his young companion. His ankle niggled him, but the stick was a nuisance and he used it almost like an oar as he waded into the water, ducked below the branches and squeezed through the gully between the "clashing rocks," as he had named them.

Did you catch a fine fish? Are you sitting there, gutting it? To surprise me, to make me ruffle your head with pleasure? Oh God, don't let it happen again—

He staggered out through the broken wood and boulders onto the reed-fringed shore, scrambling down to the water's edge as he bit back his cry of distress. Then he stood for a while, shocked and sick, staring out toward the hollowing and the huge lake creature, the frozen moment, and the dying boy.

Slowly he edged to a water-slick boulder and leaned against it, squinting against the light on the lake, the glitter of the calm lake that must have recently been in a state of turbulent disorder as the battle had raged. He could imagine how the hunters must have thrashed, out there on the water, their struggle throwing waves across the rocks so that everything was wet, everything slick, with weed and broken rushes decorating the crusted oaks and the fallen willows, the gritty sandstone teeth of the shore.

"Taaj ..." he called, but his voice was a mere whisper. Perhaps, even as he planned to help his friend, he knew that his betrayal would cost the life of the boy.

Again, "Taaj! Hold on! I'm going to help. Hold on— we'll eat a fat slice of your friend for supper."

If the boy heard, he gave no sign, not even a turn of his dark-haired head or a movement of his muscles, standing out so hard, so proud against his slim frame as he held the serpent through the jaw. It was like a blue-painted canvas, a scene from an ancient battle between a young David and the Goliath of the sea, a creature half fish, half reptile, its jaws stretched in a toothy rictus, its eyes slowly blinking, the frills and spines around its neck and gills waving, beating, slowly, like the oars of a galley. Reds and greens, and stripes of livid purple, pulsed on the coils of neck that tensed below the head, and in the small boat, Taaj knelt on one knee, the great harpoon upright, the stone point fixed in the throat of the serpent.

The tail of the beast was curled twice round the skiff, and once around the boy. Only the sting at the end of the tail moved, and it flexed in fury, suppressed and restless fury, and Richard, at the shore, intuited that somehow this battle had become a test of strength. Stalemate! The boy's weapon was close to something vulnerable in the creature. But the beast would not release its grip.

I'm afraid, Rishar. I think I have less than the day's fight in me—

Richard groaned, beat the rock with his bare hands, tugged at the cords of his plaited beard and hair, rent at the faded garments on his tanned chest.

It was as if Taaj had known of his fate. He had sensed it! That the fish would be driven from another world by a creature that was from the realm of monsters. He had *known* his destiny lay in a bitter fight to the death, perhaps one of many, and he had sensed that he was unequal to the task. He had asked his friend, the old man of Spirit Rock, Rishar, the screaming, dreaming, frantic, frightened *Rishar,* to come with him, just in case of danger.

Out on the water the monster foamed bloodily, the lake shifted, the skiff bobbed and Taaj pushed harder against the jaw, felt the muscular tail of the beast tighten, squeeze more life from him. The hollowing was a haze of white and gray—shapes moved there, out of vision, a disturbance against the dark treeline of the opposite shore.

I have less than the day's fight in me—

A day, then—*the* day—a full day to defeat the serpent, according to the story that had "birthed" Taaj from the forgotten womb of a human mind, and already the brave boy had used up most of it. There were minutes left. Richard had only one hope of helping, and that meant using Lytton's boat, the old longship, and the harpoons he had kept there, and which were still strong in shaft and point. The vessel, with its death's-head prow, was moored close by, the sail furled. There was a good breeze. The boat could circle widely and come upon the serpent from the farther side.

Stripped to his trousers, all thoughts of pain long gone, Richard boarded the sleek longship and tugged the rigging that held the white sail, catching its ends as it fell and holding them at arms' stretch, body braced behind a rail of oak, leaning back to take the strain as the breeze filled the canvas, billowed the sail, nudged the dark hull across the water. A wave rippled out, covered the sparkling gray, tossed the skiff, and the serpent foamed bloodily again, thrashed its body as much as it could, but then stiffened. The wood of the skiff creaked as the muscles tightened, as the coil slid round Taaj's braced body, scales grating at his skin, but he held his own harpoon firmly, pushed against the creature, and brought mortality closer by the sliding of an inch of stone through bone, and an inch of flesh, to a heart in the skull, to the brain itself.

I can't lose this boy. Not this boy too. His fishing is too good. I should have learned his story. I should have been ready to listen, and then I would have been ready for this.

The longship glided through the icy waters, Richard braced, leaning back, muscles taut as he held the edges of the full sail, tugging to guide the low hull, watching the shoreline as it slid across the high prow, slipping across his vision with just the *lap* and *slap* of the lake and the rumbling protest of the nearing beast to remind him of movement and goal.

"Hold on, my lad—these Vikings built for speed, not subtlety."

I can't lose him. I don't even know his culture. He's such a good fisher. He hunts so well. He sings raucously, and it reminds me of Lacan. I know he is comfortable with stone. He seems unfamiliar with metals, can launch a spear from a hollow pebble held in his palm, is frightened of the moon when it's full, talks of his sister with affection, seems to un-

derstand me. I can talk to him, although his words are meaningless. He can talk to me, though all I do is shout.

The carcass of a fish floated past, rolling in the lake, blind eyes seeing Richard, harpoon scar bleeding still. Streaks of bright purple ran along its side as far as the wide tail-fins—the dorsal fins were flecked with black. It was plump and no doubt the boy could claim the killing, but this creature of the sea had been driven here by a serpent from hell, and it would be some time yet before the catch hung out to dry . . .

He had rounded the hollowing, caught the strong breeze, shifted his stance and now built up speed again, coming in on a hard tack, prow cutting the water—

clop—swish, clop—swish, clop—

The voice of the lake urged him on, waters parting, breaking and the mast creaking with the strain, the canvas flapping when he let the tension drop, but strong again when the wind took it, tugging him forward, off balance, until he braced and the boat surged beneath his feet, listing on the water, then righting, and closing on the fisherman and his weakening attacker—

Another boy called to him, a voice from another time. "I'm going fishing, Daddy. Will you come? Will you come with me?"

He had had so many other things to do in his lifelong pursuit of doing nothing. "Have a good catch. A trout for each of us, please. I'll help gut the fish. Your mother would run screaming—"

"I'm fishing for perch. We can't really eat them. It's just to see them, really. It's fun . . ."

There was a cricket match to watch. He had waved the boys goodbye, Alex, Simon, a third lad with ginger hair. Their catch had been spectacular. Alex had hooked a pike. The greatest struggle had not been the bringing-in of the catch—who would ever want to eat pike?—but the release of the two-foot-long fish, which had given the boys a look with its piscine eyes that had haunted Alex for months.

"It was angry! It looked like you do, when you have nothing to say, because it's all been said before, and we ought to know better. Very cold."

"I do *not* give you a cold look. Do I?"

"Sometimes . . ."

"Like a pike's? Really?"

"Not so . . . fishy . . . not quite, anyway."

He had grabbed the boy, laughing, and they roughed and tumbled, but still he had only *heard* about the expedition and adventure, and that the pike was *this* long, and one of Simon's perches had had two heads—*honest!*

The water was thrashed, the longship rocked. Richard dropped one end of the sail which billowed and flapped uselessly, but momentum carried the vessel toward the struggling serpent, and Taaj allowed himself a quick, grim glance at the old man, bearing down on him.

"Don't come close!"

"I'll help. Hold on!"

"Let me go down. This was in the dream. Don't come close!"

In the dream? Had Taaj told him about the dream? If so, he'd forgotten . . .

Richard could smell the serpent now, a rank stench of weed. The huge body rippled below the scales, air puffed from its feathery gills. It was like a salamander, but its head alone was the size of a bullock. Eyes that were prominent swiveled and glared at the coming man, and the skiff rocked, the coil around the boy slid more loosely, and Taaj grunted loudly as he thrust the stone harpoon more deeply into flesh.

The longship slid by the rising neck and Richard flung the harpoon, finding the creature's watery eye, flinching as liquid spurted as the point struck. The cameo dissolved, the beast flexed, the tail shattered the skiff and Taaj was flung into the lake, still holding the spear which had been wrenched loose. The longship rocked to its side and Richard clung to the rail, wondering what he had done. The water around him foamed white and red, the air resounding to the serpent's screeching cry of pain and anger.

Its coils slid through the water, breaking the surface, then descending. Richard held the rail, stared out over the suddenly placid lake, shouting for the boy.

Taaj's face watched him from the crystal pool. He still held the spear. His arms were stretched out, his eyes wide as he slowly sank toward the deeper structure of the castle below.

"Oh no you don't. You don't escape me this easily!"

That he felt sick with fear did not register on Richard, as he stripped naked and leapt from the longship, aware of its dark shape moving past him, away toward the shore. The lake was icy. He dived down, wriggling like a fish, turning to try to find the boy and saw him as he descended, like a statue, arms out, hair streaming, face a mask of fear. Richard swam toward him and the dark eyes watched him with what might have been urgency—

Help me . . .

I'm coming. For Christ's sake why don't you swim? Alex! Reach up for me. Swim! It's too far . . . my strength . . .

The air burst from him.

Why doesn't he swim?

His ears jarred. He panicked suddenly and swiveled in the water, ascending to the reviving day.

Then down again, and swimming hard, directly down to the frozen face, the white face, the guileless features of the descending boy. He came close again, fighting the water like a thrashing catch on the line, urging himself deeper, refusing to let the lake float him up again, fighting down, reaching down, fingers in the drifting hair, trying to get a grip, to pull the boy up. Taaj smiled, his eyes wide with hope, although his arms were stiff and his right fist clenched the stone-tipped harpoon.

Fight, damn you. Alex! Swim! Don't give up now. Let the spear go. It's no use. Swim for your life. Why do you look at me like that? I'm doing my best. Help yourself too! I can only do so much.

He grasped the boy's hair. *Got you.* He reversed his swim, tugged at the youth, felt the small, tough body rise with him.

A shadow passed across the face of innocence. The immense length of the serpent flowed around Richard and descended distantly, toward the ruins. Richard's lungs began to burst. Air bubbled from him and he turned in fear and the fight for life, let go of the boy's hair and stretched for water and the light until he broke the surface and gasped for breath.

He went down for the third time to fetch his friend.

Now the boy was in the gloom above the ruins of the castle, far deeper than Richard had been able to go that time when he had swum with Helen. He glanced around, looked for the serpent, but saw only the movement of weed and eels, the occasional flash of deep light on the silver scales of fish. The boy's air was still inside him. There was still a chance. He swam vigorously, dropping vertically, pushing back the water and meeting Taaj's dying gaze. The boy's eyes watched him with great sadness. That look was so familiar! The faces were the same. He had always known it, always seen it, from the first moment the boy had appeared by the gate. There seemed to be such hopelessness there, now, and the sort of sad smile that might have been goodbye.

Lungs straining, Richard strove, kicked, flung himself through the chill and was triumphant when he felt the brush of hair on his fingers, and he spread his hand and grasped, tugged hard, tugged up, found a better grip and held the boy.

Taaj smiled and let the harpoon go. (Alex reached for him—)
We're going home. I've got you now.

Richard turned in the water and kicked, tugging at the boy's hair, feeling the body come with him.

Then the water swirled and twisted him. He looked down, saw the huge eye, the open mouth, felt the tug, the hair in his hand snatched, then torn away. Taaj's face had contorted into a mask of shock and pain. The serpent had come up from the dark of the castle and taken him round the waist. It dropped down again, fish-eye cold and expressionless. The half-boy reached from its jaws until it jerked and gulped and Taaj was gone, and only the closed maw, with its terrible grin, could be seen among the battlements, soon lost in the weeds, though light sparkled on a watching, silver orb.

The boy's air had left him. Richard swam with it, embraced it, twisted in the bubbles, scrabbling at them, consuming them, tasting the sour breath, the last of his friend. Man and boy reached the surface together, and the cry that sounded over the water was as much the pain of the drowned, released at last, as the despair of the living, who then struck for the shore and the empty camp at Old Stone Hollow.

To the Forgotten Shore

(i) Ship of Sorrows

All night Richard sat by the lake, hunched inside his clothes, staring out at the moonlit water and the haze of Wide Water Hollowing, thinking of the dead boy, and of Alex, indeed, of everything that was lost, like a life, like a story. He kept remembering Lacan's words of so many weeks ago: *harden your heart. These creatures are dying, but remember—they are alive elsewhere in the wood.*

So somewhere else Taaj was still alive, perhaps the companion to an old man who this time might not reject the boy's plea for help on the fishing trip, and the serpent would be subdued and brought home in triumph. But that other Taaj did not belong to him. It would not have the same face, Alex's face. It would not watch him with sadness, would not need him in the same way, in Alex's way. He had watched a mythago drown, and he had been watching an aspect of his own son, consumed by a creature from the icy hell of a legendary deep, bitten in half, two gulps, a brief life savagely ended. He was not unaware of the irony of the situation. During the long night he thought hard about Alex, perhaps still alive in the wood and waiting. Had Alex sent Taaj as a test for his father? Or had Taaj formed from the Old Man's guilt, a conscience in need of a kick-start, creating an echo of that time of agony when Alex had been taken from him and he had done so little to resist?

He had not felt this alone for years. When Alice left him there had been a few months when he thought he was going mad with loneliness, missing his son, missing her, despite their relationship having been quite distant. The anxiety had passed, of course; he had adapted to his solitary life and moved to London. Now, however, he felt that same claustrophobia—he was in a vast world, but without voices. He might as well have been in a dungeon, hidden from sight and sound. Night birds chorused, water lapped restlessly, and somewhere, just out of earshot, Arnauld Lacan still roared, bearlike, Helen Silverlock sang her charms to Trickster, and Alexander Lytton murmured his exhortations to the only hidden entity of the wood that mattered: George Huxley.

The memories of his lost friends were strong in Richard.

Something moved on the lake and his attention was snatched from dreams to the reality of Old Stone Hollow Station. He narrowed his eyes, concentrated on the hollowing, and saw again the gray shape moving in the haze. For a minute or more it was quite still and he thought of a sail, then it faded, although the lake became turbulent, the waves reaching the outcrop of stone where Richard huddled.

There was a presence beyond the hollowing, he felt sure, and it was approaching the lake.

At dawn, a drumbeat pulsed from the hollowing, a steady strike, two beats a second, a determined rhythm that might have come from a war-galley. As if carried on a shifting wind, the drumbeat faded for a while, then came back, and at times there was a deeper, slower rhythm superimposed, a second ship perhaps. The shape in the hollowing darkened to become an indented square, quite definitely a sail, and the lake reacted to whatever was on the other side, and the waves coming like billows, drenching the shore.

He went back to the longhouse for a while, but returned at the height of the day to find the lake literally *echoing* to the double thunder of wardrums. Shapes passed across the hollowing in a tantalizing display of shadow movement, suggesting a sea battle. Indeed, at some time in the afternoon the smell of fire came from the lake, partly the fragrance of burning cedar, partly the acrid and choking stink of pitch. As if through a sound-shutter, opening and closing, the drum-beats surged and faded, and with them came frequent sounds of screeching, like tortured gulls.

For a while, then, there was silence, but at dusk and into the early evening the dark sail ar____ ____d again. Richard stood at the lake edge, chewing dried_____ ____waiting for the drums to start.

There was a sudden screech, like metal rending . . . and the screams of men dying—

A *thunder* of drums, and a white wave surged from the hollowing, spreading widely across the evening lake, bringing with it the sharp scent of the ocean—

Astonished, Richard stepped quickly back as the water broke over his feet. The black sail deepened in the frame, became sharper as the frantic rhythm of the drum grew louder. It was coming toward him, rising, filling the hollowing, but motionless for the moment, oddly frozen.

When the galley broke through the gate it so surprised Richard that he fell backward. The ship came onto the lake at terrific speed, oars flashing in the dusk light as they rose and fell into the water, drum loud, sail straining in the last of an ocean wind, then dropping fast. High-prowed, deep-hulled, of classic early Greek design, the galley shot across the water, directly toward the frozen figure of the man on the shore. Richard heard voices scream, the sail was slackened, the oars dipped to skim the lake and slow the headlong approach, but too late, the great vessel struck the shore and with a smashing of wood and beams rode up over the rocks, into the trees, lifted from the ground, oars snapping, the mast breaking in a billow of canvas and rigging. The whole vessel came to a sudden halt, then subsided to the right. Half-armored, grim-faced men jumped from the deck, yelling; out on the lake, one mariner was swimming awkwardly to the shore; below the deck, animals screeched. The wooden hull began to sing and whine, cracking and snapping as it settled and slipped until it was suddenly and eerily silent.

A shape scampered along the soaking shore and came up to the gully. Richard found himself staring at a creature from his wildest dreams: a man's scarred body on a black beast's rump, a striking animal form that urinated copiously with fear before looking round in panic, then leaping over the rocks and into the trees. Richard scrambled into cover just as a brawny man, dressed in gleaming breastplate, greaves and leather tunic, face half-hidden behind a white, slant-eyed mask, thundered past him, carrying a slim and deadly spear. The man screamed out in anger, patrolled the rocks where the beast had vanished, then turned back to the beach in fury, flinging the javelin, which struck and stuck in the ship's hull, quivering for long seconds.

Other men were spilling from the wreck, light gleaming on the scraps of Greek armor and colored and grotesque face-masks they wore. They shed this metal to appear either naked or wearing filthy loincloths; all were old, Richard saw now. They were muscular, but heavily lined and paunchy, the flesh hanging on them; thick, dark hair spread over their chests and shoulders. A horse whinnied and was suddenly quiet. Then a woman cried out, a high sobbing sound that responded to a gruff order. A man sang sweetly for a moment, a brief lament, and somewhere below the deck there was a flurry of disturbance and distress that was soon quelled with barked orders and the sound of a lash.

A hand grabbed Richard's shoulder and he cried out, startled, rising from his crouch and turning, fists flying. The man-beast stood there, terrified. It was a centaur, of course, but like no such creature that Richard had ever seen depicted. The elements of man and horse flowed through the whole body. Richard felt he understood the being's fear— these new arrivals looked dangerous, and Richard was wary and frightened of them himself. He led the way from the lake into the narrow gully that led to the Station. The centaur followed, crying in a weird fashion. Spittle ran from its black lips and through the wiry hair of its beard. It shivered on the river bank by the Station gates, looking anxiously at the darkening trees, the defenses and particularly at the tall, grotesque effigy that guarded the entrance through the palisade.

"You'll be safe," Richard said, although he was aware that mythagos did not survive the electronic defenses. "At least, you'll be safe from me—"

The centaur suddenly cantered through the palisade and into the tall grass, following the path to the longhouse, stooping to peer inside. It dropped dung at the entrance and as if embarrassed stepped back and reached down to gather up the three hard pellets, tossing them into the wood and brushing its hands together. It prowled about the house, then curled up in its entrance. It feigned sleep, though as Richard stared down its eyes opened slightly, like a child's when sleep is necessary but curiosity remains.

Who were these new arrivals? He could hear shouting and banging, a drumbeat, and a moment later the area was pierced by the shrill tones of a horn, high-pitched, rising in note, repeated ten times while the drum was sounded. The centaur shivered, curled up on its side, its almost-human arms wrapped around its bearded head.

Richard crept back to the lake, night gathering around him. Torches burned everywhere and there was much activity. He could hear furtive movement around him and kept low in the gully, alert for any sudden attack. All he could make out in the gloom was that a skin tent had been erected, tied to the gunnels of the stranded vessel at one end and to the exposed roots of a willow at the other. A cauldron of water was heating and women's voices came from that area of activity. Two men were swimming out across the black lake, calling to each other, others were hauling lengths of rigging into the tree branches. The great sail had been dismantled and folded. Three figures, heavily built, long-haired, were lifting down a huge wooden image from the stranded ship. Richard could see a woman's face and breasts, an expression of fury carved and luridly painted. This image was erected at the water's edge, facing toward the woodland, and two tall braziers, flaming brightly, placed on each side of it.

Further along the shore, flames that glowed brighter than a cooking fire suggested a primitive forge had been established. A large man fussed over this flame-pit in the high rocks and it was he who saw Richard, as if by far sight, and moved stealthily toward him. As the giant loomed up, Richard saw that he had only one eye. The beard that fringed his broad face was gray-streaked auburn. His arms were huge, each tattooed with a winding snake. Through the white hairs of his chest a brand had marked him, a wheel around a cross, with wings on each side. He stank of sweat and honey, and breathed hard as he stepped closer and closer to the crouching man, dragging one lame leg behind him.

He was just close enough when Richard said, sharply, "Come any further and I'll kick your other leg away. Do you understand?"

The giant hesitated at the sound of the voice. From the beach he was called and shouted back. The words were guttural, strangely unfamiliar since they were no doubt a form of early Greek. Again he dragged his bad leg toward Richard, who fumbled in his clothes for Lytton's lighter, which he raised and struck, with the flame set to shoot high. To the other man it would have seemed as if the flame had come from Richard's clenched hand, and he was satisfyingly startled. Richard flicked the fire on and off twice more, then said menacingly, "Get back to your forge!" indicating the flame in the rocks.

The smith glanced over his shoulder, then frowned and began to back away.

On the lake shore, an old man in a long, dark cloak, holding a long spear, watched what was happening and called again. The glint of firelight on this tall character's eyes reminded Richard of the light on the serpent's gaze as it had consumed Taaj, illuminating a soulless curiosity and aggressive determination. Richard shivered as he looked at the man by the water.

The smith spoke to this figure again, and this time Richard thought he heard a name: *Yar sun*.

The name was familiar. He played its sound in his mind. It was *distinctly* familiar, and when the smith repeated it the sound became clear, and Richard felt a thrill of excitement as he realized who was confronting him on the shore.

Jason!

The argonauts had worked all night and by dawn the *Argo* was secure and upright, still impaled on the rocks but ready, now, for the first planks to be repaired. At the water's edge the effigy of Hera was a grim depiction of the manipulative nature of the Goddess. Her face was pinched, her eyes wide and angry, and although there was beauty there, the effect was dispowering. One would not enter lightly into a relationship with a woman whose need for gratification was so determinedly portrayed. Ten feet high, wreathed in the coils of black smoke from the braziers, the statue gazed across the bowed, crouching shape of a man in a black, wool-trimmed cloak: Jason himself, but a man now long-years-since finished with the quest for which he had become renowned.

He was talking occasionally and nodding, as if in communion with the idol. When he stood it was a sudden movement and he turned quickly to look directly at Richard, hidden among the rocks. Richard started with shock as the dark face broke into a cruel grin and a brawny hand lifted, finger extended, pointing. The idol had drawn attention to him.

This was an *old* man. Below the dark fur hood, Jason's hair and beard were gray, and the naked torso that was now revealed was sagging, the belly full over a wide sword belt, like a girdle, the thighs still strong, but loose-skinned. He was in his seventies, by the look of him, and his companions not far off, their women friends too; they formed a gap-toothed, gray-haired, crouch-boned crew of adventurers, but strong in arm, and still strong in menace.

The smith was attacking rigging rings and bolts, sending sparks flying. The dull sound of hammered bronze pulsed along the lake shore.

Richard returned to Old Stone Hollow in time to see the centaur moving furtively away up the river. It glanced back as it heard movement and raised an arm in thanks before trotting jerkily into the shadows.

An hour later the first of the argonauts edged cautiously through the gully and approached the giant effigy which Richard had constructed at the gateway to the compound. The man had no beard, just a wide mustache. His gray hair was lank, but held back by a simple purple headband. He carried a bow, a quiver of arrows and a wide-bladed cutting sword that reflected greenly as he held it at the ready. Apart from sandals and a belt fringed with leather strips, he was naked below the heavy cloak of stitched skins that he wore, opened at the front. They had come from hot Aegean weather into this brisk, chilly autumnal world.

The man stood across the river and peered into Old Stone Hollow, observing the cliff, the longhouse, the height of the palisade, the wooden Guardian. He was nervous, curious and perhaps only an advance guard. From hiding in the long grass Richard scanned the cliff top and the other paths, but he saw nothing. As the argonaut stepped into the river, to cross it and enter the compound, Richard darted quickly to the tent that protected the generator and increased its power to the wires, ground tracks and laser channels around the Station.

The effect was astonishing. The man stopped suddenly, very puzzled, then began to scream, stumbling back in the water, falling, dragging himself up onto the bank again. Around him, the land heaved, the trees shuddered. He jerked his hand away from the sudden tug of green tendrils that had emerged to wrap around him. Again he screamed, this time in terror, his voice taking on a strange quality, deepening, until it was not recognizably human. He was still standing, but he had become gray. Gradually his spine arched and he tumbled back. There was a scurrying of activity around him and ground-ivy flowed to cover him. Below this unlikely shroud he continued to struggle and breathe for some time, occasionally emitting a cry of intense pain, occasionally calling helplessly for Jason.

As he had fallen, so there had been a quick movement back toward the gully. Richard darted round the palisade and peered out, in time to see Jason and two others returning in haste, and certainly in confusion, to their lakeside camp by the *Argo*.

Later in the day, one of the women and another argonaut edged through the gully. They called out repeatedly, advertising their presence, and took a wide arc up the slope, above the river, before cautiously coming to the water's edge, grinning and nodding, there to place a gleaming jug and a roll of fleece on the ground. They were unarmed and crept away. Richard watched them go, then fetched the offerings into the compound, delighting in the fact that he was clearly regarded as some terrible creature that would need placating. He remembered the Gorgon, however, and was not unaware that to these aging adventurers, placation might only be a first ruse in the eventual tricking and destroying of the mysterious, magical life-form that they had encountered.

How did Jason and his crew regard him, he wondered? They had adventured against cyclops and titans, gorgons and sirens, the guardians of magic groves and serpents. Here, now, they had beached by magic on a cold lake shore, after passing, perhaps, through an odd storm, or clashing rocks, on the sunny Aegean. They were in a mysterious land, and threatened by a wild man, a wizard, who summoned the very earth to consume one of their men by touching a bizarre, metallic monster that hummed a single note, and whined to call for more prey.

The jug was of beaten gold. It contained a sharp wine, flavored with lavender, and he was immediately suspicious, risking no more than a taste on the end of his finger. The vessel was exquisite, decorated with figures of heroes, and the full and leafy features of the god of all things indulgent. The roll of fleece did not reveal gold, to his disappointment, but was beautifully soft, white with fine streaks of gray, and cut carefully to make a shoulder wrap, the ties at the front being the small, scaly horns of the creature that had perhaps once worn the hide more naturally. The horns were not pronouncedly like a goat's, nor sheep-like—more in the fashion of Pan, he thought.

The sounds of repair were loud. Richard heard trees being felled, the wood then chopped and shaped. The forge rang continuously and sometimes the breeze brought the smell of cooking and Richard sighed as he remembered good, tasty stews and succulent Sunday roasts of lamb and pork.

Perhaps his hunger carried on that same breeze. In the late afternoon, Jason and another burly fellow, both unarmed, both in sheepskins, brought a small copper cauldron to the river's edge and left it there. A tantalizing aroma of fish and Mediterranean herbs came from the pot. Jason's companion withdrew nervously, but the leader of the argonauts remained. He produced a wooden spoon and consumed three mouthfuls of the soup and fish, then drew back so that Richard could cross the water and take the container. Jason made encouraging sounds, grinning, his mouth full of black teeth.

"Thank you," Richard said, and added, "Daksi."

Jason shook his head thoughtfully, crouched on his haunches, eyes alert for every movement, every twitch of the forest. Richard carried the cauldron back into the compound then came to the river's edge again, dropping into the same tense crouch as his visitor. He was conscious of being explored carefully, examined in every detail, from his tennis shoes to his denim shorts, from the ragged affair of blankets that he wore around his shoulders for warmth to his braided hair and the bone slivers and egret feathers with which the boy had decorated him in recent, happier times.

Jason indicated the crumbling mound that was his dead companion and said a few words. Richard spread his hands and shook his head, before hunching forward again. "I didn't know it would happen. There's a defensive field around Old Stone Hollow—" He waved his hand behind him and repeated slowly: "Old. Stone. Hollow." Jason nodded and said, "Hollow."

Richard went on, "The field kills in different ways. It didn't kill the centaur at all, and you seem safe enough. You're mythagos. All of you. And you're all vulnerable in different ways. This is a dying place, for mythagos. It's dangerous for you to be here."

"Hollow," Jason said. "Mythaaga . . ."

"Mythagos, that's right."

Jason shook his head, looking beyond Richard, then scanning the high rise of shadowy cliff. He stood and stretched, rubbing circulation back into his tanned and muscular legs. His bones creaked and cracked as he straightened, like the *Argo* on the beach, and he grinned broadly, an acknowledgment of age. He pointed to the stew and said something encouraging, then raised a hand in temporary farewell.

As he left he glanced back twice, his face an open book of thoughtful planning.

What was Richard's significance to them? Were they afraid of him? Did he represent some goal in their adventure? Did they believe that he might be in possession of a magic that would aid their greater quest?

The *Argo* had been pulled down from the rocks, and was now suspended by ropes. Its stern was in the water, but its prow, and the damaged area of the hull, were more accessible to the carpenters and metalworkers, and Richard, watching from above the gully, could see how the planks had been cut back to expose the great tree that formed the keel.

An aspect of the Jason legend came back to him: the *Argo* was built around a sacred oak. He had always assumed that the keel had been shaped from the tree, however, not that the tree itself had been incorporated into the vessel. Yet there it was, its branches like veins, reaching up and through the narrow space below the deck, winding around like roots, a cage of branches containing strength and magic, a cage of branches within the man-formed sleek shape of the ship itself.

Two of the argonauts were at work repairing several broken branches, applying an unguent. Smoking censers had been placed inside the tree, and the vapor wafted out across the lake. Looking carefully, Richard could see movement inside the oak cage, acts of propitiation, perhaps, or repair to the main trunk.

It was as he watched the bustle of activity that he heard the sound of a girl crying out in anguish. A harsh male voice barked an order. Much of the work on the ship stopped for a moment and there was a clattering, somewhere below decks, the sound of hooves, or stamping, and then a rattle of metal followed again by the girl's shrill cry.

One of the argonauts laughed. A length of rigging slipped, uncurling as it plunged, and was caught by a man below. The new mast was up, the sail being hauled to its cross-bar. The accident broke the moment's mood, and activity began again.

Five minutes later, one of the planks at the rear of the ship began to move. Curious, Richard moved closer through the rocks and trees. The panel had been loosened by the force of the beaching. It opened along three feet of its length, and a dark, frightened face peered out at the shore. Daylight glinted on wide eyes, then a second face, this one more animal than human, glanced out anxiously before withdrawing.

The plank snapped back into place with a crack, but the sound went unremarked by the busy men around.

In the evening Richard built a fire just inside the gates of the Station and racked up the generator. On the far bank, where the argonaut had died, an odd tree had grown. It shivered despite the lack of wind, and carried four small, yellow fruits, round and shiny. Richard declined to go across the river and investigate them.

Movement in the gully alerted him and he quickly strung his long bow, then knocked an arrow. Over the weeks since he had found this weapon he had become adept at its use, though the flights and heads were getting battered now and he had so far failed to make a successful arrow himself.

From the long grass he could see the gleam of light in the defensive field, and in places the glitter of the thin wires that carried the current. Water splashed, a man's voice barked, a girl's voice protested. Richard drew back into the grass, crouching, and soon Jason and three others appeared across the river. Jason had a small, dark-skinned girl with him, chained around her neck, her face open and frightened. She wore a thin wrap that scarcely covered her skeletal limbs.

Jason called to him and Richard came out of cover. "What do you want?"

The girl immediately closed her eyes, concentrating hard. Jason just grinned and watched the other man. His companions shifted uneasily, tugging skins around their chests. One of them kept a weather-eye on the huge bow, which Richard had drawn, the arrow turned only slightly to the side. Richard felt his arm twitch with the effort of holding the weapon, but he sensed menace in the air and was taking no chances.

Again Jason spoke. He slapped his chest, his mouth, and indicated Richard. He wanted to come over the water and talk. He wanted to bring the girl. Was that permitted?

"Just you, then. Not your friends. They must go back to the *Argo*."

"*Argo?*" Jason repeated. Richard stabbed a finger at the other three men and then toward the shore. Jason grasped the message. His friends withdrew. Jason tugged the protesting girl and they waded through the deep water, shivering as they came ashore, crouching gladly by the fire in the gateway below the menacing glare of Richard's totem.

Closer to, when Richard met the gaze of Jason's prisoner and saw the etched lines of experience and humor, of pain and defiance all around the sparkling eyes, the corners of her mouth, he realized that it was only her slightness that had made him think of her as a girl, rather than the subdued but still defiant young woman that she was.

Jason produced a piece of cloth and unwrapped a rare-cooked and juicy shin of mutton. It gave off an aroma of rosemary and garlic and as Jason saw the hungry look in Richard's eyes, so Richard saw the look in the woman's. She was starving. Jason hacked off a portion of the meat and ate it, then carved a slice for Richard, who took it and consumed it with gusto. The woman accepted a small slice, behaving as if she were surprised to be offered such a treat. There was wine too, a clay amphora containing about two pints. Jason took a long draught, then Richard, and this time he appreciated the drink, with its honeyish aftertaste and warming effect on his stomach.

"Thank you," he said, and the woman repeated, "Thank you."

"To what do I owe the pleasure of this visit?" Richard went on, then frowned as the woman said, in perfect imitation, "To what do I owe the pleasure of this visit?"

Jason watched her, nudged her, but she shook her head and scowled, rattling the thin length of chain with which he held her. She looked hungrily at the lamb and the big man sliced more for her, then for Richard. She chewed gratefully, dark eyes sparkling. Her skin tone suggested the Middle East. Her hair was jet black, but cropped short. Her earlobes gaped grotesquely with holes where heavy rings had once hung, and indeed, there was a distension in the flesh of her nostrils too. A thin covering of dark hair spread from her ankles to her knees, and bushed from below her arms. She was boyish in shape, her face seeming older than her breastless body. The wrap that covered her was purple, and the designs were of broad-headed lions, winged dragons, and sharp-beaked eagles.

"Why are you repeating what I say?" Richard asked.

"Why are you repeating what I say?"

"Are you trying to understand me?"

"Are you trying to understand me?"

"My name is Richard. What's yours?"

"My name is Richard . . ." She trailed off, looked down.

Jason leaned forward expectantly, watching her. He said something and she nodded.

She murmured, "I know him now." She looked up, brows dark, head cocked. "It's a strange tongue. I know you though, I know how you speak. Many tongues muddled. What do you call it? Your language . . ."

"English. You seem to have learned it very fast."

"I already knew it—I just had to find it. It's a long-to-come language. They float in me like dreams. There are so many. The languages of the long-gone are easier. But I have him—you—I have you now. I have your tongue. You are Richard."

"Yes. And you?"

"Sarinpushtam. My sad companions, below the deck of the *Argo*, call me Sarin. This is Jason."

"Yes. I know."

"Don't trust him."

"I'll try not to."

"I'm hungry. Please indicate that I should have more meat, or this man will deny me. He's very cruel."

Aware that contact had been established, Jason tightened the chain around Sarin's neck, tugged her and growled at her. She spoke to him in his language and he glanced at Richard, nodding, then smiling grimly. He released the girl, who touched her neck tenderly and started to ask questions. He expected Sarin to translate, but the girl just watched Richard, eyes haunted. Richard pointed to the lamb and to the girl and Jason's features darkened, but he got the message, sliced a thick piece of meat and passed it to Sarin. He watched her impatiently as she ate it, seeming to chew longer than necessary, licking her lips exaggeratedly, closing her eyes in ecstasy when she wasn't watching Jason carefully and tauntingly. When she had finished she wiped her fingers on the ground, looked hard at Jason and wiggled her tongue between her lips in an odd gesture. She smiled "sweetly" as Jason passed her the wine amphora, and drank so deeply from it that Richard was surprised to hear the slosh of remaining liquid when she passed it back.

"That's better," she said. "It will ease the pain later, when he punishes me."

"Why will he punish you?"

"Mostly because I don't like him and he knows it, and I make life difficult for him. Partly because I'm a woman, or what's left of one, and ever since Medea killed his precious lover and his boys, he doesn't much like the female sex, although he doesn't prefer his lusty companions. He has very little choice. Boys, boy-shaped girls, and . . ." She sucked her fingers pointedly. "Well, I hope you don't mind eating meat from a carcass that Jason has raped."

She was grinning mischievously. Jason suddenly lashed out with his hand, a stinging blow to her cheek, drawing blood from the corner of her mouth. He spoke angrily, she translated quickly.

The business session had begun.

"What magic did you use to kill Peleus? And make Tisamenus disappear . . ."

Which one was Tisamenus, Richard wondered, but he said, "A magic that surfaces out of dreams. The dream lives in the skulls of certain men, and also in the earth. The light of the sun, and the terror of lightning, can be controlled by this magic, and made to dance at my orders."

It was sufficiently garbled for confusion, but Richard was proud of his invention. When Sarin conveyed this information, Jason began to look hungry in a different way. Predictably he asked, "What will you trade for knowledge of this magic?"

"Nothing," Richard said. "The magic is known only to me. The very earth in this place is at my command—" Jason had seen something that would not give the lie to this lie—"No one else can have the knowledge."

It was some moments before Jason answered, his gaze burning into Richard. When he finally spoke it was in a whisper, and Sarin had to listen hard as she gave voice to the old man's thoughts. "Will you come with me, then? Will you sail with me on the *Argo*, as my honored companion, and work your magic for me? If you believe this, you're a fool."

It took Richard a moment to dissect Sarin's commentary from the translation. As he glanced at her she raised her eyebrows, quickly and pointedly. He said, "No. Thank you, but the Goddess Hera directs your fortunes. You must ask her for all the magic you need."

Jason turned his head and spat angrily. His face literally darkened as he met Richard's gaze again. "Hera? She rations me. In some ways I'm no more than her shadow, and she dances at her own whim to make me move." He scratched the gray stubble on his chin, smiling thinly. "But I like the tone of your magic. I like its effect. There are places I wish to go, there are treasures to acquire, achievements that would be easier with a magician like you. I will offer you a *palace.* I carry a treasure in the hold of the *Argo* with which I could buy two such places. I will give it to you." He grinned hugely. "And gladly! Just come with me for one year. No more than that. One year. Come on—what do you say?"

Without taking his eyes from Jason, aware of the face that Sarin was pulling, Richard said, "No. This is my home. My gods watch me from the woods. The forest and myself are as one. I seek something that only I can find. My own adventure will take me deep into the wood, not onto the high sea."

Jason was very tense, the fingers of his right hand gouging at the earth. He said, "Then I will help you find what you seek. Myself, my friends. We'll be at your service for . . . two years. If you will spend just one year with me."

"No. I must find what I seek alone. There is a god called *conscience,* and he needs to be placated."

The word was hard for Jason (for Sarin, too, Richard noted). The argonaut came from a time when the notion of conscience was still raw-formed, still a confusion of the will of gods and predestined actions. Richard went on, "More importantly, there is a life called Alex, a life that is in limbo. Like Orpheus—"

"Orpheus? I'll introduce you—"

"Like Orpheus, I have to enter hell to bring him out. I can only do it alone."

Jason was angry, but he tried to hide the fury. He stood, kicked the lamb to Richard, then tugged Sarin to her feet, dragging her to the river. "You should give me the chance to help you!"

"Leave the woman here for a while!" Richard called, and he heard Sarin translate, but Jason snapped a negative and pushed the frail creature into the water ahead of him, splashing through the shallows toward the gully. As he disappeared from view, he shouted out, and Sarin's voice echoed the words: "Perhaps your magic is not as powerful as you think!"

(ii) Dancing with Shadows

Somehow she slipped her chain, and came back to the compound after dark, huddling by the glowing embers and calling softly for Richard. He ran around the grass path, peering over the weeds until he saw who it was, then went to her, picking up one of the still-burning branches and leading her by the hand to the longhouse. She was shuddering, wincing with pain, and he wondered if it might be the defenses, so he turned down the generator and indeed her agony diminished.

He had been huddled in the longhouse without a fire, but he set light to the pile of wood, now, and they sat and listened to the crackle of dry bark, watching the smoke stream up to the roof hole. There was food left, and unsurprisingly Sarin went at it like a hound. She sat cross-legged, her robe riding up her thin legs, and as the light grew with the fire Richard saw the bruising on her thighs. Distressed and disturbed for her, he reached over and tugged the cloth to conceal her wounds. Her neck was black and blue where the chain had been.

"He's sleeping. He put me back in the hold, without the chain, but there's a loose plank and I'm small enough to get through it. I mustn't let him know I'm gone. It would be too terrible for the others."

She was not the only prisoner, then. But Richard hesitated to ask her who else was locked below the deck of the *Argo*. He wanted to know more about Sarin herself. How had she grasped his language so quickly? What was her myth?

By firelight, relaxed and warm, with a friend at last, she told him about her life. To her, of course, it was a natural life that had ended abruptly when she had been taken by Jason.

She had lived in a town called Eshmun, close to a city and sacred site where the priests had ordered the construction of a great tower to reach to the gates of heaven itself. A place called Babel. As a child, she had seen her grandfather broken by the work, sent home to die once his bones had cracked and his muscles become like rags. Her father had been taken. When he too was broken by a fall, his dying words had been that from the top of the tower he had seen a place where the sun shone from every horizon.

Sarin, her mother and sisters were now alone, and unsupported. Sarin had been six. One day they had been taken by other women, and moved up to the base of the tower itself, which was so wide, so huge, so high that it blocked the light from the west. They lived among the tents. Sarin for a while had helped prepare food for the builders, carpenters and stonemasons. But soon she was old enough to follow her sisters into the tower itself, and climb one of the twenty flights of spiral stairs. This led to the ornamental rooms where jade lions watched over shallow pools of water, and those men with the *Vision of the Tower* came to bathe and relax, and take their various pleasures. And Sarin, for a year or more, was one of these.

Because of the nature of her work, because she would need to talk to men from all across the world where customs and the secret languages were different, she was trained in the language of the Tall Grass. The Tall Grass language had been the first language, spoken in the long-gone by the first adventurers. Over many generations the Tall Grass tongue had become rich and complex and all men the known world over spoke it; a small part of it, however, had become divided and secret; each and every man and woman had a secret language, which they spoke alone, to the moon, or to hidden forces, or to God.

Once Sarin had learned the ancient Tall Grass tongue, she could see deeper into the wisdom of the men of Vision, further into their hearts, further into their humor, further into their fears. She became one of the Comforting Mouths, women whose conversation and understanding was like magic. Her head was full of language, and those languages were like windows onto long-gone worlds. Sometimes, too, there were long-to-come worlds, showing themselves in dreams. This was the nature of the Tall Grass tongue: so simple that it was the key to everything human beings thought in their secret worlds. The women kept this secret closely guarded in their hearts.

One day, Sarin made the mistake—the only mistake she would ever make, until she failed to kill a man called Jason who came to abduct her—the mistake of mentioning her visions of the long-to-come.

One of the Tower Builders, aspiring to the priesthood, was jealous of her dreams. He asked her to reveal the names of God in the worlds of the long-to-come. Sarin refused. He beat her, then dragged her to the stone drop, a hole in the wall through which the blasphemous were sent to their deaths on the rocks and tents, an hour's fall below. The Builder held Sarin by the hair and dangled her from the stone drop. From here she could see the sun at every horizon, and she remembered her father's dying words, and that made her think of her grandfather, and her mother and sisters, now lost in this great structure in the service of the Builders.

She felt at peace despite the pain and hung there, talking to the memory of her father, while the Builder's arm tired. He demanded to know the names of God in the long-to-come. She asked him why he wished to know. He told her that in names there was great power, and when the tower reached to Heaven itself, those men in possession of the not-yet-known names of God would be as Kings in that great place.

That was when the tower cracked.

Sarin declined to let her secret knowledge be known.

The tower cracked again, and this time she felt the whole world shake, and reached to the Builder just as he released her hair. She clung to his arm, then found a grip upon the lintel of the stone hole. The tower trembled and the Builder was thrown out into the air, to fall for a long time, robes flapping, his scream outliving his body. As the tower began to collapse, Sarin scrambled into its ruined bulk, and scampered down the spiral stairs, dodging the rocks and stones, the cedarwood beams, the jade and golden idols. Eventually she was struck by masonry and lost consciousness, save for a dream in which, with thousands of others, she was falling through the ruins to her death below.

She woke among those ruins. Her mother was bathing her face. Everything was in chaos. The world was full of sound, and the sounds jarred and flowed and screamed, but as Sarin came to full alertness she found that she could understand those sounds. The secret languages of every man, woman and child were now the *only* languages—the greater part of the Tall Grass tongue had been torn away!— but each was different. She could understand her mother, but her mother could understand none of her daughters, save Sarin.

Sarin was the Tall Grass Lady, and she was depicted on many painted and carved surfaces, vases, and sacred stones. She knew all tongues. When she had denied the Builder his obscene request, she alone had been spared by the fateful and vengeful force that had destroyed the language of the world, the tower, and its blasphemous intent. Sarin dwelt in a temple, and was visited often, to interpret between new peoples, new clans, new tribes. Her visions continued. Her fame spread . . .

And then—to this Sarin at least—a strange thing happened . . .

Out of the long-to-come came a ship like no ship she had ever seen, men like no men she had ever seen, carrying swords and spears with terrifying blades, speaking a language that she recognized, but talking of her own life as if she was long-gone, long in the past. They were collectors, and they had come to collect her. They would sell her for a high price to a king whose desire for power could make use of this Witch of Tongues.

They took her, abused her, beat her and chained her in the cargo hold of the *Argo*.

Sarinpushtam. Tall Grass Speaker. A woman with the gift of language. One of Jason's tradable treasures.

"There are two holds," she said after finishing the last of the sour, lavender wine. It hadn't done Sarinpushtam any harm, so Richard too had indulged from the golden jug, and now felt light-headed and aggressive toward Jason. "To get to the hold where the living are chained you have to go through the dead treasure hold. It's stuffed. You can hardly move for fleeces, skulls, statues and bits of armor."

"Fleeces? Is there a golden fleece among them?"

"They're all golden," Sarin said with a little laugh. "He collects them compulsively. I don't know why— nobody seems to want them."

"What about guards?"

"They're all drunkards. They'll be vigilant during daylight, but they eat and sleep like lions, and drink like Old Vineface . . . I don't know how you remember him in your long-to-come. They'll soon drift off, but Richard, they're not fools. If they sleep readily, because of their age, they sleep lightly, they wake fast, they're stronger than they look, and they've lost none of their skills. They're mean-tempered, ferocious old men."

"I'll be careful. At least Hercules didn't come back."

"Four of his illegitimate sons are among them, though, and one of the women is his daughter. The sons of the Dioscuri are among them too. And the shade of Aeneus, of whom you should be very wary."

"The unsung heroes of Jason's later legend," Richard mused aloud, and was about to speak again, to ask who the rest of the argonauts were, when he noticed that sweat was pouring from Sarin's face. She seemed to be in pain, and almost immediately she arched back and began to howl. Richard leapt to his feet and picked her up, astonished at the fact that he could hardly feel her weight. Her breath was bad, but her eyes, now wide, were terrified. "Something's happening to me . . ."

The defenses! Christ!

"Hang on to me. I have to get you out of the Station."

She began to weep, biting back the sounds, gnawing at her lip to frustrate the anguish of pain that she was suddenly experiencing. Richard cut straight through the grass, wading through the tall grass, crossing his winding paths. He hardly glanced around him as he passed the gates, and entered the water. If Jason was here, now, then he was in trouble. Sarin's grip on his neck tightened, then relaxed and he was shocked, dropping her to the ground, slapping her cheeks, pulling her face round to see if life still existed. She was breathing shallowly. Her mouth was slack and wet. He picked her up again and stumbled up the bank, running fast toward the Sanctuary, to get her away from the humming defenses, the totems, the talismans, the forces of the earth that could so unpredictably take the life of a mythago.

He fell to the ground, his legs too tired to work anymore. He covered Sarin with his body, hugged her, his mouth against her neck not for pleasure, but so that he could feel with his lips for the pulse of life. She groaned, was sick, and he drew away, holding her hand, massaging her thin fingers, waiting for her to come back to full strength.

"What happened?" she whispered after a while. "I felt like my life was being sucked into a great hole. There were running creatures, running men, all being sucked down into a great hollow in the ground ..."

The reference was clear. She had experienced Old Stone Hollow itself. So did that mean that it was the camp's defenses that had attacked her suddenly or had something reached to her from the cave? In any case, it would be dangerous for her to return to the Station.

"How do you feel?"

She wiped a hand across her mouth. "Too much wine," she said. "I feel shaky. I don't want to be beaten again. I'm going back. From what I've heard Jason say to the others, the *Argo* will not be seaworthy for four days, perhaps five. So don't act hastily. If you really want to help, then we must wait for a good moment."

She was staring at him. It was an odd look and he couldn't interpret it. Suddenly she flung her arms around his neck and cried on his shoulder. Helplessly he patted her back, alarmed by the prominent ribs. "I *will* help," he said. "As best I can. But you mustn't come back to the compound. It's too dangerous for you."

"He'll drag me back. He needs to control you. He wants your head. Jason believes that the source of all magic is in the jelly that fills our skulls."

Clever man ...

"Richard ... ?"

"What is it?"

She drew back, peered at him through furrowed brow, licking her lips and grimacing at the taste. "If you can't help us. If it seems Jason will win ..." Her eyes gleamed with passion and desperation. "Richard. I would rather not be alive than with Jason. Do you understand what I'm asking?"

"Yes. I do."

"The knowledge has only just become important to me. I can't stand it any longer. I don't belong with him. I don't belong here. I dream of long-gone and long-to-come, but the dreams are wrong. It's as if I am not in the right world. Can you explain that?"

Richard could have spent an hour explaining it, of course, but he shook his head. Suddenly Sarin was on her feet. She slipped off her colorful wrap and merged with night shadows, a pathetically slim shape, slipping down the bank to the gully, moving like the softest breeze back to her prison in the *Argo.*

"Riiich—aaaard! Good morrr-ning. Brek-faaast, *Riiiich*—ard. Braaaaak—fust!"

The sound of Jason's call, his shouted invitation to come to the river, woke Richard from a deep and dizzying sleep. He was in the longhouse, wet and cold with sweat. Jason's voice, the accent pronounced, the laughter a clear indicator that he was amused by the strange words (no doubt taught to him by Sarin), was nightmarish.

"Riiich—aaaard!"

He dressed and ran in his crouch through the wind-stirred grass, finally peering through the gate at the crouched, cloaked shape on the far bank. Sarin was there too, but not in chains. On a skewer, Jason held two crisply black fish, plump of body. Fish for breakfast. Why not? The pain in Richard's head was a sufficient warning not to accept any alcohol, however.

He thought of turning up the generator, but the memory of the previous night, and the possibility that Sarin would not survive the destructive field, decided him against such a move. Jason as ever was unarmed, but Richard knocked an arrow and skulked forward, finally standing in the open gates.

"Why the bow?" Jason asked through the woman.

"Because I relish the idea of living to be as old as you."

Jason laughed and nodded. "But that's too much caution, Richard. Men like you are too fearful of their backs. I'm old because I don't care. I just trust to Hera. She bargained with me years ago. A long life, said I. Then pleasure me, said she. How do I do that, I asked. I like to see you *find* things, she said. The world is full of hidden treasures. And like a man finding the secret places of a woman for the first time, so to the gods there is a satisfaction in seeing men discover the secret places of the earth. Hera is my love, my life and some might say my tormentor. But what torment? I have the fullest of lives, and I am unquenchable. I have the vigor of a youth, and the experience of age. I can drink like Old Vineface, and plan a strategy for the ache in the head the next day; and at the whisper of my voice I can summon a hero to sail with me, or a king to charge me with a task. I *like* being old. Memory—experience—these are the truest sources of *power*. Make your own pact, Richard, and that way you need never look behind your back again. But for the moment, it's breakfast and conversation that I want, and a bargain, not a fight, so do put down that bow."

They ate fish, and Richard noticed that Sarin was given an equal share. Jason was treating her with much greater respect today. His old man's temper had got the better of him yesterday, but in the harsh light of retrospect he had clearly decided that a way to get Richard's confidence was to show consideration for the woman. Sarin's smile, as she ate and watched her friend, was cynical, a signal that she knew the situation.

"What's the order of business for today?" Richard asked eventually, and as if understanding him Jason laughed, slapped the woman on the back and indicated that she should talk.

"Firstly, I'm yours to do with as you want for the duration of the repair to the *Argo*."

"I accept. I could do with some intelligent conversation."

Sarin shook her head grimly. "That's not what Jason means . . ."

"So what?" said Richard with a smile. "What does it matter what Jason means? It's not what I mean. I'd like to have your company. I accept the deal. I'll find a way to get you deeper into the wood, away from him. I need company, chat, and a sense of humor, and you fit the bill. Yes please, I will have your company for the duration. If *you* agree, that is . . ."

"I agree! But don't think about smuggling me away. If I betray him, he'll kill his best friend, who happens to be mine too. I'm sorry, but this man knows his business, and there are other friends below the deck . . ."

Richard glanced at the smirking man. Did Jason follow the drift of the conversation in English? It was hard to tell.

Sarin said, "The main business today is that you are invited to inspect the *Argo,* to see its goods and treasures, the creatures that he carries, the magic that he has stolen from the earth. He wants to convince you that to join him on the *Argo* would be in your favor. Of course, the whole point is to take you and subdue you. He has already gathered that your strength only shows in this magic place, this *hollow.* He's afraid of your magic, certainly, but he has guessed correctly that your skills are limited. He still wants to use them. So if you go to the *Argo,* don't expect to come back. That's my advice, anyway."

"Thanks. I think I'll take it." Richard looked at Jason and shook his head vigorously. "Tell him that if he releases all that is living on the *Argo,* and waits a full day, then I'll talk to him again and consider his offer. Tell him I do not travel with prisoners."

Jason raised his hands, on hearing this, then patted his groin as he crouched, a clear signal that Richard could take his request, perceived as the lie it was, and post it back to Shadoxhurst.

A look in Jason's eye alarmed and alerted Richard. There had been the faintest of glances upward, the merest shake of the man's head. Richard twisted quickly, at the crouch, and was in time to see the faint shadow of a man pull back from the top of the cliff above Old Stone Hollow.

Damn! They had found a way up. Perhaps an arrow had been knocked and pointed at Richard's exposed back all the time that he had been talking. The compound was totally vulnerable to attack from above.

For a moment Jason picked at his lower teeth with thumb and index finger, examining the fragments of fish that he hooked from his blackening ivories before sucking them away. At length he said something to Sarin, who announced, "He's sorry you won't see sense, but in fact your magic is probably of less use than he'd thought. He'll not bother you again. He has a centaur to hunt, an escapee. He's sorry, but he has decided not to give me to you. The *Argo* will be repaired in a day—I can't believe that's true—and then they'll be gone. If you can help me, please help me soon. Death or release, I don't care which. That bow looks like a giant's, but if you can shoot it, shoot it."

"Be in no doubt of that," Richard said, and as he spoke he realized, was almost shocked to realize, that he *would* kill her. "I'm in no doubt that it's what you want."

"Try to board the *Argo* tonight, to talk with our oracle. It might help you plan a strategy. I'll be waiting for you."

Brutally, Jason tugged the Tall Grass Speaker to her feet. Again, as the night before, he tossed the remnants of the food to the disheveled man in Old Stone Hollow, grinning, waving a hand goodbye.

Throughout the day the noise of repair continued, and the day passed. As night drew in, and torches were lit, Richard armed himself with sword and knife and spent nearly an hour approaching the shore with the utmost caution, his eyes so acutely tuned to the darkness that not even a fly could have moved without his seeing it.

Hera watched him from between her braziers; the lake water lapped calmly; a slight breeze shifted the *Argo,* which creaked in its "dry dock," the rigging moving and slapping against the wood.

All things were quite peaceful, the argonauts sleeping below their skin tents, one man on watch, but his gaze fixed on the shimmering light of Wide Water Hollowing. Richard crept aboard the ship, past the heavily slumbering form of the smith, and swung through the deck hatch, where Sarin's tiny hands held his legs as he descended.

"Do you have the small fire?" she asked in a whisper, and Richard produced Lytton's lighter, striking flame to a compact torch, which illuminated the cramped hold and displayed the clutter of purloined goods.

The rolls of fleeces were stacked against one wall. Richard picked his way carefully through a crate of armor, mostly helmets patterned with designs that seemed to move with a life of their own. Clay discs, and papyrus scrolls were in another box, the lost languages of lost kings. There were bone horns, glass vases, gold amphorae, necklets and circlets of glittering gemstones, woven carpets with intricate and puzzling designs, such simple things as bunches of reed and rush, two sets of pipes as played by Pan, drums with patterned skins, horribly reminiscent of the shaman drum that the Sons of Kyrdu had once destroyed, and in the far corner, tossed aside as if of no interest, a set of bone pipes with a leather air sac that Richard recognized at once, and with a terrible shock.

They were Lacan's! He saw the black rings on the bass pipe, recognized the peculiarity of the design, felt sick with fear and apprehension. Lacan's favorite possession, here possessed by the butcher of the Aegean.

"What do you know about these?" he whispered urgently to a startled Sarin.

She peered at the bagpipes, then shrugged. "They came on board with Tisamenus, just two days ago. They were taken from a dead man. Jason thinks they can summon the gods, but he doesn't know which gods, nor how to make the right sounds with them. He's keeping them in case someone recognizes their function."

Richard's heart had sunk at Sarin's words. His eyes filled with tears, his mouth went dry, as he thought of the big man, with his broad sense of humor, dead now. He said quietly, "A dead man? Are you sure?"

"From a corpse. Yes. Peleus had watched the fight from a distance. I was in the hold when I heard him talking to Jason. Whoever it was, he put up a huge fight and broke Tisamenus' voice box, a rib or two, and two fingers.

Tisamenus cut him almost completely in two. I'm sorry . . .
I think he must have been a friend."

"A dear one. The very best . . ."

As he placed Lacan's pipes down, a touch of breath
passed through the bag and the deep pipe whined briefly, a
last lament, shocking Sarin and reducing Richard to a pos-
ture of frozen terror. They listened for movement above, but
after a few minutes all remained quiet. "Be careful," she
said, and led the way to the rear compartment.

In the half-light, the sad figures shifted; a centaur tried to
rise, but failed, watching Richard through eyes similar to the
creature's that had escaped two days before. This one was
female, though. A woman with small horns curled up in a
corner; two men, wearing the sort of leathers and greens that
suggested they were forest outlaws, were breathing softly as
they sat against the hull, all life gone from their eyes. They
were chained, but the most protection was afforded to a
brawny, silver-haired, silver-armed man, who was held by
arms and legs to the floor; the glint of metal on his right
arm, the gleam of silver in his mouth, the anger in his eyes,
the silence of him, all confirmed that this was Silver Arm,
of Irish myth, and Jason was lucky indeed to have subdued
him.

There were others, slender, broken shapes, some dressed,
some naked, none of them recognizable as to their mythological or legendary natures, all story drained from them,
stripped from them, leaving them not fairy-like, as Lytton
might have imagined, but dead, corrupt in that most human
of ways in which all hope is taken, and all life is made
meaningless.

A voice sang sweetly and softly, and by the faint torchlight Richard looked at the far wall and saw five heads dangling by the hair, two of them clearly rotten, two others,
red-bearded, alive but silent, watching him through furious
eyes, the fifth a thin, youthful face framed with curls of
golden hair, beardless, smiling, eyes sparkling as it sang.

But as Richard drew closer so what had seemed signs of
youth fell away, and he realized that he was looking at a
skull so drawn that it seemed smooth, and yet there *was*
vigor in the eyes, the same vigor as in the tumble of thick,

sweet-smelling hair. The mouth worked, the thin lips puckering, licked by a yellowed tongue. No breath could have supplied the voice, since the neck was ragged and blackened with blood. Still, though, the head sang, a soft voice, the words meaningless, until suddenly it sang, slowly and carefully, "Two bloody nicks . . . to the back of his . . . neck . . . all for the sake . . . of his lady's green . . . girdle . . ."

Alex's song, from the school play!

The head's eyes filled with sadness and followed Richard as he dropped to a crouch, staring at the monstrosity, asking, "Who are you?"

The sad gaze swiveled toward Sarin, who said, "It's Orpheus. He's my closest friend. Once he was Jason's friend too, but no longer. Jason says he still loves him, but he searched for a year to find the rocks where this head was wedged, after being torn off by wild women at the gates of Hades, and he stole it, and will sell it. Orpheus can see the fates, so if you help him he will help you. He can see into men's hearts."

"I know. It just happened . . ."

Behind him one of the green hunters stirred, reacting to the sound of voices. He spoke weakly, the words fluid but incomprehensible for a moment, "Kenna thow helpa? Kenna thow helpa?" until the dialect resolved into the desperate plea for help that it was.

Sarin shushed him, then turned back to Orpheus, stroking the skull through the tight flesh. "Sing for our friend. He can help us."

Orpheus spoke in his own language, and Sarin looked grim as she replied to the wounded hero. Turning to Richard, she explained, "I told him we'd take him too. We'll find a wizard to build a mechanical body for him. Does your magic extend that far?"

"I'm afraid not. Sorry. And my belief systems are stretched to credibility just seeing what I'm seeing."

Orpheus sang again, a haunting tune, his eyes closed for a moment, then opening widely and staring at Richard. The voice changed, the words were English, and spoken, now: "He is with the stone faces, in a place of stone. He is with the tree that runs and speaks. He watches and waits for his father by the oak shroud where the bird spits. He is imprisoned by his own ghosts."

"Alex? Can you see my son?" Richard crouched eagerly before the head, all thoughts of the impossibility of this situation gone as he detected a reference to Alex again. "Tell me more. Please! How do I get to him?"

But Orpheus was singing softly again, and in his own language, tears running from the hollow eyes.

A living head. No breath being pumped from lungs to activate the vocal cords, but a head, nevertheless, that sang and spoke, and gave oracles, and had seen Alex. Was this a dream? Had Jason spiked the wine with so subtle a drug that Richard was now existing in two states of consciousness, the real and the falsely lucid?

He scrambled back through the gully and into Old Stone Hollow.

A talking head! Orpheus himself, rent by the nails of the Thracian women after he had offended them in some way. Was it because he had looked back into Hades after abandoning Eurydice? Richard couldn't remember the legend. The head had been thrown into the river Hebrus, had become wedged between rocks and continued to sing for years. Jason, in his new profession as collector of oddities, had sought the oracle that was his old friend, and would trade it to the highest bidder. Richard, in his own way, needed to purloin the head, to have it, to hold it, to use it to find Alex.

But how could he alone invade the *Argo,* destroy the argonauts and liberate the oppressed creatures in its dungeon? The only way, surely, was to entice the crew of the *Argo* into the defensive field around the Station. But they would be wary, now, having seen the earth itself consume Peleus.

At dawn, the nesting herons in the woods behind the Station woke him with the clattering of their bills. A hard wind was blowing through the high grass, and from the cave below the cliff, from the hollow itself, came the sound of voices, distorted and haunting. He had spent a night dreaming of Alex and Helen, and in those dreams he had felt effective in their rescue. Now, in this breezy, mournful dawn, he felt the wood tug at him, sensed smells and detected the minutiae of movement in the forest that suggested he was becoming more attuned. His edge vision was restless again, and the breath was tight in his lungs. He felt happiest with his hands spread on the cold earth, as if this allowed strength into him. The taste in his mouth seemed to be satisfied by lapping quickly at the dew on the tall grass and he scampered on hands and feet, over a rough hummock that he didn't recognize, letting the moisture drench him, freshen him and invigorate him . . .

He stood suddenly, slapping at his cheeks.

What the hell am I doing! I can't afford to go bosky!

The bill-clattering faded. The breeze still disturbed him as he walked through the grass to the closed gates and eased them open. There was a cloth-wrapped object on the far bank, another gift perhaps from the nervous argonauts. Had they come during the night, or at dawn? He had slept so heavily . . .

His mind's eye began to clear, and the hummock in the Station resolved into the unnatural and new feature that it was. He had crawled right over it, moments ago, when he had been lapping up the sun-dew. He went back, now, back through the maze path, looking for the crushed grass that told of his bosky-transit, and there, suddenly, was the body of a man. It was overgrown. The suckers of ivy and grapevine had penetrated the crumbling flesh. The man was sprawled on his side, one arm behind his back, still holding a bronze sword. His neck was bent back, his mouth agape and sprouting dog mercury. The gray hair was still visible on the decaying skull, a purple headband identifying the dead man as one of the argonauts.

So: you brought me a gift, then crossed the river to kill me . . .

He picked up the sword, removed the headband from the skull, which puffed into dust as he struck it with the back of his hand. With the band around the hilt of the bronze sword he crossed the stream and investigated the offering; an elaborately decorated long bone, the etchings ingrained with gold, the bulbous head, where it had once articulated in a hip joint, shaped into a grinning face. Richard covered the grotesque bone, unsure whether this was intended to frighten

him, or had been offered as a gift in exchange for some of
his own magic.

Distantly, a hunting horn sounded, not the shrill, metallic
sound of the twentieth century, but a duller, more resonant
call that ranged in tone and was clearly produced by the bel-
lowing of a man through the grooved horn of an animal. The
sound came from beyond the Sanctuary. Richard's hearing
was acute, perhaps because of the isolation he had experienced for the last few months. He sensed that there were
five men running. A creature on four legs fled from them.
They crashed through undergrowth and cantered over clearer
ground, and for a few minutes Richard stood by the slope,
turning to follow the distant action.

Jason was determined to have his centaur back.

On the beach, the *Argo* was now half in the lake water.
The mast was up, the crossbeam tied, the sail rigged and
furled. The effigy of Hera had been replaced on board, and
glared inland across a deck that was piled high with supplies, ready for stowing. The tent was still pegged to the
shore, and several argonauts moved about domestic business, while a circle of four guards crouched, weapons in
hand, very alert as they watched the wood. One of them was
certainly aware of Richard, who observed the proceedings
from his special place, but the man made no movement toward him. The smith was in the small skiff with another
man, peering down through the lake waters, a hundred yards
from the shore.

The hunting horn sounded again, a fluctuating note on the
shifting, rising breeze. There was quite a wind, now. The
lake water was choppy. The fires on the lake shore shed
smoke in gusting streams. Richard eased his way back along
the gully, and approached the Station, aware of the sighing
and creaking of the forest around him. The wind was almost
sinister. The tall grass in the compound rippled: the huge effigy outside the gate swayed on its stand, rags flapping. The
gates of the Station banged on their hinges.

As Richard approached his home, the centaur suddenly
appeared. It had been lurking inside the palisade. Its eyes
were huge, its mouth slick with saliva, and it was dropping
dung uncontrollably, as if terrified.

"They haven't got you yet, then? Are you looking for sanctuary?"

"Hide me . . ." the pathetic creature whispered, repeating the request three times.

Richard tugged its mane, trying to avoid its breath. "Of course I will. Jason can't harm you inside Old Stone Hollow. There are defenses here . . ."

The centaur seemed to relax, even though it couldn't have understood the words: its request to "hide me" was almost certainly part of its education from Sarin. It shuffled nervously, its tail waving, its human chest expanded so that ribs and cords of muscle showed through the black hide. It backed away from Richard, back into the compound, eyes oddly imploring.

"The defenses," Richard said again, and the herons clattered their bills, distracting him, and a shrike called, and rooks, nesting in a high elm, cawed, while the wind brought the scents of sweat and groin, powerful smells that made Richard nervous. Yet when he looked around he could see nothing but the black man-beast, backing away from him.

The defenses . . .

He realized with a terrible shock that the humming of the generator was no longer part of the sounds of the wood. Glancing quickly to the right, he ascertained that the glint of red light, the infrared, was not there.

The generator was down!

He stepped quickly into the Station. The centaur made a sound, half fear, half laughter, then galloped behind him. Richard turned to watch the creature, which now pawed nervously at the ground by the gates, watching him, saliva streaming from its lower lip, eyes blinking furiously and nostrils twitching.

"A trap," Richard said calmly. He turned back to the compound. There was an odd sound, a swish of air, followed by a second, then a third. He saw nothing in the rippling grass or among the waving trees that hid the path to Old Stone Hollow itself, but when he glanced back at the centaur he saw an arrow protruding from the creature's mouth. The man-face was wide-eyed with shock as it collapsed onto its forelegs. A second arrow jutted from its chest, a third dangling in the shallow skin of its shoulder.

And then Lacan's bagpipes wailed, the sound like a mocking sigh, breaking into the rhythm of a mocking laugh.

The fourth arrow, loosed now, sliced the air as Richard turned back to the cave. He saw it coming, but it was too fast. It struck the superficial flesh of his left arm and passed all the way through. The pain was strangely remote, and he lifted his forearm as if nothing had happened, then held his hand against the flow of blood as the bright woodland near the cave darkened with movement, and nine men, cloaked and hooded, all but one masked, stepped into the open and walked slowly through the wind-whipped grass toward their prey.

It was a moment of silence, oddly peaceful, nothing but the murmur of wind, the susurration of the grass, and the flap and slap of skins as the nine figures moved in a wide arc, closing on Richard. Jason was foremost, carrying a spear and the bone pipes, his glittering eyes filled with amusement as he watched from below his hood. "Your magic is finished," he said in stilted English, waving a hand at the generator tent.

"Don't be so sure," Richard said, the wound in his arm beginning to hurt.

Jason shrugged. Sarin would have given him the words to speak, but he couldn't understand the reply. He simply repeated, "Your magic is finished. Richard. Hollow. Magic finished." And laughed, coming right up to Richard and striking him a stunning blow to the face. Richard fell and was sick. Jason squeezed the leather bag of the pipes, making a series of punctuated howls, like a tuneless jig, that caused laughter among the argonauts. As Richard half rose he saw one of them working the arrows from the cadaver of the centaur. When the weapons were recovered, he kicked the body into the river.

Poor betrayed beast. It had perhaps been promised its freedom if it helped entice Richard into the compound, where Jason was waiting. Its usefulness gone, its worth on the market limited, perhaps, Jason had decided to lighten the *Argo*'s cargo load. He had a new object to sell, now.

But if Richard entertained the idea that he was now one of Jason's objects of interest to the citadels of the Aegean, he was mistaken. Though led through the gully to the *Argo*, he was paid scant attention. His wound was treated and bound, and from Jason's murmured words Richard got the sense that the arrow hadn't been intended for him at all.

He was more concerned by the fact that the ship was now afloat. The below-water repairs were complete, and carpenters were working on the upper hull from the inside, braced among the branches of the sacred oak.

The wind brought rain, a dark thundercloud that poured across the lake, and made the morning seem like night. The tent was rapidly re-erected on the beach, and two small fires lit. Richard huddled in this miserable place, ignored by Jason for a while, free to run if he wanted, strangely reluctant to do so.

When Jason eventually came into this billowing shelter again, he was leading Sarin by a leather leash, tied tightly around her neck. Through the drum of rain, the woman said grimly, "The gods must have helped him with the *Argo*. The ship was unseaworthy yesterday: now it's sufficiently repaired that he's proposing to sail back through the storm channel."

"The storm channel?"

"The passage here, a raging storm between sea rocks, too narrow for large ships. It's how he escaped the war galleys of the Titan Polymnus, which were about to ram us and destroy us. The gateway is out on the lake, he knows that. But he's frightened. He thinks there must be a trick, and he believes you can help him understand the nature of what happened. If he sails into the lake, will he pass back to his own world? Will Polymnus be waiting for him? Or will he sail into another of the god's cages, like this place? Hera hasn't spoken to him for days. He thinks he's being tested, but he doesn't know for what."

Jason watched Richard all the time, his face quite expressionless, waiting for the other man's response.

It occurred to Richard in an instant that there might be a way to separate Jason from his crew. He tried not to look too apprehensive. It would be difficult to contrive.

"There are many worlds beyond the lake," he said, and Jason frowned as Sarin informed him of this. Richard described the dark lakes of Tuonela, the wild, icy seas of the Irish coast, the endless rivers through dense forest, marshes filled with brackish water that were home to heron-people, and offered no comfort at all. To pass back to his own, warm seas Jason would have to worship at a shrine. The shrine was on the hill, above Old Stone Hollow. It was a sanctuary of stones, and the farsighted might be privileged to glimpse their destination.

Jason thought long and hard, staring at Richard with an almost corrosive gaze, grumbling in his throat, winding and unwinding the leather of Sarin's leash around his brawny fingers. Richard felt his knees begin to tremble as he crouched, damp and cold below the sagging, dripping hides of this crude shelter. Jason was not convinced.

"Tell him," Richard said, "that I have lived in this place for many years. I have seen heroes pass through, some wary of me, some befriending me. He has destroyed the source of my magic, but not my vision." Sarin translated as Richard spoke. "Tell him that Hercules camped for five days in the Sanctuary and told me in detail of the quest for the fleece and that he had seen Medea dismembered and hung in pieces, still alive, from a giant cedar tree, where silver-crested crows feed upon . . ."

Jason half rose, his eyes widening. "Where? Where did Hercules see this?"

"He saw it through the shrine. There is a place of vision on the hill. Medea did not live long after the murder of your sons and second wife. A simulacrum took her place."

This clearly conflicted with Jason's own knowledge, but he was intrigued. "A simulacrum? Medea dead?" There was spittle at the edges of his mouth, and his skin, below the stubbly beard, was flushed. Tiny creases in his forehead gave the lie to his calm: he was furious, he was angry, he wanted this vision for himself.

"Medea dead!" he repeated, staring into the distance.

"Medea among the living dead, all magic gone, the object of ridicule from passing heroes."

And Jason smiled! He stood, tugged Sarin roughly to her

feet, then eased the pressure, rubbing a thick thumb over the bruising around her neck as he glared at Richard and said, "Then take me to see this place."

He bellowed orders. The sons of the Dioscuri cloaked-up heavily and picked short spears from the weapons pile, walking through the downpour to join Jason. Aeneus came too, the rain running from the smooth, yellow-metaled helmet that covered his face to the gaping mouth, where broken teeth gleamed between thin graying lips.

These three guardians followed Jason through the gully, and Richard led them to the Sanctuary, to the ruined stones.

Where was the hollowing? It had only been a few months, but the wood had changed, grown denser ...

He swept a stick through the ground elder, slapped at the carved pillars, ducked and weaved through this overgrown place of ruins. His eyes were alert for anything familiar, and he knew, too, that a hollowing led away from here, and that it was essential not to step through it.

A glimpse of red caught his eye, and he moved aside the ivy at the base of a standing stone to find a small hollowstick, a much-rotted doll, but the red fabric of its body still tightly tied. Triumphantly he picked the effigy up and held it to Jason, who backed away, raising his spear.

Now Richard could orientate. The stone was part of the original arch, but the top had fallen. Was it still the gateway that he had taken with Helen, that time in the past? He began to move about the clearing, while the Dioscuri watched him suspiciously and Aeneus stared at him through the sinister eyeholes of his helmet. Sarin smiled, chewing on her finger, half aware that Richard was trying to trap her master.

Richard moved round the arch, then faced Jason, his arms wide, his head thrown back. "It's here," he said loudly, and Sarin whispered the words.

"I can't see anything," Jason said.

"Come here, then, and look between the pillars," Richard urged, backing away and beckoning to Jason. For a moment he thought Jason would bring the woman with him, but the argonaut let go of Sarin's leash. He glanced at the Dioscuri and whispered something to them. Then, with his spear held ready and his black cloak wrapped tightly against the drizzling rain, he walked toward Richard . . .

For a moment Jason seemed to hesitate. Richard thought he had begun to move in slow motion. The light around him changed and the Dioscuri shouted in alarm, backing away. Sarin gasped and crouched, like an animal about to flee. Jason stared at Richard then spoke quickly and with meaning before his face slowly melted into a scowl, becoming a rage, the flesh blackening, the eyes deepening, radiating a terrible if futile menace, a menace touched by a sudden death's head smile.

He was still walking. He had been caught by the hollowing, and a second or so later he vanished completely from view. Richard had the sensation of being struck, but it may have been a leaf blown on the wet wind. The Dioscuri had fled. Aeneus stood, staring from behind his helmet mask, then he too turned and walked quickly down the hill.

"Where did he go?" Sarin asked in the sudden silence. "I heard the statue of the goddess, screaming."

"A long way away. Where Hera cannot control him. And for Jason there's no coming back, now. His newest adventure is one that no one will sing about." He hesitated, watching the rain-drenched woman. "What did he say? What were his last words?"

"He shouted, 'I didn't see the trap. Well done! Though it won't hold me. So now you *should* start watching your back!'"

She shuddered, arms around her body, dark eyes enthralled by the silent stones that had consumed her tormentor.

"You banished him. I thought your magic was dead. Jason killed the humming rock, the source of your power. I thought you were finished."

"He should have believed his own insight: true magic is in here, in the *jelly*." Richard tapped his head. Scents and sounds swirled around him. He was dizzy with triumph and the wood. The rain had different odors, different textures. It ran down his skin, through his hair, through his clothes, and seemed to converse with him. Sarin's small hand tugged at his arm.

"Are you leaving me?"

He stared at her, frowning. "Leaving you?"

"A spirit has you. You have the look of faraway. Are you leaving me?"

"I'm trying not to . . ."

She led him quickly back to the river, then through the gully. They had heard shouting on the shore, the sounds of frightened men. The *Argo* had been launched and was out on the lake, drifting slowly toward the hollowing, its sail furled, its oars out and steady, ready to strike. It was running away. On the shore, a motley collection of creatures huddled in the rain. Aeneus, or whoever had taken command, had decided to empty the hold of living creatures, perhaps unnerved by the thought of the magic they possessed. The two forest hunters were already moving surreptitiously around the lake, scanning the woods, looking for a pathway in. The female centaur was drinking at the lake's edge. The horned woman, wrapped now in a fleece, was cradling the open-mouthed head of Orpheus.

Even from the gully, Richard could tell that Orpheus was dead, that his singing days were finished.

The centaur bolted suddenly, disappearing among the rocks and calling out as it entered the forest. The *Argo* was rocked and the waters thrashed. Sarin cried out and hid her eyes as the serpentine tail of the lake creature wrapped suddenly and sinuously around the broken hull of the vessel, knocking men and women from the deck, snapping the oars like matchwood. The creature's head emerged and the argonauts shrieked. The *Argo* buckled, cracked, the sail spar shattered. As men and women dived for the unlikely safety of the lake the creature rolled, taking the *Argo* with it, vanishing suddenly amidst a storm and explosion of blue water.

Then one by one the swimmers heading for the shore screamed and were gone, the last being the shade of Aeneus himself who made it to the shore and was standing when the open-mawed beast flung itself suddenly through the shallows and dragged him back. Others had swum for the hollowing. Richard watched them reach the gray water and slowly vanish, emerging no doubt into the middle of a wild sea, to face a terrible drowning.

The hunters had gone, merging stealthily with the wood. The horned woman came up to the gully and gave the head of Orpheus to Sarin. Then she kissed the other woman, touched a rough-skinned hand to Richard's beard, before wading into the water and walking steadily into obscurity.

"Will I be safe?"

Sarin's words pulsed on the wind. Richard had a scent, though; it was coming on the rain. He crouched and brushed the water against his nose, smelling, lapping at it. The woman touched him, the ridges of her fingers sliding over his bristling skin. Her odor was strong, and the head of Orpheus was a faint sound as its final songs sang in the jelly of its skull, though no sound came from its mouth. The wind turned, the breeze stroked and curled, the rain shifted, the scents and touches of nature embraced Richard, and the stink-trail suddenly touched him in his heart.

He straightened and cried out. *It was her!* He sniffed hard, then breathed slowly and deeply, waving his hands through the drizzling rain, touching the play of aromas. She was signaling to him. She had touched his heart once before, now she called to him. The scent-trail rose from his groin to his throat and he cried her name. *Helen!*

Frightened, the dark-skinned woman scampered away from him, into the Hollow, through the rain-lashed grass and into the longhouse. Richard followed, a part of him wanting to see that she was safe. Then he closed the gates, howled his pleasure and moved with the scent into the overhang below the cliff, huddling there until the night came, the rain eased, the wind dropped and the stink-trail hardened, gusting from the hole in the ground, below the running creatures . . .

Bosky

The paintings flowed; they were not paintings at all. They were alive, they were vital, they were shadow herds, moving in a great, steaming mass across the rock, across the face of the world, thundering across the grasslands.

He rose to his feet, turning as the huge shapes drummed and billowed past him, and he ran with them, following the broken ground, his face wet with the rank foam that sprayed from their stretched mouths, their lolling tongues. He drew a new strength from the power of the great beasts and grasped at the thick and heavy hair that streamed from their dark hides. He followed the movement of the sun as it glinted on the curved horns and was carried by the power of the herd. Smaller creatures ran too, white-backed, gray-flanked, high-horned, slender-legged. He pranced with them on the rumbling earth, then loped with gray wolves that raced across the grassland, all moving toward the great cavern. The world was vibrant, the earth a deep and resonant drumbeat, the air thick with mud and spray, the sky darkened by huge backs. He ran with them, the scent-trail strong in his nostrils despite the dung and sweat and animal breath of the running herds.

When the earth of the hollow closed around him it was cold. The sounds of the herds became faint. He plunged through darkness into the coiling passages of the world underground, squirming and crawling through the narrow spaces, every finger alive to the smooth, damp rock, the slick stone, his body like that of a snake as he pulled himself deeper through the dark. The earth around him still thundered and shook as the herds of bison and gazelle found their own paths down into the odd world, not of dreams, or the real, but a place between the two. Water fell, hard and cold, from a high ledge in a great dark cavern, into a second system of passages, and he slipped down, following the flow, hands briefly brushing marbled human figures, his eyes glimpsing the stony faces, his nostrils flaring as he again responded to the scents of the wood that lay at the far end of the cave system, and the sweet and beckoning woman who waited for him there.

The cold water carried him. It entered him, bathed him, washed him, clothed him. He slipped and slid, ducked and crawled where the cavern narrowed, ran blindly when it widened, shedding everything that was false upon him, a trail of clothes like skins, letting the stone air and rock spray form a miasma around his taut and sensitized flesh.

He was aware that time passed, but in the absolute dark he measured its passing by the flow of dreams and voices that ebbed and surged, touching his eyes, his heart, his laughter.

At last he crawled out of the earth, emerging through the rock and the turf, clinging to the swollen root of a massive tree. He had been following the root for many dreams, through the lower darkness, embracing its softer texture where it emerged from the icy stone in which it was embedded. The trunk of the tree extended above him, filling his whole view as he rose to his feet, naked and filthy. The colors of the interlocking masks were bright despite the gloom cast by the huge spread of the canopy. He stumbled and jumped across the spread of surface roots, then scampered into the brush at the edge of the Mask Tree's vast glade, looking back at the faces carved there, old faces, weathered and stained, overlain with newer, brighter shapes. The more he looked the more he was able to see among the horned heads, the wide eyes, the oddly gaping mouths, the grins—a thousand masks etched and gouged on the black trunk of the oak, each one watching him from its own forgotten time.

The tree affected him strongly. Somewhere in the maze of faces a sweeter face watched him, a boy, an earnest child—

but he couldn't see the eyes, only sense them, and he curled down into the leaf litter, rubbed soil and crushed grass over his skin, smelled the ground and let the miasma strengthen.

After a while the vague sense of distress and loss that affected him in the glade passed away and he moved at ease through the wildwood, through the dappled light, gathering the scents of rose and wood anemone, bud and sap, gathering all of these to the miasma that flowed with him. The scent trail which he still followed was strong, and he knew the woman was close. When the land dropped toward a moist hollow, filled with thorn and hazel thickets, he knew he had found her. The place was warm and hazy, the ground marshy, in shifting light as the taller trees that crowded and loomed over the dell moved to an unfelt breeze. A stream flowed at the bottom of the hollow, separating two banks, where briar and thistle grew densely, and as he looked from one bank to the other he saw her bower, a thickening in the copse of hawthorn and hazel, where grasses and dead branches had been woven into the thicket to create a protective wall, and a warm shelter.

He went to the stream and the miasma flowed around him, attracting more scents. The light from above made the fine mist in the hollow seem to glow. Through that bright, gently shifting veil, he watched the bower, and if he concentrated he could see her moving. She watched him too, but drew back into deep cover when their eyes met.

He couldn't decide if he should approach or not, and he crouched by the stream, splashing at the water, letting the heavy stillness of the dell envelop him, learning from the faint sounds where the nests were above, and the warrens and passages through the earth and hollow boles around.

At last he crossed the stream, drawing the miasma with him like a cloak, and ascended the bank, through the briar and bramble that she had laid in lines and patches where the ground was more open. The hawthorn bower shook to her sudden movement and a dart penetrated his flesh painfully, then another, thin slivers of white wood tipped with a blue stain. He turned and scampered back to safety.

He constructed a warm, dry place in a thicket, making a

bed of ferns covered with grass, a crude roof of dead wood and the broad leaves of sycamore. From here, each dawn, he watched the hawthorn bower.

At first light the grass-covered woman slipped through her own defenses to the brook, to crouch, sing, and drink, her body tense, her head always cocked, her eyes and ears alert for danger. Her hair was black and streaked with more silver than his dream-memory of her recognized. It fell loosely around her face, where bright, dark eyes flashed and a full and sensuous mouth opened to sing or drink. She was always moist, and light sparkled on her body. She was adept at brushing small fish onto the bank, stunning them and storing them in a leaf pouch. She always carried the thin pipe with its poisoned darts and if he stirred she raised it threateningly.

His arm and neck itched infuriatingly where the fungal toxins had penetrated his skin.

Each dawn when she had finished she would return through the haze, the thick miasma of heat and scent, and it was his turn. She would watch him from cover, sometimes singing in her reedy voice.

Animals came to drink, and he learned to snare hares, the occasional, incautious fowl, a heron, and on one occasion a small pig. Without fire, the flesh was chewy, that of the hare strong and bloody, but exquisitely reviving.

The days in the dell were long, the moist warmth stifling at times. There was a silence and a stillness about the place, broken only by the brook and the restless murmur of birds. The nests of herons woke him each dawn with the clattering of their bills. Huge crows cawed and cackled from a colony nearby, and somewhere in a thicket deer were living. He could hear the male bark, the doe cough. But he never saw them, though their air flowed into the dell and mingled with the miasma of odors that formed each dawn above the brook.

Each dusk he returned to the Mask Tree and sat among the sprawling roots, staring up at the ancient faces. There were many things that tickled memories in his head, such familiarity, but no words or names came to him, only images of strange men, strange creatures, hints of stories, and the occasional thought of a bright boy running through tall grass, holding something wooden above his head that suddenly escaped him and soared into the sky, an unflapping bird.

He felt sad sometimes, but the sadness lifted as night shadow made the tree faces invisible, and only the monstrous black bole faced him. At this time he would stand against the trunk, his body almost enfolded by one of the deep channels in the thick bark. If he listened hard, if he blocked from his mind the chatter of nightjars, the rustle of voles and weasels, the furtive movement of cats and pigs, the flutter of nestlings, he could hear songs in the tree, but the words meant nothing. When he himself sang he sang with words that shaped the tune, and stirred feelings in his chest and stomach, yet meant nothing to the mind above—he had ears and eyes and thoughts only for the woman in the hawthorn bower.

One dawn, the scent miasma had changed. It stirred him deeply. It was sour-sweet, exciting, and he ran along the brook, splashing furiously, circling through the underbrush before crossing the brook and staring expectantly at the bower.

The leaves moved, eyes watched. The new scent flowed down the bank, encompassing him. His body reacted with pleasure and he closed his eyes for a long moment. But the bower remained shut. He whooped, called and sang, then returned to his shelter. When he was back, and out of harm's way, the bower opened and she came down to drink.

He watched her hungrily, silently. There was something different about her. She had tied her hair into a single frond at the back. Her breasts were naked and she washed them carefully. Her legs and waist were still thick with grass, but when she turned to run back up the bank, he saw that her buttocks were naked too, and without the usual caking of mud. When she stooped to enter the bower the breath caught in his throat before he could *whoop* his call. Sweat suddenly beaded his skin.

As he watched the strutting of birds by the brook, and later two hares on their hind legs, boxing and rolling in the grass, memories surfaced from the edge of dreams of men dancing by the light of high, roaring fires, which gave brilliance, by reflection, to the colors of cloaks and the gold of masks and helmets. As the dream dissolved he went to scavenge for leaves and feathers, to make himself the ritual garments of display, a primal urge impelling him to decorate himself.

All day he constructed his display. He used thin splinters of tough grass to sew leaves of birch down each of his arms, and of oak across his chest, and of shining beech, emerald green, down the fronts of his legs. He was careful to pierce only the surface skin and not draw blood, which would add the wrong scent to the miasma.

He selected long heron feathers for his chin, working them through the long, thick hairs of his dark beard so that they hung like a white fringe. Black crow tail feathers formed a fringe across the base of his belly. He used chalk and light clay on the exposed skin of his body, then dabbed the purple and red juices of sloe and belladonna to make eyes on the clay-white.

Instinct told him that this would make a good impression.

Finally he used a mixture of resin, sap and clay to stiffen his long hair, raising it into a crest that spanned his head from ear to ear. It took a long time, and it was almost dusk before he was ready. When he moved at last to the brook, the first of night had descended. A bright moon made the water gleam, the leaves on his body shine, his whitened skin glow. As he crawled to the brook, watching the hawthorn bower, he saw the leaves rustle and part, and he stood up slowly, arms stretched, legs apart. When the bower window remained open he grinned and wiggled his hips, then did a slow turn, and so began his first dance.

At the end of the dance he sang the first calling song. His voice was loud in the still night air and the herons clattered above him, irritating him as he summoned forgotten words and melodies from his other life.

But when the song was over, the bower window closed. He frowned, thought hard, then turned twice and started his second dance, drawing the miasma around him, feeling the condensing moisture with its stinks and perfumes of the wood. He danced a wide circle through the wood and returned to the bank of the brook. The bower window was open again. He cast quick glances at it as he turned and whistled, and when his back was to the bower he allowed a smile to touch his face. His heart was racing with anticipation.

At the end of the moon, however, she was still inside the hawthorn wall.

Disappointed and exhausted, he returned to the shelter, though as he stooped to enter the dry place she emerged and sang slowly and sweetly from the top of the bank, a brief call, thanking him.

Delightedly, he whistled back.

He couldn't sleep. The earth shook below him, sounded strange. The trees that surrounded the dell, its brook and bowers, trembled and shifted, as if a storm was coming. At some point, in the depth of the dark, a horse rode through, breathless, burdened by a man's shape, which struck at the low branches. Later, four foxes came to drink, barked, fled when something stirred in the hazel scrub. He watched that dark shape apprehensively, the faint gleam on tusks. He had sensed it, but not how big it was, and for a while he wondered if it was watching and waiting for him as prey. He was relieved when, after a few hours, he heard it move away.

At dawn, he danced again, before drinking from the cold water of the brook. Then he returned to the Mask Tree and stood with his back to the carved and painted faces, feeling the enfolding bark, letting the air and aroma drift across him, watching the day's shadows pass with the sun, the light on leaves, the movement of trees and fern, the restless passage of clouds in the far distance, at the edge of the great canopy overhead.

And then at dusk he danced for the hawthorn bower with renewed energy. He crossed the brook and ventured up the bank to the lines of briar, turned and called, sang a song that had arisen in his soul like a dream, when he had been standing by the Mask Tree.

He retreated to the stream and waited for the night and dark. When the dell was bright with moonglow he danced again, in his own miasma, singing vigorously, and this time she emerged from the bower, approaching the brook slowly, entering the scent cloak around him, her body wrapped in grasses, her hair flowing, the streaks of silver bright.

She did a quick dance of her own, then laughed as he responded vigorously, encouraging him, before bounding off, disappearing into the night, following the curving bank of the brook, out of the dell and into the deep wood.

He leapt into the air and raced after her, drawing the miasma with him.

All night she led him on a wild and sensuous chase through the deepwood. He had known her in another dream. He remembered her pleasures, and they sang to each other from oak, ash, glade and earthen bank. Soon—it was that deathly time before dawn—they came to a high stone rise, a sheer wall of gray rock, carved with grim faces, and draped with ivy. She turned back from this ruin, then led the way to a dry-earth place, among small trees without thorn or rose briar, and here she danced and sang for a while, before beckoning for him.

He stepped quickly through the trees, grasped her and they fell to the ground. She shredded the leaves from his arms and chest, tore the crow-feathers from his belly and held him. He bit through the grass knots and uncovered her, entwined his fingers with her hair, pressed his body against hers. Her mouth was soft and wet, her taste familiar and exquisite, the touch of her skin thrilling as they rolled together on the dry ground.

Midges plagued his back, biting hard; a mosquito droned faintly near his ear; an earthworm slid through the fingers of his hand as he grasped the raw earth for support; but he was in the earth with her, and the smells of earth and sweat, of blood and her mouth filled his senses, filled hers, and they moved frantically, then gently, then vigorously again, but always together, his mouth going down on hers when she began to scream, so that he drank the sound and the pleasure, sucking every cry, every tremor, every arching thrust of her body against his own, until after a long while she fell back breathless, holding his skin, his damp flesh, easing him to the edge of her body, then tugging him deep again, giggling and teasing.

When she had finished kissing him she lay below him,

peaceful, breathing gently, looking up through the canopy, at the stark light, the shifting light, but listening to furtive movement inside the cold, false stone of the ruin close by.

The miasma flowed over them as the night changed, and the deathless dawn crept through the grass and the fine roots of the trees, and the pores of the leaves. Everything was suddenly very cold, very wet. A new vibrancy flowed suddenly about the lovers and the earth wrapped them with tendrils, feeding on the chemicals on their skin before drawing back.

And as dawnlight replaced the dark, Richard rolled away from the curled woman beside him and entered a lucid dream state in which he murmured her name and his own, and began to remember who he was, and the events at Old Stone Hollow.

He was cold, and curled into a ball, and he was tired, so he dozed, aware of movement and whispering all around.

Skin of Stone

At some time during the waking of their bodies and the re-awakening of their minds, Helen had risen and left the clearing in the trees. Fully conscious again, Richard followed her and found her by the high stone wall, a grayish, naked shape in the morning haze, her long hair thrown back as she stared at the stone faces above her. Richard approached and she turned, stared darkly at him for a moment, then smiled and reached for him. They hugged for a long time, shivering slightly, rubbing each other's backs for warmth. "I have a feeling you were glad to see me," she said dryly.

"You remind me of someone I once knew. Helen Silverlock . . ."

A tighter hug, a longer shiver.

"I hoped you'd find me," she said. "It's been a hell of a long wait. I buried Dan a long time ago, back at the Station. I've missed you."

Her words reminded him of the note she'd left, in another time, a misplaced time. Should he mention it? He decided not, saying simply, "When Lacan described the process of going 'bosky' to me, he made it sound dreamlike and silent, a great deal of communing with the rustling leaves and lapping lake waters. It wasn't like that at all. First I went on a mad stampede with herds of bison and gazelles and packs of wolves, then I followed your smell, acted out some sort of mating ritual, hunted you through the wood and became totally and absolutely rampant."

"And so did I," she said quickly, perhaps sensing the apology that was about to be expressed, and silencing it with a grin and a direct look. "I wanted you very much."

"Me too."

"And wasn't it wonderful?"

"I certainly feel a lot better. Thank you."

She pinched him very hard, sharing his smile. He went on, "My mouth is full of mud and leaf mold. I'm scratched and bitten ... and I think I jabbed a crow's feather into your rump ... at one of the more passionate moments ...?"

"You did. I forgive you. Try to control yourself next time."

"I coated myself with clay and feathers. I pranced around by the brook like a prize prat, singing to you. God knows what I was singing ..."

She suddenly laughed, dark eyes wide with delight, then kissed him on the mouth. "But you were *wonderful*! I was half aware of the songs because they were familiar from *this* life, and half responding to them like a bird responding to a mating call. Sound pheromones! But you really aroused me—the primitive me—even though you were singing such funny things. That's what brought me out of the bower, dragged along by my own instincts."

"For God's sake—*what* did I sing?"

She did a little bobbing dance, arms slightly out from her sides, knees bending, silver-dark hair falling over her breasts, eyes twinkling with mischief as she sang, "Love, love me, *DO*."

"*Beatles* songs?" Richard cried. "I sang *Beatles* songs? You're joking!"

But memory came back; full, horrifying and embarrassing memory.

"Christ. I *did*. And Presley: *There's a place for us.*"

"Uh huh."

"And then suddenly *you* sang. *I can't get no satisfaction.*"

"Which at that time I couldn't. But you seemed to remember how much I liked the Rolling Stones. You chased me through the wood singing 'Jumping Jack Flash'!"

"I did ... I remember now. Oh my God ..."

Laughing, she said, "I thought that was great. You almost

blew it the first evening, though, singing Beach Boys stuff. And something about, *I am the very model of a modern Major General.*"

He groaned. "Gilbert and Sullivan? Dressed in leaves and feathers, in the middle of the night, in the middle of a wild-wood, I tried to seduce you with *The Pirates of Penzance*? Oh God. This is going to be hard to explain to our children."

"Talking of which . . ."

She pulled away from him, walked toward the stone wall. "Do you recognize this place?"

"Yes. But it feels dead."

It was a hard feeling to articulate. It was not just that it was ruined, but there was no *life* to it of any form. The trees that grew over it, the ivy that spread across its walls, the space between its stone buttresses and the nearby woodland, all these things were *silent*. There was an emptiness of spirit. It was an abandoned place.

"Dead, yes," Helen said. "But not dead enough. There's someone inside. He's been watching us. I think I know who it is . . ."

With a frisson of both excitement and apprehension, Richard whispered, "Alex!"

But Helen said, "No. Not Alex. A more recent arrival at the ruins."

In her time in the bower, in her time in the otherworldly state of nature that the Station knew as "bosky," Helen had become adept at creating warm and protective clothing from the living and dried fabrics of nature. Ivy, both thin and thick, could be used to create a clothing frame, then cross-stitched with grasses, or strong plant stems, and in-filled with soft litter, or broad leaves. She dressed them both in minutes, and though the vestments itched and scratched, the hard chill that had begun to become intrusive became limited to hands and feet.

As she worked, Richard enthralled her with details of his encounter with Jason and the *Argo*. Then he asked her about the last three years of her own life, after the Long Man had snatched him away and carried him back to Oak Lodge. "It was as if he knew where I wanted to go."

She nodded agreement. "That's what I eventually realized. I'd passed him twice, trying to find my way back to the Station, but he didn't see me. I couldn't get out of that land no matter how hard I tried. I must have been there six, seven months. Eventually I confronted the Long Man, said yes when he asked me 'Helpen?' and he took me back to the Station. That's his function in legend: to lead you home. I don't know his full story."

"McCarthy found his own way back, following shadows of course, but he died soon after. He was never very strong. And then one day, Lytton turned up. I thought he'd been killed by the Jack-chapel, but no. It spat him out . . ."

"That's what Elizabeth said."

"You've seen Elizabeth?"

"Briefly."

Richard told her of the encounter that had brought him back to Ryhope. When he described Elizabeth's abduction, Helen closed her eyes and shook her head. "Poor woman. She had it so hard those last few months . . ."

When Helen had finally returned to Old Stone Hollow, there was news of Dan. "That's why I didn't come and find you. I was missing you very much." She smiled almost wistfully. "I felt I'd known you for a long time. But I went off looking for Dan, and that was a year's journey, and I found him, what was left of him. And buried him. Lytton by then had scoured Huxley's papers again, and worked out how Alex's shadow might be loose in the wood. He sent me to get you . . . you weren't there . . . I don't understand what went wrong, yet. But anyway, I left the note, came back, and Trickster struck at us from the cave. It was no more than a shadow, all claws, tusks and destruction. It tried to eat Lytton. It killed Wakeman, and pursued me for days. I couldn't handle the confrontation. I wasn't even sure this was *my* Coyote. Then I went bosky, came here, close to the tree covered with faces, and made my home. God alone knows how long I've inhabited that dell. But something stirred in me, waking me up, when you came along. Singing your little songs . . ." She laughed again, shaking her head, then looked up at the gray stone wall.

"I think it's time to take a look inside ... Find our old friend."

They entered the remains of the cathedral through the vaulting arch where great oak doors had once opened to the sanctuary within. Richard stared into the vast, silent ruin and began to recognize it, though its name escaped him. He had been here before, however, and Alex too, a long time ago in another world, his son at that time a tiny child, awestruck and silent, staring up at the vaulted ceiling, at the light through colored windows. Alex had called out in the heavy stillness, listening to the sound of his voice passing through the high spaces, an echo creature that had delighted him as much as the grimacing faces that had watched from the stone, and the serene figures that had moved in the glass.

"I know this place—I've been here before—but I can't remember it—but I do remember these from our last journey! The agony figures. Do you see?"

He walked between the first broad columns, each with the statue of a dying man, St. Sebastian on one side, the stone of his face melting, the stubs of arrows still visible, the twisted Christ on the tree on the other, features faded as if dissolved in acid, but the musculature still defined, so that tortured limbs and a deeper pain communicated powerfully from the dead marble.

The roof of the cathedral had long since fallen in. Broken window arches made a jagged line along the walls, high above. Carved pillars, once richly colored, now gray, rose to crumbling and broken bosses, massive structures reminiscent of the majestic ruins of Greece. Crows flew noisily across the open sky. Stone cracked and fell, clattering on the heaped floor, the whole building rotting before Richard's eyes.

He walked along the nave, between pillars, through the gray, petrified trunks of trees, thinking *a wood once grew here!* but though the gnarled boughs twisted up from the cracked floor, now they flowed into the stone of the cathedral itself, all life squeezed from them, pallid, fractile organic shapes in the architecture, roots spreading, branches flattening against the limestone, leaves like flakes of chalk, falling with every footstep.

There was no frost or ice, yet the place was deathly cold and his breath misted. From the altar he looked back into the body of the building, at the shreds of paint that showed where frescoes had once told stories, at the gargoyles in the high corners, some with faces intact, but broken bodies, others just stubs of proud stone. And at the statues: here, the robes of a woman, her face blank, her hands still precisely carved; and close by, eyes and mouth in a face, surmounting the body of a saint that seemed to melt through the white marble. And everywhere the shadows of dead branches, breaking the sky. And everywhere, stone that crumbled like rotten wood.

Helen was a dark shape, watching from the door at the far end of the church, motionless but for the icy mist that formed a halo round her head.

Suddenly she stepped forward, between the statues of the martyrs, and called sharply, "Alexander?"

There was silence for a moment, and Richard called, "I thought he was dead."

Helen advanced through the cold place, walking cautiously between the stone pillars, the stone trees. "He's here all right. I saw him from my bower, watching us. Lytton! Don't be shy, now."

There was sudden movement in the fallen stone. Broken branches were dislodged from a heap of rubble, small shards of marble and rock rolled down, and a shapeless mass of rock and dust began to rise, to reveal itself as a gray man emerging from hiding, heavily dressed, holding a long staff. Through the lank hair that fell around his face, piercing eyes stared at Richard and a mouth twisted into a death-mask grin. Then the head dropped as the figure coughed violently, spots of blood falling on the dust-white chest before the man could block his mouth and stifle the sounds of pain.

When the fit was over, Lytton looked up and laughed, stepping more into the open.

"I've been here for four days," he said hoarsely. "I'm damned if I know what to do next. Your son has had the second laugh on us, Richard. But he'll come to the tree. He'll have to. He'll come to the tree. And when he does ..."

Helen had been approaching quietly, and Lytton sensed

her now. He turned quickly, his filthy cloaks swirling, his staff brought defensively down to the horizontal. As she hesitated, he backed away, turning again to Richard.

"You have the look of a man who's seen a ghost. And maybe you have. And that's a fine set of clothes ..." Lytton laughed as he spoke, but again broke down into a violent, bloody coughing fit. Staring at Richard, he wiped the red spit from his beard and lips, then looked at it. "I've been too long in the wild. It's slipping away. But Huxley will survive, mark my words. Huxley *will* survive. Damn it!" He looked up hard again, banged the staff on the broken floor. "You've *got* to get him out. One of us. Somehow. He's running us like puppets on strings, Richard. Why didn't you come *back* when we called for you?"

Richard was confused and cold, and his heart was racing. The last time he had seen Lytton, the man had shot and smashed his son, not realizing the trick, and been consumed by the shapechanger. Then Haylock had said he'd been killed at Old Stone Hollow. So indeed his words were right. For Richard, there was the distinct sense of looking at a ghost.

"Was he here? Was Alex here?"

Lytton struck at one of the marble columns, cracking the stone and watching as dust and fragments fell. The hollow sound reverberated in the space. "In the same way that a snake sheds its skin, so Alex has shed this building. Can you *imagine* that, Richard? Like the Jack-chapel that tried to swallow us, this was a *part* of your boy, living stone, living armor. Certainly he was here. But he's long gone. This cathedral has been discarded, like a dying dream. Like the White Castle—do you remember? He's moved to another place, the same place, but a *living* form of it. And it's close. And it's hidden from sight. Why he abandoned this particular nest, that I cannot tell you. Perhaps because of me. Perhaps because of fear of me—or something else that was closing in. It's probably a part of his defenses. He can create, discard, re-create. He can disguise himself in the world of the wood. So yes, Richard. Your son was here, a year ago, a thousand years ago, hard to tell. This place is as much a mythago as any of the Hooded Men, the Jacks, the Bone

Carvers we might encounter. Once the life is taken from it, it will collapse back into itself, rot down like the dead thing it is. What *we* have to do, now, is look for a wrongness in the wood—a clue as to where he's hiding."

Helen came through the drifting dust, circling Lytton widely, alert to the huge and heavy staff he carried so tensely, so threateningly. A stream of pink saliva ran from his lower lip as he watched her.

"You need a doctor," she said.

"No time for that."

"At least let me help you."

"To a poisoned dart, on behalf of Mr. Bradley, here? Thanks, but no. If I find Huxley, if I can bring him into this world, see him, talk to him, then what does it matter how ill I am? He can tell me the way to peace. He can show me the direction. I'm sure he knew it."

Richard listened to the words, the obsession, only vaguely understanding what drove Lytton. The man's breath rattled in his lungs. He had known of Helen's poisoned darts—had he been watching events in the dell?

Helen, frowning at Lytton's defensiveness, said, "I have no desire to hurt you. You should know that. Richard thinks you tried to kill Alex. Maybe you did. But if you help *us*, if you help us get to Alex, then you won't need to kill him. We should work together."

Lytton mocked, turned away from her, always cautious. He ran his tongue around the inside of his lips, emphasizing his hollow face, the emerging skull. But his eyes gleamed as he approached Richard and said, "I knew it was the Jack. But I can't deny my first impulse was to settle it there, to get rid of the cancer. That was years ago and things have changed, but the boy will still come to the tree. I'm sure of it."

"The Mask Tree?"

"You saw it. They're Alex's faces, the faces of his private heroes, his magic friends. Did you see Arthur there? And the Green Knight? And Guiwenneth of the Green? And Jason?"

"I've seen a little too much of Jason recently," Richard murmured, and Lytton hesitated, thinking, before going on: "Then you saw his pleasures. But there, also, is everything that is older, older, all the nightmares, all the elemental forms that haunted Alex as he lay kicking, terrified, in the womb. Did you see *them*? There are hundreds of them. And he'll come to them. He *has* to."

"The protogenomorph?" Richard said, glancing at Helen.

Lytton straightened, looking impressed. "Indeed. The protogenomorph. The guardian in Alex, the part of him that has waited for you, the part that has been fighting the battle ..."

"What battle?"

"Against everything that was released from him when his dreams and his imagination were sucked through the mask." Lytton frowned through his filthy, matted hair. "You've not been fully briefed, then."

"He got my note," Helen said, "but under difficult circumstances. We've only just met again ... in the dell, as I'm sure you saw."

Lytton's look darkened, his lips pinched, though his gaze remained steadfastly upon Richard. "Are you going to kill me, Richard? If I turn my back will you club my brains out for trying to kill your son, as you believe?"

"Of course not. Not unless you attack him again."

"Then I'm relieved. I can't watch you both. I'm tired, I'm ill. And I need food, and rest. However ..."

He dropped the staff, shrugged off his filthy cloak to reveal a second layer of stitched hides, with a grimy wool ruff. This he removed and tossed to Helen, who grimaced at its stink, but wrapped it gratefully around her shoulders. Below this second cloak, Lytton was wearing stained cotton shorts and a torn tennis shirt. He put his outer cloak on again and shrugged as if to say, Sorry, not enough rags to go round.

In his slow voice, breathing hard, he said, "There's a tragic painting by Manet: *The Execution of the Emperor Maximilian* ... Have you ever seen it?"

Frowning, Richard said, "Yes. Of course."

"Four attempts, Richard. Four attempts at depicting the moment of a man's death, two feet from a firing squad. A year and a half of the artist's life, of his mind, his sweat, his madness. All that time to get a single *moment*. A tragic moment. A violent moment."

"It's a powerful painting . . ."

Lytton nodded thoughtfully. "A year and a half of hell, for Manet. When he had completed the painting, he wondered, in a letter to friend, if such a moment of violence, perhaps of evil, when subjected to such concentration, to such need to be expressed, might literally escape from time itself . . ."

Richard was perplexed by the earnestness and subject matter of Lytton's conversation: why were they standing in the discarded stone-skin of one of his son's mythagos, talking Art History?

Lytton chuckled hoarsely, wiping his mouth, his gaze on the etched and cracked face of a stone green man, whose piercing eyes watched through a mask of acanthus leaves. The sinister figure peered from below the marble legs of a horse, whose body and rider had long since broken away. He said, "Because unless my understanding is wildly wrong, such a moment is waiting for *us;* in some way it's all around us; we've been inhabiting it for years. Alex has waited for you for several years of your time, but for just weeks of his. He exists *outside* of time. He's frightened. He's watching. You've felt it—McCarthy touched it on several occasions. He has constructed worlds around himself, through which you and I stumble, all of us, stumble. And at the heart of that world, there is a moment. *The* moment! He has guarded it jealously, or a part of him has. The moment of his death, or transition, as seen by the wood! When it occurs, we *must* be there. Because a primal part of Alex—which Huxley called the protogenomorph—will be looking for *us,* to lead us to the hiding place. The protogenomorph will be a shadow, and the shadow behind it is the danger. Follow the small shadow, the guardian, and you will find Alex. I'll be following it too. It's the greater shadow that we must be wary of."

"And the greater shadow is what, exactly? Or don't you know?"

"I'm certain it's Trickster," Lytton said simply, with a half-glance at Helen. "The trickster in Alex. The manipulative manifestation of our first consciousness, our first awareness of the potential for deceit. It exists in all of us, blocked by the small shadow to the best of the small shadow's ability."

"Conscience?"

"Yes—but more *control*. The part of us that always recognizes the danger in trusting to our own needs, in believing that our lies might never be found out. It's a primary quality, there are many legends and heroic figures associated with its existence. It's a gatekeeper between states of mind, states of behavior, and is very deeply buried. Like dark and light, Trickster and Control cannot exist separately. Unfortunately, these aspects of your son are free in the wood and fighting each other. The primitive Trickster has been released and doesn't wish to return—but like all mythagos it is drawn to its maker, Alex. As Alex's protector, you threaten it and it has attacked you, most notably in the form of Jack-the-Chapel."

He had talked so much he had weakened his already damaged lungs, and he collapsed suddenly to his knees, leaning forward to retch bloodily and painfully into the stone dust. Helen crouched with him, arms round his broad back.

"You're a dying man, Alexander. We *have* to get you help."

"I'm an ill man, not a dying one. I'm closing in on Huxley. He and I are fated to meet, I'm convinced of it. Something in his journals. Once I find him, my health will turn for the better."

"I'm going to take you back to the Station. There's nothing here for us. Let's go back for a while, behind the lines, and catch up on what's been happening to us in this place. Get your strength back."

Glamor

They retraced the steps of their lunatic dance to the dark glade formed below the branches of the towering Mask Tree.

Richard stared at the jumble of forms, some so old that they were little more than shadows in his consciousness, others bright and new and recognizably Alex's. He told Lytton of his experience with the tree, when bosky, of the feeling of Alex singing.

"You saw deeper than us," Lytton surmised. "The masks are there, all of them. Alex is deeply in the tree, coming slowly to the surface. In time, all the masks will emerge. What then, I wonder?" He doubled up, coughing badly, and Helen tried to lead him away, but he shook her off, quite angrily. "We mustn't leave this place," he said forcefully, and for a while he stood in the overpowering rise of the bole, his hands against the dull colors that filled out the scratching and gouges in the bark. "This is where it all began," he whispered, and beat against the faces as if by sheer brute force he could strip away the brighter colors and reveal the primal ochres, the oldest of the masks, the deepest of the journeys of the spirit that was reflected, recorded in the tree.

"This is your son," he said softly to Richard. "Look at him! Images of the higher mind. This is the history that makes us all. This is Alex. Without it, he is just a hollow man. We cannot leave it. We may never find it again."

Helen tugged Lytton from the tree and led him to the path. "You have a flair for the melodramatic, Alexander. We must

go back—we need clothes and I need an old Coyote. The
tree won't go away. We'll come back in a few days."

"The tree won't go away," Lytton murmured, defeated.
"But we might miss the moment ..."

Lytton's own route to the Mask Tree had not been through
Old Stone Hollow. He had discovered the place a year or
more ago, after searching widely, carefully, following his instincts and the map of the layers of the wood which he had
compiled at the Station. He had found the cathedral, but no
Alex, and for a year had obsessively scoured the land around
the Tree, becoming ill, becoming weak in limb, attacked by
the wild, frozen by winter.

He had returned just once to the Station, marking out a
grueling four-day trek through freezing birchwoods, raging
rivers and deep valleys haunted by shadows and heavy with
oak and elm, which closed above him until he had felt stifled
in the heat, almost too frightened to continue. When he finally reached the camp, it was deserted, the haunt of scaven-
gers, and he had retraced his steps.

Now he led Richard and Helen back along that same
route, looting a mortuary enclosure on the way, for clothes,
caps and tarnished knives of bronze.

And it was clad in this way, in the trappings of the dead,
raw with itching from the coarse cloth, that Richard arrived
at the edge of a lake on the fifth morning and recognized
Wide Water Hollowing and the Viking vessel that he had
used against the serpent. Half a mile away around the shore
was the gully to Old Stone Hollow.

Now he thought again of Sarin, whom he had abandoned
so abruptly, instants after his deception of Jason. Would she
still be in the Station, waiting for him, warm and safe? He
felt suddenly apprehensive. For the last few days he had
been dogged by thoughts of the drowned argonauts and by a
curious anxiety that some of them might have survived. And
indeed, perhaps this had been a process of premonition at
work, for as he entered the gully, aware that there was indeed someone inhabiting Old Stone Hollow, his heart was
squeezed with fear as he heard the tuneless wail of bagpipes,
sounding from somewhere inside the Station. An image of a

grinning man, wrapped in black furs, squeezing the leather bag to make the sound of dying came to him . . .

"Jason," he whispered. "Oh Christ no . . ."

The pipes whined again, a long drawn out howl of pain, a mocking call to Richard before they were discarded, their challenge finished. Noticing Richard's sudden agitation, Helen led Lytton up the bank, to cover in the rocks, before returning to the wooden palisade. "Trouble?"

"An old man with a big grudge—he must have found his way back."

"You mean Jason . . ."

Richard thought of Sarin, and of the brutal man, and closed his eyes. But perhaps it was Sarin herself who was trying to extract music from the ancient instrument. Richard dismissed the thought—she had been too apprehensive of the pipes before, believing them to be a call to the shadow world. And to confirm his anxiety, as he walked into the tall grass he saw a black cloak, hanging from the branch of a tree, washed, wet and drying. A skull mask hung over the longhouse door. Two spears and a round leather shield had been placed on one side.

The breeze rustled grass, branches, and the wet cloak. Otherwise the Station was silent. A thin stream of smoke rose from the longhouse, more dead than alive. Richard motioned Helen down and then ran quickly, bent low, to the entrance to the Lodge. He picked up the shorter spear and the shield, which had a cracked and heavy wooden back, and stepped inside, advancing stealthily into the first room. A fire had burned here recently. Its ash, the trickle of smoke, still swirled through the light from the small window. The discarded pipes lay nearby, plus two rolls of fleece and a tunic of patterned leather.

Certain that the thunder of his heart could be heard clearly, Richard stretched out the spear toward the rough curtain between entrance and inner room. When he tugged it open he saw only gloom, a deserted place, illuminated thinly from holes in the roof. He stepped forward and a hand gripped his shoulder, spinning him round.

"Have mercy! Have mercy!" Lacan roared through his

belly laugh, as Richard made to strike. "It's only me! Spare my life!"

"Arnauld!" Richard flung his arms around the big man.

"My favorite Englishman! You *stink*!"

"I thought you were dead. Oh God, I thought you were dead."

"I should be. I struck a hard bargain! Sweet Virgin, what *is* that smell?"

"I was told you'd been killed on the *Argo*!"

"I wish I had been. I'm embracing you firmly, out of joy, yet asphyxiating with nausea. What have you been *eating*?"

"Mud and leaf litter, mostly."

Lacan was beside himself with mirth, slapping Richard stunningly on his left shoulder. "I should have expected no less from the English! Terrible cooks, terrible taste in food. Ah well, each to his own."

"I could murder a hare stew, right now. Christ it's so good—so wonderful—to see you—I thought you were dead!"

Lacan detached himself from Richard's second hug. "Enough of this excessive male bonding. There are limits, even for a Frenchman. Are you alone?"

From behind him, Helen murmured, "Any hare's blood left?" and jabbed the second spear gently into the big man's rump.

"Helen!" Lacan roared, with his second peal of genuine delight, and the ritual hugging and asphyxia began again.

With Lytton fed, washed, warm and sleeping, they sat in the longhouse around the new fire, prodding at the burning wood, feeling the glow of comfort, pigeon stew, and nettle tea course through their bodies. For Richard, the whole thing seemed normal again, and it took an unwelcome effort of will to construct an idea of the world outside the wood, where time ran from one hour to the next, and the seasons obeyed the spinning of the globe.

"You said you struck a hard bargain—how do you mean?"

Lacan picked at his yellowing teeth. His hair rattled with shells, newly tied into his black locks. "One of Jason's social workers—Tisamenus by name—pursued me for my pipes. He offered to strike off my head. I struck off his arm, then divided his skull—not without difficulty— into two uneven pieces. A *very* hard bargain."

He looked at Helen who was very solemn, watching him and frowning. Lacan nodded. "Before I left I had never killed a man. This man, this Tisamenus, was my third in the years I was lost. I have rarely been frightened, but in the hours after a killing fear becomes like an illness. Fear of what, exactly, I don't know. I am just afraid, and very sick. And very lonely ..."

Helen reached out and squeezed Lacan's toes through his thick boots. There was some silent conversation between them, a reference to a time before Richard's acquaintance with them, perhaps, and he remained respectfully quiet. Helen asked. "How did you get here?"

"On the *Argo*," Lacan said. "Disguised as Tisamenus. The ship came through Wide Water Hollowing, although I didn't realize this for a while."

Lacan had been lost on the shores of a hot sea, having strayed through a hollowing two years after he had left the Station. He had adventured like Hercules, loved, lived, sinned, sunned and consumed the local wild life with a gusto that even he, now, found hard to believe. When the *Argo* had beached, and an expedition come ashore, the adventurer called Tisamenus had become envious of the pipes, which he had heard being played in the caves above the shore. The *Argo* was being pursued by two war galleys of sinister demeanor and intent. When they had appeared on the sea horizon, Tisamenus called back to the ship, had masked himself and attacked the dark-bearded man, to claim the mysterious booty.

Lacan had then struck his deadly bargain.

Disguised as Tisamenus he had entered the *Argo*—"I was lost. I had nothing better to do"—and had kept his identity behind the mask during the ensuing battle.

"I was aware that there were living beings below the deck. Richard, this man, this Jason, was the worst of men. A true monster. If not for the battle he would have unmasked me and slaughtered me—although I would have exacted a terrible price! As I'm sure you both realize."

"Terrible," Richard concurred.

"Awesomely so," agreed Helen.

"Indeed! But the *Argo* plunged through a sea cave, which turned out to be a hollowing. On the other side it was cold. I jumped for the shore. Only days later did I discover that it was this shore, this place, my old home. Someone had been here recently, but had gone. Now I realize it was you 'two! I *knew* there had been a woman here . . ." He grinned at Helen.

"Not me," she said. "Been eating earthworms for a season or more."

Lacan frowned. "Who, then?" And his words reminded Richard that Sarin should be near.

"A small woman, very thin, very chirpy," he said. "She's called Sarinpushtam. She was on the *Argo* with you, but below the deck, and too often being abused by Jason."

Lacan shook his head. "I saw none of the prisoners, only the cooks. But I heard a young woman crying out sometimes, and not with pleasure. I'm glad I was only aboard for a few hours. I would have had to kill that man."

Declining Lacan's offer of help in locating Sarin— assuming she was still in the vicinity and hiding— Richard left the longhouse to look for her.

She was hiding beyond the Sanctuary, sheltering below an arch formed of two fallen pillars. Terrified and cold, she had been about to give herself to the lake, but Richard's call reached her hearing and confused her determination. When Lacan, disguised as Tisamenus, had come to Old Stone Hollow a few hours before, she had fled, remembering the cruelty of that particular argonaut, not willing to experience it further. When Richard explained that Lacan was a good and trusted friend, she wept. When he told her that Lacan was a fine cook she stopped weeping.

"Since you left I've eaten nothing but mushrooms, dried fish and something from your house. It was in a fragile crystal vessel and I had to break it." She closed her eyes at its memory and half smiled. "It was like the food eaten by the gods. It drove me mad with pleasure. But there was very little of it."

Meacham's Potted Beef! Good God. An English horror had appealed to a Bronze Age appetite.

"There's plenty more where that came from," Richard said. "Shops full. Unsold. Unwanted." Sarin was delighted at the thought, and Richard led her back to the river.

It was close to dusk. Helen had made clothes from the cloaks of the drowned argonauts and Lacan had gone to the lake to peer into its depths. He was obsessed, now, with the idea of dredging the vessel from the castle ruins below and refloating it. Being a sensible man, he was wary of the lake serpent, but for most of the afternoon, Helen said, he had been sitting in the gathering gloom, thinking of the possibilities of voyaging aboard so famous a ship.

Sarin washed, ate heartily and kicked the bagpipes, as if to reassure herself that they were not, as she feared, the source of summoning of evil shadows (which she called night feeders).

Another shadow had to be summoned, and Helen sat with Richard and Alexander Lytton and recalled the day she had journeyed to the edge of the wood and delivered the note to Richard's home.

"I went out through the Oak Lodge. There was a strange feel to the place, like movement, like ghosts. I assumed everything was mythago. I wasn't happy about it. Arnauld's snares and probes were everywhere, so maybe they were having an effect. He always said that Oak Lodge had more than its fair share of ghosts.

"I rested in the clearing for a while, and a young girl appeared. Again, I assumed this was a mythago, although my first thought was that she was a local. But she didn't speak. She was very willowy, very moon-faced, silvery, and beckoned me. I followed her through the wood, and came out into the field, above Shadoxhurst. No sign of the girl, but she was at the edgewood when I went back in, and again vanished as I followed her. As I say, a mythago of some sort.

"At Richard's house? I noticed that a woman was living there, which irritated me." She cast a glance at Richard. "I was tempted to leave a more loving note, but I didn't." She leaned toward him, "I did *miss* you, though." And after a pause, "That's about it. It was a flying visit to Richard through the ghost zone."

Lytton had been scribbling furiously, and thinking hard. Without looking up he said, "The moon-faced girl was silent. Do you mean she didn't speak?"

"Not a word."

"And when she moved? Could you hear her?"

With a shudder Helen suddenly shook her head. "No. No, I didn't hear her, come to think of it. It was quite eerie. I followed her by light. She didn't glow, I don't mean that. She sort of radiated. Ethereal, I guess. What do you think she was?"

"An elemental," Lytton said quietly.

"You and your elementals!" Helen was amused, glancing at Richard.

Ignoring her, Lytton went on, "What I don't understand is how she got there. Except that James Keeton re-emerged from the wood by way of Oak Lodge, hours older after an absence of months. Are you *sure* he said he'd come through the Lodge, Richard?"

"Quite sure. Like Helen, he said that he'd felt the presence of ghosts, many people. It had felt unearthly."

Outside, from the direction of the wooden defenses, a sound cut into the conversation. Richard stood and went to peer into the evening gloom. "It's Arnauld. At last."

Lacan had returned and was formally closing the gate, critically inspecting the crude hinges that Richard had contrived during his rebuilding. The Frenchman entered the longhouse and flung his cloak to one side.

"We must dredge up the *Argo*," he said. "It's an opportunity too good to be missed. What's cooking? *Who's* cooking?" he added with a nervous glance at Richard.

Then he saw Sarin. For a second he froze completely. Richard began to introduce the woman properly, aware that Sarin's face had registered an expression of startlement. He was startled himself when Lacan mumbled, "Excuse me. Nature calls."

The Frenchman reached for his cloak, almost angrily, and left the house abruptly, leaving Richard puzzled and Sarin disturbed. She stared after the big man for a long time, not responding to Richard's words. She was in a dreamy state, a daze, concerned and anxious, her face, usually so thin and pretty, now furrowed. Richard touched her shoulder and she jumped, then shook her head and crawled across the floor, to curl up on her furs and think.

When, after an hour or more, Lacan had not returned, Richard went out and called for him, but without success. After dark, with the fire dead, Helen curled up against him, below the fleeces from the *Argo,* and while Lytton groaned in his nightmare sleep and Sarin chattered like a bird, twitching and shifting below her covers, they made love side by side, very gently and with almost no sound.

"I'm beginning to like you, Mr. Bradley."

"Then why do you keep calling me Next-Buffalo-Dinner?"

At some time during the long night Richard was disturbed by the sigh of the bagpipes. Helen was sleeping against his chest, her hands holding him intimately. He detached himself without waking the woman and followed the dark shape of Lacan out into the tall grass. The night shadow of the big man was fleet as it passed through the moonlight to the open gates of the Station.

"Arnauld!" Richard called softly. "Arnauld! Where are you going? What's the matter with you?"

"Leave me alone!" the Frenchman whispered furiously, his eyes gleaming in the moonlight. And with those brutal words he was gone again.

Richard couldn't sleep, and imagined that he had stayed awake all night, staring into the darkness of the longhouse, breathing the fading scents of woodsmoke from the fire. And yet at first light, when he stirred from the fleeces again, he saw that Sarin was not in her corner. He went out into the dewy morning. There was a slight breeze and the air was chill on his skin. The brightening sky was cloudless, still purple over the eastern forest. The gates to the compound were open, but it was to the overhang above the cave system that Richard went, aware that he had heard furtive movement high above him, where the rock curved out of sight.

He pulled himself up the steep path and came onto the cliff top, caught for a moment by the richness of color, the spread of fire where the sun was rising over Ryhope. Then he saw the hunched figure of the girl, a few yards away, so dark against a tree that for a moment he had missed her. She was watching Lacan, who was hunkered down on his haunches, supporting himself with a heavy staff, his ringleted hair hanging lank around a bowed head.

As Richard moved up to Sarin he saw tears in her eyes and blood on her lower lip. He put a comforting arm on her shoulder and felt her tremble through the thin cloth of her dress.

"How long have you been here?"

"Since he called me. Before first light."

"He called you?" Richard watched the motionless figure on the cliff top. Lacan might have been a statue, save for the fact that the wind rattled the shells at the ends of his ringlets, and occasionally his broad back, below the draping black cloak, heaved deeply.

"I heard his voice in my dream. I was so afraid of him when he came to the camp. He was still wearing the mask. But when I saw his face, I knew him. But I don't know from where. He just makes me feel wounded . . ."

Wounded? Richard watched the anxiety on Sarinpushtam's lean face, the furrows on her high forehead, the well and ebb of tears in her richly dark eyes. She was Lacan's mythago. That had to be the answer. But there was something more, and Lacan was in distress about it.

"Have you tried approaching him?"

"I've called to him. He just growls and crushes into himself."

"Why don't you go back to the house? I'll try and talk to our bearlike friend. Whatever it is, it can't last."

Sarin hesitated then stood and ran, almost angrily, back down the track, swinging from trunk to trunk, slipping and skidding out of sight, occasionally slapping the trees and regretting with a cry that she'd been so angry.

The sounds of her departure disturbed Lacan, who turned his head slightly, caught Richard approaching and looked away.

"Arnauld? Call me a nuisance, throw me over the cliff,

tell me to mind my own business. But tell me what's wrong, if you can. It hurts us all to see you in such pain."

"Two hours more," Lacan grunted, shaking his head. Beyond him, the sky was dazzling. He leaned on his staff and the wind blew his hair. The sun caught fire in his eyes.

"Two hours?"

"To think. To be alone. Don't worry about me. Please, just bugger off. I'll be down in two hours. Don't let her get distressed."

"Sarin?"

"Please. Look after her. I smelled blood on her, Richard. Don't let her do anything foolish."

"She was only biting her lip. She's confused. She's yours, of course. Your mythago . . ."

"Of course. Go away, Richard. I need to be alone a while longer."

A hind had come down to the lake, but bolted as Richard reacted to its presence with a cry. The hunt, with Helen, took several hours, and it was Helen's accuracy with the short bow that claimed the kill. She paunched the steaming beast with a confidence that left Richard amazed, and she rebuked the man for his teasing.

"Fresh meat, Richard!"

"It'll have to hang for a while."

"Not its liver, my man. That we'll have tonight."

"You're beginning to sound like Lacan . . ."

As they carried the carcass back to Old Stone Hollow, skirting the lakeside, they saw Lacan walking among the distant rocks, his hood drawn over his head against the drizzle. Richard called to him, but he kept walking, glancing occasionally across the wide water, his face grim.

They hung the deer, and prepared a stew pan of the liver with wild vegetables. Lytton was writing furiously in his notebook. "It's so important to record everything. *Everything.* When I write, ideas come. That's how I worked out the function of the protogenomorph, after McCarthy's shadowy encounter with it. Explanation later, Richard. And I would like to hear an account of what has happened to you as well. Alex is everywhere. Can you feel him? He's watching still. He will pick the moment to come to us, and we must be ready, not just physically, but mentally as well. Where's Lacan?"

"Still brooding. Still upset."

"Upset? About what?"

"I'm not sure."

From the other room, where Helen was stitching hides together, she called, "Matilde!"

Lytton nodded, said, "I see. Where is she?"

"Somewhere about. Waiting for him."

Without further response, leaving Richard infuriatingly confused, he returned to his notebook.

Richard went through the curtain and watched Helen at her task. "Matilde? Sarin by another name?"

Helen cocked her head. She had a length of coarse thread between her teeth, and was using a bone needle very effectively. Her dark eyes engaged Richard for a moment, thoughtfully, perhaps making a decision. Then she nodded. "I guess so."

"His daughter?"

"His wife. He'll talk when he's ready."

Lytton came through, his notebook closed. He rubbed his chin as he watched Helen work, then sat down, cross-legged on the floor, indicating that Richard should do the same.

"It's making a sort of sense, now, as much as anything in Huxley's first forest can ever make sense . . .

"The way Keeton described his sojourn in Ryhope reminds me of the land of faerie—unlike Ryhope, in the *fey* world you age *less* than the world outside, and that is what happened to Keeton, and what has happened to Alex. Alex has created his own time, and to do this he is using the elemental in him, the earliest myths, the earliest part of consciousness, when notions of time itself became defined, both in the terms we would understand it, and in the mystical time of gods and faerie that these days we would call fantastic.

"When Keeton lost his daughter in 1957 his anguish, his desperation, entered the wood as an entity *apart* from him, crystallizing—*condensing,* as Elizabeth Haylock used to say—into the complex matrix of energy and time that underlies this place.

"Is it possible that Keeton was protected by a form of 'glamor'? Held out of time by a protecting, sheltering cloak of faerie magic? When he left the wood, the glamor remained behind, an echo. It had formed into the shape of his own daughter, and lingered there for years—it's still there! When you encountered it, Helen, you followed it to the edge, you passed *through* it, because it was another form of hollowing, only this passage connected with a time eight years before. It was waiting for you on your return, after leaving the note, and again you tried to encounter the moonfaced girl, and so you passed back to the present."

Helen was hunched over her work, her head shaking slightly, the silver locks on each side glinting in the candlelight. She said, quite simply, "If that's right, then I'm frightened. Too much of my life has been interfered with by time. I've wasted too much time. Time has wasted me. Time has wasted my family. By fear, it has tricked us out of our lives. If Coyote is Time, then I'm going to be done with him now."

She looked up at Richard. There were tears in her eyes not of sadness but of anger. She reached out and touched his hand, and without even understanding what he was doing Richard folded his arms around her and kissed the moist, warm parting in her hair. "Don't lose me," she said. "Every hour, every day—it's ours, not Trickster's. Don't lose me. Don't let it all go."

While Lytton frowned restlessly, watching the kiss, unable to continue because of the sudden passion, the sudden need, Richard embraced Helen with all his heart. As their mouths parted and they smiled, their eyes lingering on each other, Richard had an image of Alex, smiling and clapping his hands in delight.

"My son's going to adore you," he said.

Alex wouldn't know about Alice. He wouldn't know his mother had gone—

"Glad you've come to believe in him."

She turned back to Alexander Lytton. "So this 'echo' Keeton created was like the 'moment out of time' you talked about, like the Manet painting. So much anguish that it formed a focus—"

"Drawing to it everything that was related to that anguish—shaped like the daughter, but calling to anyone or anything that was associated with Tallis."

Richard tried to absorb the images and ideas that were raised by Lytton's half-distracted account. The man was thinking aloud: he was unfocused, but he hardened that gaze as Richard said, "How does Alex fit in?"

"Alex was the substitute for Tallis. When Alex stared through the Moondream mask—a hollowing mask, don't forget—he was torn through it, stripped of everything but flesh and bone and *dragged* through that mask.

"Keeton's anguish, Keeton's need, his need for his child—he reached from inside the wood through the mask, reaching to the moment of his real-time death and clutched at the memories of Tallis that he could feel there—all of them in your son.

"A reflection of Alex's mind, in the wood, is in the faces on the Mask Tree. That's where the boy will come—that's where we'll see the moment of his transition, a moment that we'll follow to the cathedral, where Alex himself is hiding."

At dusk Lacan called from the river, and Richard went out through the tall grass to find him. He was aware that Sarin was among the elder bushes that concealed the deep cave. She was watching furtively. Lacan, swathed in a dark cloak, eyes glistening with cold, leaned against a heavy tree, staring distantly toward the gully. He acknowledged Richard, then walked away, up the steep bank, back to the Sanctuary, through the place where once the underfoot had been a graveyard of decaying creatures.

By the hollowing, by the marble pillars where Richard had tricked Jason, he turned and worked his staff into the ground.

"I am very lost," he said quietly. "You must help me."

Richard started to reach a reassuring hand, but drew back as angry eyes caught his. He said only, "I've offered friendship. Helen and Lytton are very discreet. I know that Sarin reminds you of your wife. I have a half idea that you've been seeking her . . . that she died, and you've been seeking her . . ."

Lacan seemed to collapse slightly, nodding, as if both relieved and comforted by Richard's simple intuition. "I remember telling you—so many years ago, now—but I remember saying in answer to a question of yours that I was looking for the moment of my death. Richard . . . if you had known Matilde . . . if you could have once seen her, heard her speak, been touched by her glamor . . . she was ethereal. I know that, now. I always have. I loved her so much. When the wood killed her, it should have strangled me with its creepers too. But it left me to mourn her, and to die and be reborn, as it were, and then to hunt for her with a force of life that is all that protects me from the shadowland."

Richard was about to make a comment, a naive interruption questioning why, if Lacan had now found his beloved Matilde, he found it so hard to speak to her. The Frenchman silenced him angrily, then apologized and walked stiffly back to a point, beyond this copse, where the ridge of the high cliff could just be seen.

Softly, he said, "I didn't expect to find her like this. I've spent so long looking, I need her so much . . . and suddenly I am aware that she is dying. She has no life, only an appearance in our world for a few days, a few weeks. Like all these things we summon, she is no more than a shadow, strong in the sun, doomed to dusk beauty and then annihilation. I've always known it. Of course I have. But I've never accepted the truth of the matter, that when I found her she would be wood and earth, she would be transient. Oh God in Heaven, I can't bear to lose her again, I can't bear to lose her again . . ." He started to shake and Richard squeezed his shoulder, helpless and distressed as his friend's emotion began to surface.

"She's strong," he whispered. "I've got to know her. She's strong."

"Not strong enough. Look at her. There's nothing on her, no flesh even for the crows. But it *is* her. After so long . . . she *has* surfaced from the wood. And I know, I just *know,* that she will never surface again . . ."

"Then go and be with her while you can. What more is there to do?"

"What more? Why, to save her from Matilde's fate, of course. I couldn't bear that. I feel lost. I think I must become lost again."

There was a fleet movement ahead of them, and both men ducked slightly, scanning the trees, the ruins. Richard strung his bow, drew a flighted arrow. Lacan glowered at the shadows, hands caressing the blackthorn staff.

He looked at Richard abruptly. His sadness was overwhelming, but now there was almost anger painting his features.

"Were you born close to this wood?"

"Far away. I moved to Shadoxhurst when I married Alice."

"There's the difference between us, then, since I *was* born near a wood like this. In Brittany. A vast forest through which you could only follow certain tracks, certain paths, much as we experience in Ryhope. It was a wonderful place. Huge stones circled it, hidden by the edge: it was a wood that had grown inside a stone circle and had reached out its skirts to hide the gray markers. It was a place of ponds and lakes, and deep, moist hollows. It was a place of magic.

"I lived in a cottage at the bottom of a hill. Some nights, winter nights especially, people came from the wood and passed along a lost track, close to my garden. They walked over the hill and to a vanishing place on the other side. Sometimes I followed them, but I could never see where they went. Perhaps I didn't have the faith, the belief in them, perhaps I simply didn't have the right way of looking.

"When I was a child I would explore the lakes, hiding in the bushes and watching the gray shapes, like mist creatures, that would come and stand by the water, staring into the depths. They were ghosts. Many of them cried silently before returning to the wood. All seemed to be searching for something. I have no idea what.

"When the war came, my father fought and came home wounded. I was too young, but eager to fight. In 1943 I left Brittany by fishing boat for England, to join a French Canadian command. I was sixteen. Before I left I went back to the lake. It was dusk. A woman came out of the shadows, a gray woman, and touched my eyes and my lips. She had appeared so fast, and she disappeared so fast, that I was too shocked to think. I remember only that I had been kissed on each eye, each cheek, each lip.

"When I arrived in England, I was there for only two weeks and suddenly the war ended. I came home, dizzy and confused, because I found that two years had passed.

"The cottage was shuttered, my parents were gone. Neighbors told me that they had followed a laughing woman into the wood one winter, and that was the last they had seen of them. I had been held safe in some sort of spell. Or had I? Two years had passed and I have memory of only two weeks.

"Then, in the edgewood, I met Matilde. I thought she was from a local village. Perhaps she was. She looked very like the woman who had touched me with her glamor, but Matilde was only sixteen. She was delicious in every way, sensuous in every way. Her laughter a joy.

"We lived together in the cottage. I stopped grieving for my parents. I was consumed with love for her, with her smell, her voice, her teasing. Then our son was born, but he was not born well. In a few months we realized that he was blind. And although he made an infant's sounds, he didn't speak as he reached the age when other children begin to chatter. He had no language. By the time he was four . . . it was terrible. I can't tell you how terrible, Richard. Matilde was—well, there is only one word: she was ruined. The boy gradually began to see— only colors at first, then shapes, then the whole world, except for shadows. He began to speak—little words at first, then wild descriptions, then haunting accounts of what his mind's eyes could see. At the same time, Matilde faded.

"In her dreams she screamed and fought with shadow creatures. She barricaded the cottage obsessively. She gradually lost her sight, until all she could see were shadows. She lost her speech. As the boy learned words, so they vanished from her, until she could only say two words aloud, my own first name being one of them, the other, something I never understood. It was such a terrible thing. She saw the world as shadows, and the shadows were alive in ways that were not right. She tried to communicate this to me. The shadows of trees chased her. The shadows of foxes prowled around her on moonless nights. It was as if she was being punished for having the badly-born child. I called him ghost-born, but as Matilde faded, so he grew stronger.

"When he slept, my passion for Matilde was always in earnest, and she responded with such need, such longing, such desperate physicality, clinging to me without break, that I began to realize that these moments of intimacy were her only way of expressing the love she felt, at a time when she was safe. And yet she never opened her eyes, never uttered sound, except for my name.

"I was heartbroken. I was dying. It was an endless battle with her to stop her sealing the house, with wood, with corrugated iron, with animal skins, with sheets of plastic, with anything she could find.

"Then one day she was gone, and my son had gone too. I searched for them desperately.

"I found them in the lake. When I dragged them to the shore, when I pushed the wet hair from their faces, when I kissed the white flesh on each face, the eyes, the cheeks, the lips, I could not tell them apart. I obliterated my son's name from my memory, because at that moment I believed he had never existed. It was the moment of my own death, and I entered the lake and fell into a sleep without pain.

"I woke in my own cottage, on the couch, covered by a blanket. I had been found by one of the villagers wandering aimlessly, not drowned at all. The man knew nothing of Matilde. He knew nothing of my son. He said I was a hermit, always barricading my cottage, and he was terrified of me. Indeed, I looked frightful.

"And the rest you know. She dwelt in my dreams continuously, but I began to snare and trap the ghosts of my wood, in the hope of finding her. I became famous for it, and word spread. One day, Alexander Lytton found *me*. I learned of mythagos. I clung to his invitation to come to Ryhope Wood because it was a last chance to resurrect Matilde. Maybe Lytton exaggerated the possibilities. He wanted what he wanted for his team and he saw possibilities in me. I came gladly, Richard. Life was then, and still is, as nothing without that lovely woman."

"Then go to her."

Lacan turned furiously. "But don't you see? After all I've said? She never existed! I was touched by something, some charm . . . my life was a charm, and Matilde a part of that charm. She was only my dream, made real. I have tried to make her real again, but she is still just that, a dream, a shadow. There never was Matilde. There never was a son. And now there is a woman who is everything my heart longs for, but she exists only because I needed to fulfill my selfish needs in *one* life. Long gone! I have created the shadow of a shadow. This Sarin is less even than a mythago. She's the hopeless object of desire of an aging Frenchman. If I touch her, she'll die, I know it. She'll die."

Richard shouted his frustration with the big man. "And maybe she won't! If you even have a few days with her, than have them, Arnauld. Sarin is very moved by you. She feels strongly for you. Tell her what you've told me. Maybe the two of you, maybe together you'll *find* the strength to survive. How can you tell until you try it?"

Lacan glanced at Richard, frowning, his eyes filled with sadness. "There is more to it," he whispered, looking away. "But perhaps only things that should be forgotten. Ryhope Wood, the wood in France: they are the same wood, they share a common time, a common space, a dimension we cannot really see, the same shadows, the same dreams. We have no way of defining it, this imaginary time, this *sylvan* time. It's beyond our language." He was in despair again, sighing deeply. "What do I do?" I couldn't bear to see her die through grief and fear, like Matilde . . ."

Remembering the encounter of a few days before, Richard said, "Sarin nearly died when I switched on the defenses, but she survived. She's strong, Arnauld. One of Jason's argonauts only lasted seconds. Don't underestimate her. Love the shadow while you can . . ."

And suddenly, perhaps because she'd been listening, Sarin was there, standing a short way away, her wiry body wrapped firmly in a thick wool cloak, her face dark with anguish and curiosity, and perhaps a touch of longing. Her gaze was fixed on Lacan. The Frenchman watched her, then smiled, extending his arm, hand outstretched to her. As

Richard took his leave, the girl came over to the marble pillar and entered Lacan's deep embrace.

Curious, which is to say nosy, Richard watched them from the shadows. The two of them cried for a while, then laughed. Lacan began to speak and they walked away from the Sanctuary, deeper into the wood. Their movement disturbed birds, but soon there was silence. An hour later, crows erupted from the canopy a half-mile or so distant. As the sun began to set a nest of herons set up a clattering of bills, a vile objection to movement below.

At dawn, Richard was woken by the strident sound of bagpipes playing a jig, just outside the palisade, where two people were washing in the crisp water of the river.

He and Helen went out to join in the icy fun, and it was then that they saw the first signs of the world dying around them.

The Triumph of Time

Winter, like a branching white scar, had begun to streak the greenwood, patches and lines of frost in the verdure that slowly spread, ice killing the summer leaf and the hardwood trunks, stone turning into the same soft, crumbling decay that had infested the cast-off cathedral.

Sarin scampered naked from the river, grabbing for her cloak. Lacan, rotund and hairy, crawled out after her, using his hand self-consciously to protect his groin. Around them, leaves fell like ash. The air was winter crisp, and their breath steamed.

From outside the longhouse Lytton shouted excitedly, "This is Alex's work! He's calling to us!"

Helen looked at the encroaching winter, frowned, then whispered to Richard, "How the hell can he always be so sure?"

"I don't know. But I'm not about to argue. Are you?"

"To what end? Lytton knows what Lytton knows; Huxley's shade whispers to him . . ."

She turned and ran to the longhouse, to find warm clothes and food supplies. Richard thought of Old Stone Hollow and curiosity took him through the ice-glazed elderwood.

Below the cliff, the paintings on the overhang had faded, the rock flaking away and taking the colors and the shapes with it. The flow of water had dried. The cavern was a barren place. Lytton entered the overhang and stared around him, taking his weight on his staff, his gray locks iridescent with frost. "I suspected as much: this place was from Alex's imagination, and like the rest, he's killed it now. What else I wonder? He'll be killing all his creations."

Anxiously, Richard thought of Sarin, but the woman, bulky in her new furs, was following Lacan toward the Hollow. She looked vibrantly alive.

"What's happening?" the Frenchman asked.

"We need to return to the Mask Tree," Lytton murmured, his face to the sky as he sniffed and tasted the winter air. "Alex is close to us again. I can feel it. He's calling to us. He's *coming* to us."

"He's coming here?" Richard asked.

Narrow eyes in a bone-white face glanced briefly, irritably at him. "No. Not here. He's trapped in the cathedral. But I think he must be breaking from the moment of frozen time ... He'll come to the Mask Tree. I'm sure of it!"

"We'll have to risk the hollowing," Helen said. "Through the cave."

"Too dangerous. Besides, Richard only got through because he was bosky, and his son was able to guide him. Perhaps he did the same for you, when *you* went through the pipe. But we can't risk the cave, now. Too many outflows ..."

"But it's a four-day trek along the land route," Richard said, appalled at the thought of the return journey to the Tree.

Lytton smiled at him, a gesture of dry amusement. "Then let's waste no time. If we miss him, Alex may have no choice but to stay hidden forever. And what he's shed to the wood will stay in the wood, and I simply can't have that."

While the rest made their brief preparations, Richard scoured the area around the Station. The Sanctuary was intact, although the white and frozen corpses of a man and a woman were crouched nearby. In the summer wood beyond he found the icy mass of a boar, the broken spear with which it had run for most of its life still embedded in its flank. From the lakeside, where Jason had landed, he watched the Viking longship become engulfed in frost and slowly crack. Warm, summer air gusted, followed by the frozen blast of deep winter. The clouds, the water, all seemed to be divided between the seasons, and Richard marveled at the way his son was drawing back his creations, sucking the magic forests, lands and creatures of childhood back toward the cathedral, and the giant elm, with its shallow faces, the place, Lytton now believed, that had been Alex's first entry into the world of Ryhope Wood.

The last thing he saw, before Helen came up behind him putting her arms around his chest and whispering, "Stop brooding. It's time to go and find the boy," was the frozen body of the serpent. It surfaced suddenly, a coiled iceberg, the head twisted up and away from the rest of its body, the haunting eye glazed-over and lifeless now. The creature floated there, melting slowly, disintegrating. As it decayed so it turned, seeming to watch the shore, then subsiding, taking the last memory of a terrible encounter, the last memory of Taaj, as it condensed back into the lake above the stone castle.

It was such an odd feeling: the realization that Alex had created both the courageous boy, a powerful reflection of himself, and the monster that had consumed him.

Richard's thoughts turned briefly to the *Argo,* on the lake bed, but if that vessel too had been Alex's creation, now consumed by frost, it held its secret in the depths.

"Come *on,*" Helen urged. She had Richard's pack, his new cloak of crudely cured skins, a hood against the rain.

He followed her, followed the others, round the wide lake shore, to the valley between high, crumbling cliffs, which led back to the dell and the carved tree.

To avoid freezing, they followed, as far as possible, the pockets and zones of spring and summer. Inevitably there were times, lasting for hours, when they were forced to trek through winter woods, deep with snow and silent, or icelocked and dangerous. A new life had begun to generate in these landscapes, to replace the vast creatures that now lay or stood like ice carvings: mastodon, cave bears, elks, shaggy bison and snarling wolves. Darker, livelier forms of these beasts of the frozen world now emerged, including dire wolves, which dogged their tracks with obvious intent and willful abandon of strategy. Lytton confidently declared that these new creatures were "condensing from our own minds, appropriate to the land around us."

As ever, he seemed in his element, trudging through snowdrifts, cloak swirling, staff bearing his slight weight, white-haired head always turned to the far horizons as he absorbed the world around him, a magus leading his doubting followers.

In the summer wood they had to use force to avoid the dire wolves, which attacked in groups of three, acting without caution, easily driven back. Helen shot game birds, but they avoided heavier meat since they were traveling fast and light. And they indulged in wary, careful exchange with the mythagos that emerged, usually at dawn or dusk, to share their food and fire, or chatter in strange tongues. There was usually time for Sarin to comprehend the languages of their guests; when she failed, she proved to be adept, as indeed was Richard, at interpreting meaning from sound and gesture.

Their most successful encounter was with a mailed knight, a young man on foot, a blue-eyed and blond warrior from the early Age of Chivalry who entranced Helen with his smile and his descriptions of the river-barge he sought, where his lady's heart was hidden in the body of the black dog Cunhaval. The hound slept on the afterdeck. A ghost steered the barge. Its destination was a fabled castle.

The knight was named Culloch. He was Durham-born, but had squired at the court at Caer Navon, before taking his oath and shipping out to fight for the liberation of the Holy City in the Crusade.

"How big is this dog?" Helen asked.

The knight licked his fingers as he finished eating and pointed to the tree tops. "As tall as the Cross, lady. It has eaten a king's ransom in gold from our new minster, and swallowed the purest heart that ever beat within the court and summer-tower of Caer Navon. I shall cut my way with iron into the body of the black dog and release that heart. The Cross will be my strength."

"Sounds messy," Helen murmured dryly. "But good luck. God's speed."

Culloch lowered his gaze. "You give me courage with

your smile and your faith in the Cross. God's speed your-selves."

Helen watched him go, a glittering shape in his iron mail, swallowed by shadows within moments.

"In his situation, I think I'd prefer a large lump of poi-soned meat."

Sarin had begun to feel the cold; her exuberance faded, her energy sapped, and Richard and Lacan took it in turns to carry her through the worst of the frozen wastes. Her loss of defiance in the teeth of winter disturbed Lacan, depressed him. He showed a side of his character that Richard found hard to accommodate, a too-easy resignation, a fatalism that perhaps was protecting him against the anticipated grief of the girl's death.

When he could, Richard bullied the man into exercising a more cheerful and optimistic attitude, at least in front of Sa-rin herself, and Lacan said, "Damn! You're right!" hugged Richard, but continued to behave in exactly the same gloomy way.

Helen whispered, "The man's tired. Deep down, he's ex-hausted. To the core. He's been too many years in his own company, too many years hoping. Give him time."

"Of course I will," Richard said irritably. "I understand Lacan well enough. It's Sarin I'm concerned for. If she needs *his* strength to extend her life, right now she's dying faster than she need."

In the summer woods Sarin cheered up, found fresh heart, fresh strength. And at these times it was she who teased the big man, and over the days Richard saw the relationship be-tween the two of them deepen and intensify.

Four days after they had begun their journey inward, they emerged in a downpour from the saturated forest into the heavy ground-haze of a clearing below wide canopy. The ro-bust and serpentine roots that flowed across the ground marked the place as the Mask Tree, and the huge, dark trunk ahead of them was the place where Alex's imagination was embedded.

Already Richard had seen what Lytton had been shocked to notice: there were no marks now, no masks, no faces on

Robert Holdstock

the trunk, nothing but ridged bark, stained with white lichen, infested with black and orange fungal growth, rotting.

Lytton cried out in frustration. "I knew we should have stayed!" But a moment later, as he moved toward the tree, he changed his tone. "No! There *is* something here."

He began to trace his finger round a shallow oval scratching, throwing his staff to one side, spreading himself against the trunk. "Yes! There's something ... Richard. Quickly! Come here ..."

He had found a single design. It was Moondream. Richard recognized it at once, from the bark mask that James Keeton had been clutching on his return from the Otherworld, so many years ago, now: half-crescent, sharply focused eyes, a half-smile, the same outline. It was Keeton's daughter's mask, his only memento of the lost girl.

Richard stared at the crudely carved face, touched its eyes, its mouth.

This has nothing to do with Alex.

He wondered aloud what had happened to the rest of the faces and masks. Had they been re-absorbed, as all of Alex's creations in the wood had been sucked back? Then why had this particular image survived?

Lytton tapped at the bark, curious for a moment, then enlightened, and he confirmed Richard's intuitive thought. "This design was not from your son." He looked back at the face, spread his hands over the shallow tracing. "But if not from Alex—then who? Who could have carved this face? You can see that it's old. But it's not ancient."

The answer was not so much obvious as suggested by memory. If Richard recollected his son's account correctly, Moondream had been Tallis Keeton's favorite mask. And it was Moondream that she had dropped for her father to find at the entrance to Ryhope Wood, at the hollowing where Hunters Brook entered the forest. Had Tallis herself, then, carved the face that was now etched across the growing and gigantic tree?

A few hours later, with the rain easing off, Sarin came running into the half-light below the spreading branches. Lacan was noisily cracking wood, constructing a temporary shelter along the lines of Helen's bower. He heard Sarin's loud call of, "Someone coming!" and pulled into deeper cover. Richard and Lytton followed him, slipping on the wet underfoot and sliding onto their bellies in the cruel embrace of thorn and briar. Sarin pointed to where the undergrowth was moving, and a man stepped out to face the Mask Tree. He seemed dazed: his hair was disheveled, his face streaked with dirt and blood.

He was wearing a red dressing gown, tied at the front. He was barefoot.

"My God," Richard whispered, "it's James Keeton. That's exactly how I found him, years ago. He ran in front of my car. James Keeton ..."

The figure of the man walked unsteadily into the clear space below the high, wide canopy. He was clutching a piece of wood in his hands, holding the object close to his stomach. He stepped up to the trunk of the tree and stared at the face, silent for a long while, shivering with cold, his right hand occasionally reaching out to stroke the heavy bark.

And suddenly he called out Tallis's name. He repeated the cry, and the name extended into a howl of pain, a wail of despair. Again and again he called for his daughter, dropping the mask, leaning against the tree, hitting his forehead against the wood. His agony reduced Sarin to tears, and Lacan, who was crouched beside her, folded her into his cloak. Richard felt moved to tears himself. He wanted to go to the man, began to do so, and almost struck Lytton when the gray-faced Scot forced him back.

"Don't interfere. This is not his moment. It's *Alex's*. If you want your son, you'll have to let him come. I *know* he'll come ..."

Lytton quickly scanned the surrounding forest, listening hard for a second approach. Helen held her head in her hands, half watching the screaming, sobbing man at the tree, wincing as the wailing grew louder, shaking her head helplessly. When Richard put a hand on her shoulder she leaned toward him, but still tried to block her ears against Keeton's appalling sadness.

The ground below them trembled. By the tree, James Keeton had stopped crying. He took a nervous step back,

then reached quickly to pick up the Moondream mask,
clutching it to his chest as he stepped away from the elm. At
the same time the air turned chill and dry, and the noises of
the world around them receded, as if the atmosphere had
suddenly rarefied.

The tree shimmered with light.

The face of Moondream stood out against the black bark,
a thin trace of silver light. No sooner had it been defined,
clearly enough for Richard to see the details of the eyes and
mouth, than it was lost below other lines and slashes that
seemed to burn out of the wood, one face after another, then
a proliferation of features, haunting, frightening attributions,
male, female, animal, some from the dreamworld. The mon-
tage of masks spread rapidly to cover the whole tree. Silver
light spilled like a fine spray up into the canopy, down to the
distended root-mass where James Keeton still stood, half
hunched, in shock and wonderment, his pale skin reflecting
the rich colors of the emerging faces.

Suddenly Keeton again screamed out Tallis's name, a raw
and primal cry of such need, such anguish, that the whole
wood seemed shocked and silent for a moment.

And then the trunk of the tree exploded soundlessly, en-
veloping Keeton in elemental shapes!

Figures streamed through from the dark trunk, ethereal
and huge, some running, some riding, some gleaming with
armor, others in a swirl of cloaks or skins, colors bright. The
ghostly forms flowed around the shattered form of James
Keeton, but as each figure reached the edge of the clearing
and entered the wood, so it became solid. Around Richard
the forest was suddenly alive with movement.

Lytton hissed, "Great God, I didn't think of this—he's
coming from *inside*!"

A purple-painted man ran toward Richard, a round shield
held in one hand, a short sword in the other, hair flying, lips
drawn back to expose brilliant white teeth. The figure leapt
across the crouching man, crashed into the underbrush, and
with an ululation of triumph raced away into the gloom,
leaving Richard with an image of faces and whorls and
swirls decorating the body from head to feet.

"What are we witnessing?" he asked loudly.

"Witnessing?" Lytton repeated. "Alex's death! The moment his history was sucked from him. You were in the room at the time. Remember? Look at it! This is an encyclopedia of what we have *all* inherited. Everything is here! And I can never remember it all. There's just too much! We must watch for the boy! Watch for the shadow."

He turned to Lacan and Helen, repeating the instruction. "It will be small, no more than the *shadow* of a boy. When you see it, follow it. Don't lose it!"

The procession of forgotten heroes continued for a few seconds more and Richard recognized what Helen had called the "Hood" form, and Jacks, and an axe-wielding Viking, and a woman with hair like flowing fire, dressed in checkered leather trousers and jerkin, leading two gray mastiffs on long leashes. This might have been Queen Boudicca, a particular favorite of Alex's. A wagon and horses came through, driven by hunched, shrouded figures. Warriors walked out of the tree, some of them Greek, some Roman, some painted, some with helmets of striking horror. Women flowed from the tree, green girls, cloaked matrons, women with the look of magic about them, or of the fight for freedom.

Alexander Lytton, his face shining with delight and color, was uttering a catalog of recognition as each hunter, warrior, crusader, wizard or wild man passed: "Peredur ... Tom Hickathrift. And that's Hereward the Wake! Fergus, from the Cattle Raid of Cooley. Where's Cu Chullain? Morgana! Jack the Hound Killer there! Guinevere. And Kei, from Arthur's court. That's the Henge Builder of Avebury! A crane hunter ... Dick Turpin! The Woman of the Mist. That's Llewelyn!"

To Richard, they were an army of blindly running ghosts, streaming silently from the tree and vanishing noisily into the woods.

The explosion of life ceased as abruptly as it had begun.

At some point in the procession, James Keeton turned and walked away. Richard was half aware of his departure, but no one had followed the man. He had stepped away, into the oblivion of memory, into an encounter that was now years in Richard's past.

Still stunned by what he had seen, Richard watched as the Mask Tree darkened; the carved faces once again had vanished. He imagined they would not return. Whatever their function, that function was now fulfilled.

And yet—a movement in the darkness told of a struggle. A moment later a small shadow burst into the empty clearing and scampered to the left. It was so fleet, so undefined, that for a moment even Lytton hesitated, his gaze on the great creature that was stretching from the trunk, striving to free itself from the tree.

Then he was on his feet and running after the shadow. Richard delayed for an instant only, astonished at the writhing tree-man, its face and body a mass of leaves, glistening branches like tusks twisting from its gaping mouth. Behind it, other twigling limbs were reaching for the cold air of the clearing. A shrill clattering began to sound from them.

Richard raced after Lytton, following the man by sound alone. To his right he could hear Lacan and Sarin taking a different path through the forest. It was only after some seconds that he realized Helen had stayed at the Mask Tree, watching the final emergence from Alex's devastated mind. He called for her, but she didn't answer, and when Lytton shouted angrily, "Richard! Come on!" he continued to follow the elusive protogenomorph through the wood.

They struggled through the tangled darkness, tripping over roots, forcing their way through thickets so dense that they almost suffocated. When they suddenly emerged into open ground, it was into an overgrown cemetery, where stained gray stones poked from thistle-covered mounds. The wall of the cathedral rose before them, white and frosted, already beginning to shed its surface layer of stone.

Richard's cry of triumph gave way to a howl of frustration and disappointment. "It's just another shell! He's tricked us again."

"I don't think so," Lytton said calmly. "Look!" He pointed to the ivy-covered porch. The depthless shadow of the boy moved there, then seemed to seep into the stone, vanishing. "This *is* the place. But how do we get in?"

To their left, Lacan burst from the wood, his hair in tangles, ribbons of briar hanging from him like a bizarre May

Day veil. Sarin crawled on all fours from the cover, her breath misting in the intense cold.

Where was Helen?

Lacan called out in alarm, "The place is dead. We've been led *off* the track . . ."

"This is the place all right!" Lytton called back. He was scanning the high windows, the jagged line of the wall where the roof had fallen, the buttresses, the porch, the steep rise of what had once been a bell tower.

And as Richard followed that gaze with his own, he saw the falcon. It stretched from below a high arched window, a rain gutter, its mouth the opened beak of the bird, which stared down at the man with an almost teasing gaze. *The bird that spits . . .*

"The bird window . . ." he whispered. "Into the chapel, disguised as a falcon . . . That's how Gawain did it in Alex's play . . ."

Lytton was exhilarated. "If this is the Green Chapel, then we may find a way through to the Otherworld. *Our* world, that is."

Lacan shouted, "We're being followed! Daurog, I think, but they're changing. We have to find safety."

"Is Helen with you?" Richard called back, but Lacan just shrugged.

Richard led the way, climbing to the roof of the porch, then ascending the slope of a buttress to gain access to a statue niche, the figure long since rotted. From here it was a dangerous climb, using fingerholds in the pitted stone, to the stretched neck of the falcon and the wide sill, carved with oak leaves and acorns, below which it extended. Behind him, Lacan grunted and heaved his weight, reaching back for Lytton, whose arms were no longer strong enough to accomplish the climb. From high on the wall, Richard scanned the black forest below, and saw how winter crept, a growing silver crystal, toward them.

He could not see Helen, and the concern he now felt for her began to make him shake.

It started to snow, the dull sky deepening into a grim, gray cover, shedding flakes that began to swirl about the church.

From the sill, Richard saw the greenwood that had grown

to fill the center of the cathedral. A wave of warmth and moisture ascended from this summer place, although the first snow crystals were already wetting the higher foliage. He called for Alex and succeeded only in disturbing a roost of rooks, away toward the closed doors, where a tangle of vegetation suggested a huge, spherical nest.

As Lacan arrived on the stone sill, there was suddenly less room than before, and Richard almost lost his grip. Lacan steadied him, pointed to the ropes of creeper that covered the inside wall, and carefully Richard lowered himself to the chapel-wood below. Lacan dropped next, then Sarin, then Lytton, who immediately pushed his way through to the massive structure. Richard followed, aware of the terrible stench that exuded from the mound of dead wood and grass. Lytton had entered the nest. He emerged, brushing black feathers from his face, looking around. "Empty," he said. "A daurog birthing place—she's shed, probably dead now." He saw something, below the statue of the crucified Christ. "There!"

The hollyjack had been laid on a crude bier. Her arms were outstretched, but had risen in the first moments of death so that her thorn-fingered hands seemed to be clutching at the open sky and the gently falling snow that was settling on her. Her mouth was hideously agape, the four branch tusks dry and moldering. The leaf on her head had turned yellow-brown. Her body gaped, was arched as if in pain. A small, dead rook was entangled in the dry ribs.

Someone had placed a small straw effigy of a bird above her head.

From the chapel-wood Lacan hissed, "Something below us!"

Richard felt rather than heard the movement below the marble flooring. The disturbance was brief and he wondered if it might be Alex, so he called for the boy again and from the far end of the ruin he heard a voice call questioningly, "Daddy?"

With memory of the shapechanging Jack freshened by apprehension, Richard forced aside the foliage and approached the altar. Something gold was gleaming there, and after a few moments he recognized a crucifix, as tall as a man, rising above the consuming swathes of holly.

"Alex? Where are you?"

The boy moved suddenly from the green. He was unkempt and naked, a frail figure, his skin as white as the snow that drifted down around him, eyes fierce in a feral face, hair to his shoulders. He was trembling like an animal caged.

Richard began to cry. Alex was so young, so old. Despite the long hair, he was almost exactly as Richard had remembered him over the years, the Alex of those last terrible months in the long-gone when he had looked at the sky with blank eyes, when he had lain listless and content on the grass, responding with nothing more than reflex actions. But this boy, this Alex, had a light in the terrified eyes that spoke of intelligence, of awareness of the long-to-come; and best of all: of recognition.

"Daddy!" he yelled suddenly, and ran to the crying man, to Richard, who dropped to his knees to gather in his son. "We're in danger!" Alex shouted. "Gawain's coming!"

The Green Knight

Green light played on the white ceiling and walls of the
hospital room. Alex lay and watched the swirling color for
a while, then rose from his small bed and walked to the
window. He watched without wonder or fear as a knight
emerged from the wood and rode across the dew-bright
lawn. The knight was huge, on a massive white horse with
flowing green trappings. His hair and beard were green,
as was his scaly armor and the rippling cloak that unfurled behind him as he cantered; he left a spreading fan
of glowing green that reached back to the tangle of the
dawn wood.

He came close to the hospital, then reined in, reared up
and turned twice on his charger, grinning at the watching
boy above him. He beckoned. Five spears were strapped
to his saddle, and a curved axe, its cutting edge smothered
in leather, swung from his belt. Tusked faces formed his
armor, which looked more bone than metal. Alex felt
drawn without really comprehending the compulsion to
follow. He saw the color and the patterns of the knight,
but felt no fear, no pleasure, no curiosity. Compelled,
though, he left his room and went out into the early morning.

Once outside he could smell the rank sweat of the
horse, and hear its heavy breathing. The ground vibrated
as the beast turned, shook violently as it reared and fell
back with a jangle of trappings. The huge knight reached

*down with a green-gloved hand. His breath smelled of
earth. Alex accepted the grasp and was swung into the
saddle behind the green man. No words were spoken. Alex
held on to the thick cloak. His legs were stretched hard
over the broad saddle. Faces of the dead, branches growing from their gaping mouths, watched him from the
armored back. When he touched one, its eyes narrowed
and it snapped at him, giggling.*

*He gasped, then, as the horse charged back to the
wood. It entered the trees without hesitation; the knight
ducked, laughing as branches tore his flowing hair. Alex
turned to glance briefly at the gray and silent building behind him. Then darkness closed about him and thorns began to tear his hands.*

*It was a wild ride. Silently, the knight rode through the
woodland edges, sometimes using a knife as long as a
scythe to cut a path. He crossed fields and roads, shouting
encouragement to his steed, uttering a shrill cry when he
saw a game bird, or hare, and running it down with almost magical speed, snatching and catching the creature
more often than he missed. The horse pounded the country
lanes, foaming at the mouth, complaining noisily when its
direction was changed so that it had to plunge into
marshy forest, or canter along shallow brooks.*

*A moment came when Alex passed his house in
Shadoxhurst. He watched, aware yet unaware. There was
movement in the garden, someone digging. He glanced
back once, but without pain or longing, only recognition.
The digging man had looked up, looked round, perhaps
aware of the distant canter. But the knight was on the
bridleway to Hunters Brook, and his green aura was dispersing in the fog that filled this lower, marshy land.*

*They were soon at Ryhope Wood. The knight rode care-
fully into the edge by the old Lodge. Here, in a clearing
by the ruin, he dismounted, to gather wood and grass, bits
of rag and bundles of leaves. As Alex watched from the
saddle, he shaped a boy on the ground, gave it Alex's features, then lifted it and made Alex spit into the wooden
figure's mouth. The false-Alex stood and ran to the edge,
then across the fields, uttering a meaningless gabble of*

sound. Alex watched it go without thought, without question.

He rested his head against the knight's broad back as they rode through the forest, his face cushioned from the bone scales and living armor by the thick cloak. This he wrapped around his body for warmth. His knuckles were white where he gripped the knight. His backside and legs were bruised and aching from the hours of cantering. He rode without a murmur though, embraced by his rescuer.

The forest opened into wide hills, then closed into stony valleys. They waded through deep snow, skidded on winter ice, were drenched with rains that soaked them for days.

One dusk, they came to a wide lake. A black barge was moored there, its sail furled. Three women stood on the shore among the tall rushes, watching. The knight kicked his horse forward, then stretched round to help Alex from the horse, down to the soft earth. The smallest of the women, a girl of about Alex's age, came forward and wrapped her red cloak around the boy. Alex stared into her eyes for a moment and she smiled. A second woman, who looked like his mother, robed in brown, turned to the barge and reached for the tethering rope. The third, clothed in black, was old. She climbed into the barge and unfurled the sail, then sat, facing the shore.

The Green Knight leaned down and tugged at Alex's hair. His breath misted as he spoke, his accent odd, "I heard your call. I was the first to come back to you. I have to find the other knight, to bring him back.

"You need time now, to heal. These ladies will take you to the place where that healing can be managed. They will heal you with Courage," he pointed to the girl, "with Love," the woman in brown, "and Magic." He scowled at the woman in black. "But mostly you will be healed by Courage. I shall send a small spirit to be my eyes and ears as you recover. Don't do anything to hurt the wolves in winter! Each nick in their flesh is a nick in mine."

And with that, he turned and rode away, axe swinging at his thigh, cloak billowing.

The girl held out her hand and Alex stepped with her aboard the barge. The woman in brown pushed the vessel from the reeds, knee deep in the mere, then clambered in. She picked up the oars and rowed the vessel across the silent lake until a breeze caught the sail and the eldest of the women leaned forward to hold the ropes.

After a while, as if in a dream, they drifted through fog, but emerged, oars stroking gently, to see tall trees and a craggy shore. The girl scrambled from the barge. She ran into the hidden land, through the mossy rocks of the shore, then came back and beckoned to Alex. As the older women stayed with the boat and watched, he held hands with the girl and let her lead him. They emerged from the wood to face the towering wall of a church. It was in a state of ruin.

"This is your place," the girl whispered. She looked round anxiously. "Go inside quickly. It's not safe on this side of the window." She kissed him, first on his cheek, then his chin, then ran back into the undergrowth, toward the lake and her companions. "Go inside!" she called again, and Alex turned to face the gray wall.

Inside the ruin he could hear the sound of birds ... They had gathered on one particular window.

The doors were all blocked. He climbed the wall and went inside. It was warm but empty, yet as soon as he arrived, the wood began to grow from the crypt below, saplings at first, then a bristling, rustling forest.

Nothing had any meaning. He explored the ruin without interest, instinctively seeking warm places, and shelter. Faces watched him from the dark benches, from the stone figures on the walls. Light caught the tints of colored glass from shattered windows. He scavenged for food, was drawn to water in a well, outside the wall.

At some time in the sequence of days and nights, he heard movement in the heavy wood, where the girl had left him. A sinister presence had arrived, that changed its shape, sometimes wolf-like and howling, sometimes tusked and giggling, sometimes a grinning knight who called to him with a mocking human cry. It meant him harm and attacked him when he came too near, and he became afraid to leave the sanctuary of the place of stone.

The hollyjack came, rustling in through the window

where a stone face with feathers spat water when it rained. And it was soon after she had come that he began to dream again. The dreams came back to him, at first ugly and distorted. But one by one they passed the giggler in the wood, creeping into him through the doors and windows of the sanctuary. As he dreamed, so things found names again, and small figures danced out from the wooden benches, and the colored window where the greenjack lived began to grow, to reveal the knight and the green man, and the great mound of green turf through which a bright land gleamed. Everything was almost real again.

He dreamed about his father.

Alex huddled in his father's arms. Richard stroked the boy's hair, touched his cheek, tugged him more tightly into his embrace.

He could hardly believe that Alex was here. He kept cradling the boy, kept looking, remembering, reminding himself that this *was* how Alex had been, this unkempt, dreamy boy, this smiling, loving boy who grasped his father in the manner of a kitten, nervous and determined. What was Alex thinking? What did he feel?

His words, as he had told his story—his dream—had been stilted, as if he was struggling to find the language to convey the wonders and horrors of his existence. He was like a child waking from a deep sleep, half-coherent, strangely real, still unfamiliar.

He was not complete.

But he was Alex Bradley, no doubt about it, and his father held him with all the energy of a man who cannot bear to lose a dream, who cannot quite believe the dream, who wants to feel the dream forever, never to wake.

Richard whispered, "You've been so missed. You've been so lost. It must have been terrifying for you to go through all of that."

Alex touched his father's face and smiled. "The hollyjack was sent by the Green Knight. She was my friend. She helped me dream. She was a small part of him, a small spirit. I thought the knight was Gawain at first. There's a window where the nest is. It grew back while I watched it. All the colors came back. All the reds and greens and golds. When the window healed, I remembered the knight. I thought it showed Gawain killing the green monster. But it's the Green Knight who's our friend. Gawain is cunning. He's the giggler. He trapped me here. He doesn't want to come back. He doesn't want you to take me away. He likes being outside."

Richard looked up from his son, focused on the far window where sunlight illuminated the fitted shards of color, predominantly green. The stained glass showed a classic duel between chivalrous knight and man-eating monster, a human form, a wild man, green-cloaked and massive, barring the way to a summer-wood, just glimpsed through the door in a mound that rose higher than the trees. Yet instead of the knight spearing the wild man, this window showed the wild man exacting the life of the knight. It could have been a portrayal of martyrdom. But Richard now saw that it depicted the triumph of nature over the despoiler.

Alexander Lytton had listened with fascination as Alex recounted this dream-like memory of his "rescue" by the knight. Now, he looked up, looked around, murmured, "His dreams came back to him by all the doors and windows of the sanctuary . . ."

Alex, exhausted, had begun to drift into sleep in his father's arms. Richard cradled him, rocked him, but watched the gaunt features of the Scot.

"Where are we, Alexander? Where the hell are we? We're in a wood, I know that. We're in a reflection of a ruin that Alex once visited, a cathedral, a sanctuary, a holy place. A *haven*. I know that too. It's the Green Chapel, in its way, and Green Knights come and go, and dreams enter and pass through—"

"Exactly," Lytton murmured. "This is the passing place. Exactly that. Old dreams pass out, new dreams enter. The Green Chapel in the old poem was a place of testing. To the medieval world, the tests were of honor, of chivalry, of courage. The Cross against the witches of the pagan world, the world of forgotten gods, forgotten lore. The Green Chapel itself was described as a burial mound, an access to the Otherworld of 'faerie.' Your boy recognized a long time ago that the Christian story was a convenience to suit its times. I remember you telling me how he subverted the story in his school play to make it not a test of honor by benevolent trickery, but a double-cross by Gawain himself, to get access to an older land and older treasures. And what treasures!

"The chapel is the frontier between instinct and conscience, the place which tests dreams, and by testing dreams, by testing the faith a mind *puts* in its dream-state, tests the mind itself. There is a magic in dreams that these days we can't value. They can express combinations of experience. They can create vision. If the vision is clear, is lucid, if it can be controlled, if its symbols can be comprehended, it gives power through something we take for granted. Intuition! But that ability has to be won against more basic instincts."

Lytton glanced at Richard and smiled. "Think of this place as your son's version of the 'passage' between primal and higher minds, between unconscious and conscious. That's certainly what the Green Chapel itself represents. This is a natural place to come when you are stripped of dreams, and need to heal. How I would love to know the *dreamtime* story of the Green Chapel. What an understanding that might give us into *insight*. Your boy was given the briefest of glimpses. So have we been. But because of the appetite of Alex's imagination, which means he absorbs a lot of junk imagery, we only get to see Jack the Giant-Killers, and Gawains, and sturdy knights et cetera, Tennyson-esque queens in barges (an interesting aspect of the mind's notion of self-healing, incidentally). The hollyjack is primitive, though. *That* was close to something very old . . ."

From the window through which they had entered the cathedral, Lacan called down, "There's something coming through the woods! Can't make it out, but whatever it is, there's a lot of it. Not creatures . . . not as such . . ."

Alarmed, Richard said, "Christ! Helen! We've got to help Helen."

Lytton grabbed his arm. "Helen stayed behind in the glade for a reason. She's a capable woman. If she sensed Coyote, you should let her be . . ."

"She's in danger. I can't lose her! Not now."

"She'll have to face Coyote on her own. You can't help her."

"She's not facing Coyote. She's facing Gawain . . . If what Alex says—"

"The greenjacks," Alex whispered. "Only it's winter. The Green Knight in winter can't be trusted. The hollyjack told me so. Until the spring comes, he'll try to kill us, just like Gawain . . ."

Increasing his grip on Richard's arm, Lytton said grimly, "Gawain and the Green Knight are part of the same creature. But they're Alex's—Coyote is not. Helen wouldn't have stayed behind unless she was sure her own time of testing was coming."

Winter developed into a storm. Snow blew hard against the cathedral, swirling icily into the wood inside the walls. Richard joined Lacan on the falcon sill, staring into the gloom, and saw the spread of movement across the black forest. Like the lights and shapes that had emerged from the Mask Tree, elemental forces were flowing toward the sanctuary, streaks and swirls of color in the blizzard, faces and forms that existed at the periphery of vision.

Richard returned to the shelter in the Lady Chapel. When he told Lytton of the impending attack, the man swore loudly, raised wide eyes to the broken walls.

Moments later the elementals seeped into the cathedral. Lacan yelled suddenly from the window-ledge and almost plummeted to the snow-covered floor below, just keeping his grip on the thick, slippery creeper. Above him, faces stretched from the stone, statues shifted, and the cracked figures in the wooden pews emerged and ran through the shivering wood.

Through it all, light pierced the stained glass making the figures of Gawain and the Green Knight appear to writhe within the crystal. Yet they remained in place, while the stone figures all around them, birds, gryphons and grinning monks, became animated, their voices emerging as a meaningless chatter, muffled by the stifling snow.

Alex laughed at the antics. His eyes glowed, despite the

cold. "It's like the first dream. They danced for me! They danced!"

Richard hugged his son, not understanding the enthusiasm, the excitement. The cathedral flowed with movement. Every thorn and hazel, all the gnarled oaks and slender birches that formed the chapel-wood seemed to move, to shift a little, to join the dancing figures.

"They're coming back to Alex," Lytton said from his hunched position in a niche where a statue had once stood.

But even as he spoke, so the effect seemed to vanish. The figures froze, the sense of a massive elemental intrusion into the sanctuary withdrew. Lytton's eyes widened. He glanced at the boy, then murmured, "Not Alex's at all! Someone watching us, someone outside."

He stood and waded through snow to the ivy-covered wall, pulled himself up the thick strands to the icy ledge. Richard followed him. Lacan and Sarin huddled for warmth; Alex was swathed in the big man's cloak.

From the falcon window, as the snowstorm eased, a figure could be seen at the woodland edge. Richard was certain that it was not Helen, nor a knight in any shape or form. It was a man in a long, black overcoat, his white head bare, his face full-bearded. He carried a staff; a backpack was slung over his left shoulder. He was staring up at the cathedral.

The air cleared, a sudden lull. The man stepped forward, shaking snow from his hair to reveal darker locks, a younger face.

"My God," Alexander Lytton breathed. "It's Huxley. It's George Huxley!"

The man by the wood turned away. Lytton called his name. The man hesitated, frowning as he glanced back, but then turned again to pursue his path through the trees.

"Huxley!" Lytton cried desperately to the winter wood. "George Huxley! Wait!" He scrambled down to the floor of the chapel, grabbed his rucksack and found his oak staff. He tied his cloak around his chest and tugged the hood over his head. "I can't lose him now . . . I've spent too long looking."

"You're mad!" Richard said. "You'll never find him in this storm. And how can you be sure it *was* him, and not a mythago?"

Lytton laughed dryly, as if recognizing the irony of the situation. "How? Because I've seen more photographs of the man than he ever knew existed. I gained access to them. I've stared into his eyes, into his soul, using a lens, using my imagination ... I've stared at that face for more hours than I've stared at my own, Richard. You could show me the shaved whiskers of his cheeks and I'd know they were his. Don't doubt me, lad. I'd know him anywhere. For Huxley, it's the 1930s. This is the middle of his deepest journey, his longest absence. I didn't expect to find him. He found *me* ... our meeting is recorded in his journal—he doesn't name me, so I can't be sure, but everything fits with what he wrote when he returned to Oak Lodge in September 1937.

"I *will* find him, Richard; he can't get far in this snow. I hardly had the courage to believe it would happen. But it has. And it's time for me to leave you."

He hugged Lacan powerfully, then bowed to Sarin. He ruffled Alex's hair and finally extended a hand to Richard. "I'm glad we *both* got our wish. I learned a frightening lesson about myself, that day with the Jack ..."

"Gone and forgotten," Richard said quickly. "As will Huxley be, if you don't get a move on."

Lytton glanced down at Alex. "Don't let your father do anything foolish. His friend, Helen, knows how to handle herself. She's a match for *any* trickster. To help her," this for Richard again, "might be to frustrate *her* wish."

"There are wolves in the wood," Alex said anxiously. Lytton frowned.

"*Scarag*. I know. The greenjacks in winter."

"Try not to hurt them. When spring comes, they'll be our friends."

Lytton smiled thinly to reassure the boy. "Laddie, I have no intention whatsoever of challenging a scarag. I saw what they did to a friend of mine."

He scaled the wall again, crossing the sill by the falcon gargoyle and skidding heavily to the ground outside. Richard followed him to the window, leaned out of the stone and watched him go, a fleeing figure, cloak swirling, entering the snowstorm again, soon lost in the wood, his final cry for Huxley sucked hollow by the winter world.

* * *

During the night the sounds and vibrations from the crypt were a constant, muffled reminder that the cathedral was not a complete sanctuary. The snow had ceased to fall. At dawn Lacan took his spear and climbed to the window to watch for danger. Sarin and Richard investigated the entrance to the crypt, but found only a sealed wall, riddled with roots and faint inscriptions. Alex wouldn't go down the stone stairs. "They're coming back to me. My friend told me. But they frighten me—"

"Who?"

"The winter-wolves. They're finding a way to get to me . . ."

Richard strung his bow, fingered the tip of one of his arrows. "We'll fight with everything we've got. Which isn't much, admittedly, but we'll use it!"

"They're our friends in the spring. Don't hurt them—"

"You seem to know a lot about them, Alex. But none of the rest of us do. You seem afraid of them, but afraid *for* them. What do I do if they attack?"

"Don't hurt them," Alex whispered, but he shivered as he said it, looking nervously across the snow-laden trees, feeling the sudden vibration of a large creature below the altar.

"What is it?" Sarin whispered apprehensively. "Something's happening."

"I don't know."

Richard took a step away from the altar. The whole wood was quivering, snow being shed from winter branches. "Arnauld!" he began to shout, but he managed no more.

The floor in front of him buckled below the spreading roots and silver trunk of a birch, forcing the tree to lean sharply. It heaved again and the birch fell. A black marble slab thrust vertically from below it, scattering snow and exposing the darkness of the crypt.

The head that pushed up from the hole was bone-white, huge, with four tusks curling from its gaping mouth. Below folds of bone and gnarled ridges, black eyes glittered as the creature looked quickly around before heaving its lithe and sinewy frame from the pit. It had a wolf's features, despite the protuberances from its mouth. Its rib cage was vast, gruesomely defined above a stomach that was hollow and taut, although it rippled as the muscles were tensed. The creature was twice the height of a man. Its arms hung heavily by its sides, fingers spread and ready as it watched Lacan on the high window, then howled at him.

Lacan hurled his spear. The scarag didn't flinch. At the last moment it snatched at the weapon, allowing the blade to make a shallow nick in its breast. It howled again and its tusks clattered. It tossed the spear across the cathedral, toward the altar where Richard watched in horror. As the haft clattered on the stone, Richard reached for it.

The scarag moved away from the vault. At once a second head appeared in the hole, this one broader, flatter, one tusk broken. The lame thing that hauled itself from the crypt was gray and bony also, taller than the first, but stooped. It watched Lacan curiously, then growled and turned to forage in the chapel wood.

A third and fourth winter-wolf emerged from the hole in the floor, each looking around as it rose, hesitating, watching first Lacan, then Richard, before stalking through the trees. The fifth scarag, a smaller version but no less menacing, remained at a crouch by the gap in the marble floor, emitting a sound like a low growl. Without moving its head, its eyes shifted restlessly, sharing its scrutiny between the huge Frenchman and the crouching trio by the golden cross on the altar. It seemed to be guarding the hole to the underworld.

The first scarag soon found the body of the hollyjack. It gathered the dry, dead evergreen into its arms and lifted it to its chest. One of the others picked up the straw bird and placed it in the open body. The wood filled with the sounds of mourning and the winter beasts moved stealthily toward the cathedral's main doors and entered the decaying nest.

Last to go was the Guardian, the shaman of the group. It pointed three times with its carved staff to the passage through to the crypt, its feral eyes fixed on Richard. Then it rose and backed steadily through the snow to the maw of the nest. Here, with a series of cries that were almost human, it turned and crawled inside.

* * *

Three days later, at the height of the day, as Richard returned
from a fruitless search for Helen, the nest by the tall doors
began to exude bird-cries and chattering. At once, Alex ran
to the ramshackle structure and stood in the wash of green
light that began to flood from the circular mouth. There was
a great deal of movement inside the nest and the same sun
that had transformed the winter world into one of spring
flashed blindingly through the crystal window above the
doors.

Alex started to move toward that light but Sarin put restraining hands upon his shoulders and looked around for
Arnauld, signaling to Richard as she saw the man drop over
the access sill.

"Something's happening," she called urgently.

Alex shrugged her off, then turned, eyes wide, lank hair
flowing about his grinning face. "They're back. They've
come!"

Before Richard could do anything to stop his son, Alex
had jumped at the hole in the mass of wood and grass and
bundled himself inside. The eerie light flickered. There was
movement and a sudden breeze, like a breath.

The entrance to the nest closed! It seemed to snap shut,
and Richard flung himself across the cathedral to stand by
Sarin. She backed away, horrified and appalled, her hands to
her mouth.

"It's eaten him," she whispered. Richard held her, shaking
and afraid.

"No. No, I don't think so. I think this is the end of it."
Dear God, please let it be so.

The nest shrank. The wood and bramble melted down, became hair, became eyes, became a nose and a grinning
mouth that opened and emitted a low chuckle. The eyes
watched stonily, the hair waved like rushes in a high wind.
Richard panicked.

"Arnauld! Quickly!"

The Frenchman came running. Richard tried to thrust his
spear into one of the Jack's eyes, but was blown back by the
stench from its mouth, and the hollow laugh. *Don't hurt
it . . .* his son seemed to say. A moment later the face seemed

to calm down. It dissolved into a kinder head, a sad-featured visage that Richard remembered from the *Argo*.

Vast, grotesque in its way, Orpheus fleetingly watched the trembling man below him, and sang words in a whisper.

"One bloody nick ... side of his head ... all for the lady ... the love of the lady ..."

Then Orpheus too dissolved, the wood and bracken crumbling into dust, the whole nest collapsing down, dissolving, dispersing into the feeding green shoots of new growth that reached from the tall doors, and from between the cold stone flooring. Soon there was just a curled human shape covered with ivy and ground elder, which writhed over the boy's naked form, then drew back, taking the black rot, the orange fungal growth, the shards and fragments of decay, taking it all back down to the root-web.

Curled on the floor, Alex opened his eyes. He unfurled like a leaf at dawn, his arms stretching, his legs flexing, his back arching. He greeted the high sun, the gray-green shadows, and smiled. He passed water and sat up, watching the steam from between his legs, slightly embarrassed. Then he looked at Richard, who was standing shocked and in tears. He stood up, brushing self-consciously at his wet thighs, trying to hide himself from his father's gaze. There was a strange fire in his eyes. Green light seemed to touch his skin.

"I need clothes."

At once, as if kicked into action, Richard ran to the boy and placed his cloak around Alex's shoulders. He could hardly speak, managing a tear-choked, "Dear God, you give me some frights!"

The nest had sucked all dead things away, including the ends of hair and strips of his nails. But there was something *whole* about the boy, now: trickster and conscience had come back. The two faces of the Green Knight had returned.

Alex stared at Richard with a searching curiosity. "Your hair's gone gray. You've got lots of gray."

Richard kissed the boy's forehead, then with his arm tightly around him led him back to the altar. "I'm getting old. Too many adventures."

"I've been dreaming, haven't I? It was such a funny dream. Can we go home?"

"Of course we can go home," Richard whispered. He glanced down. "You'll find things a bit changed, Alex. You've been in a long sleep. It's been a long dream."

"I saw Mr. Keeton. He was very sad. Is Tallis all right?"

Shaking his head, Richard said, "Tallis went away. Mr. Keeton was very sick, and he died." He couldn't help his tears. He hugged his son to his chest. Alex struggled for breath, pushed at his father's embrace.

"It's all right," he said. "I'm grown-up enough to know that Mr. Keeton was very ill."

"Mummy's gone away too. But you'll be able to visit her. It will be very important for you both."

Alex looked grim. "You were always arguing. I could hear you from my room."

"We were always arguing," Richard agreed gently. "We weren't happy."

"Are you going to argue with the new one? The Red Indian?"

"*American* Indian! We don't say 'red' anymore. And no, I'm not going to argue with her. I know what songs to sing these days ..."

"Is she a real Indian?"

Richard laughed. "Of course! Helen Silverlock is an almost pure blood Lakota. Or did she say Dakota? Minnesota? Anyway, she's Sioux. I think. Maybe Cherokee." *Damn! He couldn't remember.*

Alex was looking puzzled. "What does 'pure blood' mean?"

"She had a tough grandfather. She's got a lot of courage."

"What's Lakota and Dakota?"

Richard sighed. "I don't know. Signs and signals of my ignorance of any history that isn't our own. But what does it matter? I love the 'new one' as you call her because she's making history with *me*. Silver hair on each side of her head, feathers up her nose, Rolling Stones and all."

Alex looked blank, and Richard reflected ruefully that the boy had ridden away with the Green Knight before the Rolling Stones had given their "Mummy" her "little helpers," before the Beatles had "please, pleased" themselves. If they could ever get out of this wood again, it would be 1967 ... maybe 1968, eight years since Alex's healing had begun. And there was a climate of healing in the world beyond Ryhope now, a mood of peace, societies angry at the war in Indo-China; and the Seventies were looming, and things were going to be so much more interesting! Alex would enter that new world, that brightly blossoming world, like a young leaf unfurling to make his mark on the tree, to suck in the sun, to add his voice and his dreams to the dreams and voices that were striving so hard to make their courage and their vision known.

Richard was startled by Alex touching his eyes. "You're crying," the boy said.

"Am I? So I am. I was just thinking how much you had to look forward to. I was just thinking of being home."

"Me too. I think the Green Knight just showed us the way." Alex wriggled away, and drew the cloak around his tall, thin body. He used a piece of creeper to tie the baggy garment at his waist, and hauled the extra length up and tucked it in the belt.

He went back through the trees to the broken floor and peered down into the crypt. Arnauld Lacan crouched beside him, spear held firmly between his knees. Alex said, "When I was dreaming, I moved through strange corridors, through the roots under the world. I could dream of you. I saw you." He glanced at Lacan. "I could also dream of the hollyjacks. Sometimes I dreamed of the world outside, and I think this is the way home. It's down through the dead, but I think the dead only frightened me because they were coming back. They're all back now. There's nothing to be frightened of." He looked up at Richard. "I'd like to go home."

"I know you would," Richard whispered, looking desperately at the falcon window. Helen was still out there! He couldn't leave until she came back. But he couldn't leave Alex again, not now, not having found him. He was too precious a treasure ever to leave again.

He could hardly think straight. He wanted Alex home, and safe—he wanted Helen safe, and coming home.

Before he could speak a word, Alex looked up sharply, quite alarmed.

"What about your friend? She might be in trouble! Are you going to help her?"

"Yes," Richard said quietly. "I'm going to try and find her. I won't have to wait long. I can hunt for game. There's plenty of water in the well . . ."

"Is she hunting down a wolf?"

"Coyote."

"Sounds like a wolf to me. I've heard him crying. He's there now, out in the woods. Can you hear?"

And indeed, as Richard fell silent and raised his head, as he listened hard through the trees and stone, he could hear an odd baying, a triumphant and frightening wolf-cry. A battle was being fought. He reached for his bow, but Sarin stepped forward and held him. Her dark eyes glistened.

"Let her be. Let her *be*. If you lose her, it will be because she's dead. But if you find her, it will be because she's won. Just let her come back in the way that will give her release from her nightmare. She knows the way out of the wood. And you've already proved enough. I will never forget how you defeated Jason! Now sit between the worlds and wait, and pray, wait for what happens. Now take care of Alex. Take him home . . ."

Lacan loomed behind the Tall Grass Speaker. "I've just been down among the bones. There's certainly a hollowing below us. It has that feel. But if this giggler thing has gone, we might do better to go the land route." He sensed the awkward silence. "What's happening?"

Sarin said grimly, "I think Richard is staying. To help Helen."

Lacan smiled broadly. "Of course he is! And we're staying too. Four are better than one! Besides, what's the alternative?"

Richard said, "You could take Alex back to my house in Shadoxhurst—wait for us there . . ."

"Your house?" Lacan said, horrified. "Where no doubt there is nothing to drink but tea and medicines?"

"You might find some red wine in the sitting room."

"In the sitting room," Lacan breathed with a despairing

shake of his head. "In the light, no doubt. By the fire. In the warm. To keep it happy. A very fine vinegar, I'm sure, but if I want to drink vinegar I'll go to a British fish-and-chip shop. There is no hope for you. Please immediately return to the *bosk.* I shall save your son from the humiliation of you being his father. Come on, Alex." He squeezed the boy's ear gently, teasingly, "Come on. We have a long journey. We have to hunt before we leave the wood. To *eat,* you understand! We have to prepare for your home—and for all the horrors it no doubt contains."

Alex watched his father all the time. "I'm staying," he said, and Lacan laughed quietly.

"Of course you are."

The boy came over and took Richard's hand. Richard smiled at his son, tightened the boy's cloak across his chest, noticed what brightness of spirit, what sudden awareness and maturity had etched the edges of the smooth face that stared at him.

"Perhaps you *should* go home. Arnauld is only joking when he says the things he says."

"I know!" Alex said in frustration. "I'm not stupid. But Sarin told me that she can't live outside the wood for very long, and Arno' wants to stay with her, so they wouldn't be with me for long. So we should stay."

Outside the cathedral a wolf whined, a long, plaintive and sinister sound that made Richard's skin crawl.

"I'm frightened for you!" he said, standing.

"Don't be."

Later, Richard went up to the window, to sit and watch and wait, listening to the whining call and the mocking laughter of the creature that Helen, perhaps, was hunting.

The night deepened. A fire was burning in the distance, a single beacon which Richard watched with an almost hypnotic fascination. It was hard to tell at this distance, but occasionally it seemed that a figure passed in front of the flames.

The wolf bayed in the wildwood, then chuckled and chattered. No wolf, then.

A flight of rooks swirled noisily through the cold night,

stags coughed and barked, wide-winged water birds flapped
noisily, moonlight gray as they circled their high roosts. The
wood was a restless yet motionless expanse of dark and at
its farther end the fire burned, the figure moved, the sky
glowed, Coyote prowled. Above its nearer edge, at the
threshold that separated two worlds, Richard Bradley lay on
his side, curled up like a child asleep, thinking of the son
he'd found and the woman he loved.

He was startled by movement behind him and grabbed for
his knife. Something had been climbing the ivy ladder to the
falcon window. Half-dazed, he turned and reached down to
defend himself against the intruder.

"It's me," Alex said.

The boy scrambled the last few feet and huddled on the
wide stone ledge, shivering slightly, watching the fire in the
distance, close to where his Mask Tree grew in the forest.
"Arno' and Sarin have gone down into the crypt. I think
they're sleeping. I'd like to stay up here while you're waiting for Helen. If that's OK . . . ?" He seemed apprehensive.

Out in the wood the sound of a wolf triumphant split the
night. An instant later the sound was cut off. There was
something chilling, something very final about that sudden
silence.

"*Is* it OK?" the boy asked.

Richard smiled and reached to pinch Alex's pale cheek.
He glanced back to the fire, which had now begun to fade.

"It's OK," he said.

Appendix

Editor's note: *George Huxley recorded numerous folk tales, myths and legends, mostly obscure, which he heard or interpreted during his explorations of Ryhope Wood between 1928 and 1946. He dates* Jack His Father *to 600 BC, an early Celtic version of a much older* Kurgan *tale.*

R.H.

Jack His Father

Jack was sowing the last of the summer wheat when the smell of smoke told him of the raid on his village. His sister, who had better hearing than a hound, yelled "Horsemen!" and ran quickly to the cover of the woods. From the treeline she called to Jack to hide. The boy followed her as far as the first tree, but stood with his back against it, strong against the coming storm. In the distance he could see the smoke rising from the enclosure where his father's house would now be burning.

"I still have a father, a mother, a sister and three brothers," he said desperately to the birds that circled the field. The ravens departed noisily, mocking him. The geese descended to eat the summer seed, and Jack's heart sank.

The armed runners came first, searching for crops and cattle. They led three calves with them, and two horses, which trotted in silence since their jaws had been tied. These men were young. The horsemen and the warlord's chariot came after, riding suddenly from the trees, hooves drumming, chariot wheels creaking. Two of the horsemen saw Jack and galloped down upon him. Jack stood his ground, his right fist clenched around the last of the wheat. He saw the sacks that were tethered and slung across the withers of the horses, and thought at once of the pigs and fowl that he and his sister had so carefully raised.

"Don't tell them I'm here!" whispered his sister from hiding. "Since you're so stupid that you won't hide, then your head it'll be, but don't give me away."

"You'll give yourself away, if you don't shut up."

The man in the chariot was Bran, resplendent in dark leathers and a red cloak. He wore a crested war helmet, and the silver curve of the moon was stitched into his corselet. He was black-haired, big-handed, clean of face. The blue and black symbols of his clan, the Boar and Eagle, spread richly across his cheeks and chin. Now he crouched in front of Jack, amused by the boy, and of a mind to bargain.

"I see you wear good shoes," he says. "Cowhide, is it? Well-stitched, I think."

But Jack blows a hard breath at the man. "Take them from me or leave them on me, it makes no difference. If you've done us harm I'll follow you faster than cloud shadow."

The horsemen laugh, but the man with the crested helmet does not.

"That's a fine talisman, that bone carving, that boar, on the leather there, around your neck."

But Jack blows a hard breath at the man. "Take it from me or leave it on me, it makes no difference. If you've done us harm I'll come at you from a hawthorn thicket faster than the breeze."

The horsemen shift nervously now, horse-chains rattling, sacks of booty swinging in the cooling day. The crested man draws a small bronze dagger and meets the defiant gaze.

"That's a brave tongue you wag at me, that lip-licker, there, that loud proclaimer."

But again Jack blows a hard breath. "Cut it from me or leave it in me, it makes no difference. If you've done us harm I'll sing in your ears as the crows feast on your eyes."

The dagger points at Jack's right hand. "I'll have what's

there, then. I'll have what you hold, or cut it from you, that clenched hand."

"Cut if from me, then. It's the only way you'll get it, and what I hold will vanish."

"What does that fist conceal?"

"Seeds," says the boy.

"What sort of seeds?"

"The seed of a tree that takes no more than a day to grow and can make a house where there's always a feast of pork roasting on the fire."

"I'll certainly have that," says Bran hungrily. "And I'll have more. What else?"

"The seed of a tree that takes no more than a day to grow and can make a boat fit to cross any haunted lake."

"I'll have that too, and more besides. What else?"

"The seed of a tree that grows faster than the hair on a man's face, and can give shelter and fruit to a host of men. From its top can be seen the Isle of Women."

"I'll have that, and twice over!" says Bran, his eyes lively, his hand patting his balls. "Or die in the trying."

So Jack says, "What will you give me for them?"

He can hear the sound of women crying. A cold wind brings the smell of smoke and slaughter over the fields, where the geese stalk the new seeds, and the ravens cast dark shadows.

And Bran says, "I'll give you the best singing voice a man could wish to hear."

Jack laughs. "I'll certainly take that from you. *And* I'll have more."

"Then I'll give you the prize of all pigs taken in this raid."

"I'll certainly take that from you," says Jack hungrily. "And I'll *still* have more."

"Then I'll give you back your father," says the helmeted man, this Bran, with a scowl, slapping his knees to signify an end to the bargaining. "And promise to make you a better man than him. There, now, it's done, this game. That's all."

Jack agrees and holds out the seeds to the chieftain, who takes them and looks at them angrily. "This is wheat!"

"Not everything is as it seems," says Jack with a laugh.

"Indeed, but that's right, that's very true."

The chieftain shakes his head and scowls, then goes to his chariot and fetches a sack, which he tosses to the boy. When Jack opens it, his father's head, half-lidded and bloody, grimaces at him from its cold grave.

Bran and the horsemen laugh and turn to ride along the river. The chief calls from his wicker chariot, "Indeed, Jack, you were quite right there, correct in what you said. Not everything is as it seems. But I kept my part of the bargain, that bargain there just now, which you cheated on! Your father was the wild pig of your clan I prized the most, and he sang for his life more sweetly than your three brothers, who I'll be taking with me, in those sacks, there, which you thought were pigs. And since he's dead, your father, then it takes no magic to make you the better man!"

When they've gone from sight, though, Jack kisses his father's face and consoles his sister. Then he crosses to the field where the fat geese are almost finished with the wheat.

"You've taken my last seeds!" he shouts at the birds. "Now you must pay for them. There can never be a better man than my father, so make me my father now, and return me to that chariot, that armored man, who killed him, to follow him."

And he catches a goose by its legs, holding the bird down, while the crows circle and chatter with amusement at Jack's cleverness. The goose is ashamed at its greed, the eating of the wheat while Jack had fought for his life. The air is suddenly full of feathers, and the sound of the Screech Owl that has been summoned, and by her magic Jack takes the shape of a raven which feeds upon the sad eyes of his father. Then the raven becomes the head. Only a goose is strong enough to carry the head in its sack, and this goose flies up above the furrows, and then to the west, following the chariot. Jack's sister takes their father home, to the burned village.

When the goose is above Bran's chariot, it lets the sack fall.

Then Bran opens the sack, and Jack-his-father opens his eyes. And he says, in his father's voice, "Give me back my sons."

"Never!" says the chief, but he ties the sack again and

rests his foot upon it as he rides, frightened by what has happened.

The first night after the raid they camped on open land. Bran planted one of the seeds, more by way of humor than expectation, and pissed upon it. But Jack-his-father rolled unseen from the chariot and changed his shape again. He sang as he grew, a head becoming a tree, a strong oak, spreading out over the camp, reaching boughs to the ground and using leaves as a roof. When he had enclosed the raiders and their horses, he made the fire spring up and the wood spit and hiss with the rich fat of a spitted pig. He made sap run as honeyed ale and watched as the men below him fell into a pleasant stupor. The crows in Jack's branches flew down and stole back the severed head of his eldest brother. "Carry it safely," Jack said, and the sound of his voice woke Bran, but too late to stop the birds from flying off, out of this unknown region.

On the second night, Jack-his-father taunted Bran. "One of my sons is safe again, taken home. Give me back the others."

"Not even if the flesh rolls from my bones and I catch my death of a cold."

They were by a lake. Jack waited until Bran planted a second seed and pissed upon it, crying, "To see the Isle of Women, that would be a fine raid!" then, when the man had laughed scornfully and retired to sleep, he rolled from his sack and grew into a strong willow. He reached out over the deep water and shaped his prow, then his hull, and used branches as oars. He became a low, sleek galley, and the raiders found him in the morning and imagined it had drifted to the shore by night. They clambered aboard and rowed to the middle of the lake, toward the forest trail beyond that led to their own land.

But halfway across the lake, Jack opened the branches that formed the hull and the galley foundered. Man and beast swam to the shore, but a great pike caught the hair on the head of Jack's second brother and carried the head up the river, out of this unknown region, back to the land of his birth. Jack-his-father was gathered in and slung across the neck of a horse, to be carried on. He felt like singing, but kept silent.

A third night, then, and Bran placed Jack-his-father in the ground, placing the last of the wheat seeds from the bargain into its mouth. "If you make a tree that can shelter and feed my companions, and from which I can see the Isle of Women, then you shall have your third son back."

Jack grew. He was the oldest of oaks, wide and strong, trunk dressed with creeper and a place big enough for a house in the angle of every branch. The host of men camped below the spreading lower branches. There were fallow deer here, plump geese, and sweet, young pigs. The hunting was good. Sharp-juiced apples grew from the middle boughs. Strong-breasted fowl nested higher, within bow-shot. Wild wheat bristled from the swathes of ivy, and made good bread. It was a great place to be, below this solitary oak, and they stayed here for the better part of the season, growing fat and thinking themselves on the Island of Ease.

Each day Bran climbed higher into the tree, but turned back before reaching the top out of fear, not liking the way the birds sang. But all the time he was thinking of what the Bold Boy had said to him: that he would be able to see the Isle of Women from the higher branches. It was a place Bran hungered for. To know its direction would give him great power over the land. He would not be caught by the spirit tracks that confused mortal men if he knew where, in the west, he was heading.

Jack-in-the-tree waited.

One evening, when the skies were clear and the air still and warm, Bran climbed the tree to the very top. From here he could see to the edge of the world. He saw the Isles of the Mighty, the Land of the Young, the Isle of Women, and when he had learned how to get to them all he began to climb down. But as fast as he climbed down, so Jack-in-the-tree grew, until the oak became so heavy above the ground that it began to wave and bend in the wind. Soon it cracked across its roots, and fell heavily to the rocks on the shore of the Isle of Women, where the body of Bran was smashed and broken.

Jack became himself again, the Bold Boy, Loud Proclaimer, and picked up the head of his youngest brother. He could never run faster than the hound, so he became a hound in form, and ran from this unknown place, back to the lake, back to the open land, back to the ploughed field and over the rise of forested ground to the place of his father's lodge. His brothers were there, but his sister had disappeared the summer before, and he would not find her again for many years.

He spat out the last of the seeds and planted them, then re-built the house. A town flourishes there now, and it is still the best part of the island for growing wheat. A white figure, carved on the hill, marks the place of Jack's defiant stand against the raiders. From its head, looking toward the setting sun, his sister's strange tomb can sometimes be seen at dusk.

If you and/or a friend would like to receive the *ROC Advance*, a bimonthly newsletter featuring all the newest and hottest ROC books and authors, on a complimentary basis, please fill out this form and return it to:

ROC Books/Penguin USA
375 Hudson Street
New York, NY 10014

Your Address
Name _____
Street _____ Apt. # _____
City _____ State _____ Zip _____

Friend's Address
Name _____
Street _____ Apt. # _____
City _____ State _____ Zip _____